I0592174

James Boniface Mackinlay

Saint Edmund - King and Martyr

A history of his Life and Times

James Boniface Mackinlay

Saint Edmund - King and Martyr
A history of his Life and Times

ISBN/EAN: 9783743406766

Manufactured in Europe, USA, Canada, Australia, Japa

Cover: Foto ©Raphael Reischuk / pixelio.de

Manufactured and distributed by brebook publishing software (www.brebook.com)

James Boniface Mackinlay

Saint Edmund - King and Martyr

SAINT EDMUND

KING AND MARTYR

A

HISTORY OF HIS LIFE AND TIMES

WITH AN ACCOUNT OF

THE TRANSLATIONS OF HIS INCORRUPT BODY, ETC.

From Original MSS.

BY THE

REV. J. B. MACKINLAY, O.S.B.

Utque cruore suo, Gallos Dionysius ornat,
  Græcos Demetrius, gloria quisque suis ;
Sic nos Edmundus nulli virtute secundus
  Lux patet, et patriæ gloria magna suæ.
Sceptra manum, diadema caput, sua purpura corpus
  Ornat ei, sed plus vincula, mucro, cruor.
              (Ex libro Abbatiæ de Rufford in Bibl. Cott).

LONDON AND LEAMINGTON

𝔄𝔯𝔱 𝔞𝔫𝔡 𝔅𝔬𝔬𝔨 ℭ𝔬𝔪𝔭𝔞𝔫𝔶

NEW YORK, CINCINNATI & CHICAGO: BENZIGER BROS.

1893

TO

THE SONS OF MY ALMA MATER,

WHO TRAINED UNDER

SAINT EDMUND'S PATRONAGE

ESTEEM IT THEIR GLORY TO SHOW FORTH

HIS HEROIC SPIRIT

IN A LIFE OF SELF-SACRIFICE

AND

HIS KINGLY VIRTUES IN A ROYAL PRIESTHOOD,

THIS TRIBUTE

TO OUR GREAT MARTYR

IS HUMBLY AND RESPECTFULLY

DEDICATED.

PREFACE.

THE materials for the following history have been collected during the past ten years, in intervals of leisure from busy work in monastery and college, and subsequently on the mission. This desultory method of storing and arranging material will account for many faults, which, it is feared, mar the work, but which, it is hoped, will meet with the reader's kind indulgence.

The work is purposely entitled a *History of the Life and Times of St. Edmund.* A mere Life of the saint could be compressed into a few pages, but the mass of historical and traditional lore, which illustrates his character and position in the England of his day, calls for wider treatment. Hence the endeavour to interweave the history of East Anglia, the narrative of the Danish invasion and the customs of Saxon times, into the great martyr's biography.

For centuries St. Edmund's incorrupt body exercised a living influence over the nation, and kept his personality ever present. To end his history with his martyrdom would leave unrecorded this important place, which he occupied in the hearts of the faithful and in the annals of the country. Accordingly, the sacred body has been traced through the vicissitudes of a thousand years to its present resting-place, and his other relics enumerated and described. Distinct chapters treat of the miraculous power which the people believed him to wield, and of the devotion which his life and character inspired; while a brief sketch of the magnificent memorial which rose over and around his shrine finishes the work.

Parallel with this long and continuous history of the saint run the numerous and varied records, in medieval manuscript and modern print, which furnish the materials. To omit all description of these interesting documents and their authors would rob St. Edmund's history of one of its most beautiful features—the tribute which literature has paid to him through the ages. Their introduction, however, remained a difficulty. They admitted of three methods of treatment—(1) a mere enumeration in the preface, (2) a dry appendix, or (3) an account of each of them in turn with the chapter to which it related. Following at least two notable examples,[1] choice has been made of the third method, and in the *Authorities* at the head of each chapter the reader will find a concurrent history of the literature which perpetuated the name

---

[1] Butler's "Lives of the Saints," and Green's "Short History of the English People."

and memory of the martyr king of East Anglia.
St. Edmund's Bury has at last found a place in
the Rolls Series, and the first volume of "Memorials of
St. Edmund's Abbey" has recently seen the light.[1]
The editor, Mr. Thomas Arnold, M.A., in the introduction, p. xiii., thus compares St. Cuthbert and
St. Edmund : "Although nearly two centuries divided
the death of St. Edmund from that of St. Cuthbert,
and there is no reason, except the common possession
of sanctity and heroic endurance, for supposing any
special resemblance in their characters, yet when we
inquire into the development of the *cultus* which was
consecrated to their memory, we are struck by some
remarkable points of likeness. Of both the incorruption of the mortal remains was confidently believed ;
over the tombs of both arose, first chapels, then
churches, then magnificent cathedrals. Eardulf the
bishop, and Eadred the abbot, dreading a visit from
the ruthless Northmen, took up the body of St. Cuthbert from Lindisfarne in 875, and wandered about
with it for seven years, settling at last at Chester-le-
Street. Egelwin the priest, alarmed for the safety of
the treasure of which he was the guardian, when
Thurkill made a descent in the Orwell in 1010, took
up the body of St. Edmund from its resting-place at

---

[1] "Memorials of St. Edmund's Abbey," edited by Thomas Arnold,
M.A., University College, Oxford, Fellow of the Royal University
of Ireland ; vol. I. Published by the authority of the Lords Commissioners of Her Majesty's Treasury, under the direction of the
Master of the Rolls, 1890.

Beodricsworth, and wandering up to London, remained there three years, till the state of Suffolk was quiet enough to allow of his returning home. Miracles prevented St. Cuthbert's body from being carried over to Ireland; miracles prevented St. Edmund's body from becoming a prey to the pious cupidity of the Londoners. On the completion of Abbot Baldwin's new church at Bury in 1095, there is a solemn translation of the body of St. Edmund to the shrine prepared for it, Bishop Wakeline, and Ranulf the king's chaplain, being the presiding functionaries. On the completion of Durham cathedral in 1104, there is a yet more solemn translation of the body of St. Cuthbert from the cemetery in the cloister into the church, the same Ranulf, now bishop of Durham, presiding, and the ceremony being crowned by a visitation of the relics, which verifies their reported incorruption. A similar visitation of the relics of St. Edmund, resulting in a similar verification, is made by Abbot Samson in 1198."

Mr. Arnold is not so happy in his further remarks. We doubtless know a great deal more of St. Cuthbert's real life and character than of St. Edmund's, but it is an exaggeration to write that we know "next to nothing" of the latter. To assert that St. Abbo drew on a free and strong imagination for his description and character of St. Edmund is scarcely justifiable, considering that the martyr's person and exploits were well known in St. Abbo's day. The present

writer has not started on the supposition that the
greater part of the information regarding St. Edmund
is myth, the concoction of men "whose information
is scanty, and their imagination strong." Judging
from references in existing manuscripts that the old
scribes drew from sources long since perished, the
compiler of these pages takes their works as a safe
basis. He examines them fairly, tries to supply what
is wanting from other sources, compares their facts
with ancient and modern traditions, traces their
agreement with the general history of the times, and
thus endeavours to piece together the lost history of
St. Edmund. It is not, however, maintained that no
myth has grown around St. Edmund's name, or that
in the course of a thousand years no legend has crept
into his history, but abundant facts remain in connection with the saint's life which are credible and
authentic. For instance, Ethelwerd and the Anglo-
Saxon Chronicle refer to a king of East Anglia
between St. Ethelbert and St. Edmund, and therefore
support Gaufridus, who gives his name and the
particulars of his reign. Gaufridus thus becomes a
reliable authority on one point, and may be equally
considered reliable in his account of the parentage
and fatherland of St. Edmund, which fits in with
Charlemagne's known protection of English exiles
and other facts of contemporary history. The supposition of Battely, that a certain Florentius invented the
parentage of St. Edmund one or two centuries *after*

Gaufridus, is baseless and far-fetched. North Hamburg, not Nuremburg, as the place of St. Edmund's
birth, and the local traditions of Hunstanton further
fix the probability of the narrative of Gaufridus.
The legend of Lothbroc or Lothparch has at least a
substratum of truth. Mr. Sharon Turner's identifica-
tion of the Lothbroc of St. Edmund's history with
Ragnar Lodbrog, who, he says, met his death in
Deira between 862 and 867, cannot be accepted in
the face of all the Icelandic writers who assign his
death to the *eighth* century and not the ninth.[1] On
the other hand, Adam of Bremen's testimony, the
local traditions of Reedham, Caistor-St.-Edmund's and
its neighbourhood, Hinguar's avowed object to invade
East Anglia (which is mentioned by all chroniclers),
and the name of Bern or Wern in the list of the ten
sea-kings establish the identity of Lothparch, and
confirm all that Gaufridus relates. His manuscript
is therefore an historical fragment of great value.
Similar records supply evidence of a like character,
which cannot reasonably be considered fictitious,
merely on opinion of what should be.

Two views of St. Edmund's martyrdom are current,
but easily reconciled. The first—represented by
the Saxon Chronicle, Asser, Ethelwerd, Matthew of
Westminster, and several of the St. Edmund's Bury
annals—states that Edmund fought bravely and
manfully ("atrociter pugnavit.") According to the

---

[1] Introduction to " Memorials of St. Edmund's Abbey," vol. I.
p. xix.

second—represented by St. Abbo, Florence and Malmesbury—the saint, when attacked by the Danes, made
no resistance. Each view is correct from its own
standpoint. In one, St. Abbo and those who follow
him aim at illustrating the meekness, self-sacrifice
and resignation of the saint. They accordingly dwell
chiefly on the martyrdom, and describe the Danes
and their two invasions in general terms,[1] merely to
contrast the pagan savagery with the Christian
Edmund's gentleness. The various attacks and the
consequent battles are foreign to their purpose and
they ignore them. The second view is more historical.
It pictures the invasion of East Anglia in 865 by
Hinguar, and Edmund's valiant stand; and the second
invasion of 870, crowned by the final struggle, and
the holy king's surrender of himself to the enemy in
order to save his people from further bloodshed.
Together, the two views give a perfect delineation of
St. Edmund's character, which was one of heroic and
unselfish bravery.

In closing this introduction I desire to tender my
heartfelt thanks to the numerous friends who have
aided me in my work. I gratefully acknowledge the
assistance of the late Father Lazenby, S.J., of Bury-
St.-Edmund's, who encouraged me to write and placed
his notes at my service, a kindness continued by his
superiors after his death. The librarians at Oxford and
Cambridge always showed courtesy and a willingness

---

[1] St. Abbo speaks of the two invasions as one.

to oblige, due no doubt to my introduction by
Father Stevenson, S.J. I cannot forget the hospitality
accorded me in London by a family, whose friendship
I then made and have always valued since. My
special thanks are due to the Right Rev. Abbot
Snow, O.S.B. for his revision of my manuscript, and
to others whose valuable hints will gain for these
pages any success which they may deserve.

Lastly, in giving the history of St. Edmund to the
public, I beforehand condemn and unreservedly retract
any expression or opinion which may be contrary to
the teaching or spirit of our Holy Mother the Catholic
and Roman Church.

J. B. MACKINLAY, O.S.B.

BLYTH, *March* 19, 1893.

CONTENTS.

CHAPTER IX.

ILLUSTRATIONS, PLANS, ETC.

PRAYER TO ST. EDMUND.

O precious charbouncle of martir's alle,
  O hevenly gemme, saphir of stabilnesse,
Thyn hevenly dewh of grace, let dou falle
    In to my penne, enclosed with rudnesse :
    And blissed martir, my stile do so dresse,
Undir thi wingis of proteccion,
That I nat erre in my translacion.

O richest rube, rubefied with blood
  In thi passion, be ful meek suffrance
Bound to a tre, lowly whan thou stood,
    Of arwes sharp suffryng ful gret penaunce,
    Stable as a wal, of herte in thi constaunce,
Directe my stile which I have undirtake
In thi worshepe, thi legende for to make.

O amatist, with peynes purpureat
  Emeraud trewe, of chastite most clene,
Which, nat withstandyng thi kyngli hih estat,
    Ffor Cristis feith suffredist poynes keene,
    Wherefore, of mercy, my dulnesse to susteene,
Into my brest sende a confortatiff
Of sum fair language t' embelisshe with thi liff.

Send dou, of grace, thi licour aureat
  Which enlumynyth these rethoriciens
To write of martirs, ther passions laureat :
    And causith also, these fressh musiciens,
    Ffals lust avoided of epicuriens,
Of glorious seyntes the tryumphes for to synge
That suffred peyne for Crist in ther levynge.

Now glorious martir of Bury cheef patron,
  In Saxonie born, of the blood roial,
Conveie my mater, be my proteccion,
    Githe in thi support myn hope abidith al,
    Directe my penne of that I write shal,
Ffor so thi favour fro me nat ne twynne
Upon thi story ryght thus I will be gynne.

LYDGATE, (Harleian MS. 2278, fol. 9 b,
collated with Harleian MS. 4826.)

PRAYER TO ST. EDMUND.

O precious charbouncle of martir's alle,
 O hevenly gemme, saphir of stabilnesse,
Thyn hevenly dewh of grace, let dou falle

Couuete my maiet, be my proteccion,
 Githe in thi support myn hope abidith al,
 Directe my penne of that I write shal,
Ffor so thi favour fro me nat ne twynne
Upon thi story ryght thus I will be gynne.

LYDGATE, (Harleian MS. 2278, fol. 9 b,
                    collated with Harleian MS. 4826.)

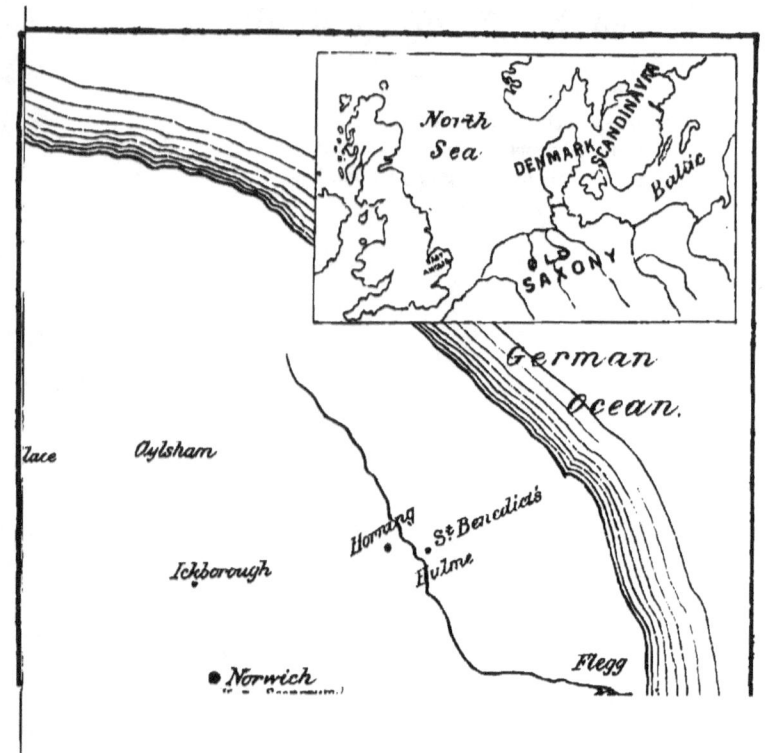

SAINT EDMUND,

KING AND MARTYR.

CHAPTER I.

Introductory—St. Edmund's Kingdom—Its Rulers and Saints.

[1] *Authorities*—St. Bede's "Ecclesiastical History" is the chief authority for the events of this chapter to the year 731. The Anglo-Saxon Chronicle, William of Malmesbury's "History of the Kings" and "History of the Prelates," Ethelwerd's Chronicle, and similar annals supplement St. Bede's History. Nicholas Harpsfeld's "Historia Anglicana Ecclesiastica," Duaci, 1622, and Blomefield's "History of Thetford," printed at Fersfield 1739, are secondary though valuable authorities. For well known historical facts in this and the following chapters, only standard works like Lingard's "History of England," and Green's "Short History of the English People," have been referred to. For geography throughout the work consult Camden's "Britania," with McCulloch's "Geographical Dictionary," or Bell's "Gazetteer of England and Wales."]

THAT portion of England which bulges out into the German Ocean in the form of a peninsula, and comprises the present counties of Norfolk, Suffolk, and Cambridge, was called by the early Anglo-Saxons East Anglia or East England. The sea encompassed this district on the north and east. On the south the river Stour separated it from the neighbouring kingdom of Essex. Impassable woods, "deep lakes and stagnant pools,"[1] protected its western frontier. The fens and marshes, two or three miles in breadth, which cover the flat lands of the west, stretch a distance of sixty or seventy miles from the Cam to

Geographical position of East Anglia.

---

[1] William of Malmesbury.

Wisbeach, and descend in river and morass to join the wide estuary of the Wash. These marshes, together with the dense forests of the south-west totally secluded East Anglia from the mainland. One clear and open space alone connected the peninsula with the rest of the island, and this the East Anglians afterwards defended against the frequent incursions of their neighbours by four ditches with corresponding lofty walls of earth. The principal of these, called St. Edmund's ditch, runs across Newmarket Heath. The common people call it "Devil's Dyke," its gigantic proportions marking it out as the work of evil spirits rather than of men.[1] The dykes completed the boundaries of the province over which Providence destined St. Edmund to reign— a man who, according to William of Malmesbury, was "devoted to God and ennobled by descent from ancient kings."

St. Edmund's kingdom under the Britons.

Previous to the Christian era, St. Edmund's kingdom was inhabited by the Celtic tribe of Iceni, the Cenimagni of Cæsar. Traces of the first inhabitants still survive in the names Ikensworth, Ickworth, Ickborough, Iken, Icklingham, and lastly Ikenild Street, the great consular road of the Iceni. The last king of the Iceni was Præsutagus, the consort of the famous British queen Boadicea, whose valiant resistance and tragic end finally brought East Britain under the sway of the Romans.

---

[1] It is doubtful who constructed these great walls. Some attribute them to Canute (A.D. 1017), who certainly made them the boundary of St. Edmund's Liberty. The Anglo-Saxon Chronicle mentions them as early as A.D. 905, and Matthew of Westminster makes them the site of a battle fought in that year between Edward the Elder and Ethelwald the Rebel. St. Abbo, who wrote thirty years before Canute's reign, also mentions the dykes. Most probably St. Edmund himself, whose names they bear, raised them as a defence against the Mercians and Danes.

The Roman governor Agricola, in dividing Britain Under the Romans. into provinces, made the territory of the Iceni part of Flavia Cæsariensis. In a few years the consular roads Ikenild Street, Jeddar Way, Stone Way, Via Devana, and perhaps Ermine Street, linked it with the important cities of Bath, Chester, Verulam, York, and London, while its general fertility, its clear and bracing climate, its picturesque scenery and nearness to Gaul, its hunting-grounds and rich pastures, attracted thither every class of citizen. East Britain thus became a favourite field of Roman civilization. Camp, station, and town, places like Brancaster, Sitomagus (Thetford), Caistor, Venta Icenorum (Norwich), Villa Faustini (Bury - St. - Edmund's), soon sprang up on plain and river-side. Vestiges of Roman art, Roman remains unearthed from time to time all through the district, show that the ancient civilization worked as great a change in East Britain during its 300 years' occupation, as modern civilization has done in the same or shorter time in America and Australia.

The Roman province of Britain flourished till the middle of the fourth century, when it fell before the attacks of the barbarians. At first Rome attempted to defend its most western province. The Count of the Saxon Shore pitched one of his chief camps at Brancaster on the Wash, in order to guard the exposed coasts of East Britain and North Gaul. All precautions, however, proved ineffectual. The waves of barbarian invasion still came on, forcing the Roman legions to retreat to the capital, and abandon Britain and all outlying provinces. The Britons with the Iceni thus found themselves utterly without resources to resist the savage hordes who poured from the northern mountains of the island upon their cities and plains.

The Barbarian
invasion and
conquest of
Britain.

The helplessness of the Britons after the departure
of the Romans, together with the incursion of the
Picts and Scots, conspired to bring about the formation of St. Edmund's kingdom. At the time there
dwelt among the marshes of Friesland and the Elbe,
or in the peninsula which parts the Baltic from the
North Sea, three kindred tribes of low-German Teu-
tonic race. The first tribe, the Jutes, lived on the
north of the peninsula, on the dry and sandy heaths
of Jutland, called in early times Zealand, because of
the purple waters which fringed the green meadows
of its coast; to the south of the Jutes, in the rich
farm-lands of Sleswig, or Angleland, as the great
Alfred delighted to call it, the Angles had settled
down; further south again, amid the sand-flats and
fen-lands of the Weser and the Elbe, and on the
very borders of the Roman empire, hovered the Saxons,
—the only name by which southern Europe knew
the other two tribes. All three, Jutes, Angles, and
Saxons, practised piracy on the high seas. In war-
ships, contemptuously named *chiules*, or keels, they rode
the wildest billows of the ocean, "in tempests dread-
ful to others, but to them a subject of joy." They
were thus scouring the North Sea when the Romans
abandoned Britain, and the Picts and Scots swarmed
down from the wilds of Caledonia. To invite them to
land and give assistance in repelling the invaders
from the north was the last despairing policy of the
British chiefs, who little thought of the consequence
of admitting the sea-pirates into the island. The new
allies quickly drove Pict and Scot back to their
mountain-fastnesses, and at once began a war of
conquest and extermination unparalleled in the barbarian invasion of any other country of Europe. Every
vestige of Roman civilization in Britain vanished
before the sword of Angle, Jute, and Saxon. Towns

and villages, palaces and cottages, were levelled to the ground. The inhabitants fled as from a devouring conflagration; the nobles made their escape to the continent or the western hills; the common people took refuge in the churches; but the enemy set fire to the holiest sanctuaries, and the victim who escaped the sword perished by the flames. In a hundred years the old race had entirely disappeared before the conquerors' advance.

The Jutes first began the conquest under Hengist and Horsa, who founded the kingdom of Kent. Then other bands, eager for plunder, put to sea from their German homes. The Saxons (A.D. 477) under Ælla and his three sons coasted along the hills and dark woodlands from Beachy Head to Selsey Bill, disembarked, and after a fierce struggle with the natives founded the kingdom of the Suth-Seaxe, or Sussex. Five years later the war-ships of Cerdic ploughed the Channel waters as far as the Isle of Wight. Their crews landed at Portsmouth, took possession of the neighbouring country, and founded the kingdom of West-Seaxe, or Wessex. Before Wessex extended its conquests to Oxford and Gloucester, the Middle-Seaxe and East-Seaxe crept up the Thames, and on its northern bank established the kingdom of Essex. *Formation of Kent and of the Saxon kingdoms.*

The advance of Jutes and Saxons, however, is of minor importance compared with the later advance of the Angles, "the fiercest in battle of all the barbarians." Owing to the superior prowess of these Angles, the three tribes assumed the common name of "English." By that name they were first known to the Britons, and fifty years later to Pope St. Gregory,[1] when he met their slaves exposed for sale in the Roman market-place. *The formation of the English Kingdoms.*

---

[1] St. Gregory in his letters styles them the "gens Anglorum," "the English people."

The Angles put to sea from the original Angleland, when the conquest of South Britain had almost ceased. A fleet of their chiules, under the command of Seomel, sailed up the Humber, took York, and founded the kingdom of Deira. Ida, another chief, with forty of the rude war-ships of his race, followed in the wake of Seomel, and founded, north of the Tees, the kingdom of Bernicia. Bernicia and Deira with the Frith of Forth as their northernmost boundary formed, in after times, the single kingdom of Northumbria. Up the southern tributaries of the Humber, the water gateway of North Britain, other "wolves, dogs, whelps from the kennel of barbarism," as St. Gildas from his abbey in Brittany styled them, penetrated into the heart of the island. They sailed up the Trent, took possession of Nottinghamshire, and, striking off along the Soar, colonized Leicestershire. Thus by degrees the whole district of central England grew into the kingdom of Mercia, so named either from the marshes of Lincolnshire on its borders, or from the marks or boundaries which on every side defined its frontier.

The formation of East Anglia.

The first of these English conquests and the one which mostly concerns this history was on the east of Mercia. It was preeminently Anglia, or England. Full twenty years before Ida and Seomel overran Northumbria, and three score years before Mercia became a kingdom, the East Angles drew up their long keels on the wide sand-flats of the coast of the Iceni, or left them secure in its numerous river creeks. The eastern coast, on which the pirates first landed, presented no high and rugged cliffs or walls of rock, like Bamborough or Beachy Head. On the contrary, its numerous estuaries, the many navigable streams which flowed through the broads and sand-banks, rather invited than opposed invasion. The

Angles accordingly ascended the Stour, and, leaving
their kinsmen in Essex undisturbed, spread themselves over the land to the north. Some rowed up the
picturesque and wood-flanked Orwell ; others swarmed
up the Yare, the Waveney, and the Ouse. Once in
the country, the Roman highways led them to spacious
cities and to rich fields for plunder. No record is left
of the struggle with the inhabitants. Many fled, while
others were either massacred or died in slavery.
Hardly a trace of them remained to guide the new
nation, whose history now began where theirs had
ended.

The land thus roughly seized did not differ consider- Physical
ably from the old country which the English had East Anglia.
just abandoned. In area both districts measured about
5,000 square miles ; both were from 70 to 80 miles in
length and breadth. They also resembled each other
in natural features. Even now the two countries are
wonderfully alike. The snug and homely farm-houses
of Sleswig, the hedgerows, the cattle quietly feeding
in the meadows, carry us in imagination to the east
of England. The low sea-coast of Yarmouth, the
level fen-lands of North Cambridgeshire, the salt
marshes of the Lincolnshire border, the scarcity of
wood, the general flatness, with only slight undulations
here and there, the sloping grass-land on the banks
of the Waveney,—all have their counterpart in the
old home of the East English. The new conquest
possessed other advantages of which the wild half-
cultivated fatherland could not boast. Roman art
had transformed into a paradise a land by nature
similar to their own, by laying it out in gardens and
groves and pastures and hunting-grounds ; Roman
engineers had linked together its numerous towns
and villas by a network of magnificent roads, unsur-
passed save by our modern railways. Finally, a dry

and salubrious climate added its attractions. True, the east winds were sharp and keen in winter and spring, but the air which blew over the land from the sea, unimpeded by mountain or wood, was clear and bracing. It suited the temper of the invaders, and doubtless aided in forming those "merry, pleasant, jovial" East Anglians of William of Malmesbury's Chronicle, who gloried in being St. Edmund's subjects.

The kingship established in East Anglia.

In the country whose early history and natural features are thus faintly outlined, the Angles settled down, family by family, kinsfolk by kinsfolk, in their "ham," or "ton," or "wick." Each freeman had his freeland; each settlement of freemen had its wise men or eldermen, who administered justice and framed laws under the sacred tree, or on the moot-hill—the original of our modern market-place,—round which home and farm clustered. So far in habits of life and government the invaders preserved their primitive traditions. Fresh circumstances, however, begot fresh requirements. The friendly feeling between kindred and kindred which existed on the shores of the Baltic made war almost unknown there. Captains or chiefs were seldom necessary. In time of danger, indeed, the Angles would choose a leader to marshal them for battle; but, the danger over, he stepped back into the rank and file. Now things were different: the Britons hovered on their borders; the limits of the neighbouring kingdoms were undefined; invasion or war frequently threatened them. Under these circumstances a permanent chief became a necessity. The division of plunder, too, and the partition of land called for a supreme and stable ruler. Wessex in similar difficulties elected Cerdic its *konning, can-ning,* or ableman; Kent chose Hengist. In imitation of these the North Folk and South Folk of East Anglia chose Uffa as king, and their sovereigns down to St. Edmund's time they styled Uffings.

All our chroniclers agree that St. Edmund sprang from the "ancient and noble stock" of the Uffings. Something in those bold leaders and their dauntless followers gave early promise of the martyr king who closed their illustrious line. They all possessed natural virtues of no mean order. Respect for authority, reverence for purity, bravery and fearlessness in war, boldness in the cause of right, frankness and love of truth were their distinguishing characteristics. Qualities like these, guided and perfected by the faith of Christ, produced the saintly and heroic kings whom history presents to us as the worthy progenitors of St. Edmund, their crowning glory, as he was the fairest blossom of their stock and the fulfilment of all their promise. The grace of God, it is true, energised his own individual labour, and primarily made Edmund a saint; but in the order of nature the traditions of his house had a share in moulding his character. The example of his ancestors stimulated him; he emulated their virtues; he modelled himself on them as on men renowned throughout the Churches. This will be made evident by a glance at those ancestral portraits which the youthful Edmund always had before his eyes.

During the reigns of King Uffa and of Tytil, his son and successor, no wave of that Christian teaching which formed the future saints of their line reached the shores of East England. Even Redwald, the third Uffing, can scarcely be regarded as a Christian king. Policy rather than conviction actuated his religion. He accepted the baptism of the black-robed strangers at Canterbury merely to please Ethelbert, his overlord, to whom Pope St. Gregory wrote: "Hasten to infuse into the minds of the kings subject to you

Character of the Uffings.

St. Edmund's ancestry.

the knowledge of one God, Father, Son, and Holy Ghost." Redwald while in Kent assisted at the solemn sacrifice, and listened to the religious chant of the Roman monks, but on returning home "he departed from the sincerity of the faith," writes Venerable Bede, "and, like the ancient Samaritans, seemed at the same time to serve Christ and the gods whom he had served before; for in the same temple he had an altar to sacrifice to Christ, and another small one to offer victims to the devils." Accordingly, when he became bretwalda or overlord by the defeat of Ethelfrid of Northumbria, the cross gained no victory. Redwald's sons, however, were of a different stamp. The eldest, Regnhere, fell in battle a devoted follower of the cross. St. Eorpwald the Martyr, [1] another son, was a disciple of St. Paulinus of York. He embraced the faith of Christ in the court of Edwin of Northumbria, a king who owed his crown to Redwald, and on returning home and succeeding his father began the conversion of his people with all the ardour of a neophyte. But a pagan revolt stopped his work, and Eorpwald, stabbed by a hired ruffian named Richbert, "poured out his immaculate spirit to God" a Christian martyr.

St. Sigebert the Learned, A.D. 630.

His half-brother St. Sigebert next ascended the throne. St. Sigebert was the apostle, the teacher, the father of his people. During the three years' anarchy which followed his brother's murder, he lived in exile in Burgundy. There he received fuller instruction in the Catholic faith at the feet of the then successor of St. Germanus of Auxerre, and was baptized. With the faith he drank in all the secular knowledge which

---

[1] Also spelt *Earpwald* and *Eorpenwald*. See Butler's "Lives of the Saints," Oct. 4. Between Redwald and Eorpwald Matthew of Westminster places Wibert. See his list of early E. Anglian kings and his manner of spelling their names (Bohn's edit. vol. i. p. 433).

the cloisters of Burgundy could provide. An accomplished scholar, a brave soldier, an earnest yet prudent son of the Church, Sigebert, succeeded to the crown, thoroughly fitted for the work of converting and civilizing his kingdom.

He commenced his reign by inviting St. Felix, whom he had met in Burgundy, to preach the faith to his subjects. [1] Felix received episcopal consecration from St. Honorius, archbishop of Canterbury, and fixed his see at Dunwich, [2] then a place of great importance. With his aid the work of conversion advanced with rapid strides. Sigebert was even enabled with teachers from Canterbury to establish the schools on the Cam which Henry III. afterwards raised to the dignity of a university.

St. Felix, the apostle of East Anglia.

---

[1] St. Felix, O.S.B., the apostle of East Anglia, landed at Babingley in Norfolk about A. D. 630, where he is said to have built his first church. Thoke, the great lord of these parts when St. Felix came to convert the East Angles, embraced Christianity and built the second church at Shernborne, and dedicated it to SS. Peter and Paul. Of Babingley succeeding ages made St. Felix the patron. The memory of St. Felix and his mission still lingers about East Anglia. On the mountains of the Christian Hills he is said to have preached. Flitcham, the ham or dwelling of Felix, Flixton, Felixstow, Felixston, and many other places in Norfolk and Suffolk were named after him, their first bishop. His feast is kept by the English Benedictines on March 8. See Montalembert's "Moines d'Occident," vol. iv. chap. iii. ; also "Historia Eliensis," published by the Anglia Christiana Society.

[2] Dunwich was a place of importance among the Romans, and immense quantities of bronze antiquities belonging to that people have been and are still washed out of the cliffs by the ever encroaching sea. At the time of St. Felix it was thoroughly fortified, but not strong enough to resist the inroads of the ocean, and now ships can float over the site once occupied by the city. The royal forest, which extended for miles south-east of the town, has been quite submerged ; and so the episcopal city, for 270 years crowded with hospitals, monasteries and churches, is now only a fishing village with a population of 250 souls.

Especially to this holy and learned king East
England owed its monasticism.   He welcomed to
his realm the Irish monk St. Fursey and his companions,[1] and built for them to the glory of God,
under the invocation of the Apostles SS. Peter and
Paul, the monastery and church of Cnobbersburg.[2]
Venerable Bede describes this first monastery of
East Anglia as standing on the summit of a hill
overlooking on three sides the dark forests of the
interior and on the fourth the broad expanse of
water formed by the junction of the Waveney and
Yare.   On this Mount Thabor, the Irish monks tarried
awhile, it is said, at the command of an angel.   To
join in their chant or holy conversation, St. Sigebert
would often steal away from the gaiety of the court.
He delighted to sit, a privileged disciple, at the feet
of Abbot Fursey and listen to his narrative of visions
as sublime and awful as those which Dante has

[1] St. Fursey was the son of an Irish king and abbot of an Irish
monastery.   With his brothers Ultan and St. Foilan, and the
Irish priests Gobban and Dicuil, he left Ireland and established
monastic life in East Anglia, where he adopted the Benedictine
rule of his bishop, as well as the Roman observance of Easter.
His fervent preaching and heroic virtues did much to convert the
people and to strengthen them in the faith.   In fact, Baronius
("Annals," viii. 313) attributes the conversion of East Anglia
chiefly to these Irish saints.   It is recorded that St. Fursey
established various double monasteries (Mabillon, "Acta SS.,"
vol. ii).   After twelve years' sojourn in East Anglia, leaving St.
Foilan to govern the monasteries he had founded there, St. Fursey
followed his other brother Ultan to France, where he built the
great monastery of Latiniac near Paris.   As vicar general he
governed the diocese of Paris for many years, and died at Froheins
(*Fursei Domus*), in the diocese of Amiens, while superintending
the building of Peronne Abbey.   His feast is kept in the north of
France on Jan. 16.   See Montalembert's "Monks of the West,"
and Cardinal Moran's "Irish Saints in Great Britain."

[2] Cnobbersburg, formerly a Roman camp, now Burgh Castle, or,
according to some, Blythburgh.

immortalized. For St. Fursey had been caught up into
heaven and seen "the choirs of angels, and heard the
praises which they sing;" endowed with angelic
vision, he had looked down upon the earth and
watched the struggle of good and evil in the world;
his miraculously gifted eyes had pierced the dark
abyss and gazed into "the fire which burns those
whose works and desires have been evil;" the recording angel's book even had been opened to him, and
in it he had read the judgments of the Son of God
on men. Touched by the burning words of this man
of God, the king resolved to resign his kingdom and
spend the rest of his life in contemplation of the
world to come. For this purpose he built a monastery
in honour of the ever Virgin Mother of God on a
certain gentle slope looking towards the east, and
washed by the little streams Linnet and Larke,—a
hallowed spot, destined in after days to be the resting
place of St. Edmund's body and the site of his vast
and magnificent abbey-shrine. Here King Sigebert
sought his long-wished-for solitude; here he unbuckled
his sword, put off his royal insignia, and donned the
black monastic cowl; his crown he laid upon the altar,
wearing in its place round his shaven head a simple
rim of hair, to remind him of his Saviour's diadem
of thorns and of the imperishable crown laid up for
him by the just Judge. Then he took his place in
the lowest stall in the monastic choir, the first of the
long list of Anglo-Saxon princes who forsook the
palace for the cloister. Short had been his reign, but
great his work. Everywhere he left memorials of
his practical wisdom and goodness. Under his rule
pagan and barbarian East Anglia passed away; in
its place arose a Christian commonwealth with bishops,
priests and faithful people, and churches, monasteries
and schools.

Sigebert was not allowed, however, to breathe his last in the retirement of the sanctuary. A terrible enemy of the cross threatened his kingdom and his work in the person of Penda, king of Mercia, a sworn champion of the old heathen worship. Penda would permit no Christian teacher to enter his dominions with impunity, and, if a neighbouring prince received the faith of Christ, he considered it as a challenge of his policy and a declaration of war. Accordingly, when Edwin of Northumbria embraced the faith, Penda attacked him and slew him in the fight of Hatfield Chase. The progress of the faith now brought this upholder of paganism into East Anglia at the head of an army of Mercians and Britons. Egric, the successor of St. Sigebert, prepared to take the field against him, but his soldiers, mindful of the courage and experience of their former sovereign, dragged Sigebert from his cell and put him at their head. The saint, faithful to his profession, refused to unsheath the sword or wield the battle-axe, and he entered the battle-field with no weapon save a small wand. Thus armed, he was slain with King Egric at the head of the Christian army.

King St. Annas,
A D. 649.

St. Annas, son of Eni, Redwald's brother, at once took up the reins of government. He worthily filled the throne of St. Eorpwald and St. Sigebert, endeavouring with Bishop Felix and Abbot Fursey to consolidate what his predecessors had begun. In spite of nineteen years of almost perpetual war with Penda, Annas succeeded in raising fresh monasteries, embellishing the old ones with more stately buildings and enriching all with valuable treasures of books and vestments. Annas' influence spread beyond his own kingdom: his court became the refuge of Penda's victims, and there princes like Coinwalch, king of

Wessex, flying from the Mercian tyrant's vengeance, received the faith of Christ.

From around St. Annas' throne shines out a galaxy of saintly children. [1] His queen, the holy Hereswide, sister of St. Hilda, the celebrated abbess of Whitby, bore him St. Sexberga, who, married to Erconbert of Kent, became the mother of St. Ermenhilda and St. Earcongota, and the grandmother of St. Werberga, the patroness of Chester. St. Ethelberga, [2] abbess of Faremoutier, [3] and St. Etheldreda, the foundress of Ely, were the first and third daughters of St. Annas. Both are

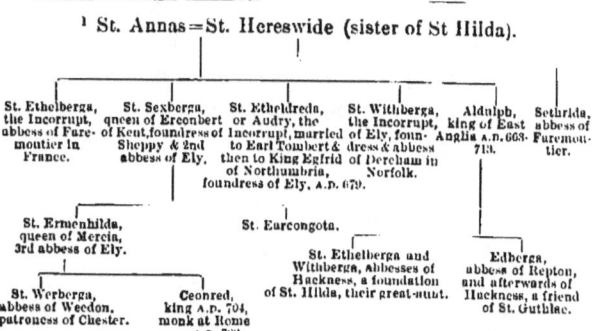

[1] St. Annas = St. Hereswide (sister of St Hilda).

St. Ethelberga, the Incorrupt, abbess of Faremoutier in France.

St. Sexberga, queen of Erconbert of Kent, foundress of Shepoy & 2nd abbess of Ely.

St. Etheldreda, or Audry, the Incorrupt, married to Earl Tombert & then to King Egfrid of Northumbria, foundress of Ely, A.D. 679.

St. Withberga, the Incorrupt, king of East foundress of Ely, foun- Anglia A.D. 663- Faremoudress & abbess of Dereham in Norfolk.

Aldulph, king of East Anglia A.D. 663- 713.

Sethrida, abbess of Faremoutier.

St. Ermenhilda, queen of Mercia, 3rd abbess of Ely.

St. Werberga, abbess of Weedon, patroness of Chester.

Ceonred, king A.D. 704, monk at Rome A.D. 709.

St. Earcongota.

St. Ethelberga and Withberga, Abbesses of Hackness, a foundation of St. Hilda, their great-aunt.

Edberga, abbess of Repton, and afterwards of Hackness, a friend of St. Guthlac.

Some authors (compare Butler, April 30, Wharton's " Hist. Epis. Lond.," Capgrave, April 30, and Leland's " Itinerary," vol. viii. p. 72.) make St. Annas the father of St. Erconwald, the founder of Chertsey Abbey and bishop of London, and of St. Ethelberga, his sister, the first abbess of Barking. The confusion arises from not distinguishing St. Ethelberga daughter of St. Annas from St. Ethelberga sister of St. Erconwald. Erconwald and his sister were children of Offa, king of the East Saxons, sometimes incorrectly called East Anglia, or the country of the East Angles, even by ancient authors.

[2] Called in French St. Aubierge. St. Bede styles her the natural daughter of St. Annas, which in his time had not the present meaning, but was used in opposition to his *adopted* child, Sethrida, of whom St. Bede is also speaking. Montalembert seems to have forgotten this fact.

[3] Founded by St. Fara, A.D. 616. There being few abbeys in England at this period, many noble virgins entered the monasteries in Gaul, especially Faremoutier, Chelles and Andelys.

celebrated for their unblemished chastity, and their bodies remained incorrupt after death, the one in England and the other in France. St. Withberga, the youngest virgin-daughter of this extraordinarily holy family, founded Dereham in Norfolk, over which she presided as abbess for many years. Aldulph, Annas' only son, showed himself little inferior in holiness to his devout sisters. The worthy father of three abbesses, his contemporaries recognised in him the virtues of a truly Christian prince.

St. Annas closed an honourable reign by a martyr's death. With his brother, St. Firminus,[1] he fell in a last struggle with the heathen Penda (A.D. 654), and his subjects buried him in the priory, now an ivy-covered ruin, at Blythburgh. His tomb is still pointed out in the north aisle of the neighbouring church of Broad.

Ethelhere, the successor of Annas, for a moment broke the tradition of loyalty to the cross and holiness of life so remarkable in the royal line of East Anglia. He made a league with Penda, and fell in battle with him and thirty other royal princes on the field of Winwoed, near Leeds. In that battle King Oswy terribly avenged the death of his brother, St. Oswald, and the death of St. Sigebert, St. Annas, Edwin and Egric, all kings sacrificed to the pagan gods by the Mercian sword.[2] After the fall of Ethelhere his brother Ethelward reigned nine years. Ethelward saw the old heathenism pass away for ever, and left the throne to King Aldulph, when the triumph of the cross was complete.

Ethelhere.

Ethelward.

---

[1] St. Firminus, whose shrine together with that of St. Botulph stood attendant on the shrine of St. Edmund, was a brother of St. Annas, and not a son, as some state.

[2] "At the Winwed was avenged the slaughter of Annas,
 The slaughter of the kings Sigebert and Egric,
 The slaughter of the kings Oswald and Edwin."
  Henry of Huntingdon (Bohn's edition, p. 57).

Few rulers in Saxon times stand out more gloriously King Aldulph. from among the Christian kings of their age than Aldulph. In his childhood he had seen the broken idols which once stood side by side with the Christian altar, but after his nineteen years of vigorous rule no vestige of Woden or Thor existed in the land. Over the dust and ruins of crumbled paganism he raised innumerable churches and religious houses. Ely Abbey especially owed some of its splendours to him. He directed the workmen in the building of that stateliest monastery of his realm, and, when the minster was reared, he welcomed to its cloisters his sister St. Etheldreda. On another solemn occasion the old chroniclers picture him at the abbey gates in company with King Wulphere of Mercia, King Egbright of Kent and a crowd of noble followers, taking part in the dedication to God's service of his niece St. Werberga. So well known were Aldulph's piety and devotion to the Church, that the prelates of the time elected to meet in council in his territory rather than in any other. According to some writers, St. Theodore of Canterbury held his famous synod for the canonical organization of the English Church, not at Hertford, but at Aldulph's royal city of Thetford. [1] At that important council, Bisus, then bishop of the Angles, took his rank first after the arch-bishop. Among other business St. Theodore's synod divided East Anglia into two sees, fixing the second at North Elmham, and leaving the aged Bisus to preside over the older see of Dunwich. [2] Aldulph, after seeing

---

[1] See Blomefield's "History of Thetford," p. 24, where the question is discussed.

[2] *The early bishops of East Anglia.*—The first episcopal see for the kingdom of East Anglia was placed at Dunwich in Suffolk on the consecration of

ST. FELIX, the first bishop about A.D. 630.

THOMAS, who had served as deacon to St. Felix, succeeded in 653.

Malmesbury writes of him *ex Girviorum provincia oriundus.*

his kingdom politically and ecclesiastically organised, passed to his reward. Of his two immediate successors, **Elfwold and Bernred**, the scanty records of the time give little more than the names. The next king, the good and virtuous **Ethelred**, is principally remarkable for his long and peaceful reign of fifty years (A.D. 748). His son, St. Ethelbert the Martyr, succeeded.

Medieval chroniclers bestow unstinted praise upon the young and accomplished Ethelbert, a king amiable in disposition, handsome in countenance, graceful in body, prudent in mind. As a child this holy prince loved the monks' chant in choir more than the games of boyhood; unlike other sons of kings, he delighted not in the glitter and dissipation of the court, but preferred to minister to the sick and feeble, to relieve the poor with alms, to retire and converse with God and His saints in prayer. In him as a sovereign, mercy and justice met. One saying of his especially reveals the secret of his amiable character. "The higher our rank," he would remind his attendants, "the more gentle and lowly should be our bearing." No wonder this pious disposition led him to prefer a life of perpetual chastity. His wise men, however, hoped by his marriage to secure an heir to the throne and thus preserve the tranquillity of the kingdom. Accordingly, at their entreaty, in the forty-fourth year of his reign, Ethelbert set out for the court of Offa of Mercia to seek the hand of that sovereign's daughter Alfrida.[1] On arriving with his retinue on the frontiers

Marginal notes:
Elfwold and Bernred.

Ethelred.

St. Ethelbert the Martyr, A.D. 792.

BONIFACE, the next bishop, died in 669.   He is called Bertgus in Cott. MS. Vesp. B. 6, and Beortgils in MS. Tiber B.5.

BISUS, BISI, or BOSA was the next bishop. About the year 673, as stated in the text, his diocese was divided into two, at the national council held by Archbishop Theodore at Hertford.   One see continued at Dunwich, the other was fixed at North Elmham in Norfolk.

[1] Called also Etheldreda.

of Mercia, he sent before him presents and letters to announce the object of his visit. Offa received his overtures with favour, invited the East Anglian prince to the palace of Sutton Wallis, four miles from the present city of Hereford, and there entertained him with great show of pomp and ceremony. The day's rejoicing over, attendants conducted the royal guest to his bed-chamber, but not to rest. As he knelt in prayer commending himself to his heavenly Father's keeping, Wimbert, a court official, summoned him to a conference with Offa. While the unsuspecting stranger made his way through the dungeon-like passages of the castle to his host's presence, a band of hired assassins suddenly rushed out and stabbed him to death. At the news of their sovereign's murder, horror and dismay seized upon his attendants They mounted their horses and fled. Offa on his side pretended to bewail his royal brother's death, but his immediate seizure of Ethelbert's kingdom branded him with the crime. On him and his God avenged the death of His saint. Offa died within two years, and the torrent of the river Ouse at Bedford, in a strange and unaccountable rising, unearthed and swept away his corpse; his sons died without issue; his daughters became widows and beggars; and his queen, at whose door history chiefly lays the murder of Ethelbert, met a most miserable death three months after her crime. A few years after St. Ethelbert's martyrdom, the race of Offa had passed away for ever, and East Anglia, which he had so forcibly possessed, became the tomb of each successive Mercian sovereign who claimed dominion over it.

At first the faithful secretly buried St. Ethelbert's The shrine of body not far from the scene of his martyrdom, in the St. Ethelbert. village of Marden, on the river Lugg, where a miraculous well still marks its first resting-place. Later on, as the saint's tomb became famous for the number of cures wrought at it, the clergy and faithful translated the sacred body to a church at Fernby, or Fern Heath, which in course of time developed into the cathedral of Hereford.

Meanwhile the East Anglians, at first scattered and disorganised, quickly rallied again, and chose for their leader a prince of the royal line named Offa, a namesake of their Mercian persecutor. This Offa was the immediate predecessor of St. Edmund.

Offa

Such is the noble and illustrious line of kings who lead up to St. Edmund. As his ancestors and predecessors, they form a brilliant background to the royal martyr, who stands out among them as the most striking figure in the picture. For St. Edmund embodies in himself all the characteristics of the East Anglian dynasty: like Uffa and Redwald, he was a fearless warrior; like St. Sigebert, a patron of learning and of the Church; like St. Annas, a defender of his kingdom and subjects; like St. Ethelberga, St. Etheldreda, and St. Withberga, a lover of virginity; like St. Eorpwald and St. Ethelbert, a martyr. The ancient antiphon composed in his honour saluted him as king, warrior of Christ, white lily of virginity, red rose of martyrdom. "Hail, king of the Angles," it ran, "soldier of the King of angels, Edmund, the flower of martyrs, resembling both the rose and the lily, pray to the Lord for the salvation of the faithful."

King Edmund.

CHAPTER II.

Saint Edmund's Parentage and Birth.

[*Authorities*—Gaufridus de Fontibus' "De Infantia Sti. Edmundi" holds the first and foremost place among the authorities for the events of this chapter. A 15th century copy of this work exists in Bibl. Pub. Cantab., Ff. 1.27, § 29, p. 628-624, which Thomas Arnold, M.A., has recently edited for the Master of the Rolls in his "Memorials of St. Edmund's Abbey," vol. i. Hardy conjectures that Gaufridus was identical with Godefridus de Fontibus, a Franciscan friar and guardian of a convent of his order in Paris, who died Bishop of Cambrai in 1238. This, however, is impossible, since Gaufridus dedicates his work to the noble Lord Abbot Ording, who ruled St. Edmundsbury from 1148 to 1156, thirty years before St. Francis of Assisium was born. According to Arnold, he "belonged to the house of regular canons in the patronage of St. Edmund at Thetford." More probably he was a monk of St. Edmundsbury, afterwards bishop of Ely, the same who graced by his presence the translation of St. Frideswide, Feb. 12, 1180. From the prologue of his work, the reader gathers that he often revisited his former brethren, and, when the conversation turned on St. Edmund, he gave them the fruit of his researches. At last, urged by Prior Sihtric and Sub-Prior Gocelin, who met him at Thetford, he committed to writing what he had heard *(quædam ab aliis mihi tradita)*, and what he had read *(quædam viva lectione cognita)*, dedicating his work to Abbot Ording, whose obedient servant he calls himself. His MS., treating of the parentage, birth, and early life of St. Edmund, is valuable, because he had access to records and genealogies long since lost. With Tanner's "Biblioth. Britan.," p. 304, compare Battely's "Antiquitates Sti. Edmundi Burgis," p. 76. The next important and most complete narrative extant of St. Edmund's life is the "Vita et Passio S. Edmundi Regis et Martyris una cum miraculis ejusdem," MS. Bodl. 240, ff. 624-677 vell folio XIV. cent., a compilation from all the chronicles, histories and legends of the saint then in existence and within reach. At intervals, in the margin of this MS., the compiler refers to the following authorities: Henry of Huntingdon, Simeon of Durham, St. Abbo, Gaufridus, Nicholas Prior of Wallingford, the chronicles of Westminster, Ely, and Norwich, Samson Abbas, Hermannus, and Osbert de Clare. After the life, the early incidents of which are word for word from Gaufridus, follow the narrative of Abbot Baldwin's translation of the saint's body, and then the earliest and latest records of St. Edmund's miracles. The whole MS., though called a compendium, fills 53 folio pages of small and closely written matter, and, if put into modern type, would fill a handsome volume. Another ancient "Vita S. Edmundi Regis et Martyris," MS. Cott. Tiber E 1. f. 283b suffered so materially in the fire of 1731 as to be now unreadable. Capgrave, however, has preserved it in his "Nova Legenda Angliæ," f. 107, and a copy of it exists in the Bodleian library, MS. Tanner 15. The introduction of this "Vita" is taken from Gaufridus de Fontibus; the other part from Herman's narrative, ending with the erection of St. Edmund's Church in Canute's time. From the MSS. in his abbey library, John Lydgate, the monk-poet of St. Edmundsbury, wrote in verse the "Life and Acts of St. Edmund the King and Martyr," a poem varying in different MSS. from 300 stanzas of seven lines each to twice that number. Lydgate, by far the most famous versifier of the 15th century, according to Prof. Craik ("English Literature and Language," p. 175), was born (A.D. 1380) in the village of Lydgate, from which he takes his name. After studying in the university of Paris and travelling in Italy, he returned to his abbey, intimately acquainted with the literature of the countries through which he had passed, and stored with the learning of his age. After his return to his monastery, he spent the rest of his life, like St. Bede, in teaching and studying. A master of the English tongue, he rivalled Chaucer, whose disciple he was, in the smoothness of his verse.

His wit, says Camden, the very muses formed and modelled. Craik considers him a mercenary rhymester, because he received one hundred shillings from Abbot Whethamstede for putting into English verse the Latin legend of St. Alban, as if payment, then as now, did not rather commend a poet than condemn him. The same professor calls attention to Lydgate's diffuseness, but it is hard to agree with him that the monk-poet possessed very little strength or originality of imagination. Gillingwater in his History of Bury mentions some of Lydgate's poems, and Ritson gives a list of about two hundred and fifty of them. Several have been printed at various times; among others his nine books of tragedies translated from a Latin work of Boccaccio's and printed at London in the reign of Henry VIII. A selection of Lydgate's minor poems, edited by Mr. Halliwell, was printed by the Percy Society (London, 1840). Lydgate wrote the poem of St. Edmund's life, as he himself tells us, "Whan the Sixte Henry in his estat royal, with his sceptre of Yngelond and of ffraunce held at Bury his feeste principal of Crystemasse." "The Abbot William," he continues, "gaff me chaarge to doon my attendaunce, the noble stoory to translate in substaunce out of Latin." There are extant as many as nine original MSS. of Lydgate's beautiful poem. None have yet been printed. MS. Harl. 2278, presented to Henry VI. on his visiting Bury, and ornamented with 120 limnings, is considered one of the richest illuminated manuscripts in the world (see a description of it in vol. ii. of the Harleian Catalogue, pp. 639-649). MS. Ashmole 463 was dedicated and presented to Edward IV. Most of the MSS. of Lydgate's "Life and Acts of St. Edmund" not only vary in length, but differ verbally. The MSS. used here are Harl. 4826, for the copying of which the author is indebted to a London friend, and Harl. 2278. Though richly imaginative in his descriptions, Lydgate is a valuable authority on St. Edmund. He had at hand in his abbey library the most authentic lives and traditions of the saint, and he used them "folwying myn auctours in e'ery manere thing, as in substaunce folwyng the letter in dede." For further remarks of Lydgate's poems on St. Edmund see chapters x. and xii.; see also chapter xii. for an account of "La vie Seint Edmund le Rey," a life in French verse by Denis Piramus, a courtier of Henry III., which has much in common with Lydgate's].

THE last chapter sketched the history of a brave and saintly dynasty, no less remarkable in our annals for its martyr and virgin spirit than for its bold and haughty blood. This chapter will treat of the descent and birth of St. Edmund, the last of that noble East Anglian line.

The country of St. Edmund's birth.

Old Saxony, not the Saxony of the present day, claims to be the country of St. Edmund's birth. At the end of the eighth and the beginning of the ninth century, the period of our saint's early history, Old Saxony comprised the district which lies between the Ems and the Elbe, and stretches from Cologne to the northernmost part of Schleswig-Holstein. Its connection with the early English kingdoms is a well known fact of history. The kindred races of the two countries were in frequent communication with each other. In the time of St. Boniface, of St. Willibrord and of the parents of St. Edmund, whole colonies of English passed over from Britain to Old Saxony, and the Saxons in their turn constantly sent their sons to be

brought up in England.   It is not surprising, then,
that the East Anglian nobles on the murder of St.
Ethelbert looked to Old Saxony as to an easy and
convenient refuge.   At first they hoped to rally
again in their own land, but Offa pursued them in
their flight from Sutton Wallis, overtook them as
they crossed the plains of Ely, and annexed their
country, as he had previously annexed Kent and
Wessex.   They never submitted, however, to the
Mercian tyranny, choosing rather a few months'
voluntary exile among friendly kinsmen in Saxony.[1]

The whole event brought them in contact with Charlemagne
Charlemagne.   Their land of exile, in fact, fills an ^and Old Saxony.
important page in the annals of the great Frankish
emperor's reign.   The Saxons had invaded and ravaged
the imperial dominions over and over again.   At last,
after their attack on the Rhine Provinces, during his
campaign against the Saracens, Charlemagne finally
conquered them.   Later on, in the year 782, when
they revolted, he forced their king Witikind and his
chief followers to become Christians as the sole condition of peace.   Although from that time Witikind
and his subjects remained faithful to their religion
and firm in their allegiance, other Saxon bands, during
a space of thirty-three years, continually made war,
and were as frequently vanquished.   Charlemagne
had just succeeded in crushing one of these rebellions
at the time of St. Ethelbert's murder, and the two
events conspired to bring him into connection with the
East Anglian nobles.   In him they found a powerful
and willing protector.   With open arms the great Charlemagne
emperor received any English prince whom the ^and England.
rapacity of Offa of Mercia drove to his court.   Perhaps

---

[1] See "Annales Ecclesiastici et Civiles Britannorum, Saxonum,
Anglorum, &c.," R. P. Michaelis Alford (alias Griffith), vol iii.,
anno 841.

the influence of Alcuin, the famous English scholar
from Bede's school at Jarrow, made him ready to open
his palace-gates to his favourite's compatriots; more
likely, fear of a neighbouring rival power and a secret
wish to add England to his empire induced him to
offer hospitality to the enemies of Mercia. In any
case, Offa's victims invariably fled to Charlemagne's
court for protection. Thither came Eardulph of
Northumbria after his vain contest for the crown with
Ethelred, the husband of one of Offa's daughters.
Egbert, the claimant of the throne of Wessex, driven
from his kingdom by another son-in-law of Offa's,
likewise sought an asylum in the Frankish emperor's
dominions. 'Kent also appealed to Charlemagne against
Offa's invasion and tyranny; lastly, the East Anglian
princes and thanes received a welcome from him. The
emperor was particularly kind to his English exiles.
He advanced them to posts of trust in his empire; he
pushed their claims, and materially assisted them in
their war of independence; and he trained their youth
in the art of war and educated them in his palace-
school.

Charlemagne and St. Edmund's father.

Among those thus brought into contact with
Charlemagne through the seizure of East Anglia by
the Mercians, were two cousins in whose veins flowed
the royal blood of the Uffings. One of these, Offa, the
namesake of Offa of Mercia, the exiles elected to
succeed St. Ethelbert; the other, named Alcmund,
Divine Providence destined one day to become the
father of St. Edmund. Alcmund, though an exile and
stranger in a foreign land, could thus claim a near
relationship with the reigning house of East Anglia.
Lydgate styles him the "cousin," other chroniclers
the "consanguineus," the *blood relation*, and "cognatus,"
the *near kinsman*, of Offa of East Anglia. Besides his
royal blood Alcmund possessed qualities of mind and

body of no ordinary character. As a mere boy he distinguished himself among the English on the continent, and while still a youth Charlemagne thought him fit to govern part of his new conquest of Saxony.[1]

The Protestant Dean Battely (followed by Arnold) asserts that the parentage of St. Edmund is all a myth—the make-up of one Florentius, abbot of the church of St. Adalbert in "Egmundâ," who in the year 1296 came on an embassy to England and visited the place in which lay the body or relics of St. Edmund the Martyr, once king of the Angles. This devout abbot wished very much to get some clue to the genealogy and acts of St. Adalbert and of his brothers in the flesh, and so among other works he searched into the chronicles of the kings of England, and in them he found it recorded that Adalbert (Ethelbert) had reigned over the Angles thirty-seven years and seven months before his brother Edmund obtained the kingdom. The two brothers had a sister named Brictiva, who was buried at Frankenwoerde. Their father's name was Alemund, a prince of noble and ancient Saxon stock. Behold Alemund the father of St. Edmund.—So far Battely.

It is answered : First, the facts connected with the parentage of St. Edmund are given, *not* on the authority of Florentius, but of Gaufridus, who wrote at least a hundred years before Abbot Florentius visited St. Edmundsbury. With abundant materials at hand, Gaufridus compiled the historical fragment a copy of which has survived to our own day. Now there is nothing positive to refute his evidence. To say that he drew upon his imagination for his facts is a rash and unwarrantable assertion. He mentions the sources from which he drew, viz. the records and traditions of the time. And, if the sixteenth century vandalism destroyed the sources, that is no reason for holding that they did not exist. Moreover, as the text shows, his facts accord with the events and customs of the age as related in other annals, and also with whatever traditional or written history of East Anglia exists, scanty though it be. Secondly, Abbot Florentius made the grave mistake of confusing St. Edmund's brother, Adalbert, with St. Ethelbert. From that mistake follows a host of blunders. For instance, St. Ethelbert became the son of Alemund. He was in fact the son of King Ethelred of East Anglia. Adalbert became a king and a martyr, and both Adalbert and Edmund were made to live in the eighth century instead of in the middle of the ninth. Florentius blundered, but it is hard to see how that militates against Gaufridus' facts. See, however, the chronicle of John Wallingford, Gale's "Hist. Brit., Saxon. Scriptores, xv." vol. iii. p. 534.

The character of
King Alcmund.
Alcmund was not altogether unworthy of the trust reposed in him. Some of the old St. Edmundsbury registers style him saint, and one chronicle at least calls him Alcmund the great. [1] Noble in birth, handsome in person, manly in his bearing; in battle courageous, in council prudent; above all, blameless in his private life and with the fear of God ever before his eyes,—thus the chroniclers paint the father of St. Edmund. Kingship he regarded but as a nearer and more responsible service of the King of kings; he looked upon himself only as the minister of God distributing His justice and mercy and proclaiming His laws. From the example no less than from the teaching of so saintly a father, his sons learnt to realize that higher sovereignty than the highest on earth, the sovereignty of Him who maketh kings and casteth them down, in whose sight the earthly sceptre and crown are of no avail when He chooses to put down the mighty from their seat and to exalt the humble. Charlemagne recognized the worth of such a man, and therefore, says the poet, Alcmund was "set in a chair of kingly dignity."

The mother of
St. Edmund
Siwara was Alcmund's queen. If the tree is known by its fruit, then all that ancient writers say of Siwara only faintly depicts her admirable qualities. She was "meek as Esther," sings the old monk-poet, and "fair as Judith." Of a strong yet winning character, exceedingly fair, yet matronly and dignified, she added to these queenly virtues more than the ordinary kindness and gentleness of womanhood, being ever full of tenderest pity for the afflicted, and making it her delight to feed and clothe the poor, and to comfort the sick and sorrow-laden. [2]

---

[1] See Leland, and Bodl. MS. 240, which spell his name Ulkmund.

[2] Dean Battely has started another theory with regard to Siwara. The Life of St. Botulph, he says, mentions a certain

Siwara bore King Alcmund three sons and one daughter.[1] Cerne Abbey in Dorsetshire perpetuated the memory of the eldest son, St. Edwold.[2] Edwold came to England with his brother Edmund, and remained in East Anglia for some years. After the martyrdom of Edmund, the popular voice elected him to fill the vacant throne, which he refused. Fearing compulsion, he fled and hid himself in the valley of the Cerne. There beside the silver fountain known as St. Augustine's well, secluded from the rest of the world by the lofty chalk hills surrounding his hermitage, he gave himself up to a life of austerity and prayer. One 28th of November, he passed away to the other world. Soon after his death, the fame of miracles wrought by his intercession attracted pilgrims from all parts of England to his grave. The devotion of the faithful translated his body to a rich shrine, over which they raised the noble abbey of Our Lady, St. Peter, and St. Benedict, of whose former glories the present ancient gateway alone remains.[3]

St. Adalbert, or Elbert,[4] the third son of Alcmund and Siwara, is best known in connection with the Benedictine abbey of Cormin in Holland, where his body rested for many centuries after his death. Of

---

Ethelmund, king of the South Saxons, whose mother's name was Siwara. The monkish historians, he continues, writing the legend of St. Edmund, make Siwara, the mother of Ethelmund, mother of St. Edmund. "John Wallingford," concludes Battely, "confirms my suspicions." The theory is ingenious but improbable.

[1] See Leland's "Collectanea," vol. i. p. 245, and vol. ii. p. 219, and Harpsfeld, p. 174. Capgrave speaks of St. Edmund as an only child. Gaufridus mentions two sons, of whom Edmund was *natu posterior*.

[2] Also spelt Ewold and Ewald.

[3] See Leland's "Itinerary." vol. viii. p. 71.

[4] Ibid. See also Mabillon's "Acta Sanctorum," sæcl. iii. tom. i. p. 645.

his sister Wilgena little more than the name is recorded. [1]

St. Edmund
the child of
promise.

St. Edmund was Alcmund and Siwara's second son and their child of promise. His birth, like Isaac's in the Old Testament, and St. John the Baptist's in the New, was announced by an angel. Miraculous signs similar to those related in the lives of St. Dominic, St. Columbanus, St. Thomas of Canterbury, and other saints appeared at his birth, as if to mark his future greatness. He was in a special way the fruit of prayer. Alcmund often besought God to grant him a numerous and saintly family. In answer to his prayer, an angel from heaven admonished him to undertake a pilgrimage to the tombs of the Apostles, [2] for there God would reward his devotion and grant his petition. [3]

Alcmund's
pilgrimage to
Rome.

Then, as now, every pious Catholic desired to visit Rome, that city hallowed by so many sacred memories, which St. Cyprian apostrophised as "the mother and mistress, the root and foundation, of all the Churches of the universe." Thither, as to a new Jerusalem, the Mount Sion of Christendom, the newly converted kings and nations flocked to offer their homage and allegiance to Christ's Vicar, the father and teacher of all the faithful. At this time more than thirty English kings had made the pilgrimage to the tombs of the Apostles, and many, like Ina of Wessex and Coinred of Mercia, put off the crown and abdicated the throne in order to spend a life of prayer and good works within the precincts of the eternal city. Joyfully, then, in obedience to the angel's voice, Alcmund set out to visit the churches of Rome.

---

[1] If she were the same as Brictiva, her burial-place was Frankenwoerde.

[2] "Ad limina apostolorum," writes Gaufridus.

[3] Bodl. 240.

Apparently, while in the holy city, he did not lodge in the English school or home of hospitality which Ina founded and supported with the first Peter-pence. In visiting the centre of Christendom to study the pure Catholic faith at its very source, English kings and princes, as well as bishops, priests, thanes, and freemen, usually stayed in Ina's hospice. But Alcmund scarcely belonged to England ; he therefore sought a lodging elsewhere, and became the guest of a Roman widow of wealth and high patrician rank. This lady, after her husband's death, devoted her life to works of piety. One day, while conversing with Alcmund, she noticed on his breast a brilliant sun, whose rays, darting towards the four points of the compass, threw a miraculous light on all around. Moved by the vision, and filled with the spirit of prophecy, Alcmund's pious hostess declared that from him should arise a child whose fame, like to the eastern sun, should illumine the four quarters of the world, and whose example should spread God's glory everywhere, and enkindle in the hearts of men greater love of Christ.[1] After this, Alcmund did not tarry long in Rome. The object of his pilgrimage seemed already attained, and he prepared at once to return to his kingdom.

A brilliant sun shines on his breast.

On arriving in Saxony after his long absence, Alcmund made his way to Northemberg, or North Hamburg,[2] a city pleasantly situated at the mouth of

St. Edmund born at Northemburg, A.D. 841.

---

[1] The second nocturn lessons of St. Columbanus' office relate a similar wonder : "Columbanus, natione Hibernus, jam inde ab utero matris quæ illo gravida solem radientem sibi in quiete gestare visa est, futuram claritatem præsignavit."

[2] Leland gives Norembregis, Dugdale Nuremburg, Curteys' Register and the Douai MS. Northemberges, Lydgate Northemberge, Camden Norinberg. It is hard to say for certain what city is meant unless the present Hamburg. Nuremberg is not in Old Saxony ; Norden in Friesland, and Nordenham on the Weser are

the Elbe, and claiming Charlemagne as its founder. The northern Genoa, and later on the rival of Venice, Northemberg held the first place among the towns and cities of Old Saxony. Alemund made it the capital of his kingdom, and there, some months after his return from Rome about the end of the year 841, Siwara gave birth to St. Edmund.

On his mother's side Edmund descended from the ancient Saxon kings of the continent : " Ex antiquorum Saxonum nobili prosapia oriundus,"—"*from the noble stock of the ancient Saxons he sprang*," writes his principal biographer. Through his father he inherited the blood royal of East Anglia, whose people St. Abbo calls his " comprovinciales," "*fellow-countrymen.*" In after years his subjects loved to remember that the martyr king belonged to their own race ; and our Catholic forefathers made it their loudest boast that the great Edmund was an Englishman.

The child thus nobly descended received in baptism the name of Edmund. His biographers see in this name a token of the saint's character and virtues. *Ed*, they remark, signifies *blessed*, and *mund*, *clean ;* one part of his name foreshadowed his pure and innocent life here on earth, and the other his blessed one with God in heaven. *Ead* or *Ed*, says another author, means *happy*, or, if derived from the Saxon *cath*, *easy*, *gentle mild*, and *mund* signifies *peace ;* so Edmund is happy, gentle, peace—a name most suitable to one who willingly sacrificed his life for the peace and happiness of his subjects.

From Edmund's earliest years his parents trained

---

not important enough. Alemund's capital, says Battely, quoting from a codex MS. in his time in possession of Stillingfleet, bishop of Worcester, was a most celebrated city. North Hamburg, or Hamburg, as given in the text, alone answers in every respect to what is recorded of Alemund's capital.

him in the Catholic and Roman faith.[1] In that faith
St. Augustine, St. Paulinus, and St. Felix had instructed his ancestors, and in it generations of his
people lived and died. Alcmund first learnt it at
his mother's knee, then in the court of Charlemagne,
finally perfecting it in Rome itself. Both the traditions
of his house, therefore, and the education of his father
secured Edmund's being brought up in the true faith.
To complete his teaching, Alcmund often spoke of
his pilgrimage to Rome, of the sacred places he then
visited, and of the sovereign pontiff, Christ's Vicar,
with whom he had conversed. On his father's knee,
or seated at his feet, the boy Edmund listened with
eager attention to the history of those renowned
Churches whose saints had prayed for him before his
birth. Doubtless from his father's lips he heard the
legend of St. Ambrose and the emperor more powerful
than Charlemagne, who humbly and reverently accepted
the holy bishop's reproof. The youthful saint often
heard tell of the terrible invasion of Attila, and of how
Pope Leo checked the barbarians in their headlong
course. As he listened with earnest childlike interest
to these stories of the saints, there were planted deep in
his soul a love and reverence for the Church and her
pastors, a courage and boldness against force and rapine,
which bore abundant fruit in after years. Edmund
took special delight in the stories of the Christian
soldier St. Sebastian and of the brave boy St. Pancra-
tius, both of whom he afterwards so closely resembled.
No wonder that, as he pictured to himself the amphi-
theatre, and contrasted the fierceness of the wild beasts
and of the maddened spectators with the placid bearing
of the martyrs, his whole soul glowed with the desire

---

[1] "A primæva ætate cultor veracissimæ fidei."—MS. Harl. 2802
f. 226.

to fight and conquer in the cause of God and truth. In fact, so enthusiastically did he admire the heroic deeds of the martyrs, that he affirmed not long before his death that from childhood his wish had been to die for Christ.

His mother's influence.

To his mother's influence he owed that purer and and deeper sense which gave calm and wisdom to his earnestness. Through her care, his soul, while it lost none of its fire and resoluteness, grew in gentleness and prudence. In other words, she taught him to realize that which sobers yet elevates the wildest natures — the supernatural though invisible world around us. She trained his broad and noble mind by showing him how to live in the greatness and vast- ness of the other world, and to view the circumstances of life with the light of eternity upon them. Not only at morn or eve did she bid him lisp his infant prayers, but through the day often speak with the angels and saints and converse with the Virgin Mother and her divine Son. One devotion especially Edmund imbibed with his mother's milk—his love for the holy name of Jesus. In his childhood that name was ever on his tongue ; in his youth he repeated it as the name of his dearest master and friend ; with that name on his lips he gave up his soul to God. This love for the holy name affected the whole conduct of his life. "From his earliest youth," writes St. Abbo, "he followed Christ with his whole heart"—"*a primevo juventutis tempore, Christum toto secutus est pectore.*" [1] So, "day by day," sings the monk-poet, "by the grace of Christ, as he waxed in age he always increased in virtue," "demure in port," "angelic of visage," "comely to behold." As :—

" Ifro freesh hed sprynges renne streemys crystallyne,
    So yong Edmund, pleynly to declare,
    Shewyd how he cam from Alkmond and Siware."

[1] Office of St. Edmund, MS. Bodl. Digby 109.

Alcmund had seen the value of learning in the The saint's education. palace-school which Charlemagne instituted for the education of the young princes of his court. When he became a ruler himself, he therefore gave a ready welcome to his court to all scholars. He surrounded his sons with competent teachers, so that at an early age prince Edmund learned to read, a rare accomplishment in those days. Alcmund had him also instructed in the Latin tongue, and, while still in Saxony, the child-saint began to learn by heart the psalter of David,[1] a study which he completed after his arrival in England.

Beyond this little is known of St. Edmund's childhood, till he reached the age of twelve. He was then a golden-haired, blue-eyed Saxon boy, tall for his age, graceful and cheerful, and prudent beyond his years. Thus formed and gifted, Providence drew him forth, like his divine Saviour, from the obscurity of his early days. But the event which changed the whole course of his life and started a new epoch in his history may appropriately begin a fresh chapter.

---

[1] " Psalterium quod in Saxonia cœperat," writes Gaufridus.

CHAPTER III.

King Offa of East Anglia—St. Edmund succeeds him—
St. Edmund is anointed and crowned.

[*Authorities*—Ganfridus de Fontibus, the Bodleian MS., and other authorities referred to at the beginning of the last chapter, still continue to be useful. St. Adamnan, "De Locis Sanctis," (Migne's Patrologia, vol. 88) is the great authority on the Holy Land at this period. St. Bede quotes St. Adamnan's Diary in his "Ecclesiastical History," bk. v, c. xv., as valuable and reliable. On the Holy Places at this period see also Lingard's "History and Antiquities of the Anglo-Saxon Church," vol. ii. chap. x. 1st edition. The description of St. Edmund's coronation is principally drawn from the ancient English pontifical of Archbishop Egbert of York (A.D. 745), printed by the Surtees Society, vol. 27, the preface to which gives a learned disquisition on the Anglo-Saxon pontificals. To Egbert's pontifical Dom Edmund Martène refers in his "De Antiquis Ecclesiæ Rit.," tom iii. ordo 1 and ordo 2. It is certainly "the most ancient ordo ad benedicendum regem" known, and was in use in St. Edmund's time. For any side remarks on the customs of the Church at this age, see Martène and Lingard in the works mentioned above, and Dr. Rock in his "Church of Our Fathers"]

King Offa, the predecessor of St. Edmund.

ALTHOUGH East Anglia fell a prey to the tyranny and rapine of the Mercian nobles after the martyrdom of St. Ethelbert, it remained a short time only in their hands.[1] The East Anglians soon combined for resistance. Taking advantage of the misfortunes which befell the royal house of Mercia, and supported by the Emperor Charlemagne, the exiles returned to England and started a war of independence. The young and valiant Prince Offa, whom they had chosen (A.D. 793) to succeed their late sovereign, headed them in this glorious struggle for freedom. Our best known chroniclers mention this famous king of East Anglia, without, however, giving his name.[2] Their omission is supplied

---

[1] See John Brompton, "Chron.," p. 748 quoted by Battely, p. 11, "Historiæ Anglicanæ Scriptores, x." (Gale).

[2] Butler, the Little Bollandists and others, confuse Offa of Essex

by the biographers of St. Edmund. Gaufridus writes
that the king who reigned sixty-one years before St.
Edmund, rivalling in this respect our Henry III. and
George III., was named Offa. After this statement, he
proceeds to warn his readers against confusing Offa of
East Anglia " with that Offa king of the Mercians who
iniquitously beguiled and slew Blessed Ethelbert, or
with that other noble Offa, the illustrious king of the
East Saxons, who, out of love of Christ and the
kingdom of the gospel, left wife and children and
country to go on a pilgrimage to Rome, there to receive
from Pope Constantine the tonsure and monastic habit,
and whence, after death, he reached the vision of the
blessed Apostles in heaven."

As a ruler and warrior Offa of East Anglia was in no *The reign of King Offa.*
way inferior to other kings of his royal line. Gaufridus
calls him "justitiæ cultor et pacis amator," "*a respecter
of justice and a lover of peace.*" He began his reign
with the support of the Emperor Charlemagne. Charlemagne had previously despatched Egbert from his court
to be king of Wessex, and Eardulph to sit once more
on the throne of Northumbria.[1] He now lent his
powerful aid to Offa and the thanes of East Anglia, to
enable them to throw off for ever the Mercian supremacy. Once in possession of his country, king Offa
took up both sword and sceptre with a firm hand. In
819, he engaged in battle with Cenulf, the only
sovereign since the murderer of St. Ethelbert who
wielded the Mercian sword with any effect. Victory
crowned his arms, and he left Cenulf and the flower of
his army dead upon the field. Five years afterwards,
the threatening attitude of Mercia sent him and his

---

with the predecessor of St. Edmund, although he died ninety
years before his namesake became king of East Anglia, and a
hundred and forty before St. Edmund's birth.

[1] See Green's "Short History of the English People," p. 41.

wise men to the court of their once fellow-exile, Egbert
of Wessex.[1] As a result of this interview Offa persuaded Egbert of the mutual advantage of an alliance
against Mercia. The two kings at once carried war
into the heart of Mercia; they fought side by side in
the battle of Ellandune on the banks of the Willy,
where they utterly defeated the forces of Bernulf, the
successor of Cenulf. When Bernulf attempted later on
to wreak his vengeance on East Anglia, Offa and his
men met him on the frontiers of their kingdom, and
single-handed routed his army, and slew him and five
of his dukes. Ludecan, the successor of Bernulf, continued the contest, and likewise fell by the sword of
Offa, the third victim whom God seemed to require for
the blood of His servant Ethelbert. Towards the end
of his reign a more formidable enemy challenged King
Offa in the form of a party of Danes, who, entering his
kingdom from the Lincolnshire fens (A.D. 838), endeavoured to push their way to the Thames. The king
boldly attacked them, and, though they effected their
design, it was only, says Ethelwerd, after great slaughter
had been made of them in East Anglia.

Offa seeks an
heir to his
throne.

Defensive warfare did not prevent Offa from devot-
ing himself to the more peaceful work of government.
All his reforms, however, were likely to fall to the
ground, unless he could leave a successor firm and
unflinching as himself to continue his work. He
knew well from the history of Northumbria, how rival
claimants to the throne desolate and lay waste the
fairest kingdoms. Yet he had no heir. His son by
Queen Botilda, the saintly Fremund,[2] had renounced

---

[1] See Ethelwerd's "Chronicle," A.D. 824-825, etc., and Lingard
on the reign of Egbert.

[2] St. Fremund, according to Capgrave, was the son of Offa of
East Anglia, and Lydgate in Ashmole MS. 46 f. 54, writes: "To
King Offa Fremund was son and heir, reigning in Northland

the kingly dignity for a hermit's life. Offa looked around in vain for some one who should take his place, and whose rule would be universally acknowledged. His anxiety for the future increased on learning that the Norsemen swarmed the high seas in greater numbers, and were actually plundering the mainland of the south. Meanwhile the infirmities of age crept silently but quickly upon him. In his trouble and distress this valiant prince, as renowned for piety as for prowess and kingly wisdom, whom God had raised up to avenge the death of his saints, often lifted up his hands in prayer to heaven for guidance and direction. At last, under a sudden inspiration from heaven, he resolved to make a pilgrimage to Jerusalem "to adore in the place where the feet of the Lord had stood."[1] God, he argued, would not be deaf to prayers offered up in those holy places which the life, labours, and death of His Son had sanctified.

He resolves on a pilgrimage to Jerusalem.

The aged king took advantage of his pilgrimage to visit his cousin Alcmund, whose counsel he judged would assist him in prosecuting his arduous journey.[2]

And visits Saxony on his way.

[Norfolk], the story beareth witness. His mother, Botild, right goodly and right fair." Lydgate, quoted by Yates, is made to say that Botild was St. Edmund's sister. According to Harpsfeld quoted by Cressy, p. 739, Fremund was son of Count Algar of Essex by his wife Thova, and so brother to the unfortunate wretch Leofstan, who irreverently opened the coffin of St. Edmund, and was in consequence struck with madness and disease. Leland ("Itinerary," vol. viii. p. 72), in making Erconwald, bishop of London and Ethelberga, his sister, the offspring of Offa king of East Anglia, confuses Offa of the East Saxons, who died A.D. 708, with Offa of the East Angles, who died in 854. The East Saxons were quite distinct from the East Angles, a fact not adverted to by even our most reliable annalists. See the lessons of St. Erconwald's feast in the Benedictine Breviary, the "Annales Benedictini," vol. i. bk. xvi. p. 539, and Hardy's "Materials," vol i. pt. 2, p. 522.

[1] "In loco ubi steterunt pedes Domini adorare."—Gaufridus.

[2] "Cujus perutile didicerat fore consilium ad perficiendum illud iter tam arduum."

Old Saxony lay most conveniently in his route to the Holy Land. Thence he could travel overland directly and safely through Charlemagne's dominions to one of the southern European ports, and thence take ship for the east. He accordingly set sail with a goodly retinue of knights and serving-men for the mouth of the Elbe. He had sent news of his coming before, and most of the noblesse of Saxony assembled at Northemberg to give him a royal welcome.[1] His ships anchored in the lakes of Alster, and he and his suite disembarked to enjoy the hospitality of King Alcmund.

He meets St. Edmund.

To wait as pages upon his royal guest, Alcmund selected a certain number of the most illustrious youths of Saxony, among them his two sons Edmund and Adalbert. All endeavoured to serve the venerable Offa with readiness and fidelity, but Edmund especially was always at his side willing to oblige and to please, so that he made a great impression upon his aged uncle.[2] Struck by the young saint's blithe and winning manner, his heavenly countenance, his graceful carriage, his sweet and modest speech,[3] Offa applied to him the words of Solomon: "Hast thou seen a man swift in his work ? He shall stand before kings and shall not be in obscurity."[4] The king saw in the boy a virtue and discretion far beyond his tender years. He remembered, too, Edmund's descent from the royal line of the Uffings, and therefore his eligibleness to the throne of East Anglia. Already the old king's prayers seemed answered. Edmund possessed every princely qualification of birth and heart and mind. What better or more suitable successor could he have ?

---

[1] " Utpote rex, et regis Saxonici cognatus."

[2] Strictly speaking, Offa was St. Edmund's cousin, but on account of his age and dignity he is often called St. Edmund's uncle.

[3] MS. Harl. 2802 says of the youthful Edmund that "polleret bonis moribus."

[4] Prov. xxii. 29.

So strongly did this idea grow upon him that, before continuing his pilgrimage, Offa resolved to adopt Edmund as his son and heir. According to William of Croyland,[1] instances of similar adoptions were not unusual. The Saxons frequently entrusted their sons to the English to be educated, and very often in the case of royal princes adopted children succeeded to the throne. Accordingly, before bidding farewell to the Saxon king and his noble retainers, Offa, whose heart expanded with affection towards the youthful Edmund resolved to publicly adopt him as his son. In the presence of the whole court he pressed the boy to his heart and kissed him; then, taking a ring, he placed it on the lad's finger. "My most beloved son Edmund," he said, "accept this memento of our kinship and mutual love. Remember me as one grateful for your service, in reward for which with God's permission I hope to leave you a paternal inheritance." Edmund received both gift and promise with boyish glee. His father, however, who understood the full meaning of the ceremony, seemed taken by surprise. Pleased, however, with the favour shown his boy, he quickly explained to him the nature of the proposal, and formally asked his consent. "Consider, Edmund," he said, "the offer of the East Anglian king. Are you willing to accept him as your father in my place? Shall he provide for you as his son, and you regard him as your father, so as in

And adopts him as his heir.

The ceremony of adoption.

---

[1] Miserunt Anglis puerum Saxones alendum,
  Qui restauraret quod rapuêre patres,
  Edmundus felix, &c.
  Anglorumque puer fines habitavit Eöos
  Ut consanguineus alumnus Ophæ.
Et postea, Affectans prodesse magis præesse sepulti,
  Supplendas patrui suscipit ille vices.
      William of Croyland, quoted by Battely, p. 22.
  See David Chytræus' "Saxonia" for a list of kings whom Old Saxony gave to England.

future to live in my house another's son ?" Whatever
answer Edmund gave, and probably he submitted
wholly to his father's guidance, the words delighted
Offa, for he embraced the boy again, and covered his

Offa shows
Edmund his
signet ring.

cheeks with kisses. Then, in the presence of his East
Anglian thanes and of the whole Saxon court, he drew
from his finger his coronation ring, "to him most
special and entire." With that ring the holy successor
of St. Felix had wedded him to his kingdom.
With tears coursing down his furrowed cheeks, he
showed it to prince Edmund. "Son Edmund," he
said, "observe closely this ring, notice its design and
seal. If, when far away, I intimate to you by this
token my wish and desire, do you without delay
execute my order. As the noble crowd assembled
bears witness, I intend to regard you as my most
beloved son and heir."

The East
Anglians
continue their
pilgrimage.

Satisfied with the happy issue of his visit to Saxony,
Offa made his final preparations and started once more
on his journey. Crowds of spectators lined the streets
to see the royal pilgrimage set out. Alcmund and a
long procession of clergy and nobles devoutly accompanied it some way out of the city. Then the brother-
monarchs bade each other farewell, and parted never
to meet again on earth. Alcmund continued to guide
and direct his court and realm as in the past. Offa
proceeded towards the Great Sea, intending to take
ship at Genoa or Venice for the Holy Land.

St. Edmund's biographers say little of other incidents
in King Offa's pilgrimage. That his journey was slow
and perilous compared with what it is now-a-days
there can be no doubt. The roads were uncertain and
but rarely trodden. In spite of the vigilance of Charlemagne and his successors, robbers infested the woods
and mountains. Thanks, however, to treaties and the
reverential protection afforded to pilgrims, rich and

poor, the East Anglian king and his followers reached
the Holy Land in safety.

St. Adamnan, the writer of St. Columba's life, has The Holy Land,
A.D. 853.
left a description of the holy places at this period, from
which it is easy to conjecture at what port the pilgrims
from England landed, what hallowed scenes they
visited, and in what sacred churches they prayed
during their sojourn in the most historic country of
the world. Landing at Joppa, the principal port of the
East, they set out without delay for Jerusalem. Of
the six gates of the holy city they entered by the
western, called David's gate. If it were about the 15th
of September, they perhaps saw the miraculous rain
which, according to tradition, the Great Creator made
to fall copiously at eventide to cleanse the city of his
beloved Son from the filth and refuse of the autumn
fair. The streets presented a strange and novel sight
to the visitors from the west. Camels and mules
thronged the gates; men and women in flowing eastern
robes met them at every step. But the English
strangers hurried past the picturesquely dressed loiter-
ers, past the many stately buildings for which the city
was then renowned, towards the round church of the
Holy Sepulchre. In this church three walls and three
ways, one encircling the other, enclosed the gold and The church
of the Holy
Sepulchre
marble roof which rose over the tomb wherein the
body of the Lord reposed from its burial to its
resurrection. Twelve lamps in honour of the twelve
Apostles burned day and night in this temple of the
Anastasis. Two other royal and magnificent churches
adjoined. In the one called the Church of Golgotha,
Offa knelt before the great silver cross fixed in the
very rock which once held the wooden cross whereon
suffered the Saviour of mankind. Suspended aloft,
a great brazen wheel supported a circle of lamps,
which burned day and night around the sacred spot.

The other church, called the Church of the Martyrdom, stood over the spot where St. Helen the Empress discovered the cross of the King of Martyrs. Offa and his attendants kissed the sacred ground on which the Saviour's cross lay buried for three hundred years ; then, with other pilgrims, they turned aside to the altar of the silver double-handled cup which our Lord blessed with His own hands when He supped with His Apostles the evening before He died. Within the cup lay the sponge once saturated with the vinegar and hyssop which our dying Saviour tasted. In the portico of the basilica the English pilgrims were privileged to gaze upon the spear which opened their Redeemer's heart, and to view the linen cloth on which Christ our Lord's head reposed in the sepulchre. This linen cloth the Jews once stole. When the Christians claimed it back, the Saracen judge, in order to end the dispute, commanded his men to throw the sacred relic into a fire especially kindled to consume it. But the fire harmed not the precious cloth, and the Christians in solemn procession triumphantly carried back their treasure to its shrine. The pilgrims venerated one other relic before they left Constantine's churches,— the linen winding-sheet which enclosed the Virgin Mother's body after her death, and which the Apostles found in the empty tomb after her assumption into heaven.

The valley of Josaphat.

On leaving Jerusalem, devotion led the pilgrims to the church over the tomb of our Lady in the valley of Josaphat. Beside that tomb stood the sepulchre of Simeon, the prophet who held in his arms the " Light for the revelation of the Gentiles." Again, not far off they saw the tomb of St. Joseph, our Lord's guardian and foster-father. Crossing the valley of Josaphat, Offa repaired to Mount Olivet, on which at this time stood two churches. One marked the scene of Jesus'

agony; the other, on the summit, the spot whence He
ascended into heaven. The print of Christ our Lord's
last footsteps on earth, protected by a railing of bur-
nished brass, remained visible in the centre of the
second church. Above, the roof, left open to the sky,
revealed as it were the very spot through which, on the
day of His Ascension, our King of Glory, drawing aside
the curtain of heaven, entered into His kingdom. From
the Mount of Olives the pilgrims passed on to Bethania
to see the tomb of Lazarus; then they turned towards
Bethlehem, a little village perched on the brow of a
grassy hill with a green valley all around. In Beth- Bethlehem.
lehem they venerated the spot where "the Word was
made flesh, and dwelt amongst us;" there they saw,
adorned with gold and precious stones, the manger of
the Infant Jesus, which the faithful afterwards removed to Rome. In the neighbourhood of Bethlehem
guides pointed out the tombs of the four patriarchs,
and of Rachel, David and St. Jerome. From Jerusalem
and Bethlehem the pilgrim descended into the valley
of the Dead Sea, and, passing through Jericho, made
his way to Galilee, breaking the journey at Jacob's Galilee.
well and Samaria. Nor did King Offa and his suite
pass by unnoticed the village where our Lord met
the ten lepers, or the gates of Naim, where He raised
the widow's son to life. Thus they arrived at Nazareth,
nestling quietly and peacefully in its verdant bowl-
shaped valley. Two churches graced the modest town.
One canopied the cottage in which the angel Gabriel announced the Incarnation to the Virgin Mother; the other
the house in which the boy Jesus grew up to manhood.
From Nazareth Offa and his knights visited the woods
and flowery heights of Thabor. Passing through the
thick and beautiful verdure that covered its sides, they
reached the three churches on its summit, the three
tabernacles, as it were, which Peter would have built to

his Lord, to Moses and to Elias. From the monastery-tower on the top of Thabor, the travellers gazed out over the sea of Galilee, on the margin of whose shores at irregular intervals they beheld the historic towns of Tiberias, Magdala, Bethsaida, and Capharnaum. Far beyond the sea they caught a glimpse of the desert where the Son of God fed the multitudes,—touching image of the most wonderful of His sacraments. A journey of seven or eight days through higher Galilee, by the sources of the Jordan, and through the cedar groves of Mount Libanus, brought the party to the plain of Damascus. There they contemplated the scene of the great Apostle's conversion ; in imagination they saw the bright light and heard the divine voice which changed Saul the Zealot's heart. Passing through the delightful gardens, which stretched all around, they entered into Damascus, the capital of Syria. A week within its walls ended their pilgrimage.

The return by Constantinople. But travellers to the Holy Land thought their journey incomplete unless they venerated the true cross, which at that time the walls of Constantinople guarded. In embarking, therefore, at Joppa to return home, King Offa resolved to visit the city of Constantinople, the capital of the Eastern Empire. A fifteen days' voyage first brought him and his suite to Alexandria, but, leaving that city and its cathedral with its empty shrine of St. Mark unvisited, they sailed at once for Crete, and thence to Constantinople.

Illness and death of King Offa. Either before or after paying his devotions to the true cross, Offa fell sick. The storms and trials of eighty winters had whitened his beard and bent his once stately form. The fatigue of his pilgrimage had told upon a constitution already weakened by age and by the mental and bodily troubles of a long reign. Offa well knew that his twofold pilgrimage was drawing to a close. A holy calm, however, possessed the aged

monarch. His last great act of piety and religion had
gained him an heir worthy of his throne, and destined
to be the greatest glory of his kingdom. Edmund, the
reward of a pilgrimage to Rome, God now gave to East
Anglia in reward of a pilgrimage to Jerusalem.

As Offa sailed through the Hellespont, the scenery
drew his thoughts more than ever to his own land.
Dark and luxuriant foliage fringed the shores, the
trees dipped their evergreen branches into the clear
waters. Through similar scenes had he glided on those
rivers of England, whose streams flow swiftly towards
the ocean—similes of his own transitory life making
quickly for eternity. He grew seriously worse as the
vessel neared the celebrated monastery and church
dedicated to St. George which at that time crowned
the heights overlooking the Hellespont or Dardanelles
Without delay, under the shadow of the monastery
which gave the name of " Brachium Sancti Georgii,"
or "St. George's arm," to the neighbouring waters,[1]
King Offa confessed his sins for the last time, and
received the Holy Housel and the solemn anointing.

As the hour drew nigh when he was to leave this His last message
to St. Edmund.
world, the dying king summoned his followers to his
bedside. His earthly career, he knew, was drawing to
a close. He wished to confer with them before he died
on the peace of his country and the succession to
the crown. "You know," he said, "what dissensions rival ambition and greed for power bring upon
a nation. It behoves us to consult for our kingdom,
in order to avoid this diabolical snare, and establish
a government of peace and justice. To prevent all
rivalry in your choice of a king, I name as my

---

[1] Petits Bollandistes, tom. iv. 23 avril ; Butler, April 23. Roger
of Hovedon, Rolls Publ., vol iii. p. 47, says, "Et alter Brachium
Sancti Georgii—quod est apud civitatem Constantinopolim." In
the Glossary "Brachium St. Georgii" is interpreted Archipelago·

successor one whom you know, Prince Edmund, the
son of my cousin the king of Saxony. God has given
him grace of body and wisdom of mind worthy of a
throne. High and low will love and favour him as
one able to rule firmly and well." Thereupon he
handed them his signet ring, bidding them take it to
Saxony as a sign and token of his will.

Kneeling round the bed of their dying sovereign,
the East Anglian knights solemnly promised to deliver
the ring to Edmund, and with it the message of their
lord. So Offa's soul passed away in peace. Tearfully,
and with what dirge and requiem they could procure
in a strange land, his thanes laid him to rest on the
shores of that Hellespont which Xerxes had crossed by
his bridge of boats, and at whose mouth the ruins of
ancient Troy mournfully stood sentinel. [1] Then, turning sorrowfully away from the grave, they hastened
back to Saxony to greet their new sovereign.

St. Edmund
accepts the
throne of East
Anglia.

On reaching the court of Alcmund of Saxony, the
East Anglian nobles announced the sad news of Offa's
death. At the same time they presented the royal
signet ring to Prince Edmund, and urged his speedy
departure for England. Edmund's father, however,
hesitated. He considered his son of too tender an age
to undertake the onerous duties of a kingdom. He was
unwilling, moreover, to give up so suddenly his own and
Siwara's favourite child. At the same time, fearing to
act against the providence of God, which evidently
pointed to a high and noble destiny for his son, he
withdrew to his chamber to meditate and pray over
the matter, as well as to mourn the death of his royal
cousin. Meanwhile he summoned the bishops and the

---

[1] The events of Offa's life may be dated thus : Birth about A.D.
770 ; election to the kingdom of East Anglia, A.D. 793 ; defeat of
Cenulf of Mercia, A.D. 819 ; conference with King Egbert, A.D.
824 ; visit to Saxony and adoption of St. Edmund, A.D. 853 ;
death in St. George's Bay, A.D. 854.

wise men of Saxony to meet him at Northemberg.
Putting before them the last will and testament of the
late king of England and the request of the East
Anglian deputation, he asked their advice as to the
course which he should pursue. They answered with one
accord that Edmund should go to East England, there
to be crowned as "born next in the kingly line," for
clearly God's finger pointed thither, and against God's
will "may be no resistance nor counsel which may
avail."[1] "He ordaineth by marvellous ways the
palm of princes and the crowning of kings." Alcmund
now remembered the Roman widow's prophecy that the
lustre of Edmund's virtues, like the rays of the sun,
should spread from the east to the west. Recognising
God's will in all that had occurred, Alcmund at last
acceded to the request of the East Anglian embassy.

It now remained for the royal father to take all
necessary precautions for his son's safety and well-
being in the country of his adoption. He therefore
assigned to the young prince a force numerous and
powerful enough to support his claim to the throne,
should it be called in question. For Edmund's body-
guard he added to the retinue of the late king several
thanes all notable in his realm for wisdom and chivalry.
Not satisfied with this, Alcmund determined to select
for his son a counsellor who by his age and prudence
would worthily take his own place. He possessed in
his kingdom at the time a noble named Sigentius,[2]
remarkable for his integrity of life and knowledge of
men. He was experienced in the use of arms, and,
though advanced in years, endowed with that calmness
and cheerfulness of disposition which quickly win the
respect and affection of youth. This knight Alcmund

St. Edmund's expedition to England.

---

[1] Prov. xxi. 30.
[2] Alford gives a deed of gift made by St. Edmund to Sigentius
in the year of the saint's landing in East Anglia.

made Edmund's chief guardian. The young prince's retinue further consisted of priests and clerics to offer up the daily mass, to chant the divine office, and to instruct him in all holy doctrine. Lastly, Alcmund assigned his son all such household attendants as became his rank. In fact, he omitted nothing that Edmund's dignity required or his claims demanded. [1]

Before the expedition set sail, the child of God knelt down upon the ground to receive his father's and mother's blessing. Then he embarked, and the ship weighed anchor. A sorrow which no words can describe affected the whole land at his departure, for all had learned to love the bright and guileless Edmund. His mother especially bewailed his loss. Of her the poet sings : "A tender mother's love will out; tears and weeping are tokens of her heart's bitterness ;" as Siwara kissed her brave and noble boy, " salt tears bedewed all her face," and " no word could she utter for pain and bitterness of parting." She watched the vessels sail down the river, disconsolate, and gazed out upon the sea, till the fleet dwindled to a speck on the horizon.

He lands at Hunstanton.   St. Edmund sailed for the eastern coast of England. The voyage was neither long nor dangerous. The English and Saxons were, then as now, expert seamen ; and frequent intercourse made them fully acquainted with the shoals, sandbanks, and other perils of the neighbouring seas. On this occasion, however, they needed neither skilful navigation nor knowledge of the high seas. Wind and weather favoured, and St. Edmund in the autumn of 855 reached the land where two royal crowns awaited him.

The fleet touched at the north-east point of the Norfolk coast, where a cliff sixty feet high and a mile in length juts out into the sea. This cliff, now

---

[1] Speed (fol. 329) says that Alcmund maintained his son's election and sent him with a power to claim the kingdom. See Alford also.

called St. Edmund's Head or Point, shelters on its west a wide and beautiful bay, from whose shores the amber-coloured buildings of modern Hunstanton look out smilingly upon the sea. No more suitable spot presented itself for St. Edmund to land his forces, and on this part of the East Anglian coast the young prince put ashore.[1] About an arrow's flight from the place of landing the expedition crossed the dry bed of a river which had once flowed into the sea. Beyond lay a wide and barren plain. Here, at the very entrance of his kingdom, the youthful stranger prostrated on the ground and prayed God to bless his coming and make it profitable to the land and its people. From that hour the soil round about proved the virtue of the saint's prayer. Sandy and sterile before, henceforth it bore the richest crops in all East England. As the saint rose and mounted his horse, twelve springs[2] of sweet and crystal water gushed forth from the earth as

---

[1] "St. Edmund," says Camden, "being adopted by Offa to be heir of the kingdom of the East Angles, landed with a great retinue from Germany in some part not far from St. Edmund's Cape, called *Maidenboure*. But which it should be, is not so certain : Heacham is too little and obscure; nor does Burkham seem large enough to receive such a navy upon that occasion, though it must be confessed that their ships in those days were but small. Lynn seems to lay the best claim to it, both as the most eminent port, and because that is really *Maiden-boure*, St. Margaret the Virgin or Maiden being as it were the tutelary saint of that place." ("Brit.," p. 470). A better explanation which Camden might have brought forward in support of Lynn's claim occurs in MS. Bodl. 240 f. 674, where mention is made of a chapel of St. Edmund at Lynn, and of miracles wrought therein by the intercession of the saint; but Gaufridus de Fontibus, with whose work Camden was probably unacquainted, leaves no doubt about Hunstanton being the place of St. Edmund's landing.

[2] Gaufridus says twelve springs; Lydgate says five; Capgrave "Nova Legenda Angliæ," fol. cvii., merely states, that a fountain sprang up, curing many infirmities. The springs are now called the Seven Springs.

tokens of God's favour. "These springs," adds Gaufridus, "to this our own day excite the admiration of the beholder, flowing as they do with a continuous sweet and cheering murmur to the sea. Many sick," he continues, "wash in these fountains and are restored to their former health, and pilgrims carry the healing water to remote parts for the infirm and others to drink."

Memorials of St. Edmund at Hunstanton. The whole neighbourhood of Hunstanton is still full of memories of that landing. After his coronation he founded the royal town or fortress of Honestones-dun, or the town of the honey-stones, so called from the colour of the stone of which he built it, or, according to an old chronicle, from the character of his followers who first dwelt there. For, as honey signifies sweetness and stone hardness, so Edmund's followers were notable for two qualities—gentleness in time of peace, and manly courage in time of war :—"in peace like lambs, in war like lions." On the promontory overlooking the bay and still called after him, Edmund built a palace, a favourite and frequent residence of his. From its founder it took the name of Maidenburie—*the abode of the maiden*—"maiden" signifying in old English a chaste, pure, unmarried person of either sex,[1] and "burie," from the Saxon *bur*, an inner chamber or place of shade and retirement. What a flood of light this name sheds over the character of the chaste and youthful king, who chose this place of retirement and meditation by the clear and boundless ocean, which symbolised to him the Divine eternity and immensity, in the light of which he viewed all the events of life. The piety of the faithful in after ages

---

[1] "Maidenhood is both in men and women. Those have right maidenhood, who from childhood continue in chastity. They shall have from God a hundredfold meed in life everlasting."— Aelfric's "Homilies," quoted by Lingard in his "Antiquities of the Anglo-Saxon Church," vol. ii. p. 11, 2nd edition.

turned the royal residence of Maidenburie into a chapel,
the ruins of which, called St. Edmund's chapel, are
visible to the present day, close by the lighthouse
which crowns the cliff.   St. Edmund's springs are
situate about a quarter of a mile from the ancient and
beautiful church of St. Mary in Old Hunstanton.   In
Catholic times the devout clients of St. Edmund flocked
to their crystal waters, as pilgrims journeyed to St.
Winefrid's Well on the western side of the isle.   Now,
however, the holy wells of Hunstanton belong to the
forgotten past.   Farmers, indeed, for miles round send
their water-carts to be filled at them, and one of the
springs supplies the new town with its sparkling water;
but, though marvellous cures are said to be wrought at
them, few recognise their miraculous power, and only
now and then does a solitary pilgrim linger over the
spot, and recall to memory the stranger prince who
knelt there to pray for his country.

After landing his forces, Edmund proceeded to Attle- St. Edmund
borough, a city founded by the Saxon prince Atheling, Attleborough.
from whom it derives its name.   At this period the
East Anglians regarded Attleborough as the capital of
Norfolk.   Under Offa it was the chief royal residence
and the centre of government.   Edmund in taking
possession of it thus unmistakably asserted his claim
to the throne, and proclaimed the object of his
expedition.

A few weeks later the young prince visited the court He is present
of Ethelwulph, king of Wessex, probably in order to wulph's court.
get that monarch's support to his claim. [1]   While in
Wessex, he attended the great meeting which Ethelwulph called together on November 5, A.D. 855, to confirm his famous charter of immunities to Holy Church.
Before the high altar of the cathedral of St. Peter at

---

[1] Ingulph (Bohn's edition, p. 35).   See also Roger of Wen-
over, and Lingard's "Anglo-Saxon Church," vol. i. p. 247.

Winchester, the highest magnates of the realm affixed
their signatures to a charter in honour of the glorious
Virgin Mary, of the blessed Apostles and of all the
saints," in order to solicit the protection of God, through
the psalms and holy sacrifices of religious men and
women, against the repeated descents of the northern
pirates in those times of alarm and peril." The solemn
and magnificent assembly which thus bore witness in
the presence of God to the king's generous gift to the
Church comprised the chief bishops, abbots, abbesses,
earldormen, thanes and lieges of the land. Conspicuous
among them, on the steps of their father's throne, stood
Ethelwulph's sons, Ethelbald, Ethelbert, Ethelred and
the boy Alfred, each destined to hold in turn the royal
sceptre. Edmund stood side by side with the king of
Mercia. Together these royal princes form an historic
group; all will become famous within the next fifteen
years for their valiant struggle with the savage Danish

St. Edmund and
Alfred the Great.
hordes. The two youngest, Edmund and Alfred, especially command attention. Both by their wise government and brave resistance to the pagan invader merit
the title of Great. Edmund fell a martyr in the
struggle; his death gave new life to the cause for
which he died, and his name became the rallying cry
of the Christian English against the heathen Dane.
Alfred, now a boy of seven years, who looked up
wistfully into the handsome princely face of East
Anglia's greatest glory, history knows as a victorious
conqueror. He reaped the fruit of Edmund's martyrdom. The fatality which hung over the invaders of
St. Edmund's kingdom delivered Gothrun, a comrade
of Hinguar and Hubba's,[1] into his hands, and ended
the struggle, for some years at least, in favour of the
English. Gothrun's defeat marked still more clearly

---

[1] Hinguar, Hubba and Gothrun were three of the sea-kings who
ought against St. Edmund.

the triumph of Edmund's principles. Through the
martyr's prayers not less than Alfred's persuasion,
Gothrun embraced the faith of Christ. After baptism
he ascended St. Edmund's throne, and in his person
and in the Christian spirit of his government the cause
of his martyred predecessor finally triumphed.

On Edmund's return to Attleborough the nobles and
people of Norfolk, with Humbert, bishop of Elmham,
at their head, formally acknowledged his sovereignty.
This took place on Christmas day, 855. To quote
Asser, "in the year of Our Lord's Incarnation, 855,
Edmund, the most glorious king of the East Angles,
·began to reign on the birthday of Our Lord, in the 14th
year of his age." But Edmund's authority did not
extend much beyond the neighbourhood of Attleborough. According to the custom of the English of
that day, a prince had to deserve well of the people
before they freely and unanimously elected him king.
Edmund, who respected the traditions of his countrymen, made no attempt to force his sovereignty upon
them. He awaited God's time, remaining quietly in
Norfolk for a whole year.

He spent that period in retreat and meditation. He
now learnt by heart the psalter of David, the subject
of his study in Saxony. The fact of his committing the
psalter to memory was not extraordinary, for chroniclers mention similar instances in the lives of other
ancient saints. St. Frideswide, for example, when
quite a child, proved "so apt a pupil that in five or
seven months she learnt by heart the whole of David's
psalter;" and, indeed, what richer poetry could be given
to a child, or what prayers more sublime to a Christian?
The psalms are no mere human invention, but varied
and soul-stirring aspirations, inspired by God Himself.
Once learnt by heart, in days when books were scarce,
they supplied the place of written prayers. They

comforted the aged in their loneliness. They relieved
the monotony and gloom of the blind or dim of sight.
They enabled the devout to join in the monastic choir.
To a St. Bede or an Alcuin their verses, full of expressions of every feeling of joy, of gratitude, of fear
of God's judgments, of trust in God's mercy, were a
source of cheerfulness and consolation in hours of pain
and languor. St. Edmund had a special reason for
learning the psalter. He knew no higher example of
kingly virtue than David, "the man according to
God's own heart." But David's great soul lay hidden
in his poetry, which Edmund therefore studied, in
order to form himself on the model of Israel's
famous king and prophet. Afterwards his biographers pronounced him *Deo acceptus,*—a man accept-
able to God. They beheld as the motive power of
his life the principles and piety of king David,
which, during the first year of his reign, he had
learnt under the tutorship of Bishop Humbert from
the book of psalms. [1]

The East
Anglians
hesitate to
elect Edmund. Hitherto the South Folk of East Anglia had withheld
their allegiance. The kingship in East England
being elective rather than hereditary, they considered
themselves free to choose any prince to rule over them,
provided the royal blood flowed in his veins. Edmund,
indeed, had a prior right from nearness of kin. He
could also point to the will of the late sovereign.
Other aspirants, however, better fitted by age to command, started up to contest the throne, and defer the
final election.

The Church
takes up his
cause. But in spite of his tender years something in St.
Edmund plainly betokened the ruler. Hence, the

---

[1] "Historia Eliensis" (Anglia Christiana Soc. Publ., p. 79).
"The psalter used by the saint was religiously preserved by the
monks of Bury-St.-Edmund's, and it is said to be still in St. James'
Church library of that town."—Butler, Nov. 20.

Church took up his cause. St. Humbert, who had
received the young prince on his landing at Hunstanton, still filled the episcopal chair of Elmham.[1] He
now threw all his power and influence on the side of
the young claimant, and a bishop's authority in the
days of the heptarchy was of no little importance even
in secular affairs. In virtue of his office, the nation
regarded him as the king's spiritual father and chief
adviser. His word like the king's did not require
the confirmation of an oath. Nobles and people deferred to his superior wisdom and piety in every trial and
feud. He attended the principal courts of justice. As
the expounder of the civil law, he sat with the earldor-
man in the shire-mote. As the upholder of God's law,
he often stepped in between litigants whom no earthly
power could have reconciled. In East Anglia St.
Humbert held the position which bishops and archbishops held in the other English kingdoms. From

---

[1] The Bishops of East Anglia after the division of the diocese,
continued from page 17 :—

Bishops of Dunwich.	*Bishops of North Elmham.*
ETTA, AECCE, ECCI, or HETA, consecrated in 673.	BEDWINE, or BEADWINE, also called Eadwin, consecrated in 673. He died in 679.
ASTWOLPH, AESAWLF, or ASTULFUS.	NORTHBERT, also called Rod-berht.
EADFERTH, EALDBERCHT, EARDRED, or EDRED.	HEATHOLAC, or ETELAT, called by Malmesbury, Netholacus. He was bishop in 731, when St. Bede finished his history.
CUTHWINE. ALBERTH, or ALDBERHT.	AETHILFERTH, or EDELFRID. LANFERTH, called in Cottonian MS. Vesp. B. vi. Eanferd.
ECGLAF. HEARDRED, or HENDRED. AELFHUN, or ALSIN. TIDFERA, or WIDFRED. WEREMUND, or WARMUND, who died or was martyred in 870.	AETHELWULF occurs in 811. ALCHAERD, called also Unferth. ALHERD, or Eatherd. SIPLA. HUNFERD, ALHERD, or HUFRED, living in 824. HUNFERHT, HUMBERT, or HUMBRICT, called also St. Humbert, consecrated in 826 and martyred with king Edmund 870, in about the 80th year of his age.

After 870 both sees were again united under Bishop Wilred, the
successor of Weremund.

him the young Prince Edmund sought help and advice.
In his company the royal youth attended Ethelwulph's
council at Winchester.   Afterwards, on Edmund's return to Norfolk, Bishop Humbert assembled the Wite-
nagemote, or meeting of earldormen, thanes and higher
clergy, at Attleborough, and induced them to acknowledge the boy-king's sovereignty.

The friendship
between
Edmund and
Bishop Humbert Under these circumstances sprang up that close and
lasting friendship between prince and bishop which
forms so beautiful and touching a feature in St.
Edmund's life.   Their relations as pupil and master still
more closely knit them together, for, judging from the
custom of the time, St. Humbert acted not only as
the young prince's spiritual father and temporal adviser,
but also as his preceptor and his instructor in the
divine psalmody.   The bishop was thus brought daily
into contact with the saintly boy, whose manly yet
amiable disposition quickly won his affection and esteem.
Edmund on his side loved and revered the kindly
prelate with all the devotion of a boy's pure and im-
passioned heart.   This "inseparable" companionship of
the fair boy-king and the venerable pontiff lasted in
life and death.   Together they ruled East Anglia,
together they resisted its invaders, together they received the crown of martyrdom.   What nobler models
could youth or old age propose to themselves!   St.
Humbert in his devotedness to a boy's interests, in his
knowledge of a boy's nature and consideration for it is a
pattern to all who have the charge of youth; St.
Edmund, on the other hand, in his respect for and
confidence in his priest and master justly stands forth
as the patron of the young and especially of students.

Bishop Humbert
furthers St.
Edmund's claim. In the beginning of their friendship St. Humbert
succeeded, as stated above, in persuading the North
Folk of East Anglia to acknowledge Prince Edmund's
claim.   Now that he had had ample opportunities of

studying the character of his young sovereign, he determined to promote his cause among the South Folk also. Accordingly he sent messengers to the chief men of the whole kingdom calling upon them for the good of the realm to meet and discuss the question of a successor to King Offa.

Some time elapsed before the bishop's summons reached the more distant parts of the country, and then the nation quickly responded. A rumour was abroad that the Danes threatened the eastern coasts, and the people anxiously sought for a leader in case of invasion. Another circumstance called for the speedy settlement of the question. Petty claimants all over the land began to exercise a tyrannical and unbridled power. The firm hand and strong arm of supreme authority could alone check their lawlessness or frustrate their pretensions.[1] Bishop Humbert thoroughly realized all this. As an argument in his mouth, it quickly convinced the wise men of the realm of the necessity of a king. He had next to propose Prince Edmund as the The South Folk
elect him King. proper object of their choice. By birth Edmund stood nearest to the throne. The will of the late king, to which the twenty thanes who had returned from the Holy Land bore witness, gave him a double right. He possessed, moreover, the signet ring, the symbol of supreme power, which the dying Offa had entrusted to him as his son and heir. Edmund's genuine and well known virtue, his high character and royal bearing no one could gainsay. The bishop failed not to press home these arguments. He anticipated the objections of those who desired an older and more soldier-like sovereign. Was not Edmund stalwart and valiant? By braving the seas and commanding a successful expedition into the country, had he not proved himself capable of leading even veterans to battle and victory? The

---

[1] See John Brompton, "Chron.," p. 748, quoted by Battely, p. 11.

eloquence and reasoning of the venerable Humbert prevailed. [1] The assembly unanimously approved of King Offa's choice. "The pious youth," writes Matthew of Westminster, "was elected king by all the nobles and people of the kingdom, and compelled in spite of great resistance on his own part to assume the reins of government. [2]

Edmund makes a progress through his kingdom.

. After this Edmund began a royal progress through his kingdom, attended by the magnificent and numerous retinue which had accompanied him from Saxony. Everywhere his youth, his bright and charming manner, the halo of sanctity about him gained the hearts of his subjects, while his manly bearing, his deep and penetrating gaze, his wise and tempered words inspired a confidence which remained unshaken even in the most trying times.

He is anointed and consecrated at Sudbury.

For the place of his coronation the newly elected king fixed upon Bures, more correctly spelt by Lydgate Burys, a town on the frontiers of Suffolk and Essex. Ganfridus speaks of it as a "royal town" situated "on the Stour, a river flowing most rapidly in summer and winter." Bures was in fact the southern capital of East Anglia as Attleborough was the northern; hence its more common appellation of Sud-bury, or the South borough.[3]

---

[1] "Curis et industriâ Humberti Helmahamensis episcopi ad regnum evectus est Edmundus."—Propre de St. Sernin, A.D. 1672.

[2] See also Roger of Wendover (Bohn's edit., p. 186). St. Abbo writes : "Qui atavis regibus editus, cum bonis polleret moribus, omnium comprovincialium unanimi favore non tantum eligitur ex generis successione, quantum rapitur ut eis praeesset sceptrigera potestate." ("Vita Sti Edmi. R.," Migne's Patrol., vol. 130.)

[3] See Battely, p. 15, and Yates, p. 31. A marginal note in MS. 4826 of the Harleian collection gives Sudbury or the *South-borough* as the town of St. Edmund's coronation. Camden, Leland and Hearn are likewise in favour of Sudbury in preference to Bury or Bures-St.-Mary. This latter town, though situated on the Stour, is as much in Essex as in East Anglia. It has never been a place

The boy-king arrived in Sudbury towards the close of the year 856. There he probably spent Advent— the forty days of waiting which, St. Bede affirms, the English Church set aside before Christmas as well as before Easter for special prayer and penance. Such a time accorded well with King Edmund's desire for quiet and meditation. He employed it in preparation, not only for Christmas, but also for his consecration and coronation, which he appointed to take place on that day. As the festival of Our Saviour's birth drew near, Edmund listened in the church to the great vesper antiphons of the season, applying to himself in a special way the lessons which they taught. The "O Sapientia" —"O Wisdom"—reminded him of King Solomon, who chose wisdom to reign in preference to all other gifts. The antiphon ended, "Veni ad docendum nos viam prudentiæ,"—"Come and teach us the way of prudence." Edmund deeply felt his need of prudence in the difficult task of ruling. Again the Church sang : "O Key of David and Sceptre of the House of Israel," "O Orient Sun of Justice," "O King of Nations our Law-giver ; "—each title expressive of longing for the coming of Christ Our Lord found a corresponding echo in the young king's heart. Oh, how fervently he besought the eternal Son of God to come and be the Sceptre of his reign, his Sun of justice, and the law-giver of his kingdom !

of great importance, much less a "royal town" or a residence of the East Anglian kings. Why any author should have suggested Bury-St.-Edmund's, Bury in Lancashire, or Burne in Lincolnshire, is unaccountable. Not one of them is situated on the river Stour. Bury-St.-Edmund's was Beodricsworth, not Bury, in the time of St. Edmund's first biographers. Bury in Lancashire has no connection at all with King Edmund of East Anglia. Burne is evidently a copyist's blunder. Ganfridus' statement is so explicit that there can be no doubt that Sudbury was the town of St. Edmund's coronation.

Christmas Day,
A.D. 856.

At last Christmas day, 856, dawned. The choir chanted the night song; and after each nocturn a cleric removed one of the three coverings of the altar, first the violet or black, then the red, and lastly the white. The three masses of Christmas day began, solemnized by the English Church, according to St. Gregory the Great,[1] in honour of the three comings of Christ,—His coming into this world in human flesh, His coming in spirit into our souls, and His coming in glory and majesty at the last day. Crowds of people attended each mass. Then they joined the eager spectators who in spite of the bleak weather thronged the town. The boats fringing the river banks, the din of voices, the tramp of feet, the streets lined with people all proclaimed the nation's interest in its sovereign's coronation. And now the time draws near for the third mass, at which Bishop Humbert will anoint and crown the king. All along the route from the palace to the church the "merry and jovial" East Anglians wait good-humouredly for the procession to pass.

The coronation
procession.

Soon there issue forth from the dim precincts of the church boys in white with smoking censers and the vase of holy water; then others bearing aloft Christ's rood, the holy cross, and carrying burning lights to do it honour. A long line of white-robed priests follows, and last comes the saintly pontiff, crozier in hand, blessing the kneeling people. Through the streets, clean swept and strewn with reeds or tapestry, the procession makes its way to the king's lodgings, singing the Roman chant which Felix and Sigebert first taught the people. Arrived in the royal presence, the procession forms again. Before the king a thane walks bearing the golden sceptre, and then another with the rod of justice; next a throng of priests and monks; nobles follow carrying unsheathed swords, the royal

---

[1] 8th Homily.

insignia, the coronation robes and the crown of gold
and precious stones; last of all, amidst a crowd of
warriors and thanes, and of wise men and earldormen,
and of freemen with flowing hair, and of serfs newly
freed, walk the boy-king and the aged bishop side by
side under a silken canopy held aloft on the spears of
the four bravest knights of East Anglia.

The procession reaches the church, which was built, The procession reaches the church,
as St. Bennet's masons built Wearmouth and Jarrow, in
stone rough hewn, with walls of great thickness, semi-
circular arches and massive columns. Each royal
domain and even the lands of earldormen and thanes
rejoiced in many such churches.[1] The kings of East
Anglia from the time of St. Eorpwald, St. Sigebert and
St. Annas, to the time of St. Ethelbert and Offa
imitating the example of the kings of Northumbria
and Wessex, raised temples as worthy as possible
of the God whom they adored. Their subjects, too,
moved by what they heard or witnessed of the solemnity of worship in Rome, despising all considerations
of labour and expense, vied with each other in erect-
ing churches in which no ornament or decoration
they knew of should be wanting. Walls of polished
masonry and roofs of lead took the place of oaken
planks covered with reeds and straw. Lofty towers
added dignity and majesty to the building, windows
of glass, to the astonishment of the still half-savage
multitude, admitted light yet excluded wind and rain.
Rough and wanting perhaps in symmetry of form, the which is splen-didly decorated.
East Anglian church lacked to-day nothing in richness
and grandeur. The interior, washed with lime, rivalled
the fresh fallen snow in whiteness. The walls displayed in all magnificence the most valuable spoils
taken from the Mercians in the late wars. Curtains

[1] See St. Bede "Hist. Eccles.," bk. iii. c. 22 and 30; bk. v. c.
20 and 45.

of silk, pictures of Our Lord's miracles, paintings of
the Blessed Mother of God and of the twelve Apostles
hung around. The altar, always profusely decorated,
sparkled on this occasion with gold and gems. A
lofty crucifix surmounted it, and above all hung the
pharus, filled with rows of lamps which shed their
mellow light over the sanctuary, making the dim nave
and aisles look dimmer in the wintry mist. Here and
there, suspended from ceiling and arch, burning censers
filled the sanctuary and nave with perfume. Archbishop Theodore and Abbot Adrian had introduced the
organ from Italy, and, as the royal procession left
the open air and entered the dark portico which
covered the doorway, the "thousand voices of the
organ" and the humbler sound of the harp pealed
through the building. Meanwhile the joy-bells, such as
Cumeneas, abbot of Iona, wrote of, rang out over the
country around.[1] So priest and people conducted their
young prince to the church, the sound of their chant
growing louder and louder and filling the church as
the singers entered and grouped themselves within the
precincts of the sanctuary.

Edmund makes   Arrived at the altar, the boy-king kneels before the
the three
mandata,   mitred pontiff, and with hands upon the book of
gospels, written may-be like St. Wilfrid's in letters
of gold upon a purple ground, and bound in gold and
precious stones, solemnly pronounces the three man-
dates still preserved in the English coronation service.
They are a promise on the part of the king and at the
same time a proclamation to his subjects, a species of
compact between monarch and people, ratified by the
Church's blessing. "In the name of the Holy Trinity,"
sweet and clear sounds the young king's voice, "in all
the days of my life let God's Church and all Christian

---

[1] See Lingard's "Anglo-Saxon Church," vol. ii. p. 369, 1st edit.

folk be held in peace and honour and reverence." All
around answer: "Amen." "Let all rapine and every
sort of iniquity be interdicted to all classes of my
subjects." The same solemn "Amen" ratifies the
second mandate. "Justice and mercy shall be observed in all judgments, that the great and merciful
God may of His everlasting mercy forgive us all."
Again bishop and thanes and priests and all the voices
of that great assembly answer "Amen." For a
memorial they place a copy of these solemn promises
upon the altar. [1]

Then began the celestial and mysterious sacrifice *And assists at Christ's Mass.*
wherein the elements of the bread and wine are,
through the unutterable "hallowing of the Spirit, made
to pass into the mystery of Christ's Flesh and Blood." [2]
To-day every vessel used in this sacred action is of
gold or silver. Richly embroidered and jewelled vestments clothe the ministers at the altar. The liturgy is
the old liturgy brought to the island by St. Augustine,
in essentials differing nothing from that of Rome, the
mother and ruler of all the Churches, and familiar to
the Catholic of the present day. Like every rite of
holy Church, the solemn function speaks of another
land and of another world, even of heaven and of the
invisible angels. The language is not the language of
every day, but the holy Latin tongue of God's kingdom
of saints and martyrs. The sacred ministers, no longer
of the earth, apparelled in white raiments flowing and
graceful, ascend and descend around the altar like
the angels in Jacob's vision. Truly the whole scene
reveals the nearness of Him to whom the angels are
ministering spirits.

---

[1] In some copies of Archbishop Egbert's Pontifical these three
mandata are given at the end of the coronation ceremony. Martène
and Lingard both put them at the beginning. Collectively they
are spoken of as the "primum mandatum regis ad populum."

[2] See Venerable Bede's "Hom. in Epiphan."

Bishop Humbert anoints the young king, After the gospel, which told of the divine and human generations of the King of kings,[1] the pontiff pronounced a blessing over the kneeling prince. Immediately the chanters sang the antiphon, "Unxerunt Salomon,"—"They anointed Solomon,"[2]—following it up with the psalm, "Domine in virtute tua lætabitur rex," —"In Thy strength, O Lord, the king shall joy; and in Thy salvation he shall rejoice exceedingly." Meanwhile the bishop poured the horn of oil on the boy-king's head and breast and arms: on his head to signify the glory of the kingship; on his breast to signify the strength of the warrior; on his arms to signify the necessity of working with knowledge and wisdom for his people. At each anointing the venerable pontiff prayed that the Almighty would sanctify this youth by the unction of oil, as He sanctified His servant Aaron and His priests and kings and prophets to rule over His people Israel. And all the time the choir sang the prophetic verses of the twentieth psalm:

"Thou hast given him his heart's desire, and hast not withholden from him the will of his lips.

"For Thou hast prevented him with sweetness. Thou hast set on his head a crown of precious stones . . .

"Glory and great beauty shalt Thou lay upon him.

"Thou shalt give him to be a blessing for ever and ever . . . For the king hopeth in the Lord."

And clothes him in the royal robes. The anointing finished, Edmund, seated on his throne, assumed the royal robes. The venerable bishop clothed him in tunic and dalmatic, the vestments of the sacred ministers of the altar, reciting at

---

[1] John i. There was a special mass for the crowning of kings, but probably, according to the immemorial custom of the Church, only a commemoration was made from it on so great a feast.

[2] 3 Kings i. 39, and Ant. Mag. Dom. vii. post Pent.: "They anointed Solomon king, in Gahon, Sadoc the priest and Nathan the prophet, and going up they said rejoicing, The king live for ever."

the same time the prayers, to which priests and people answered, "Amen." Two thanes, approaching, knelt and put sandals on the king's feet; others threw over his shoulders the royal mantle; then the bishop, attended by the chief nobles, put into his hands the golden sceptre of mercy and the iron rod of justice, both emblematic of the office of judge. Next, to remind him of his duties as knight and warrior, attendants handed him the naked sword, by which to strike down the rebel and the oppressor, and put on his head the helmet, the symbol of the divine protection. Sceptres of gold and iron, sword and helmet, are now laid aside, and the king proceeds to the altar to receive the ring of righteousness and the crown.[1] At this point, Bishop Humbert earnestly exhorts the young prince not to accept the last emblems of kingly power and office, unless he is resolved to observe what the Church now so publicly and solemnly ratifies. Edmund answers that boy though he is, by the grace of God he will fulfil all the duties of a good king. His after history will show how faithfully, even by the sacrifice of his life, he kept the promises of his coronation day.

The prince himself then took the crown from the altar and handed it to the pontiff. St. Humbert, without hesitation, put it upon the boy-king's head, saying ' May God crown thee with the crown of glory, with the honour of justice, with the power of strength, that by our blessing, with strong faith and abundant fruit of good works, thou mayest obtain the crown of

The coronation.

---

[1] Lydgate writes :

> "The ryche crowne was set on his hed,
> To rewle the peple thorugh his noblesse,
> And held the swerd to kepe hem undir dreed
> That wolde be wrong, the poore peple oppresse,
> The sceptre of pees, the ryng of ryghtwysnesse,
> Conserve a kyng in his estat most strong."

E

an everlasting kingdom, by His gracious gift whose kingdom remains for ever and ever."

The enthronement. With crown on head, with the sceptre of peace placed once more in his right hand and the rod of iron in his left, with incense burning before him, King Edmund with firm step walks to his throne and takes possession of it. Pontiff and sacred ministers, knights and thanes accompany him. Thrice the bishop and his assistants, standing before the throne, entone the "Long live the king," and thrice thanes, knights and people take it up; thrice they all repeat the confirmatory, "Amen, amen, amen," and then approach to receive their sovereign's kiss. Hardly had the last thane received the royal embrace, when the voice of the pontiff again prayed aloud that God, the Author of Eternity, the Leader of the heavenly hosts, the Vanquisher of all His enemies, would bless His servant Edmund, whose head was humbly bent in lowly worship before Him, would shed His grace on the newly crowned, and keep him in health and happiness during his earthly sojourn.

The mass proceeds. The bishop now continues the holy sacrifice. He offers the *oflete*, or white round loaf of unleavened bread, which has been baked under the very eye of a priest. The sacred ministers meanwhile pour wine through a strainer into a chalice, and mingle with the wine a few drops of clearest water to signify God's union with our nature. The pontiff holds aloft the chalice also, afterwards making with it the sign of the cross over the place where it is to rest, a rite emblematic of the laying of Christ upon the cross.

The king's offering in the mass. Here the king left his throne for the foot of the altar, in order to make his Christmas and coronation offering. In Saxon England the oblations of the faithful on Christmas day differed at each mass. At the midnight solemnity they offered lights—emblems of that true light which on this night first shone in the darkness. At the mass at dawn of day they gave bread, because Christ on Christmas day became our bread, our source of life, in Bethlehem, which signifies the House of Bread. At the mass in the middle of the day they offered money, to signify that the Eternal Son became united to our nature as an image is impressed upon a coin. King Edmund, therefore, kneeling on the steps of the altar, made the offering to the bishop of a large coin of purest gold, the same being the usual offering at a coronation.

The mass proceeds. The choirs sing the "ter sanctus." *Edmund receives the Holy Housel.* The celebrant beseeches the most clement Father, through His Son Jesus Christ, to bless and accept the unspotted gifts; he makes the remembrance of the living and of the dead; invokes the saints; prays for the king in preface and canon.[1] The many mystic signs of the cross are formed, the bread and chalice consecrated, and offered to Him to Whom alone is all honour and glory. Lastly the pontiff breaks the Host and prepares to eat the heavenly bread and to drink of the chalice of salvation. As the celebration of the sacred mysteries thus drew to an end, the king approached the altar to receive the Holy Housel, "the saving victim of the Lord's Body and Blood."[2] As he knelt at the foot of the altar, the venerable pontiff placed upon his tongue the sacred Host, and put to his royal lips the chalice of Christ's Blood: "May the Body and Blood of our Lord Jesus Christ guard and protect thee," said the bishop. Both king and pontiff added, "Deo gratias."

Quickly now they finish the mass. Quickly the *The ceremony ends.* crowds hasten from the church to await outside the

[1] Egbert's Pontifical, besides assigning a special collect, secret, and post communion for the mass at a king's consecration, also assigned a place in both the preface and canon for the sovereign's name.

[2] St. Bede.

royal procession. With a magnificent retinue the
newly crowned sovereign comes forth and passes in
triumphal procession through the streets amidst the
acclamations of the people. Returning to the church,
he puts off his royal robes, assumes lighter ones, and
then proceeds to his palace. A banquet closes the
day. Thus, "in the year of our Lord's incarnation
856," writes a contemporary, [1] "Humbert, bishop of
the East Angles, anointed with oil and consecrated
as king the glorious Edmund, with much rejoicing
and great honour," in the royal town of Sudbury,
"in which at that time was the royal seat, in the
fifteenth year of his age, on a Friday, it being Christmas day."

---

[1] Asser, Bohn's edit., p. 50.

CHAPTER IV.

St, Edmund's Sovereignty—His Character and Rule.

Authorities—St Abbo's " Vita et Passio Sti. Edmundi " is the most ancient and valuable narrative illustrating St. Edmund's position in the England of his day and his character and influence in East Anglia. At least thirty manuscript copies of this important " Vita" exist. The British Museum possesses sixteen, the Oxford libraries six, Cambridge one. Several are lodged in the Royal Library at Paris. Copenhagen, Gotha and Vienna possess one each. The cathedral library of Lucca (Bibl. Canon.) preserves two not mentioned by Hardy, and the initial letter of one of them contains a portrait of St. Edmund. The Lives of St. Edmund by Osbert de Clare and Hermannus are also transcripts of St. Abbo's work with a few verbal alterations. Of St. Abbo's compositions in honour of the royal martyr, Bodl. Digby 109 vell. small folio xiii. cent. is certainly the most interesting. It begins with the letter to St. Dunstan, the life and passion of St. Edmund follows, then come the antiphon " Ave Rex Anglor m " set to music, and the proper office for St. Edmund's feast. The antiphons of the office, all set to chant, are most touchingly worded, and the lessons full of devotion and feeling. St. Abbo's " Vita et Passio Sti. Edmundi " remained unprinted till the 16th cent., when the Carthusian Surius brought it out among his *Vitæ Sanctorum* (Nov. 20, vol. iv. 440) where, contrary to his usual practice, he does not alter the style, considering it sufficiently good. In fact, in spite of one or two middle age expressions, St. Abbo wrote in a style worthy of the praise of Mabillon. Remarkable for his realistic expressions, he charmingly displays his talent for exposition throughout his works. It is to be hoped that his minuteness of detail will lose none of its charm by being occasionally put into an English dress. Migne also prints Abbo's Life of St. Edmund in his Latin Patrology, tom. 139, and a translation of it occurs in a work entitled " Vies de plusieurs saints illustres des divers siècles," by Arnaud d'Andilly. Lastly Arnold edits it for the Rolls Series in his " Memorials of St. Edmund's Abbey," vol. i. St. Abbo seems to have also written a life of St. Edward the King and Martyr, and an account of the translation of St. Benedict's relics to Fleury.

This illustrious biographer of St. Edmund was one of the most enlightened and active-minded men of his age. From his Life by his disciple Aimoin (Migne tom. cxxxix. and from the exhaustive " Histoire de Saint Abbon " (Lecoffre fils et Cie, Paris) by Abbé Pardiac, we learn that Abbo was born at Orleans about the year 940. His parents offered him in his childhood to St. Benedict, and saw him receive the monastic cowl in the famous abbey of Fleury-sur-Loire. Fleury was then closely connected with England. From it the new monastic advance initiated by St. Dunstan received all its vigour; thither St. Ethelwold of Winchester sent his disciple Osgar to imbibe the true Benedictine spirit, and to study in its famous school. St. Odo, archbishop of Canterbury, brought over from Fleury a body of Benedictines to assist him in the government of his diocese. St. Oswald, bishop of Worcester and archbishop of York, when a young man, took the habit in its sanctuary and afterwards applied there for monks to start Ramsey abbey. In answer to his appeal Germanus came as abbot, and St. Abbo, who had studied both at Rheims and Paris, who had superintended the school at Fleury, and was already renowned for his works on mathematics, liturgy, history, grammar and poetry, came to organise the abbey school. Not only at Ramsey, but also at Canterbury, York, Cambridge and St. Edmund's Bury, Abbo founded schools. At St. Edmund's Bury he heard the history of St. Edmund and gained his great devotion to him. At Canterbury he again heard the narrative from his intimate friend St. Dunstan. St. Dunstan himself heard the story of the royal martyr's life and martyrdom when a young favourite at court, from an old man bent and decrepit, who asserted on oath that he was St. Edmund's sword-bearer on the day of the holy martyr's death, and who related it as an eye-witness " with simplicity and full of faith" to the glorious King Athelstan (A.D. 925). In later times Archbishop Dunstan often repeated the narrative, and once related it with tears in his eyes to Aelfstan, bishop of Rochester, to the Abbot of Malmesbury, St. Abbo and others. At the request of the monks of Ramsey Abbo committed the narrative to writing. St. Abbo is therefore a reliable authority. In order to protect himself against all inaccuracies, he took the precaution of sending his manuscript to "his holiness," *tua sanctitas*, St. Dunstan, praying him to correct anything contrary to historical truth. Yates, however, in his History of Bury (p. 25) seems to think that St. Abbo's work is of little value, since he did not see St. Dunstan till A.D. 985, *i.e.* 50 years after the archbishop had heard the history of St. Edmund. The prelate himself did not hear the narrative till 60 years after it happened, and then from a man of an age when the memory is defective and treacherous. Yates, besides being incorrect in his statements, forgets that other eye-witnesses, independent of the old sword-bearer, often related the same facts. Again, St. Abbo and even St. Dunstan when at St. Edmund's Bury, could, and probably did, consult the records kept by the contemporary guardians of St. Edmund's shrine who treasured up every incident in the life of their royal patron. Abbo wrote his "Life and Passion of St. Edmund" in the 7th year of King Ethelred's reign, *i.e.* A.D. 985. On leaving England he became Abbot of Fleury. In 1004 he undertook the reform of the monastery of Reole, where he met his death, Nov. 13 of the same year, through a deep spear-thrust in the left arm which he received in a rising of the Gascons against the French. The church at Reole still honours him as its patron. Besides Abbé Pardiac's book, see for St. Abbo's Life and works, Mabillon's "Acta Sanct. Ord. Bened.," vol. xiii. 35. Migne's Latin Patrol, vol. 139, the introduction to the "Memorials of St. Edmund's Abbey," p. xxii.

The "Vita Sancti Edmundi Regis et Martyris" MS. Harl. 2802 a large xii. cent. folio volume, also contains f. 226 b. useful matter on St. Edmund's character and reign. The author of this piece has not been ascertained. It begins, "Gloriosus Rex Edmundus ex-antiquorum Saxonum nobili prosapia oriundus," and ends, "Ad laudem Domini nostri Jesu Christi, cui est honor et gloria in secula. Amen."

Lydgate still continues useful, and Alban Butler and Dom Cressy, O.S.B. both describe in short the character of St. Edmund's rule.]

St. Edmund's age on his accession to the throne.
CHRONICLERS of St. Edmund's life differ with regard to his age on coming to the throne and the subsequent events of his reign. Their disagreement chiefly arises from a difference in the dates from which they start. Some, for instance, begin the young king's reign from the death of King Offa, others from the landing at Hunstanton, from the election at Attleborough, or from the royal consecration at Sudbury. Hence one records that Edmund ascended the throne in his thirteenth year, another places that event in his fourteenth or fifteenth year, and William of Malmesbury strangely puts it in the saint's sixteenth year. Asser, a contemporary writer, mentions two accessions of St. Edmund, but removes all ambiguity by giving the dates and circumstances of both. Edmund, he says, began his reign in his fourteenth year, on Christmas day, 855, a few weeks after his return from the court of Ethelwulph; and the Christmas following, in the fifteenth year of his age, Bishop Humbert anointed and crowned him king of the whole country. Had

other writers been as explicit as Asser, no confusion
could have arisen with regard to St. Edmund's age or
the date of his accession.

Edmund once king becomes a prominent figure in the St. Edmund's
sovereignty.
history of his day. The few scanty records of his
country which have survived treat of him as the greatest of East Anglian sovereigns. Malmesbury and
William of Croyland, while lamenting a century's
anarchy and disorder previous to St. Edmund, hail his
accession as the beginning of a new era. With a
strong hand, writes Simeon of Durham, Edmund held
the supreme power. Records which hardly meant to
speak of him describe his rule as that of no ordinary
petty sovereign, but worthy to rank with Ina's, Offa's,
Egbert's or Alfred's in the annals of our country. The
Danish invaders, recognising him as the most redoubtable of the English kings, brought all their force
to bear against his kingdom. His sturdy resistance
and final victory on their first landing, and his alliance
with Mercia under the walls of Nottingham more than
ever convinced them of the absolute necessity of subduing the defender of East Anglia before making any
attack on Wessex or Mercia. Having subjugated
Edmund, they hoped to find the rest of England an
easy conquest. What the nation thought of the valour
of Edmund's life the exceptional worship paid to him
after death testifies. Other kings fell victims to the
Danish sword, but neither their holiness nor their
prowess merited the distinction which England bestowed on the royal martyr of East Anglia.

Some writers speak of St. Edmund as a tributary and He was not a
tributary prince.
dependent sovereign. The contrary was the case.
Simeon of Durham[1] and Roger of Hovedon, while
stating the fact that "Rex Edmundus ipsis temporibus
regnavit super omnia regna orientalium"—"*In those days*

---

[1] Surtees Publ., p. 50, no. 51.

King Edmund ruled over the whole of East Anglia,"—
make no mention of his subordination to any other
sovereign. Lydgate unhesitatingly asserts that "he
had of Estyngland *holly* the governance." And Matthew
of Westminster,[1] as well as Florence of Worcester,[2]
speak of his succeeding to the *supreme* power. Add to
this the remarkable omission of East Anglia in the contemporary lists of kingdoms tributary to Ethelwulph
of Wessex. That monarch, on succeeding his father
Egbert as king of England, made over to his son
Athelstan the provinces of Kent, Essex and Sussex.
On the death of Athelstan he resumed the government
of Kent, Sussex and Essex, and resigned the western
portion of his kingdom in favour of his second son King
Ethelbald. In his last testament he bequeathed Essex
Kent, Sussex and Surrey to his third son Ethelbert.
In none of these instances do the contemporary chroniclers mention East Anglia.[3] King Edmund had indeed
graced the court of Ethelwulph on the memorable 5th
of November, A.D. 855, but neither Ethelwulph nor his
sons treated him as an under-king. His claim to East
Anglia rested on his Uffing blood and the choice of the
people. There is no record of any neighbouring power
supporting him. At his consecration and coronation
at Sudbury he took no oath to a suzerain. As independent of Wessex as Northumbria was, he ruled a
traditionally independent people. Under this impression the Danes treated with him. He professed to
them that he had been consecrated by God in the
solemn rite of coronation to rule and guide his people,

---

[1] Bohn's edit, vol. i. p. 404, A.D. 855.

[2] "Monumenta Historica Brittanica," vol. i. p. 547, 552.

[3] See Asser's "Life of Alfred," A.D. 855. Ethelwerd's Chron.,
bk. v. chap. i. collated with the Angl. Saxon Chron. A.D. 855. See
also Matt. of Westminster, A.D. 861, and Lingard's Hist. of England,
vol. i. A.D. 836 et seq. on the successors of Egbert.

and to God only was he tributary. To no over-king would he do homage. In fact, no English kingdom demanded his allegiance. Northumbria was too torn with dissensions to attempt it. Mercia had tried and failed. Ethelwulph and his sons found their own frontiers threatened with bands of sea-pirates, and had no wish to assert supremacy over a kingdom which might rival their own. They preferred to leave the long coast-line of East Anglia, the first to greet the pirates fresh from the North, to its brave king and his equally brave subjects.

St. Edmund worthily filled the position which Divine *His royal person* Providence assigned to him. His personal appearance showed him every inch a king. From birth to manhood nature had favoured him with her gifts. His face was young but manly, his complexion fair and fresh, his forehead lofty, his hair light and flowing. A somewhat prominent nose enhanced rather than marred his beauty, and eyes deep and blue beamed with the joy of a soul which saw in every event of life the wisdom and clemency of God. Tall of stature, of firm and symmetrical build,[1] he possessed before he reached maturity, "the strength and robustness," say the old Sarum lessons, "of one in the flower of his age." The majesty of his mien impressed all who beheld him. "Imperium tenebat," writes the Ely Chronicler,[2] speaking rather of his personal bearing than of his mode of government; and Abbo pictures him noble and stately as an emperor, but with a serenity of disposition which gave a grace to his every speech and action.

In his private life Edmund observed the utmost *His private* simplicity. His unassuming manner charmed all who *character.* came in contact with him. He was affable and cour-

---

[1] Roger of Wendover, Bohn's edit., vol. i. p. 195.
[2] "Historia Eliensis," Anglia Christiana Society, p. 79.

teous to the poorest and the lowliest.[1] However tried or
occupied, he never lost his equanimity or his kindly
sympathy for others. Yet with his fellow princes as
with his own thanes his superiority asserted itself, not
by outward haughtiness, but by an inherent gentleness
which none could resist. His parents had educated
him to become a saint and a martyr rather than a
prince of the world. Throughout his career, but
especially in his less public life, this early training
showed itself in an ardent striving to form his soul for
God, and in an unflinching resoluteness in the performance of duty. " Toto conamine virtutis arripuit gra-
dum," "*with all his might he strove after virtue*," writes
his earliest biographer.[2] His chaste and celibate life is
a standing proof of his high spiritual perfection. In his
daily conduct he guided himself by the commands and
will of God, whom alone he desired to please, and in
this he swerved "neither to the right nor to the left,
either by extolling himself for his merits or by suc-
cumbing to human frailty.[3] All day long, at home
and abroad, his mind was fixed on God. "Heaven-
ward soared his soul," sings the poet of his life.
He was "ever adoring God," exclaims Simeon of
Durham. And, in order that the distracting occupa-
tions of his office might not gradually weaken this
union with his Creator, the saintly king frequently
withdrew to some country retreat, there to refresh
his soul with meditations and pious exercises. By this
means he maintained the high tone and vigour of his
spiritual life.

His love for
field sports.

Edmund took great delight in field sports and all out-
door exercises. He threw into them all the earnestness

---

[1] " Erat omnibus blando eloquio affabilis, humilitatis gratia
præclarus, et inter suos coevos mirabili mansuetudine residebat
dominus absque ullo fastu superbiæ."—St. Abbo.

[2] St. Abbo.   [3] MS. Harl. 2802.

of his nature. The hunting and hawking, however, of his leisure hours were with him no mere purposeless killing of time. Besides being often the alternative of idleness, of which, says one of his biographers, he was "the declared enemy," these recreations prepared him for other duties. The young king, like the ancient Cyrus, used them to acquire boldness, coolness and strategy in the field, and thus to inspire even veteran warriors with confidence in his leadership.

The virtues of his private life made Edmund a most successful ruler. In the beginning of his reign he put himself under the spiritual guidance of St. Humbert, to whom, next to God, he mainly owed his humility, his purity and his Christlike affability. With this training and that of Sigentius, his father's old adviser, he grew up into the model of a perfect prince. Of all his public virtues a winning graciousness of manner chiefly distinguished him. According to Richard of Cirencester,[1] he always had before his eyes the words of Ecclesiasticus: "Have they made thee ruler? be not lifted up; be among them as one of them."[2] At the same time he administered justice with a firm hand, taking the law of God as the unerring standard of right and wrong. Before giving judgment he would examine with his own eyes and hear with his own ears. Thus, with dovelike simplicity, yet with the prudence of the serpent, he frustrated the evil designs of flatterers and informers. In matters of importance he invariably took counsel of others. Like Solomon, a special child of wisdom, he had won a throne by his discretion and prudence, but he did not on that account think himself capable of governing his dominions, narrow though their limits, without the aid of others. He exemplified throughout his reign the inspired

His character as a Ruler.

---

[1] Rolls Publ., vol. i. p. 331 et seq.   [2] Ecclus. xxii. 1.

proverb, " He that is wise hearkeneth unto counsels." [1]

St. Edmund's desire to grant the just demands of
even the poorest of his subjects brought him early in
his reign in conflict with the rough spirits whom the
late unsettled state of affairs had multiplied throughout the land. King Offa had successfully repressed the
lawlessness and disorder consequent on the Mercian
wars. In his later years, however, Offa had been weak
and infirm. For three years at least he had been absent
from the kingdom, and no supreme ruler had taken
his place. Consequently, oppression of the poor,
open murder and rapine, the tyranny of the strong
over the weak had again become the order of the
day. Edmund boldly attacked the evil. So well
had he learnt the lesson of his coronation, that,
while cherishing his quiet and obedient subjects
with the sceptre of peace, he hesitated not to unsheath the sword of justice and to wield the rod of
iron against the wild and rebellious. " Benign to the
submissive," Malmesbury writes of him, " severe to the
rebellious." Yet he acted with a tact that gained the
love and veneration of all. In the rough times in
which he lived, several kings devoted to duty lost their
lives in opposing lawlessness and injustice. Such had
been the fate of his predecessor St. Eorpwald, and later
on his namesake King Edmund I. fell by the dagger of
an outlaw. If St. Edmund was anything he was an
" upholder of the law of God "—" *divinæ legis apprime
tenax*,"—a most impartial administrator of justice, a
fearless guardian of the happiness and prosperity of his
people ; yet no discontented subject raised a hand
against him in vengeance or hate. Wrong-doers suffered
from the firmness and resolution, hard and unflinching
as a rock, with which he punished them ; but his

---

[1] Proverbs xii. 15.

unimpassioned manner and the kindness with which he
tempered his severity conciliated the hardest criminal.[1]

In his work of reform St. Edmund called in the help *St. Edmund and the Church.*
of the Church. Wise policy dictated the employment
of the Church's individual care and training of his
subjects as a power for good; but the young king's
appreciation of the Church and its priesthood was not
mere policy. Religion and piety had become part and
parcel of his nature. "He was most sincerely devoted
to the Christian faith," writes St. Abbo. His earnestness nowhere more conspicuously displayed itself than
in his endeavour to repair the havoc of the Mercians
in church and monastery. Wherever his predecessor
had left unrestored a broken altar or a dismantled
cloister, Edmund hastened to build it up again. The
clergy he supplied with sufficient and even abundant
means for the becoming performance of the divine
service, at the same time furthering among them to
the best of his power that spirit of ecclesiastical
discipline and piety which the troubles of the
time had so seriously impaired. While, however,
no one had a loftier idea than King Edmund of
the Church's authority, or the influence it should
exert in a kingdom, his frank and candid nature revolted from anything like hypocrisy or dissimulation,
and the insincere could never count on his sympathy
or protection. The annals of his country proclaim him
" conspicuous in Christ and in his Church,"[2] the "Fidei
Christianae cultor,"—"*the promoter of the faith of
Christ.*"[3] "He was raised up by God," exclaims St.
Abbo in the office for his feast, "to be the defender of
His Church." Even beyond the limits of his own king-

---

[1] "Divinæ legis apprime tenax, et subditorum felicitatis studiosis-
simus, omnium sibi amorem ac venerationem conciliavit," Harl.
MS. 2802.

[2] Harl. MS. 2802.   [3] Hist. Eliensis, Angl. Christiana Soc., p. 79.

dom he advanced the cause of God and religion.
By his presence at the council of Winchester he supported its charter of gifts to the monks and clergy;
and later on under the walls of Nottingham he
pleaded with his brother monarchs for the abbey of
Croyland. Finally, in defence of the altar and for the
faith of Christ he generously laid down his life.

St. Edmund's court.

The court of this Christian king presented a pattern
to princes. At early dawn the king and his attendants
paid their first homage to their common Master and
Lord by assisting at the holy sacrifice. During the
day the law of God ruled the household. Even rough
warriors, moved by the example of their youthful
sovereign, made it their first endeavour to give God due
reverence. No loud voice of rioting or dissipation
disturbed the royal halls. No oath or quarrel broke the
harmony in its precincts, for all feared the king's
displeasure as much as they valued his friendship.
Through Edmund's influence, love of truth, generosity
to the needy, gentleness, moderation of language
reigned in the palace. The words of Venerable Bede
admirably describe the East Anglians under St.
Edmund's government. "Departing from the rude
and boorish manners of their ancestors," he writes,
"they began to be exceedingly civilized and polite."
So, when some of them settled in Hunstanton, the
name of the place memorialized their gentleness of
temper no less than their bravery. The holy king,
according to Roger of Wendover,[1] instructed his
attendants in every grace of speech and behaviour;
and, in order to preserve the internal tranquillity of his
kingdom and defend it, if necessary, from external
attacks, he trained all his thanes in strict military
discipline. With one stroke of the pen Matthew of
Westminster[2] gives a picture of St. Edmund's court

---

[1] Bohn's edit., p. 193.   [2] Bohn's edit., vol. i. p. 412.

on the occasion of the Danish chief Lothbroc's introduction to it. "Lothbroc was much pleased," he
writes, "by the graciousness of manner of King
Edmund, and by the admirable state of his military
discipline, and by the numerous retinue of servants
who stood by, whom the industry of the king had
made fully accomplished in all honourable actions and
in every variety of knowledge." And all that he
saw so fascinated the Dane that he earnestly begged
to remain with St. Edmund, "in order to be more
fully instructed in the king's discipline."

From St. Edmund's person and court flowed forth The royal
charity.
charity to all in need. His poet sings :

> " Against poor folk shut was not his gate,
> His wardrobe open all needy to relieve,
> Such royal mercy did his heart move
> To clothe the naked and the hungry feed.
> And sent he alms to folk that lay bedrid." [1]

"He was the father of his subjects, particularly of the
poor," writes Alban Butler, quoting from Florence of
Worcester,[2] "the protector of widows and orphans and
the support of the weak." Again and again our
annals address him as the "clement father,"[3] the
"benefactor of the poor," the "kind father of orphans
and widows." There are, indeed, few recorded facts
to support this unanimous testimony of St. Edmund's
biographers. Incidentally, however, the saint's pane-
gyrists relate events which show that they do not
eulogise at random. The chance mention of Sathonius,
the king's old pensioner, the tears of the aged sword-
bearer, the eye-witness of his martyrdom, the devotion
of the Danish chief to the saint, the history of the
murderer Bern bear witness that Edmund was a just
ruler, a strong-souled Christian man, whose reign could
not fail to bring glory and prosperity to his country.

---

[1] Lydgate.   [2] Bohn's edit., p. 59.   [3] Harl. MS. 2802.

The monk
Lydgate on
King Edmund's
polity.

Summing up the merits of his hero's government, the old Benedictine poet compares St. Edmund's king-dom to a beautiful and well-proportioned human figure of which the king himself forms the head. With the two eyes of prudence and reason the young prince watched over the whole *body* politic, taking heed that no quarrel or dissension disturbed its action. No class of society, no subject, however humble, no branch of government failed to receive the holy sovereign's attention. Edmund regarded his knights and warriors as the *hands and arms* of the state, to whom it belonged to defend the frontiers, to protect maidens and widows, "and save the Church from mischief and damage." As the soul which quickened and animated the fair form, the king cherished " folk contemplatiff "—" sober of their lyving "—" expert in konning," who, by chaste example, holy doctrine and the dignity of their sacred office, " with lyght of virtu did his people enlumyne." He considered the plough and the labourer as the *feet* and *legs* of the state, without which it was helpless.

> " Thus evry membre set in order due,
> Ther was no cause among hem to compleyue :
> Ffor ech of hem his offyce did serve.
> The hed lyst nat at the ffoot dysdeyne.
> Ther love was oon, they partyd not on tweyne ;
> Ech thyng by grace so dewly was conveyed,
> Hed of the membrys was nat dysobeyed.
> And as the ruby, kyng of stonys alle
> Rejoyssheth ther presence with its natural lyght
> Ryght so king Edmond in his royal stalle,
> With crowne and sceptre sat lyk an hevenly knyght
> To hyh and lowh moost agreeable of syght.
> This woord rehersyd of evry creature
> Longe might he leve the kyng here, and endure."

A glorious and
peaceful reign.

Thus, to the admiration of posterity the youthful monarch throughout his reign maintained, in a bar-barous age and with subjects rough and lawless, that happy state of tranquillity in which "justice and peace kissed."[1] Few kings in early England so boldly attacked the savage and half pagan spirit of the country as Edmund of East Anglia. And he subdued it not by physical force, but by the assertion of Christian principles.

By his virtues, not by the sword, St. Edmund gained his influence. Holiness as irreproachable as it was solid and practical won the admiration and respect of his people. They beheld their prince of an age when the violence of the passions is strongest, and in a position which placed him above the usual restraints of the law. Yet, dead to all sensual pleasures, he led a life upright and stainless amid the disorders of the times. Awe-struck and subdued, they regarded him as a superior being, and obeyed him as though he were an angel from heaven. Unlike most princes, he needed no vain display of pomp and ceremony to impress his people. Both his person and his manner strongly attached the nation to him :

Through the influence of his holiness.

> " In his estat moost godly and benygne ;
> Hevenly of cheer, of counsayl provident,
> Shewyng of grace ful many a blyssed signe ;
> * * * of wourthynesse the glorye,
> * * * * * * * *
> And in persone passing delynnesse. "

Everyone,

> " Lovyd hym of herte that lokyd on his fface. "

The best of monarchs have used similar powers of fascination to enlarge their empire. Not so St. Edmund, as Pierre de Caseneuve, his French biographer, remarks. The noble and gentle king of East Anglia was only ambitious to achieve the designs of Providence. " Ever to godward hool was his entent."[2] He limited his efforts to the simple every-day duties of a petty

---

[1] Ps. lxxxiv. 11.   [2] Lydgate.

king, so long as God signified those to him. When the
divine Will called him to higher duties, Edmund just
as gladly and willingly obeyed even to the sacrifice
of his life. The invasion of the Danes required him,
lover of peace though he was, to take up arms in
defence of his religion and country. Like another
St. Michael, he unhesitatingly joined battle with the
enemy. No English king made a more gallant stand
against the Danes, none deserved better of his countrymen, none fell more heroically than Edmund of East
Anglia. But in all he designed and did he sought
not his own glory. With mind and heart he looked to
heaven. He gave no thought to self or earth.

CHAPTER V.

St. Edmund and the Danes.

[*Authorities*—The connection of the Anglo-Saxons with their kindred on the continent is a well known fact of history. Of St. Edmund's individual relations with Denmark and of his reputation there, Gaufridus, the compiler of Bodleian MS. 240 and Lydgate give the fullest particulars. The chief authority, however, for this and the following chapters is Pierre de Caseneuve, an Augustinian canon of St. Sernin's basilica at Toulouse, who flourished in the 17th century. His "Histoire de la vie et des miracles de St. Edmond Roi d'Estangle, ou Angleterre Orientale," printed "chez Pierre Bose" at Toulouse in 1644, is full of historic research, and numerous marginal references to the most reliable English and foreign annals greatly enhance its value. In his dedication to "Monseigneur Monseigneur l'Illustrissime et révérendissime Messire Charles de Monchal Archévêque de Tolose," Caseneuve mentions the occasion which suggested his writing the Life of St. Edmund, viz. the solemnity of translating the sacred bones of the royal martyr from a sepulchre of stone to a reliquary of silver, vowed to the saint by the men of Toulouse during a plague which afflicted their city. "Heaven and the angels," he writes, "have hitherto for many years been the only witnesses of the triumphs of St. Edmund. Now it is man's turn." This learned French biographer of the English martyr king has thoroughly sifted the history of Lothbroc or Lothparck, and satisfactorily cleared up the many difficulties raised by Polydore Vergil, Turner and others. Devotion and erudition combined make de Caseneuve a worthy chronicler of the events of St. Edmund's life. Most of our English chroniclers, and notably William of Malmesbury and Matthew of Westminster, cursorily refer to the other events of this chapter. For the question of Lothbroc the student should further consult Richard of Cirencester (Rolls Pub., vol. i. p. 333), Polydorus Vergil (Caxton Publ., vol. 36, pp. 141-142), and Adam of Bremen. Two other valuable documents worthy of mention here are the "Vita et Passio Sti Edmundi Breviter Co'lecti," found in the "Liber Coenobii S. Edmundi," of the municipal library of Donal, and the "Vita abbreviata," in Abbot Curteys' register, a cartulary now happily in the British Museum (Additional MSS. 7096, 14848). Hardy omits both these pieces in his "Materials," though they contain several important incidents. The "Liber Coenobii Sti Edmundi," which was written while William Excter ruled St. Edmund's Bury (1418-1429), contains on the first page the stamp "Bibliotheca Benedictina Anglorum Duaci--S. Gregorius Magnus." On the fly-leaf occur the names of its former owners, "Roberte Woode,"the famous archaeologist, and "Johannis Smithi Londiniensis." In 1836 Sir John Gage and Thomas Stapleton came expressly from London to examine this precious MS. Though full of matter of the most interesting character to the antiquarian and historian, no savant has yet edited it. On page 30 begins the account of the "Translatio Sti Edmundi," in the reign of William II., to which reference will be made in chapter ix. On page 32 occurs the Life of St. Edmund used for the compilation of this and the following chapters (see Catalogue of Douai MSS., by Dehaisnes, 543). The second, "Vita et Passio Sti E'mundi Regis, abbreviata et sumpta de prolixa Vita ejusdem Sancti," takes up twelve folio pages of the register which bears the name of Abbot Curteys, who ordered its compilation to prove the privileges of his monastery:—"Quia quidam . . . affirmavit quod monasterium Sti. Edmundi ante *edictionem* . . . . Decretorum non fuit ab omni jurisdictione episcopall exemptum ; . . . . . Pater Williclmus Curteys Martyrium S. Edmundi. compendiose compilatum hic inseri feeit." King Stephen made the publication (edictionem) mentioned in this note in Abbot Ording's time (1148-1156). Abbot Curteys, however, traces the privileges of his abbey still further back, going to the very basis of its exemption, by giving an abridgement of the "Prolixa Vita," which contained the first privileges granted to the guardians of St. Edmund's body. The "Prolixa Vita," of which the MS. Bodl. 240 partly supplies the place, probably perished in the 16th century. Abbot Curteys put forward the "Vita Abbreviata" as the strongest proof of the privileges of his abbey. As no one disputed its facts, it may be accepted as reliable.]

UNDER King Edmund's firm yet gentle rule East Anglia presented a marked contrast to the rest of England. Anarchy reigned supreme in Northumbria, internal troubles afflicted Mercia and Wessex. East Anglia alone could boast of peaceful borders, a contented people and an undisputed throne. Round the crackling fire in the halls of many a Hafford bards could sing of the peace and plenty brought to their shores, and of the noble king whom serf and freeman loved. Monks wrote his good deeds in monastic chronicles which have long since perished. So the virtues of "Blessed Edmund, of Christ's own man," spread their refulgence far and wide. [1] In that age men travelled by land and sea, almost as much as they do now, though without the same facilities. The race was young and restless. Its people revelled in any enterprise which took them beyond the limits of their own narrow homes. In these expeditions the conversation naturally turned to the young king of the East Angles. England soon rang with his praises. Even foreign kings held him in veneration. The fame of his prowess and, writes Roger of Wend-

---

[1] " *Whoo* can or may kepe cloos or hyde
A cleer lanterne whan that it is lyght,
Upon a channdelabre whan it doth abyde ?
Or of Appollo dyfface the beemys bryght ?
Or whoo kowde hyndre goddys owne knyght
This blyssed Edmund, this crystes owne man,
Thorugh many a kyndham but that his fame ran,
Off his noblesse thus was the repoort,
In Est yngelond how ther was a king
Off whoom the renoon, by many a strannge poort,
Was rad and songe his virtues rehersyng ;
His governance, his knyghtly demenyng
Which cessyd nat fro that it was be gonne
Tyl in to Denmark the noble ffame is ronne."

Lydgate.

over, "of his incomparable bodily size and stature," reached beyond the seas. Bishop Humbert in his letters to his fellow bishops on the continent probably dwelt upon the high qualities of his sovereign. The imperial court, also, closely watched Edmund's policy together with that of all the English kings of the period. According to the medieval idea the emperor presided over the whole earth in temporal matters as the pope did in spiritualities. Charlemagne acted on this principle, when he supported Egbert of Wessex or recognised Offa of Mercia so far as to treat with him for the protection of English pilgrims. The new emperor, Lothaire I., could not fail to recognise the growing popularity of the East Anglian king, whose youth and success often formed the theme of conversation in his court. Especially Old Saxony, the land of his birth, rejoiced in the renown of its young prince. The happy issue of his expedition had filled the Saxons with delight. They loved to talk of the success of their bright and gentle Edmund, the choice of his people, the glory of his land. Where "he reigned, no man sought for justice and failed to get redress, nor did any innocent man cry in vain for mercy." Under his strong and just rule "a boy might drive a mule laden with gold" from Lynn to Sudbury, or from Thetford to Yarmouth, and "none dared molest him." Thus they spoke of him in the land of his birth.

On the north of Old Saxony lay Denmark, at that time swarming with bold adventurers. The report of their neighbour's enterprise and its prosperous result spread rapidly among them. They regarded Edmund in the light of a daring and fortunate adventurer, and in their schemes of invasion or conquest naturally discussed his method of success. Finding it Christian in every

detail, they were filled with an apostate hate,[1] and
thought of East Anglia only to ruin it. In Edmund
they beheld a Christian king whom their swords could
bring to the dust, and in his kingdom a fresh field for
plunder as soon as occasion offered. How terrible
a danger thus threatened Edmund and his people a
rapid glance at the Danes and their country will show.

Denmark and
the Danes, A.D.
8.0.

By the Danes or Norsemen in the ninth century
were meant all the countless tribes that peopled the
Scandinavian peninsula, the islands of the Baltic and
present Denmark. They were of a kindred race to the
Angles and Saxons, but Christian civilization had
hardly yet affected them. Untamed and savage, they
possessed all the wild daring and barbaric habits of
the English who scoured the northern seas three
centuries before. A line of vigorous sovereigns was
now, however, striving to reduce Scandinavia and its
dependencies to some settled order. Their policy, as
well as an absurd law by which the eldest son inherited
the whole patrimony to the exclusion of the rest of the
family, forced thousands of free and independent spirits
to seek their fortune on the high seas. Once more
the northern ocean was darkened by the black ships
of pirate chieftains who despised storm and tempest,
and loved the sea best when the wind lashed it into
a fury resembling their own mad licence. Any
thriving country was considered lawful prey. Any
chivalrous Christian king was deemed a fit object for
their pagan hate. In hordes these Norsemen ravaged
the coasts of Europe, and slaughtered the inhabitants
Their ships when descried on the sea-line spread universal panic. With them invasion meant the conflagration of town and village, the slavery of women, the
murder in cold blood of men and children. They struck

---

[1] Many of the Danes apostatised from the Christian faith about
this time.

down the priest at the altar. They left monasteries
and churches heaps of smouldering ruins. Government, arts, letters, religion, all lay crushed in their
wake. Having wasted one country, they steered to
another to repeat the same horrors. Winter alone
stopped their ravages. Then they retreated with the
spoils of the year to some safe harbour to give themselves up to rioting and lust. Throwing off their
lethargy with the spring breezes, they put to sea again.
In later times fleets of these pirates crowded up the
Seine, and, with Ralph the Ganger at their head, wrested
the provinces on both sides of the river from the
French king. Other bands desolated the banks of the
Tagus. Others sailed through the pillars of Hercules,
and founded a kingdom in southern Italy. But a century before these events the fame of King Edmund had
attracted their thoughts towards England.

In the annals of East Anglia occurs an episode of Lothbroc
this period which illustrates the habits of the Danes, the Dane.
and introduces several characters who play important
parts in St. Edmund's history. On that southern part
of the coast of Denmark which is washed by the northern sea ruled a chieftain named Lothbroc,[1] or more
correctly Lothparck. Some chroniclers style him king,
by which they probably mean no more than that he was
a man of position. By piracy he had accumulated
great wealth, which, added to his blood connection
with the ruling house and his known cunning and
villainy, gave him an unenviable notoriety. He must
not, however, be confused with the more famous Ragnar
Lodbrog, who was put to death on the coast of Northumbria in the year 805.[2] Both were Danes, both met

---

[1] Gaufridus writes it Lodebrok (odiosus rivus), "*loathed brook.*"
Leland gives Lothbrig and Lothbric ; Speed, Lothbroke, which
signifies, he says, *Leather briche.* The Douai MS. and Matthew
of Westminster spell it Lothbrocus ; Lydgate, Lothbrokus.

[2] Lingard. Butler says he met his death in Ireland.

a tragic death in England, both were avenged by their sons. But Lothbroc never swayed the nation like the sea-king Ragnar Lodbrog, who commanded the most terrible barbarian fleet that ever darkened the northern ocean, and bore down with thousands of savages upon England. Neither did Hinguar and Hubba avenge Ragnar's death, but his son Agner, whose name the carelessness of north-country annalists has confused with that of Hinguar. In fact, Ragnar's death occurred upwards of thirty years before St. Edmund's birth, and sixty before Hinguar and Hubba invaded England.

The identity of the Lothbroc or Lothparck of St. Edmund's history is fully established by Adam of Bremen.[1] "The kings of the Danes," he says, "who infested the coast of France were Horig, Ordinig, Gothafrid, Rodulph, and Hinguar; the cruellest of them all was Hinguar, the son of Lothparch, who wheresoever he went subjected the lives of Christians to the most horrible cruelties." This notice of Lothparck, while it distinguishes him from Ragnar Lodbrog, after whom he has been carelessly named, saves the following narrative, strange as it may read, from being considered a mere fable.

Lothparck had two sons, Hinguar and Hubba,[2] remarkable even in that rough age for fierceness and savagery. Of all the leaders who infested the coasts of France, Hinguar held the palm for merciless cruelty. His brother to other crimes added witchcraft. Unwilling to settle down in their father's district, these men chose a life of adventure on the high seas, heading the most desperate crews of their fellow pirates in raids upon the coasts of Europe. None could make a

The identity of Lothbroc established under the name of Lothparck.

Lothparck's two sons Hinguar and Hubba.

---

[1] Migne's Latin Patrol., vol. 146, p. 486, cap. xxx.

[2] Gaufridus says, "Ex quo rivo [Lodebrok, *i.e.* odiosus rivus] emanavit . . *tres*, videlicet filii ejusdem Hinguar, Hubba, et Wern."

louder boast of the success of piracy. Unloading
their ships, they would ask: "Who is there that by
right or wrong, by craft or force, has gained renown
or collected treasure as we?"[1] On one occasion they
spoke in this strain in the hearing of their father: "Is
there any living man, king or prince, on land or water,
as bold as we? No one dares to meet us sword
with sword. Be we right or wrong, all yield before us,
ploughman and merchant, horseman and ship." Lothparck, swelling with envy, or perhaps, as others sup-
pose, repenting of evil deeds which had brought him
a remorseful old age, scornfully replied that they had
achieved no success comparable with that of Edmund
of East Anglia. "I know one," he said, "not yet a
score and five years old, who surpasses you by a worthy
life as the sun the little stars. In England there
reigns a king whose goodness all folks commend. His
fame, so report says, extends all the world over. Whatever your boast may be, his prowess transcends it as
the high moon the scudding clouds. His knights are
brave; his government strong; and yet he does no
violence. His prudence puts to shame your daring.
Not many years ago, a mere stripling here in Saxony,
he sailed to England with a few followers and won a
kingdom. What have you to show compared with
that? You waste your life in crime which all good
men execrate. King Edmund wins the love of high and
low by virtuous deeds." Stung to the quick by these
rebukes, and jealous of their rival, Hinguar and Hubba
determined to wipe out the seeming reproach. "Being
angry at their father's reproof," writes Blomefield,[2]

Lothparck praises King Edmund,

And rebukes his sons.

---

[1] Leland's "Collectanea," vol i. p. 245. Also Polydorus Vergil,
Caxton Publications, vol. xxxvi. pp. 141-142 et seq.

[2] History of Thetford, p. 28. St. Abbo writes: "Ad eum
(Inguar) fama pervenerat, quod idem rex gloriosus, videlicet
Eadmundus, florenti ætate, et robustis viribus, bello per omnia
esset strenuus."

"they resolved to conquer St. Edmund or to kill him."
An unfortunate circumstance favoured their designs,
and gave an excuse to the two brothers for bearing
down upon the English coasts at the head of a host
of barbarians.

The legend of
Lothparck.

It appears that Lothparck, in his fondness for hunting, often went alone with hawk on wrist to enjoy
the quiet sport which his age and country allowed.
Love of sport one day prompted him to embark in
a little boat which was moored in the river near his
settlement. He intended to hawk in the islands lying
just off the mainland, which at that time abounded in
every kind of wild bird. But hardly had he got out to
sea when the sky darkened, and a fierce and sudden
storm broke overhead.[1] For several days and nights
the wild billows tossed him to and fro, till finally
fortune, wind and waves cast him, half dead with
hunger and fatigue, on the coast of England. His boat,
driven by the wind up the river Yare in Norfolk, ran
ashore among the reed-grown marshes which gave to
the village in their midst the name of Reedham, or the
hamlet of the reeds.[2] The inhabitants sighted the little
boat, and, on drawing it to land, discovered its occupant
prostrate and exhausted. With Christian kindness
they fed and tended the stranger, till at last he
opened his eyes to find himself in the kingdom of that
Edmund whose goodness he had heard of and extolled.
Edmund was probably then keeping his court not far
from Reedham at a town which had once been one of
the most flourishing in Britain and a residence of the
kings of Iceni. The Romans afterwards fortified it,

---

[1] Speed writes (p. 398) that Lothbroc was on the sea-shore, and
his hawk in flying for game fell into the sea, which made Lothbroc
go into his cockboat to save her ; and so he was driven out to sea.

[2] This was, of course, when the cliffs watered by the Waveney
formed the old coast line, and before the sea had silted up the
long low land which lies between the Waveney and the sea.

and from them it received its name of Caistor, *castra*,
or the camp.[1] Following the custom of the kings
before him, Edmund made Caistor one of his royal
residences. After his martyrdom the faithful built
and dedicated a church there under their holy king's
invocation, from which it received the name of Caistor-
St.-Edmund's. To Caistor, then, came the news that
the tide had washed ashore a boat from Denmark,
containing in an exhausted condition a single occupant.

With St. Edmund it was a sacred custom to receive _{St. Edmund's reception of the stranger.}
hospitably all strangers and pilgrims. He therefore
invited the hapless Dane to his court. Lothparck found
himself honourably received in the royal palace; for,
though he concealed his real estate, the extreme
elegance and beauty of his person and his imperious
carriage made the king suspect his rank. Edmund
listened attentively while Lothparck related in Danish,
a dialect at that time near akin to English, the accident
which had driven him to the Anglian shore. His tale
finished, the Dane found the king a generous host.
When the tempest wrecked Ragnar Lodbrog, the
conqueror of Paris, on the Northumbrian coast, King
Ella put him to a horrible death. Very differently
acted the merciful and Christian Edmund. He treated
Lothparck as a welcome guest. Though his officers
whispered that the Dane was a spy, he charged them
to show him every courtesy. He took upon himself
the duty of consoling the stranger in his distress,
and promised him a safe return to his own
country. The pagan chief, on his side, was won
by all he saw in the East Anglian court. The _{Lothparck tarries at King Edmund's court.}
gentle yet manly bearing of the king, the prowess and
skill of his knights, the light-hearted and cheerful
household, in a word the peace and order which reigned
throughout the royal palace wonderfully affected the

---

[1] Camden's "Brit.," p. 463.

Dane's uncultured mind. So touched was he, especially with the king's graciousness of manner, that he
earnestly begged to be allowed to tarry some days at
the English court. Edmund willingly agreed. He
hoped to bring one more soul under the sweet yoke
of Christ. In the Danish pirate he saw a fit subject
for his prayer and zeal.

The longer Lothparck remained in East Anglia the
more was he charmed with its king and " with the
admirable state of his military discipline ; with the
numerous retinue of servants who attended him, all fully
accomplished in all honourable actions and in every
variety of knowledge," through the industry of the
royal master who had trained them.[1] To Edmund's
great satisfaction his pagan guest took a childlike
interest in his new life, and showed an undisguised
admiration for the civilized ways of a Christian
country.

He is murdered
in Heglesdune
forest. Noticing Lothparck's fondness for sport, the king
associated him with Bern, the master of the hunt, in
order that they might visit together the best fields for
game on the royal domains. Bern, though a skilful
hunter and clever falconer, soon discovered that the
Dane surpassed him. By the river, in the open field,
in wood and on plain, success equally attended the
stranger's efforts. Bern, whose chief duty lay in pro-
viding the royal kitchen with provisions, now had a
rival who anticipated his every exertion, and frequently
enriched the king's table with the rarest dishes. All
the royal household talked of the new huntsman's skill.
Only Bern kept a sullen and jealous silence. Envy
of Lothparck and an unreasonable resentment against
Edmund filled him with rancour. To such an extent
did feeling overcome him that one day in the hunt he
waylaid the Danish favourite in the densest part of

[1] Matthew of Westminster.

Heglesdune[1] forest, and, coming suddenly upon him
from behind, stabbed him to death. After hiding
the corpse among the bushes and leaves of a
wooded dell, Bern blew his horn, assembled his hounds,
and rode home as if nothing had happened. One dog,
however, remained behind. It was a greyhound, a
present from the king, which the Dane had fed and
trained with affectionate care. Now it kept faithful
watch by its dead master's side, expecting him to wake
from his last sleep.

The day of the murder and the next the king
remarked the Dane's absence from the common table.
Again and again he made anxious enquiries about him.
To Bern all looked for an explanation. The murderer
replied that yesterday, when he returned home, the
Dane remained behind, and he had not seen him since.
Scarcely, however, had he spoken, when Lothparck's
faithful hound bounded into the hall. As the dog
wagged his tail and fawned upon them, especially on
the king, Edmund and his men concluded that the
Dane was not far off. With his own hand the king
fed the animal, waiting all the time for the approach
of its master. He waited in vain. Having satisfied
its hunger, the hound broke away from the royal
caresses, and ran back to keep its watch by the murdered corpse. No master appeared, nor did the dog
return. The king grew suspicious. Some whispered
that the spy, after finding out the secrets of the country, had gone back to Denmark ; others hinted at foul

Discovery of Lothparck's corpse.

---

[1] Now Hoxne in Suffolk. No name in the geography of England has probably gone through more changes than Heglesdune, or
illustrates more strikingly our tendency to shorten words. Eglesdune, the eagle's *dune* or down, is written in different chronicles
Eglesdune, Eglesdene, Eglesdon, Æglisdune, Æglestoun, Hegils-
dune, Heglesdune, Hogeston, Hoxtoun, Oxen, Hoxon, till in our
day it is written Hoxne. Alms, from *cleemosyna*, is perhaps the
only word that will bear comparison with Hoxne from Heglesdune.

play. Three days after the hound had first come, it reappeared and whined piteously; even the dainty morsels from the royal table failed to console it. It ate a little, then left; this time the king ordered his servants to follow the animal. In its track they entered Heglesdune wood, and penetrated into the hollow overgrown with brushwood, in which lay the lifeless body of the unfortunate Dane, stiff and cold, the pale face upturned to heaven, the eyes staring and glassy, and the dead limbs partly covered with leaves. The truth quickly reached the ears of the king. Edmund was deeply moved. A crime of the blackest dye had been committed on one whom he held in favour; the rights of hospitality had been disgracefully abused in a Christian land; a soul had been sent to judgment without the baptismal robe. The king ordered the body of the murdered man to be buried with honour, while he mourned as for a long-tried and faithful friend. Meantime inquiries were instituted to discover

The trial of Bern the murderer.

the murderer. Bern had last seen the murdered man, and on him suspicion fell. The attitude of the dog confirmed the evidence of his guilt. Being confronted with him, the animal growled savagely, and with difficulty could the bystanders keep it from flying at the guilty huntsman. Still the evidence was not conclusive, and Bern denied the crime. In doubt what course to pursue, Edmund called together his counsellors and asked their advice. At this time the English were accustomed in cases of this nature to refer the decision to God, by subjecting the accused to some ordeal. They made him pass barefoot over hot ploughshares, or pick up with his hands a red-hot bar of iron, or plunge the arm in boiling water. Sometimes they threw him bound hand and foot into a lake or river. If he came forth unscathed from an ordeal either of fire or water, the hand of God was thought, to have determined his innocence. In the case of Bern all agreed to leave him to the judgment and decision of God. The legend states that the king's men, placing the criminal in the very boat which bore Lothparck to their shores, sent him adrift without sail, oar, rudder, or food. There was little doubt of Bern's guilt. If he were innocent, God would protect him.

Wind and waves carried the unfortunate man far out into the northern sea. The legend does not record what dangers and perils he met with, but the monastic chroniclers affirm that Divine Providence brought him to the very shores of his victim's country.[1] It is certain that he found his way to Denmark. The Danes, recognising the boat, inquired after the chief whose mysterious disappearance had excited the wonder of the whole district. Bern answered with apparently deep emotion. The storm, he told his listeners, had cast Lothparck ashore in England, alone and half dead. The inhabitants had taken him to King Edmund, by whose command he was thrown into prison, and afterwards cruelly murdered. On hearing this, the indignant people brought the English stranger before Hinguar and Hubba. He told the same story to them. Willingly would the two pirates listen to any accusation against a foreign prince. It gave a colour of justice to their pillaging expeditions. Although they had every reason to disbelieve the charge of murder against Edmund, yet they determined to discover from Bern where their father really was. For this end they put the informer to the torture as

Bern accuses St. Edmund of the murder of Lothparck.

---

[1] An extraordinary instance of a boat and its occupant drifting to shores hundreds of miles away has occurred in our own day, in spite of skill in navigation and the frequent traffic on the high seas. The newspapers of the second week of February, 1886, gave the history of the *Columbine*, a fishing-smack, which drifted for eight days from Scotland to Norway with one poor creature on board.

a spy and traitor. Full of malice, Bern maintained his former statement. King Edmund, he called the Christian God to witness, had slain their father out of hatred to their race.

The indignation of Hinguar and Hubba.

No pen can describe the savage fury and grief which now took possession of Lothparck's sons. Passion to avenge their father's death intensified all the hate which his former reproofs had engendered. They solemnly swore to do all the mischief possible to King Edmund and his subjects. Their sisters wove a sacred banner to place at the head of their forces and inspirit them in the fight. Without delay the two brothers sent messengers throughout the neighbouring districts to spread the story and to rouse the indignation of the country· They called upon other Danish leaders to join their expedition. Adventurers of every class quickly flocked to their standard, and Lothparck's sons enrolled them without hesitation in the formidable army which was soon mustered to punish the murderers of their father. Thus, adds St. Abbo, commenting on God's employment of the wicked for the greater glory of the just, "Edmund, eminently adorned with good deeds in the sight of Christ and His Church, like holy Job was destined to undergo a trial of his patience at the hands of the enemy of the human race, who envies the good in proportion to the perversity of his own will. Therefore by divine permission he excited his agents Hinguar and Hubba to force the holy king, if possible, to break out in impatient murmuring, and, by depriving him of all things, to make him in despair curse God and die."

CHAPTER VI.

The Struggle with the Norsemen.

[*Authorities*—Our principal historians only cursorily refer to the part which St. Edmund played in the English resistance of the Danes or Norsemen, though it is among the bravest in our annals. Most English chroniclers, however, in describing the terrible conflict with Hinguar and Hubba, give the prominent place to Edmund of East Anglia. His courageous stand, crowned by his martyrdom, forms the striking event of that destructive invasion. Ethelwerd's Chronicle, the Anglo-Saxon Chronicle, Asser, a contemporary writer, Richard of Cirencester, Matthew of Westminster, William of Malmesbury, Ingulph of Croyland, the Histories of Ely, Peterborough and Ramsey, all speak of St. Edmund's part in the struggle. The biographies of the saint enter into the minutest details. Of these the principal are the Donai MS., the "Vita Abbreviata" of Curteys' Register, the Bodleian MS. 240, and Pierre de Casenenve's History. Abbo gives a picturesque account of the Danes and of the parley between their leader and St. Edmund. Leland, Blomefield in his "History of Thetford," Speed, Camden, and others, borrow their narratives from the above.]

HINGUAR and his brother had now some shadow of a reason for attacking their rival of East Anglia. The murder of their sire gave a colouring of justice to their undertaking; and no difficulty arose in drawing the wildest and most daring adventurers to their standard, for vengeance and greed of plunder equally attracted them. The descent upon England thus promised to become an easy task. *The causes of the invasion of A.D. 865.*

Besides the murder of Lothparck, another event gave Hinguar and Hubba the aid and authority of no less a personage than the king of Denmark, and swelled their ranks with the best blood of Scandinavia. A Wessex thane named Osbert had for some years disputed the throne of Northumbria with Ella, its lawful heir. While on a hunting expedition, Osbert called at the castle of the nobleman Bocader, in whose absence he and his retinue were most hospitably *The dissensions in Northumbria.*

G

entertained by the lady of the house. Before leaving,
however, he had the discourtesy to grossly insult his
hostess. Bocader, on hearing from his wife what had
occurred, pursued the guilty prince, and, supported by a
numerous party of friends, upbraided him to his face
before his whole court; then, fearing the consequences
of his boldness, the outraged noble fled to Denmark,
where he had spent his youth. He was connected by
marriage with the Danish royal line, and he now urged
the king of Denmark, Goderic or Eric II.,[1] to assist
him in avenging his wife's dishonour. He represented to him the distracted state of Northumbria,
the dissensions of its two rival parties, and the easy

prey it offered to Danish enterprise. Goderic, anxious
to give some settled form of government to his rough
and disorganized kingdom, saw in Bocader's proposal
an outlet for the restless and unmanageable spirits who
threatened to ruin all his plans of reform. He determined to authorise the invasion of England. Hinguar
and Hubba furnished opportune instruments for carrying out his policy, and their absence from Denmark
would be advantageous to its peace. Goderic accordingly approved of the expedition, but induced them to
include the north of England in their scheme under
pretext of the Northumbrian incident. He even urged
the most powerful, and hence the most dangerous, of
his subjects to join their ranks. Thus in a short time
a host of twenty thousand men, under twenty jarls and
eight sea-kings, besides Hinguar and Hubba, was ready
to sweep down upon the western isles.

This was not the first occasion on which the savage
Norsemen had invaded England. From the year 787,
when the crews of three of their ships landed at
Dorchester, their raids upon the English coast had

---

[1] Afterwards converted by St. Anscharius. See Butler, Nov. 20.

been almost incessant. Every year they planned fresh
expeditions more or less formidable. Twice they
ravaged Northumbria, and once they overran the
Isle of Thanet. Towards the end of King Egbert's
reign they annually attacked one part of Wessex or
another. In 832 they took and plundered the Isle
of Sheppey. The following year a fleet of five-and-
thirty sail entered the mouth of the Dart, and Egbert
had the mortification of seeing his West Saxons turn
their back to the invaders and fly. The next year
Cornwall became the scene of their ravages, and only
after a life and death struggle did Egbert succeed
in driving them back into the sea. A little later
their ships were swarming in the northern seas, and
literally surrounding the whole island. Not an inch
of the coast-line was secure from attack. In the
reign of Ethelwulph, Egbert's successor, one horde,
bolder than the rest, ventured into the fenny lowlands
of Lincolnshire, destroyed the Christian army under
Ealdorman Herebryht, and pushed its victorious career
through East Anglia to the Thames, in spite of the
slaughter of a considerable part of their force by
Offa, the predecessor of St. Edmund. Three terrible
struggles at Rochester, Canterbury and London within a few months, and the obstinate resistance of
Ethelwulph at Charmouth for a while stemmed
the tide of invasion. Attracted by plunder more
easily to be obtained, they turned aside to resume
their ravages in France.

For ten years they left England in comparative The invasion of
A.D. 851.
peace. On returning in 851, they found the English
kingdoms prepared to meet them. Even the clergy
had armed to resist these formidable enemies of the
cross. To the consternation of all, however, they
took forcible possession of the Isle of Thanet, sailed
up the Thames, sacked Canterbury and London, and

defeated the king of Mercia. Ealhstan, bishop of Sherbourne, won a momentary triumph at the mouth of the Parret, and then Ethelwulph, stimulated by the warnings of St. Swithun, bishop of Winchester, summoned up all his courage, and by one supreme effort overthrew the Danes with a loss greater than they had ever before sustained. Again and again in the course of the year the English repulsed them, first in one part of the country then in another, so that this was called *the prosperous year;* and a second time their reckless onsets ceased.

The great invasion of A.D. 865. These earlier Danish forays were, says our chief English historian,[1] mere preludes to the storm which broke over the country in the reign of St. Edmund. This third and most disastrous invasion of the Danes occurred in the ninth year after Edmund's coronation at Sudbury, in the eleventh after his landing at Hunstanton, and in the twenty-fourth of his age. Ethelred had just ascended the throne of Egbert, and Burrhed reigned in Mercia. The army of 20,000 Danes, under the leadership of its ten sea-kings, came, writes William of Malmesbury, "to devastate the kingdoms of Northumbria and East Anglia." Hinguar and Hubba had been entrusted with the chief command, having under them the leaders Halfsden,[2] Oskitel, Bagseg, Hosten, Eowils, Hamund, and Gothrun, names but too familiar to the old chroniclers. The perjured Bern[3] made the tenth sea-king, and acted as guide to the expedition. The twenty jarls or under-captains directed each a thousand men under their ten superior officers.

The first year of the invasion. This formidable host, with an equal number waiting

---

[1] Lingard.

[2] Halfsden, says the Anglo-Saxon Chronicle, A.D. 878, was a brother of Hinguar and Hubba.

[3] Gaufridus spells his name Wern.

UNIVERSITY OF ST. MICHAEL'S COLLEGE LIBRARY

in Denmark to follow, sailed for East Anglia. Contrary winds, however, drove them north as far as Berwick-on-Tweed, where they landed. They at once began the work of destruction. They spared no Christian, old or young; men, women and children were indiscriminately slaughtered. Churches and monasteries, the special objects of their hate, were given to the flames. Wherever they marched, the barbarians left behind a wilderness of black ruins and blazing homesteads.

At the approach of winter the greater number collected their spoil and fortified themselves in the north with the intention of wintering; but Hinguar, in his thirst for revenge, pushed southwards to East Anglia. He carried with him the famous Reafan, or standard of the Raven, which the three daughters of Lothparck had woven for their brothers in one moon-tide. Wherever the two chieftains marched, this banner went before them. [1] Previous to every battle they observed if the sable bird embroidered upon it flapped its wings, for in that case it was an omen of victory; if, however, the bird hung motionless in the air, it betokened defeat. To fight under this magic standard many willingly put to sea again; others, greedy of plunder, flocked from the main land. Thus, in command of a numerous fleet, [2] Hinguar spent the year 866 coasting about East Anglia. He made frequent forays into the country, principally with the object of capturing horses, that his men might learn the art of riding and be more equally matched with the English. In a few months their knowledge of horsemanship

---

[1] Asser.

[2] "Cum magna classe," writes St. Abbo, who has unwittingly confused this maritime attack of A.D. 866-7 with the land invasion of 870.

considerably increased their facilities for plunder.
Then, leaving his fleet on the shore under the care of
a few followers, Hinguar would land his forces, make a
sudden raid on the adjacent towns and villages, and
carry off whatever he could lay hands on. At other
times, with some seaport [1] for a base of operations, he
would carry war into the very interior of the country.

St. Edmund
takes the field.
It was now that King Edmund showed forth the
courage and prowess of a Christian warrior. "Heathen
physical force," writes Carlyle, "Danes coming into
his territory proposed mere heathenism, confiscation,
spoliation, and fire and sword. Edmund answered,
that he would oppose to the utmost such savagery." [2]
The high-souled king would not suffer with impunity his dominions to be laid waste, loving subjects
to be massacred, and homes and altars to be razed
to the ground. On his coronation-day he had taken
in his hand the naked sword, and vowed to defend
the land and people whom God had committed to his
keeping. The presence of these sea-robbers on his
coasts called upon him to fulfil his vows. Without
hesitation he marched to meet the invader. He, too,
had his banner, upon which was worked the tree
of good and evil, under whose branches stood Adam
and Eve eating the forbidden fruit. Above the tree
the Lamb slain from the beginning poured forth His
precious Blood to wash away the original sin and
to give new strength to fallen man. The device
taught both king and people not to put their trust
in sinful nature but in Christ, the victor over sin
and hell. [3] With this standard at the head of his

---

[1] E.g. Lynn.   See Arnold's "Memorials of St. Edmund's
Abbey," p. 9.

[2] "Past and Present," p. 47.

[3] St. Edmund's banner was well-known in after times.   Like
other Anglo-Saxon kings, he probably used it in his royal
progresses as well as in the battle-field.

forces, Edmund hastened to the encounter. In skirmish after skirmish he dispersed the enemy. But
each defeat made Hinguar and his men burn more
fiercely for revenge. Unable to effect their end by
force, the invaders had recourse to cunning. Here
again the valiant warrior of Christ, whose sword
brought so many of their comrades to the dust in
the open field, was equally able to meet them.
When they thought he was within their grasp, he
often took them by surprise and routed them with
great slaughter.

The "Liber Cœnobii" gives the following story of
one of St. Edmund's expedients in time of danger.
On a certain occasion the enemy surprised the king
in one of his camps,[1] and so hemmed him in that
there seemed no means of escape. The siege was so
protracted that famine threatened both the besieged
and besieging. Edmund determined to keep the Danes
ignorant of his own probable distress, and thus force
them to disband in search of food. For this end he
ordered a fatted bull which was being grazed in the
fortress to be fed abundantly with clear good wheat,
and then straightway to be turned loose outside the
enclosure. The Danes seized the beast with avidity.
To their surprise, on killing the animal they found its
stomach full of fresh corn. Naturally concluding that
the beleaguered city could be in no want of provisions,
they raised the siege in despair. The king stealthily
followed them. Waiting till they separated into
foraging parties, he attacked them now in the woods,
now in the villages, and put half their number to
the sword.

On another occasion Edmund's knowledge of the
country, no less than his tactical skill, saved his person
from capture, and enabled him to inflict considerable

The story of the bull.

The battle of Berneford or Barnby.

---

[1] Probably Thetford.

loss on the enemy. Bern, being well acquainted with the king's habits, surprised him with a few attendants in the woods and low grounds of Lothingland, [1] better known now-a-days as the Oulton and Mutford Broads. Hemmed in by the river Waveney, by the deep lake Lothing and by impassable marshes fed by four streams, there seemed no possibility of escape. Edmund, however, knew the neighbourhood better than his enemy. Crossing a ford near Barnby, known only to himself, and afterwards called Berneford, [2] because "the king escaped from Bern by it," he joined the main body of his forces, surprised the Danes in the marshes and cut them to pieces.

The Danes sue for peace.

Beaten on every side, and dreading the approaching winter, the pagan leader now anxiously sued for peace. He feared lest, if he continued the struggle, his retreat might be cut off and his army demoralised. Edmund, writes Caseneuve, looked upon the prospects of peace as a favour from God. Glad to give his harassed subjects a brief respite, he willingly came to terms. A treaty was made with conditions few and simple. Edmund allowed the pagans to winter in the camp which they had raised at Thetford, and to retain a certain number of horses. [3] The Danes on their part solemnly promised to discontinue their depredations and to leave the country at the first approach of spring. Edmund, however, still kept on the alert. He dealt with a treacherous enemy, on whose word he could place no reliance. He refused to disband his army,

---

[1] The district of Lothingland consists of the N.E. corner of Suffolk, and lies between the Waveney and the sea. It is supposed by Blomefield and Speed to have received its name from some connection with Lothparck, who was cast ashore in that neighbourhood.

[2] See Speed, p. 198. Derneford, in the Lambeth Codex quoted by Battely, is evidently a copyist's mistake.

[3] Henry of Huntingdon, lib. v.

ordered the towns to keep watch, and openly gave
the Danes to understand that he would force them
to observe the articles of the treaty. The result
showed the king's wisdom.

In the month of February of the new year 867, *The glorious King Edmund*
the third of the great invasion,[1] the Danes prepared *drives the pagans from*
to leave East Anglia, but not without one more effort *East Anglia,*
to possess the country. Their final defeat quickly
drove them back to the north. The saint's biographers
thus relate the incident: King Edmund had made
Framlingham Castle[2] his base of operations throughout the past conflict. From its battlements he kept
a look-out on the Danes, who still infested the kingdom. Framlingham stood impregnable on high ground
defended by an impassable mere, which it overlooked.
In spite of promises and treaties, Hinguar resolved
to capture this fortress and, if possible, the king also.
It was a bold idea, but not easy to carry out with an
opponent so wary as Edmund. One day, however, the
Danes surprised one of the old pensioners whom the
saint at his own expense lodged and fed in the castle.
This blind and decrepit man, by name Sathonius,
was induced by a bribe, and probably much more
by the fear of torture, to betray a weak part of the
castle walls, which he himself in his younger days

---

[1] The years of this terrible invasion are thus numbered by the
St. Edmund's Bury annalists : In the *first* year 865, they landed
in Northumbria ; in the *second* 866, they harassed East Anglia ;
in the *third* 867, they returned to York ; in the *fourth* 868, they
marched upon Nottingham ; in the *fifth* 869, they wasted Northumbria ; in the *sixth* 870, they martyred St. Edmund.

[2] Framlingham was a Roman fortress. It was rebuilt by Redwald, and has since always been a place of historic importance.
The present strong and enduring walls are Norman work. From
the conquest to 1634 it was in the hands sometimes of the Dukes
of Norfolk, sometimes of the crown. Purchased of the Norfolk
family by Sir N. Hitcham, it was bequeathed by him to Pembroke
Hall, Cambridge. See R. Loder's "History of Framlingham."

had helped to build. Hinguar now watched his chance. No sooner had his spies brought him news

After frustating their treacherous designs.

of the king's presence at Framlingham than he ordered his men to advance secretly upon the place. The king, aware too late of the treachery of his grey-haired dependent, saw no escape but in a bold flight. Mounting his swiftest charger, he galloped out through the open gates, and past the ambuscades of the enemy, who were hiding in bands in the neighbourhood. Some of the Danes saw him ride by, and, not suspecting who he was, gave chase, in the hope of getting some information about the king. As they shouted to him at a distance, Edmund, like St. Athanasius on a similar occasion, turned and answered: "Go back as fast as you can, for, when I was in the castle, the king whom you seek was there also." They quickly turned back to Framlingham, only to find how easily they had been deceived. The fearless king lost no time in collecting his forces. Then, falling upon the baffled Danes, as they were furtively retreating, he cut them to pieces without mercy. "It was thus," records an old manuscript,[1] "that through the various events of war, and after great labour and exertion, the saint and his army compelled the enemy to fly from the country."[2]

The third year of the invasion.

The vanquished Norsemen made their way to Northumbria, where, by money and promises, Hinguar had

---

[1] "Liber Cœnobii."

[2] Polydorus Vergil (lib. iv.), after correctly narrating this incident, adds : " Some say that the king ran away, then, turning round to meet his Danish pursuers, who asked him where the king was, he answered: ' When I was in the palace, Edmund whom you seek was there also. When I left, he did the same, and God only knows if he will escape from your hands.' The Danes, having heard from an interpreter that he had named God, were convinced that he was the king, and took him prisoner." This latter account is opposed to all the earlier and authentic records.

kept alive the flame of civil war.   It seemed at last The Danish victory at York, A.D. 867. as if Northumbria would fall an easy prey into his hands.   But the two rival claimants, Osbert and Ella, on the former of whom it was nominally the object of the Danish expedition to wreak its vengeance, now suddenly laid aside their private quarrel, and united their forces against the common foe.   On the 21st of March they surprised the two bodies of Danes outside York, and drove them into the city.   Then, making a breach in the walls, they pressed into the streets.   The day was almost theirs, when the efforts of the barbarians, redoubled by despair, turned the tide of war. Frantically the Danes drove the English back.   They slew Osbert and the bravest of their assailants, and captured Ella.   York was lost for ever, and with it the independence of Northumbria; and the barbarians remained in possession of the whole of that province south of the Tyne.

At the end of the year Hinguar turned his thoughts once more towards the south.   He feared, however, to again attack East Anglia, for its defender was still watching his movements.   So, leaving a small garrison at York, he marched with the greater part of his men into Mercia, and, in the beginning of the year 868, took possession of Nottingham, the strongest position in mid-England.

Before attempting to dislodge the pagans from their The fourth year of the invasion. St. Edmund at the siege of Nottingham. rocky stronghold, Burrhed, the Mercian king, begged the aid of the neighbouring princes.   Never behind in the cause of God, Edmund, the brave and heroic victor of the east, was the first to answer the call. Following his example, Ethelred of Wessex and his half-brother Alfred hastened to join the alliance against the common enemy.

Under the walls of Nottingham Edmund induced He procures a charter for Croyland. King Burrhed to grant a charter of gifts to the abbey of Croyland. Burrhed's predecessor, ostensibly to carry on war against the Danes, had plundered St. Guthlac's monastery at Croyland of all the jewels and sacred treasures with which former sovereigns had enriched it. Earl Alfgar the younger, who afterwards fell so gloriously in battle with the Danes, tried in vain to have this spoliation made good. St. Edmund now brought his influence to bear to save the great abbey from future sacrilege. Ingulph gives the charter in full which Edmund procured, and which is dated the 1st of August in the year of our Lord 868, and was signed in the camp at Nottingham. In the order of signatures the archbishops, bishops and abbots take precedence, a striking instance of the faith of the age. After the spiritual fathers and guides follow the kings and the noblest thanes. The royal signatures tell the history of the deed :

✠ Ethelred, King of Wessex, I have given my consent.
✠ Alfred, brother of the King of Wessex, I consent
    thereto.
✠ Edmund, King of East Anglia, I have procured it.

Through St. Edmund's action Croyland thus obtained its charter,—a solitary example, indeed, of his love of God's service, but one which shows at a glance the influence for good which he everywhere exercised. No doubt the saint's presence brought God's blessing upon the Christian arms as Josaphat's did upon those of Israel. The English kings quickly surrounded the Danes, cut off all escape, and forced the starving enemy to capitulate. Hinguar surrendered the town, only stipulating that he should be allowed to remain till favourable weather enabled him to march back to the north.

The Danes ravage the North:

While the walls of Nottingham thus kept the main body of invaders from doing further harm, a party of those left at York crossed the Tweed and

ravaged the far north. The dread which they inspired
may be imagined from the scene which they witnessed
at Coldingham. One horde had penetrated thus far
north, and attacked St. Ebba's Abbey. The holy abbess,
fearing nothing save the loss of her virginity, cut off
her nose and upper lip, and persuaded the sisters under
her charge to follow her example. The Danes, breaking into the cloister, beheld the ghastly sight which
these brave spouses of Christ presented. Amazed
and disconcerted, they put the nuns to the sword, fired
the abbey, and quickly departed to continue the havoc
elsewhere.

At the opening of the spring of 869, the pagans
left Nottingham and joined their comrades in the north.
Then began the wholesale destruction of every great
abbey in northern England.[1] Lindisfarne, once hallowed by the presence of St. Aidan and St. Cuthbert,
saw its monks seized and slaughtered. A few only
contrived to escape with the body of St. Cuthbert,
which now began its one hundred and twenty-six years'
wandering. Tynemouth Priory, St. Bennet Biscop's
twin monasteries of Wearmouth and Jarrow, the latter
the home of Venerable Bede, Strensall, which St. Hilda
built near her own abbey of Whitby, all were reck-
lessly plundered and given to the flames. The
approach of winter alone interrupted the work of
destruction, and the exhausted enemy, sick of the
carnage, fell back on York to rest awhile.

With the spring breezes of the year 870, the sixth
of this terrible invasion, the Norsemen began to move
again. Once on the march, they rushed southwards
like an unchecked flood, wrecking all before them.
Thirst for vengeance, whetted by three years of unbridled licence, urged the barbarian leaders to attack

The fifth year of the invasion. The wasting of Northumbria.

The sixth year of the invasion. The final conflict with Edmund.

---

[1] For a saddening and vivid picture of these onslaughts of the
Danes, see Lingard's "Anglo-Saxon Church," vol. ii. c. xii.

again the dauntless Edmund of East Anglia. To his presence Hinguar and Hubba attributed their partial failure at Nottingham. That Edmund should calmly and successfully defy them was a reproach which their savage pride could not brook. Besides, he stood in

The sacking of Eastern Mercia.

the way of any attempt at subduing Mercia and Wessex. Gathering together their army, therefore, they crossed the Humber into Lincolnshire, in direct route for East Anglia. Only by one pass and that on the west could the enemy without great difficulty enter St. Edmund's kingdom. For that they made, leaving the frontier of the country in ruin and waste. Landing at Lindsey, they first attacked the rich abbey

Bardney.

of Bardney, massacred the monks, and gave the buildings to the flames. To oppose their progress the ealdorman Alfgar gathered around him the bravest youth of the land of Kesteven, but, though three of the robber kings fell by his sword, he could not even by the sacrifice of his life stem the impetuous torrent. It was midnight when the news of Alfgar's defeat reached the ears of the venerable Theodore, abbot of

Croyland.

Croyland. The cries of the messengers broke in upon the office of matins; the burning homesteads around lit up the abbey windows with a lurid glare, and cast a weird light over nave and aisle. Theodore hastily collected the charters, jewels, relics and other treasures of the sanctuary, and sent off the younger monks to the neighbouring woods, while he himself with the elder brethren and the children continued the chant, awaiting the heathen approach. Abbot Theodore, writes the chronicler of the abbey, as if describing the great solemnity of our own day, sang the high mass, that terrible dawn assisted by Brother Alfget the deacon and Brother Savin the sub-deacon, with Egelred and Wulric as acolytes. Hardly was the mass finished and holy communion given, when the Danish

chief Osketul burst into the choir, and, seizing the
venerable abbot by his white locks, struck off his head
at the foot of the altar. Neither the looks nor the
fresh bloom of youth saved the boys of the monastery
from the sword of the barbarians; the monks were
reserved for torture before death, and their corpses
were left to be consumed in the flames of the
burning abbey. In the light of the conflagration
of Croyland, the savage horde sped on to repeat the
same tragedy at Thorney in Cambridgeshire. Thence Thorney.
they hurried to Peterborough, the pride of Saxon Peterborough.
architecture, the patrimony of St. Peter in England,
founded by kings, enriched by generations of princes.
The inhabitants of the neighbourhood had sought the
protection of its thick and massive walls. And at
first it seemed as if the abbey, fortress-like, would
effectually resist the savage onslaught, but, a stone
having struck Hinguar in the first attack, the Norsemen, mad with rage, redoubled their efforts and
captured the place. Thirsting for revenge, they broke
into the cloisters, and without mercy slaughtered the
women and children. Hubba with his own hand
immolated the abbot and eighty monks on one stone,
to avenge his brother's wound. They divided the
plunder, and then set fire to the abbey. For fifteen
days the conflagration proclaimed far and wide the
ruthlessness of the enemy who had passed that way.

The line of march to the entrance of St. Edmund's Ramsey.
kingdom next brought the Danes to Ramsey in
Huntingdonshire. From the ashes of Ramsey, they
marched to the Isle of Ely, in the midst of which stood Ely.
St. Etheldreda's abbey. The nuns had scorned flight;
they relied for protection on the extensive marshes
and the deep and impassable lakes which surrounded
their convent. The sisters, however, without leader
or defender, could not resist their formidable foe,

who was not to be deterred by mere physical obstacles.
The intrepid virgins of Christ, the daughters of the
noblest Saxon families of England, were sacrificed to the
cruellest of heathen tortures, and the flames soon
devoured every building within the Isle of Ely.

The taking of the dykes.

Leaving Hubba with ten thousand men to conduct
the sacking of Soham, and to deposit the accumulated
spoil for safety in the Isle of Ely, Hinguar pressed
onward to Newmarket Heath, the entrance to East
Anglia, hoping to take King Edmund by surprise. He
found the royal warrior of Christ ready to meet him.
A skilled general, Edmund had thrown up across the
heath the dykes known centuries afterwards as " Holy
Edmund's fortifications." [1]   A trained army under
Ealdorman Ulfketul defended these two or three lines
of lofty earth-works, while the king with a second
army held himself in readiness to march either to the
seaboard of the east or to the woods and marshes of
the west, according as the invasion of the barbarians
might require his presence. Thus at the very gates
of the kingdom a fearless Christian band opposed
Hinguar's further progress. At first Ulfketul repulsed
the enemy, but overwhelming numbers step by step
won the ground, and after a protracted resistance

The ravaging of East Anglia.

the English leader and his followers were slaughtered
to a man. The invaders rushed over their blood-
stained corpses into East Anglia. The mad war-cry
that broke in upon the stillness of night, the burning
villages that lit up the sky, the flying people, heralded
the enemy's approach. In addition to the usual acts
of violence and bloodshed which everywhere marked
the invader's passage, they now put to death every
able-bodied man who was likely to assist the sovereign

---

[1] There were two—according to some, three—of these fortifications.   See Matthew of Westminster, Bohn's edition, vol. i.
p. 457.

in his resistance. Thus they depopulated the greater part of the north-west of East Anglia, and were able to swell their ranks with the strong force which they had left behind on the sea-coast or inland to cover their possible retreat.

The Danish chief made directly for Thetford, the capital of East Anglia.[1] Messengers meanwhile reached Edmund with news of the enemy's point of attack; but scarcely had he set out at the head of a numerous force to hurry to the assistance of his brave general, when he heard of Ulfketul's defeat and of the barbarian advance into the heart of the country. The Danes on arriving at Thetford at once set to work to enlarge the famous camp,[2] now known as Castle Hill, which they had constructed during their former invasion. They now raised it high enough to overlook the besieged city and to command a view of the opposite hills, from which direction they expected that Edmund's force would appear against them. The city soon fell into their hands. By stealth a few of them made an entrance into the place, and to the consternation of the surprised citizens it was soon enveloped in a mass of flames. As the savages patrolled the streets in disorderly gangs, they cut the throats of the children and threw them on one side to die. No prayer moved them to pity or stayed their knife; they slew alike the old and young; matrons and virgins were dragged to shame and death; husband and wife sank dying or dead at the threshold of their homes; children snatched from the breast were slaughtered

The sackage of Thetford.

[1] St. Abbo refers to Thetford, and not to Bures, as Arnold suggests, in the words, "ab urbe longius,"—the city some distance from Heglesdune.

[2] This artificial mound is 110 yards in diameter, 260 in circumference, and 110 feet high, with very steep-pitched sides. See Rye's "Tourists' Guide to Norfolk," p. 114.

H

before the eye of distracted mothers. The impious marauders sacrificed the whole population to the cruelty of their bloodthirsty chief.

Hinguar en
quires after
St. Edmund,

At length, fatigued rather than surfeited with the carnage, Hinguar summoned to his presence a few of the old serfs whom he considered unworthy of his sword, and inquired of them the king's movements. He knew by experience as well as by report that "the glorious King Edmund, in the flower of his age, robust of body, and skilled in all martial exercises,"[1] would not be behindhand in taking the field. He wished, however, to make certain of the king's strength before encountering him in battle. Edmund was halting on his march at Heglesdune, a place some distance from the capital, one of his favourite retreats, and a convenient position for reconnoitring the enemy. Hinguar's prisoners, well aware of their sovereign's movements, tremblingly answered that the king with a large army tarried at Heglesdune on the banks of the Waveney. Then, knowing the royal character, they added that he would soon continue his march. The Danish leader at once called in his marauders, who were scattered over the neighbourhood. He hesitated to meet Edmund on equal terms. His followers, he knew, cared for plunder rather than fighting. They preferred the concealment of the forest or the protection of camp and hill, till they could make their raids under the cover of darkness and without fear of opposition. Only when taken by surprise or cut off from their boats could they be brought to bay, and then they fought with all the energy of desperation.

And contem-
plates his
submission.

So Hinguar on this occasion cunningly thought to avoid a struggle. Inflated with success, he imagined he could awe Edmund into submission by threats

---

[1] St. Abbo.

and promises. The history of his victorious career
in the north would, he flattered himself, bring the
royal warrior to agree to any terms he might deign
to dictate. Accordingly he resolved to demand half
the treasures of the kingdom, then, to show his
clemency, to allow Edmund to reign as his vassal.
The tyrant also purposed to force the saint to renounce the faith of Christ. In course of time he
hoped that some pretext would arise for completing
the humiliation of his enemy and supplanting him
altogether. Thus he could spare his troops and
satisfy both ambition and revenge.

Full of caution, for he recognised the comparative
fewness of his numbers, and trusting to the power
of insolence and boast, Hinguar despatched one of
his roughest followers with a message to King Edmund.

When the messenger arrived at Heglesdune, and
was ushered into the royal presence, he vauntingly
represented his master's absolute power by land and
sea, the dread in which the nations held him, and
the recent submission of Scotland, Northumbria and
Mercia to his invincible hosts. He had now returned, he said, to subject East Anglia to his sway
and thereby to complete the subjugation of Britain.
The envoy then peremptorily laid down the terms
upon which alone peace was possible, viz., the surrender by Edmund of half his treasures, and the
subordination of himself and kingdom to Hinguar.

The messenger proceeded to demand instant submission to these merciful terms. "If you resist,"
he insultingly added, "your obstinacy will let loose
upon your country our countless hordes. Your folly
will render you unworthy of kingdom or life. And
who are you," concluded the haughty pagan, "who
dare to match yourself again and again with us,
when the fiercest sea-storms impede not our oars,

He sends an insolent message to the saint.

when the thunders of heaven and the river cataracts refuse to hurt us and all the elements declare in our favour. Submit to our leader, whom nature herself obeys. He knows how to spare the humble and to break the neck of the haughty."

The hopeless-ness of the Christian cause. This bold ultimatum caused no little consternation among the king's attendants. Their case seemed hopeless. Half the forces of the country had been cut to pieces; future defeat or victory would equally ruin their cause, since the enemy was exhaustless, and Hinguar's latest policy deprived them of all means of repairing their losses. No alternative presented itself but to sacrifice their Christianity and accept the paganism of the invader.

The holy king is calm and fearless. Edmund alone remained calm and self-possessed in the midst of his followers. He bade the messenger retire; then, turning to the aged bishop of Elmham at his side, he asked what answer would be expedient. The bishop, out of love for his prince, instanced the example of some who had yielded to the torrent by flight. The saint with head bent in thought and eyes fixed upon the ground listened in silence. When the bishop had finished speaking, he paused a moment, and in his humiliation a groan escaped him. "O bishop!" he murmured, "that we should live to see this day! Behold! with drawn sword a barbarous invader threatens our noble people with destruction and our poor country with ruin! Would that, even at the cost of my life, those of my subjects who fear a struggle with the enemy might save their lives for the present, in order to restore one day our homes and fatherland!" The king thus bravely hoped, by a bold resistance on his own part and on that of his faithful soldiers, to preserve a remnant of his people, and save his country from the enemies of his faith and his God.

Bishop Humbert entertained no such hope. He knew too well the number and obstinacy of the Norsemen tribes. "Who of your subjects will survive?" he asked. Then he argued that, since for five years the victorious hosts of the enemy, wherever they met opposition, had spared neither town nor village, neither rich nor poor, neither young nor old, they would make no exception of East Anglia; already they had depopulated half the kingdom and levelled its capital to the ground; their swords were blunt with the massacre of his soldiers; now they attempted the king's person and liberty. "O king! half of my soul!" pleaded the bishop, apprehensive for his sovereign's life, "unless you bend to the storm by taking refuge in the court of some neighbouring prince, or by disgracefully surrendering yourself to a heathen vassalage, capture with torture and death awaits you."

The alternative of martyrdom which Humbert put before him presented no terrors to the strong-souled Edmund. "The supreme wish of my life," he fervently exclaimed, "is to die for my people. I desire not to live and see the inhuman pagans slay my beloved subjects."

The majority of the wise men of the realm approved the course of action suggested by the holy prelate. The blood mantled to the monarch's cheeks as he answered them: "What do you suggest? That I should tarnish my fair name by flight? If I defend not my people or abandon them in my own safety, I am a traitor to my country, and my life will be unbearable."

He was equally immovable on the point of reign- ing under Hinguar. "The Almighty Disposer of all things be my witness," he said, "that under Christ only will I reign. To Him I belong by baptism, wherein I renounced Satan and his heathen followers.

Be it said to the praise and glory of the Holy
Trinity, I have been consecrated to God by the
threefold unction of chrism : first, after receiving the
white robe of baptism ; then, by the pontiff's sign
of the cross upon my forehead at confirmation ;
lastly, when your acclamations and those of the
whole people called me to the kingly office in the
solemn rite of coronation. Thus appointed by God
and consecrated to rule and guide my people and to
bring them to Christ, I spurn to bow my neck
save in the divine service."

Or to surrender his country to heathenism.   He made little difficulty about relinquishing half
his treasure. Would that he could purchase
peace and prevent bloodshed at so small a cost! But
these unbelieving Danes told him that he must be
dependent upon them for the life and riches which
God had given him. They demanded that he should
rule his subjects no longer as God's, but as their
vicegerent. Was he free to do so? What did his
Christian faith and conscience tell him ?—that it was
wrong to renounce the service of God and transfer
his allegiance to a pagan, and sinful to deny the
rights of his Creator and acknowledge them in
the creature. And who could tell what the enemies
of the true God, besotted with idolatrous principles,
might demand of him after he had become their
vassal? He made up his mind to refuse Hinguar's
terms unless he embraced Christianity. From that
decision he swerved by no second thought.   " I
have vowed," he said firmly, "to live under Christ
alone, to reign under Christ alone."

St. Edmund's answer to Hinguar.   Edmund's dauntless words kindled an unwonted
enthusiasm in the breasts of his soldiers. Political
prudence, or rather cowardice, no longer prevailed.
All resolved never to submit to paganism, and, if
need be, to die for God and their country. The

king now gently bade the Danish envoy approach
and hear his answer. "You deserve," he said, "instant death for coming here with your hands reeking
with the blood of my people; but, having before
my eyes the example of Christ, my Master, I will
not stain my innocent hands. Now, therefore, return
quickly to your leader and take him our answer.
His threats and promises affect us no more than
those of the evil one of whom he is the principal
follower. His insatiable greed may consume the
wealth of the country, and even break to pieces the
fragile vessel of our bodies, but our Christian liberty
we shall never subject to him. It is more glorious
to maintain our liberty, if not by arms, at least by
the merit of our cause, than to sacrifice it with
ignominy, and afterwards to incur the penalty of
treason if we should dare claim it again. We will not
make ourselves the slaves of God's enemies, or
allow impious superstitions to obtain in our land.
And, if the worst comes to the worst, from its
prison-house my soul shall fly to heaven free. As
you have treated my servants, you may treat me,
drag me from the throne, deceive, insult, load me
with blows, put me to death. The King of kings
will mercifully regard these sufferings and translate
me, as I hope, to eternal life to reign with Him.
Know therefore that, unless your master first become
a servant of the true God, for no love of temporal
life will the Christian king Edmund submit to him.
He prefers to remain standard-bearer in the camp of
the Eternal King!"

Like another Judas Machabeus Edmund now prepared for battle. Bishop Humbert, won by the saint's
heroism, helped and encouraged him. The soldiers,
reassured by their commander's bold front, received
the order to arm with that quiet but resolute emo-

Edmund fights
the battle of
Thetford.

tion which the "Arm! arm! ye brave," of holy
Machabeus inspired.   "How noble and necessary
a thing it is," exclaimed the king, as he mustered his
forces in order to continue the march to Thetford,
"to expose our lives for our religion and country,
and not to desert those whose defence the love of
God bids us take up!" The Christian army soon
reached Thetford plain.   The Danes had fortified
themselves in their huge and lofty entrenchment.
Edmund with his men crossed the river Waveney
and occupied the opposite hill.   It was a dark and
bleak November morning when the two armies joined
battle on the plain between Melford and Carford
bridges, a place still dotted over with the Tuthill
and the some ten or dozen other mounds which
cover the bones of the slain. For seven hours the
battle raged, each party alternately hoping and fearing.   The royal saint showed himself a formidable
champion that day.   His strong arm mowed down
the enemy like grass.   The Danes fled when they
caught sight of his tall form and piercing eye.
Everywhere his sword seemed to glitter in the mêlée.
Many a Dane fell in that struggle side by side with
Christian martyrs.

As the early gloom of the wintry afternoon came
on, Hinguar and his men took refuge in their camp,
leaving Edmund master of a field red with the best
and noblest blood of England and Denmark.   Sorrowfully and with a heavy heart the holy king gazed
upon the dead and dying that lay around him.   He
mourned for his own soldiers, though he hoped to
meet them in heaven, for had they not died for the
faith of Christ? But he more deeply grieved for
the Danes, many of whom, it was well known, had
embraced the Christian faith in Denmark, and afterwards abandoned it. Now it was to be feared that

their lot would be cast with the rebellious and defiant angels.   The carnage on every side, the groans of men passing to judgment, his own sword wet with blood, so affected the saintly monarch, that he determined not to follow up his victory, but to retire to Heglesdune with his few surviving men, there to prepare himself [by] prayer and counsel for what might happen next.

CHAPTER VII.

St. Edmund's Passion.

[*Authorities*—The Bodleian MS. 240, in the absence of the "Prolixa Vita," is the most complete collection extant of the Acts of St. Edmund and gives in full the traditional last words and prayers of the saint which St. Abbo embodies in the holy king's parley before the battle of Thetford. The monk of Fleury's "Vita et Passio Sancti Edmundi" is, however, the most authentic narrative of the martyrdom, though it omits some minor details, only to be picked up here and there in other independent records. The Benedictine Lydgate puts into verse all the touching details of the royal martyr's last sufferings, which he gathered from the accumulated traditions and manuscripts in his abbey library. Richard of Cirencester among others has enriched his Chronicle with a beautiful and finished history of Edmund's martyrdom. Mr. Thorpe in his "Analecta Anglo-Saxonica," pp. 119-126, has printed the Anglo-Saxon "Passion of St. Edmund," MS. Bodl. N.E.F. 4. 12. f 62 xii. cent., as an interesting specimen of the dialect of East Anglia. Of this Anglo-Saxon narrative the British Museum possesses three manuscripts of the 10th and 12th centuries, but two of them are mere fragments preserved from the fire of 1731. A fourth copy, to which however the prefatory letter to St. Dunstan is wanting, Archbishop Parker gave to the public library of Cambridge, where it may still be seen, MS. I.I. 28, f 297. Mostly translations from St. Abbo, they serve to show the popularity of the royal saint with the laity. Casenenve, the last of the great martyr's biographers, gives a detailed account of St. Edmund's passion, taken chiefly from Matthew of Westminster, from whom Cressy borrowed his description. English medieval chroniclers almost without exception, and later historians of the 9th century also record the glorious martyrdom of "Blessed King Edmund of East Anglia" with more or less detail.]

St. Edmund returns to Heglesdune,

On his way back to Heglesdune with the remnant of his army, Edmund still pondered over the terrible bloodshed in which he had taken so active and yet so unwilling a part. Had not the voice of conscience bidden him defend the trust which God had committed to his keeping? Had not duty called upon him to oppose to the utmost the relentless destroyer of the homes and altars of his country? God, he well knew, hated the unnecessary spilling of blood, but only in the service of the God of Armies had he carried war into the camp of the enemy. Otherwise, throughout his reign he had especially avoided the shedding of blood, desiring thus to honour the passion and the death of Christ, the remembrance of which now. prompted the heroic desire to lay down his life for his people. As our Divine Saviour delivered himself up to the Jews to be put to death, so he determined to likewise surrender himself to his persecutors to die for his nation.

Shortly after his arrival at Heglesdune the news came of a fresh Danish inroad into the country. Hubba, having completed the destruction of Ely and Soham, had set out with his army to relieve his brother at Thetford and to aid him in the subjugation of East Anglia. An additional army, numbering ten thousand men, was thus let loose upon the kingdom. With such odds it would have been madness for Edmund to continue the struggle. The flower of his army had perished. The invaders had scattered the brave men on whom he might reasonably have relied for further help. Resistance and defeat made the Danes more desperate, and the fresh addition to their numbers placed the whole land utterly at their mercy. One thought alone now occupied the saint's mind. How could he most effectually protect his country from further outrage ? How give it peace ? How preserve for his people the Christian faith ? The venerable Bishop Humbert again besought him, if only for the sake of bringing back to the land the faith of Christ, to save himself by flight. But blessed Edmund knew that his flight would not save the people. The invaders would only more ruthlessly put to the sword every man who might help him to return.[1] His death alone would end the conflict and stop the slaughter.

And resolves to surrender himself for his people.

He refuses to fly.

---

[1] St. Edward the Confessor would often quote St. Edmund's principle, "malle se regno carere quod sine labe et sanguine obtineri non posset." (Brev. Rom., Oct. 13.)

Hinguar, who entertained a personal hatred against
him as a rival and enemy, would be doubly
satisfied with his life. Never before had the
fearless blood of his race flowed more gloriously
through Edmund's veins, as with heroic charity he
simply said, "O Bishop Humbert, my father, it is
needful that I alone should die for my people, and
that the whole nation should not perish." "Generous
soul," exclaims Caseneuve in the enthusiasm of his
southern nature, "worldly glory prompted him to
seek death in the breach at the head of a few followers; on the other hand, the love of God and
duty to his subjects promised him nothing less than
eternity, should he imitate Him who renounced the
aid of legions of angels, and for mercy's sake willingly
met torments and death. I leave you to think
whether this soul, who from infancy breathed only
for heaven, would choose this world or the next."

The saint pre-
pares to meet
his persecutors. Having made up his mind for that heroic act than
which none is greater, [1] Edmund prepared without
delay to meet his death. A little band of faithful
soldiers still clung to him. Before bidding them
farewell, he recommended submission to God's severity.
While explaining his own willingness to die, the
resolute martyr forbade further resistance and bloodshed on the part of the rough warriors who would
gladly have defended him with their life. But, as
big tears rolled down their cheeks, he calmly dismissed
them to make their retreat in safety. Then, by the
advice of Bishop Humbert, he bent his steps to the
church, "to show himself a member of Christ." [2] He
unbuckled his sword and laid down his spear. "Laying aside his temporal arms," writes Matthew of

---

[1] St. John xv. 13 : "Greater love than this no man hath that
a man lay down his life for his friends."

[2] St. Abbo and Matthew of Westminster.

Westminster, " he put on the armour of heaven."
Prostrate before the altar, with his forehead on the
pavement, he poured out his soul in prayer. " Sweet
Saviour!" he murmured, "behold me a willing sacrifice. Whatever torments Thy enemies inflict I am
ready to endure for Thy name. By sufferings like
Thine I desire to come to Thee, my Jesus. Give
me firmness and strength. With the burden of a
crown I charged myself with the imperfections of
my people ; may my death propitiate Thee to remove
the scourge with which Thou afflictest them for my
sins."

Meanwhile Hinguar, no longer concerned at the
slaughter of his troops, had left Thetford, and with
his whole army moved towards Heglesdune. The
king's resolve was kept no secret from the Danish
leaders. The Christian Edmund would not submit
to heathen masters, nor would he fly ; he would be
no party to the shedding of more Christian blood,
but most willingly offer his life for Christ's faith
and his people's safety. The pagan host, increased
by Hubba's ten thousand men, was actually surrounding Heglesdune, while Edmund, with his heart and
soul "fixed on Christ, his Saviour," knelt unmoved
before the altar with St. Humbert only by his side.
No defence was attempted. The gates of the palace
stood open. With orders to touch no one but the
king, the pagans rushed in, and with loud shouts
made their way to the church. [1]

The pagans take him prisoner.

---

[1] An oft told fable falsified by authentic history relates that
St. Edmund fled before his martyrdom and concealed himself
under the arch of a bridge, where he was discovered through his
golden spurs by a newly married couple, who betrayed him to the
Danes. This old woman's story is altogether opposed to historical
evidence, and at once dishonourable to our saint, who " *yielded
himself* to their torments to save more Christian blood," and dis-
ditable to his loving subjects. It would have been totally

The passion of
St. Edmund.

Then "the most merciful King Edmund" entered upon a passion closely resembling that of our Divine Saviour. Dragged from the church, as was his great Exemplar from the garden of Gethsemane, bound with cruel thongs, the innocent king stood before the impious leader, as Christ stood before Pilate. [1]

The martyr's
trial.

In this position of ignominy the Christian champion lost none of his royal dignity. Though his bearing had nothing in it of the self-conscious hero, it became a martyr, while it displayed the majesty of a prince. Hinguar reproached the saint with the murder of Lothparck; he accused him of perjury and the violation of those laws of charity which were enjoined by the religion which he so loudly professed. Hinguar's self-constituted tribunal had no authority to oblige Edmund to render an account of his actions. He therefore refused to answer before it or to make useless declarations of innocence. He remembered the conduct of Christ before Herod, and, conscious that God at least was witness of his guiltlessness, kept silence.

His firmness.

By mockery and threats the pagans next attempted to move him from his allegiance to Christ. "Living or dead," he answered, "nothing shall separate me from the love of Christ." Rejecting bland promises, he fell back on those eternal truths which he had learnt in youth, and remained staunch and immovable. Menaced with frightful torments and death, he boldly addressed the tyrant: "My body you can break; my

---

ignored in these pages, had not the bridge over the Golden Brook, as it is called, been rebuilt to perpetuate the fable. It is to be hoped that the true origin of the Golden Brook may be discovered, and form an addition to the facts of history, without lessening the reputation of one of the noblest and bravest of our Anglo-Saxon kings, whose popularity East Anglians have ever lovingly tried to increase by cherishing all the traditions of their country regarding him.

[1] St. Abbo.

soul's liberty you cannot bind. Triumphant, I shall ascend to reign with the Eternal King." Removed from every friend, and with none but rough soldiers around him, the saint's firmness never wavered. "Christ's faith," sings the poet of his life, "was his mighty shield." Unshaken he stood, his eyes fixed upon heaven, commending himself "unto the grace of that Lord both one and two and three."

The Danish soldiers struck him with their cudgels even in the mouth [1] as they led him to the outskirts of the wood close by, where the scene of his martyrdom was to be enacted. It was a cold and cheerless Monday in November. A leaden sky hung overhead, and the wind moaned through the gaunt and naked trees. To an oak on the borders of the forest the savages bound their victim fast, having first stripped him of every mark of royalty. [2] In the open space around, the stage on which the tragedy of a king's murder and a saint's martyrdom was to take place, stood several groups of the worst men that the pagan army could produce. Some of these, skilled bowmen, clanged their bows and whetted their arrow-points; others held in their hands whips and clubs; a few guarded the aged Humbert. Around the open space had collected a crowd of spectators, thousands of Danes, imbrued with the blood of English priest and thane, and here and there among them stealthily and timidly some of the martyr's own subjects. Thus many eye-witnesses, like the saint's own sword-bearer, could tell in after days the story of King Edmund's martyrdom.

At a sign from Hinguar the sharp lash descended on the shoulders of the innocent king. No spectator dared utter a word of pity, and the saint made no

The scene of the martyrdom.

The Danes cruelly scourge the saint.

---

[1] Some of the martyr's teeth were found wanting afterwards.
[2] They left on him his camisium, or under-garment.

complaint. The silence was only broken by the
thud of the whips and a tearful voice murmuring,
"Jesus! Jesus!" Hinguar, as he watched the signs
of pain on the saint's face, and the tender body
quivering under the heavy blows, again and again
called upon his victim to renounce the faith of
Christ. The glorious champion only answered by
invoking the holy name with greater fervour.

They make him
a target for their
arrows,

Vexed by the martyr's constancy, the soldiers
ceased their scourging to leave him as a target for the
sport of the archers. Soon arrow after arrow whizzed
through the cold, damp air, and unerringly reached
their sacred mark. Deep they penetrated the tender
flesh; earnest and quick the martyr uttered the cry
of "Jesus!" The bowmen skilfully directed their
shafts, so as not to inflict a mortal wound, but yet to
literally cover the martyr's trembling form with arrows,
so that, writes St. Abbo, he resembled "an urchin
whose skin is closely set with quills, or a thistle
covered with thorns."[1] A last time Hinguar pressed
the martyr with the promise of life and kingdom
"to turn from the faith of Christ and the confession
of the Holy Trinity."[2] Edmund's thoughts were then
far away from earth. He answered only by invoking
the name of Christ.

And finally cut
off his head.

Baffled by the king's endurance, Hinguar summarily
ordered his head to be cut off. With his own hands

---

[1] "Jam loca vulneribus desunt, nec dum furiosis,
  Tela sed hyberna grandine plura volant."

"Though now no place was left for wound, yet arrows did not fail
These furious wretches; still they fly thicker than winter hail."
    Weever's "Funeral Monuments," pp. 463-4.

St. Abbo writes: "Eum toto corpore sagittarum telis confo
diunt, multiplicantes acerbitatem cruciatus crebris telorum jacti-
bus, quoniam vulnera vulneribus imprimebant, dum jacula jaculis
locum dabant."

[2] Matthew of Westminster.

he dragged the martyr from the blood-stained tree.
As if raked by iron teeth, the saint's flesh hung
gashed and pierced upon its frame. The red blood
soaked his garments and ran down in streams
upon the ground. With dying lips he prayed:
"O Lord, who of Thy high mercy didst send Thy
Son to earth to die for us, grant me patience unto
the end. I yearn to change this world's life for
Thy blessed company."[1] While he stood, as a chosen
victim separated from the flock, waiting for the

---

[1] *St. Edmund's Last Prayer.*

"O Lord which of great benevolence,
Thy blessed Sone sentyst to erthe don,
To ben incarnat for our greet offence,
And for our trespace to make redempcion,
Upon a cros suffre dyst passyon,
Not of our meryte but of thyn hyh pyte,
Now grannte me, Lord, of Thy magnificence,
Off Thyn hyh mercy, and benygnite,
In my deying to have meke patience,
And in my passyon for to grannte me
By meke example to followe the charyte,
Which Thou haddyst hangyng on the roode,
Whan Thou lyst deye for our aldir goode.
Now in myn ende grannte me ful constance,
That I may deyen as Thy trewe knyght:
And with the palme of hool persevannce,
Performe my conquest oonly for Thy ryght,
That cruel Ynguar which staut in Thy syght
May nevir reioysshe nor put in memorye,
Off my soule that he gat victorye.
Un to tyrauntys is not victoryous,
Though they Thy servanntys sleen of fals hatrede,
Ffor thylke conquest is more gloryous
Wher that the soule hath of deth no drede,
Now blyssed Jesu for myn eternal mede
Oonly of mercy medlyd with ryght
Receyve the spirit of me that am Thy knyght."

Lydgate.

Beneath Lydgate's, Abbo's and others' language the line of
thought given in the text may be traced.

I

deathblow, the vision of interior light already refreshed
his soul. Roughly Hinguar commanded; meekly the
king obeyed and stretched forth that consecrated
head which had so honourably worn the royal
diadem. While the martyr commended his spirit to
God, the executioner at one blow severed the head
from the body. The head rolled on the grass, and
the body sank upon the ground. "And so," runs
the narrative of his passion, on the 20th of November, in the year of our Lord 870, "Edmund, a sweet
holocaust to God, purified in the fire of suffering
with the palm of victory and the crown of justice,
entered into the assembly of the heavenly court."
He had reigned fifteen years, and had not yet completed the twenty-ninth year of his age. [1]

The martyrdom of St. Humbert.

To feast their eyes upon another martyrdom, they
next led into the arena the aged Bishop Humbert,
Edmund's inseparable companion and counsellor.
Humbert had welcomed the young prince into East
Anglia, crowned and consecrated him king, supported
him in weal and woe. It was becoming that he
should share in his glorious triumph. Animated
with the courage of his royal pupil, and on the
ground red with his blood, the venerable priest
offered himself as a second holocaust to God. The
Danish sword struck off his bowed head and Humbert hastened to receive in heaven the reward of
his long and faithful service on earth.

The pagans throw the re-mains of the two martyrs outside the camp,

The pagans threw the two bleeding trunks and the
head of St. Humbert among the camp refuse, as prey
for carrion birds or prowling wolves. St. Edmund's
head they kept, so that they might revenge themselves

[1] William of Malmesbury writes that he was in the sixteenth
year of his reign, which he dates it from the autumn of 855, when
Edmund landed in England. As the saint is said to have been
born on Christmas day, he was not thirty years complete on the
day of his martyrdom.

still further on the tongue which had so constantly sounded forth the name of Christ. The
saint's characteristic sweetness, fixed on every feature
of the pale face, touched no human chord in Hinguar **Except St. Edmund's head,**
or Hubba's breast.   They tossed the sacred head
of their conquered rival from one to another with
savage delight.   At last, tired with their inhuman play-
thing, they threw it outside the camp.   There it remained, till, at the suggestion of the wretched Bern,
some of the horde carried it into the depth of
Heglesdune forest and secretly hid it amid the
tangled briars and underwood.   Every precaution **Which they conceal in the forest.**
was taken to hinder the few surviving Christians
from decently burying it with the martyr's body;
but, by the providence of God, a native Christian
watched the proceeding, and, though ignorant of the
exact spot where the pagans had thrown the precious
relic, he saw enough to afterwards guide a party in a
successful search.

CHAPTER VIII.

Edmund the Saint, " Kynge, Martyre, and Virgyne."

[*Authorities.* -All the annalists of St. Edmund's Bury sing the praises of their royal patron. The chroniclers of England's other greater abbeys join in the chorus. St. Abbo especially, in his office for the feast of St. Edmund, brings out the martyr's glories. Lydgate's " Life and Acts of St. Edmund the King and Martyr," Harleian MS. 4826, and more particularly his preface of twenty-two stanzas, are one song of praise. Scattered everywhere throughout other works bearing on the history of the saint occur innumerable encomiums of our ancestors on his holy memory.]

The martyr's panegyric.

THE panegyric of St. Edmund's virtues cannot be more opportunely written than now, while the events of his life and martyrdom are fresh in the memory. The extraordinary cultus afterwards paid to the martyr king arose not from the many or few exploits of his life, but from his strikingly Christian character. Edmund in his life and martyrdom illustrated the highest principles which can guide a man and ruler. The Church placed before the English people this rare model for their enthusiastic admiration and imitation.

St. Edmund's holiness.

Apart from the heroism of his death, posterity would have justly pronounced Edmund a saint. Had he never received the crown of martyrdom, the Church would doubtless have venerated him as one rivalling in beauty and holiness of character the blythe and gentle Edward the Confessor.

From his earliest years God surrounded His servant Edmund with the signs by which He is accustomed to distinguish those whom He designs to make the special objects of His grace. Edmund was a child of promise; miraculous signs ushered in his birth. In his baptism he received that Catholic faith which alone can and does produce saints. Parents who were fitted to educate children to reach the heights of sanctity had trained him in the spiritual life, and at an early age familiarised him with the name of Jesus, the sign of the cross, the mystery of the Holy Trinity, and the psalter, the foundation of the Church's liturgy.

The psalms of David filled the young prince with that spirit of prayer which was conspicuous through-out his life. His thoughts were always heaven-wards. His bright, calm and clear eyes had a depth in them that told of sublimity of thought and fre-quent communing with his Creator. Only a saint's love of prayer kept him in retirement during a whole year previous to his coronation, and so often afterwards withdrew him from the busy high-way of the world to one of those favourite retreats where he could be alone with God. And, when the end came, his persecutors found him kneeling at the altar and fortifying himself by prayer against the suffering and death which they were preparing to inflict upon him. *His spirit of prayer.*

He attained an equally heroic degree of humility. He came of a proud and haughty stock; in majesty of mien, in strength of body, in grace of form, in beauty of countenance he possessed more than the ordinary endowments of his race. His superior intelligence and shrewdness won him the favour of King Offa; his prowess and manly bearing gained him the allegiance of a kingdom of warriors. In the ordinary course these qualities of mind, accom-panied with more than usual success in life, would have made the young monarch self-willed and im-perious. But those who knew him well have handed *His humility.*

it down that he was affable and gentle to every one, that by his kindly sympathy he won the affections of all with whom he came in contact, that he fulfilled in himself the words of the Wise Man: "Have they made Thee ruler? Be not lifted up, be among them as one of them." His humility was markedly displayed in his love of counsel. Distrustful of self, timorous of being the tool of designing men, he always sought the advice of others before acting, though, when once his course was clear, he pursued it firmly, yet without ostentation.

His other
virtues.

Love of the poor, earnestness in the pursuit of virtue, devotion to the Church, self-sacrifice for duty were among the other characteristics of this royal saint, while his spirit of study and veneration for his elders mark him out as the patron of young men and students, and his bold and courageous defence of his people, his brave resistance to the pagan inroad rank him with St. George, St. Maurice, St. Eustace and St. William as a patron of soldiers.

St. Edmund's
three crowns.

St. Edmund's chief glories are symbolised under the figure of three crowns. With arrows through them saltierwise these crowns form the arms of old St. Edmund's Bury, and, unembellished, those of East Anglia. They typify St. Edmund's kingship, martyrdom and virginity. Lydgate assigns them a heavenly origin by picturing them as glittering upon the banneret which St. Edmund bore in his hand at the slaying of King Sweyn:

> " In which [banneret] off gold been notable crownys thre,
> The first tokne, in cronycle men may fynde,
> Grauntyd to hym for Royal dignite :
> And the second for virgynte :
> For martyrdom the thrydde ; in his sufferyng
> To these annexyd, Feyth, Hope, Charyte.

In tokne he was martyr, mayde, and king,
These thre crownys King Edmund bar certeyn,
When he was sent be grace of Goddis hond,
At Geyneburuh for to slew Kyng Sweyn."

In the concluding verses of his description of the
saint's death the poet again enumerates the dignities
represented by the three crowns :

"And with that woord he gan his nekke enclyne,
His hed smet of, the soule to hevene went ;
And thus he deyde, kynge, martyre, and virgyne."

No further words are needed to show how St. Edmund *Saint Edmund "Kynge."*
wore his kingly crown. He regarded his
royal office as a trust from the King of kings, under
whom he undertook to administer mercy and justice,
and to whom, as to his superior Lord and Master,
he was prepared to render an account. He preferred to die than to rule under a master whom he
regarded as an enemy of God, and whose probable
exactions his conscience told him that he could not
submit to. Edmund came into closer contact with his *His love for his people.*
people and country than sovereigns do now-a-days.
His subjects numbered only a few thousands, and
his kingdom embraced no more than two or three of
our present English counties. His specific duties were
not therefore so very different from those of many
a great landowner of the nineteenth century. Carlyle,
while holding him fit to govern an empire, delights
to call him "Landlord Edmund." How did he live
this life to which his Maker called him ? How did
he discharge those duties of his station by which he
became a saint ? He had difficulties, but instead of
making them greater he overcame them in a "man-
like and godlike" manner. He rose to favour not
by rigour, but "by doing justly and loving mercy."
He walked "humbly and valiantly with God; strug-

gling to make the earth heavenly as he could;
instead of walking about sumptuously and pridefully
with mammon, leaving the earth to grow hellish
as it liked."[1]   And so it happened that, petty sovereign
though he was, he gained universal love and admiration.   Englishmen proudly ranked him with Constantine, Theodosius and Charlemagne.   East Anglians
considered him the equal of Alfred the Great.
Christendom honoured him with St. Edward the
Confessor, St. Stephen of Hungary, St. Ferdinand of
Castile, St. Canute of Denmark, St. Louis of France,
as a royal national patron.   On earth he was one
of those of whom it is written, "The kings of the
earth shall serve Him."[2]   In heaven with the four
and twenty ancients he pays homage to the Saviour,
"casting down his crown before the throne and
adoring Him who liveth for ever and ever."[3]

"Saint Edmund a Martyre."   Martyrdom graces St. Edmund's brow with a second
crown.   The St. Sebastian of England, St. Abbo
styled him, and the "Flos Martyrum,"—the Flower
of English martyrs.

In the ninth century the Norsemen threatened
the Christianity of England with utter destruction.
Edmund stood forth as its defender, and in his
death bore witness to the greatness and holiness of
the name of Jesus, and to the mystery of the
Blessed Trinity.   The pagans captured him, scourged
him, pierced him with arrows, beheaded him, but
they gained no victory.   He held to his sacred
principles to the last.   And his death gave the
Christian cause new life.   His fearlessness roused the
flagging spirits of the English; his martyrdom put
clearly before his contemporaries the interests at
stake.   By his example our after kings were spurred

---

[1] "Past and Present," pp. 45 et seq., edit. 1843.
[2] Ps. lxxi.   [3] Apoc. iv. 10.

on to an uncompromising resistance. Finally Edmund prevailed; for, when Alfred made peace with the enemy, Christianity had won, and when the Danes returned to rule East Anglia, they did so on the terms which Edmund had dictated with his last breath.

The royal martyr did battle also for the liberty of his people. The East Anglians always remembered him as their protector against slavery. When king or noble attacked their liberties, they confidently had recourse to "Father Edmund." So four hundred years after the martyr's death the barons of England knew no more appropriate place of meeting than beside his tomb, to draw up under his auspices the great charter of English freedom, the basis of Britain's present constitutional liberties. *The martyr of English freedom.*

England honours seven royal martyrs: St. Eorpwald, St. Sigebert, St. Annas, St. Oswald, St. Ethelbert, St. Edward, St. Edmund. Of them all St. Edmund held the first place in the devotion of our forefathers. The poet of Rufford Abbey indicates his reputation among his countrymen in the following lines: *The chief of royal martyrs.*

> "Utque cruore suo, Gallos Dionysius ornat,
> Græcos Demetrius, gloria quisque suis;
> Sic nos Edmundus nulli virtute secundus,
> Lux patet, et patriæ gloria magna suæ.
> Sceptra manus, diadema caput, sua purpura corpus
> Ornat ei, sed plus vincula, mucro, cruor."

> As Denis by his death adorneth France,
>   Demetrius Greece, each credit to his place,
> So Edmund's virtue doth our land advance,
>   A shining light, the glory of his race.
> Crown, sceptre, robe, his brow, and limbs enhance,
>   But bonds and blood and sword still more his person
>   grace.

Virginity adorns St. Edmund in Catholic eyes with the most precious of his crowns. William of *Saint Edmund "Virgyne."*

Malmesbury bears witness that, "though he presided
over the province for many years, yet never through
the effeminacy of the times did he relax his virtue."[1]
Nobler than his kingly honour or his martyr's
courage was that life-long continency by which he
overcame the direst of his enemies, and graced his
person with the purest of dignities. So Christendom
revered him as pre-eminently the chosen and beloved
follower of Christ, another St. John the Evangelist.
Medieval England loved him as the St. Aloysius of
his country. In memory of his angelic purity, posterity named his palace by the clear blue waters
of the ocean, a fitting picture of his own soul,
Maidenboure, or the *Virgin King's House*.[2] For,
sings the monk-poet, "he was martyr, mayde and
kyng." And "he deyde kynge, martyre and
virgyne."

St. Abbo's
testimony. In sublime language St. Abbo proclaims this
crowning glory of our saint, and its reward on
earth. "We can gauge," he writes, "the saintly
martyr's holiness in life by the spotless beauty, as
it were of a risen body, which his mortal flesh bore
stamped upon it after death. The Catholic fathers,"
continues the great abbot of Fleury, "extol those
endowed with the glorious gift of virginity by pointing out the singular privilege which is granted to it.
As they say, even unto death, these saints, by a
continual martyrdom of themselves, preserve their
flesh inviolate. After death they are justly recom-
pensed by the enjoyment even here of perpetual
incorruption. What is greater in the Christian
faith," concludes St. Abbo, "than for a man to
obtain by grace what an angel has by nature?

---

[1] Bohn's edit., p. 242.

[2] Maiden is the old Saxon for a person of either sex who is
chaste, pure and unmarried.

Hence according to the divine promise virgins shall follow the Lamb wheresoever He goeth.[1] Consider then for a moment what kind of man the incorruption of Edmund's flesh reveals him to be. In the height of kingly power, surrounded by the riches and luxuries of the world, he zealously overcame himself by trampling the petulancy of the flesh underfoot. Let his household[2] in paying him their human homage endeavour to please him by that purity of life which his incorrupt members show that he always loved. If they cannot offer him the spotless flower of virginity, let them at least keep the love of pleasure within them continually mortified.[3]   That unseen and impassable[4] presence of his holy soul will be offended by the foulness of any one of his attendants. Upon such a one it is to be feared will fall the prophet's terrible threat: *In the land of the saints he hath done wicked things, and he shall not see the glory of the Lord.*[5] Moved for fear of that tremendous sentence, let us implore the patronage of holy Edmund the king and martyr, that he may obtain for us and for those who worthily serve him the pardon of the sins for which we deserve punishment, through Him who liveth and reigneth for ever and ever. Amen."

Finally St. Abbo celebrates the zeal, valour, mortification and innocence, the principal virtues of St. Edmund, in an antiphon which the monks sang in ancient days in the saint's great abbey-church, the holy king's purity and martyr-spirit being respectively

St. Abbo's antiphon sums up the martyr's virtues.

---

[1] Apoc. xiv. 4.

[2] "Familia."

[3] St. Abbo is speaking to the first guardians of the martyr's shrine, some of whom were probably married.

[4] Illocabilis.

[5] Ps. xxvi. 10.

symbolised under the appropriate emblems of the white lily and the red rose :

Ave Rex gentis Anglorum,	Hail, King of the Angles,
Miles Regis Angelorum,	Soldier of the King of Angels.
O Edmunde, Flos Martyrum,	O Edmund, Flower of Martyrs,
Velut rosa vel lilium !	Like to the rose and to the lily !
Funde preces ad Dominum	Pour forth prayers to the Lord
Pro salute fidelium.	For the salvation of the faithful.

CHAPTER IX.

The Translations of St. Edmund's Body. The Witnesses of its Incorruption. The Martyr's Relics.

§ 1. The Finding of the Martyr's Head and Body and their Burial at Heglesdune (Hoxne) on Monday, Dec. 30, A.D. 870.

[*Authorities*—The earliest record extant of the finding of St. Edmund's head is that of the saintly and learned Abbo. He received it with the rest of his narrative from St. Dunstan, who himself heard it from an eyewitness. Other writers borrow from St. Abbo. William of Malmesbury "subjoins" the "unheard-of" miracles as evidencing "the purity of St. Edmund's past life," and Malmesbury, according to Archbishop Usher, is "the chief of our historians." Leland calls him "an elegant, learned and faithful historian." And Sir Henry Saville in his preface ad Gul. Malmsby expresses the opinion that amongst all our ancient historians he holds the first place both for the fidelity of his narrative and the maturity of his judgment. The Protestant centuriators of Magdeburg (tom. 9. 3c. 12), brought face to face with witnesses like William of Malmesbury, and unable to reasonably question their statements, honestly and frankly write : "Edmund, king of the English, warring against the Danes for the defence of the Christian faith, was at last overcome and suffered martyrdom. His head, which had been hid amongst shrubs, called out to those who searched after it." Protestant historians write to the same effect. See Camden's "Brit.," f. 414, Hollinshed, lib. vi. c. xii. Fox alone, without adducing any arguments, rashly pronounces all the miracles fictitious. Besides William of Malmesbury, Matthew of Westminster also gives a full account of the finding of the royal martyr's head, and the monk Lydgate puts the whole narrative into his flowing verse.]

After the martyrdom of King Edmund the pagans met with no further opposition. Secured from attack, they at once prepared to settle down for the winter in their saintly victim's kingdom. Hinguar and Hubba broke up the camp at Heglesdune and within a few weeks moved their united forces to Thetford, where Gothrun, another of the ten sea-kings, joined them with a third band. Then the Christian people ventured forth from their hiding-places in the woods and marshes, and their first impulse led them to

The Danes retire from Heglesdune.

search for the body of their good and gentle king. They found it lying headless and unburied, exposed to sky and weather, in the open field where the champion of Christ had fallen. Reverently they lifted the martyred corpse and with tears and sobs washed its ghastly wounds. But, when they could nowhere discover the head, the plaint of the assembled people became loud and heartrending.

The Christians search for the martyr's head.

A monk [1] in the crowd then opportunely related how he had seen the Danes carry it into the thick of the great forest; and under his guidance they began hurriedly to search the neighbouring woods. Had the Providence of God frustrated the enemy's plans? Would the long grass, the briars and the dense underwood protect the anointed head of their beloved king? Had the prowling wolves desecrated or devoured it? With these thoughts in their minds they anxiously sought for their missing treasure under the gaunt bare trees throughout the whole day. When the shades of evening fell, they signalled to each other by shouts or blast of horns, so that every inch of ground might be examined without being traversed twice. Suddenly in the gloom they heard the voice of their beloved sovereign crying, "Here! Here! Here!" They stood still in astonishment, and then hurried to the spot whither the voice still summoned them. And behold, in

They find it guarded by a wolf.

a dark glade of the wood, a strange sight arrested their steps. Under the shadows of the trees a huge grey wolf couched [2] motionless, and between its paws rested the king's head, placid and unharmed. [3]

---

[1] "Quidam nostræ religionis," writes St. Abbo.

[2] "Procumbebat."

[3] Butler states that a pillar of light revealed St. Edmund's head. No chronicler mentions this fact. Oswald Crawfield picturesquely describes "The Finding of the head of St. Edmund" in the first number of "Black and White" (Feb. 6, 1891, p. 8), in order to

As they ran up the wolf gently retired, as if its duty had ceased.

Devoutly taking up the precious relic, with tears of joy they bore it to the body; and, though forty days had passed, neither body nor head was touched or tainted with corruption. The great wolf, "an unkouth thynge, and strange ageyn nature," followed the sacred remains to the very grave. Then it went back to the woods, and never again did the inhabitants see so terrible and fierce a beast. [1]

---

explain a very fine engraving of the event in that journal. He writes that after the search "by hill and valley, by river-side and by the shore of the sea, the monk Anselm, a man who had been much favoured by King Edmund, and the king's squire Swithin continued the quest when the others gave over. All that fortieth day they spent in the great forest, still hopefully seeking for the missing head; and towards nightfall, coming to a dark glade in the wood, they heard a voice that seemed to them to be the voice of their master himself, and it cried, 'I am here!' but they perceived nothing, only the shapes of wolves that passed to and fro among the shadows of the trees, and they heard the howlings of these savage beasts. They pursued their way to where the voice had spoken, and lo! a strange thing and against nature; for there stood a great wolf, and at its feet lay the head of the king with a halo of light above it, and the wolf harmed not the head, but guarded it from his fellows; and, as the men ran up, went from them gently and left them. Then Anselm and the Squire Swithin, reverently taking up the king's head, bore it to the church at Hagilsdun." The saint's biographers are silent on all names or details beyond those in the text.

[1] The part played by the wolf has its parallels in sacred history. In the presence of God's saints the most ferocious beasts have re-gained that tameness which they showed towards Adam before his fall. Over the corpse of the prophet of Bethel the lion stood and touched neither him nor his ass (3 Kings xiii.) The lions injured not the prophet Daniel (Dan. vi.) In the Christian dispensation the wild denizens of the forest have equally shown reverence for the saints. Pagan Rome beheld the fiercest beasts grow gentle in the presence of the martyrs. A lion prepared a grave for St. Paul the Hermit. A crow, St. Augustine and St. Prudentius relate, defended the body of St. Vincent of Saragossa. An eagle, as the Bollandists record (April 23), guarded for thirty

The lifeless head spoke.

St. Abbo thus comments upon "the pleasing intervention of God" for the honour of his saint: "The lifeless head emitted a voice, and called upon all who searched for it to approach. Remark, the holy king's head lay far from its trunk; the organs of speech received no aid from the sinews of the throat or from life; yet, while those who sought the head shouted to one another at each step, saying, *Where are you? Where are you?* the martyr's head revealed its hiding place by answering, *Here! Here! Here!* And it repeated without ceasing the self-same word, until it brought all who were in quest of it to itself. The dead tongue formed a word as though it were alive, showing forth in itself the power of the God of language." Hallowed tongue! Blessed in life a thousand times! Blessed in the torments of martyrdom by Jesus' loved and oft repeated name! The great Creator justly ordained that it should bring honour to the saint to whom for His sake it had brought death. [1]

days the body of St. Adalbert, the martyr and apostle of Prussia. Three eagles protected from beasts and birds the scattered pieces of St. Stanislaus' body (Brev. Rom., May 7).

The following further history of the wolf is taken from a letter of the vicar of Hoxne to the present bishop of Shrewsbury : "In digging in some foundations at Bury St. Edmund's, a small stone chest was found, which was supposed to contain the bones of a child ; but it was soon seen that they were not human bones. They were thought to be the bones of a dog. However, they were collected and sent to London to be examined by the savants, who, knowing nothing about the circumstances, came to the conclusion after much consideration that they were the bones of a wolf ! — doubtless the wolf which had guarded the king's head, and was slain and afterwards (so to speak) honoured with Christian burial. —Such is the story."

[1] The Benedictine Lydgate thus describes the finding of the saint's head :

"The lord of lordys celestial and eterne,
Off his peple havyng compassyon,
Which of his mercy ther clamours can concerne,

"Praising God, with hymns and canticles," the faithful people placed the head with the body, and there, on the scene of his triumph under the shadows of Heglesdune forest, laid the king to rest in a fresh-dug grave. Over the mound they built a rough

The faithful bury the head and body.

Relese the langour and lamentacion,
Herde of his goodnesse ther invocacion
And gaf them comfort of that they stood in drede,
Oonly be grace to ffynde ther kynges hede.
With wepying teerys, with voys moost lamentable
So as they soughte, walkyng here and there,
Wheer art thou lord ! our kyng most agreable !
Wheer art thou Edmond ? shewe us thyn hevenly fface,—
The hed answeryd thryes—heer—heer—heer :
And nevir cesyd of al the long day
So for to crye, tyl cam wheer he lay.
This hevenly noyse gan ther hertys lyght,
And them releve of al ther hevynesse,
Namly whan they hadde of the hed a syght,
Kept by a wolff forgetyng his woodnesse.
Al this consydred they mekly gan him dresse,
To thank our lord, knelyng on the pleyn
Ffor the greet myracle which that they had seyn.
They thoute it was a merveylle ful unkouth
To here this language of a dedly hede.
But he that gaff in to the assys mouth
Suych speche of old, rebukyng in his dede
Balaam the prophete, for his ungoodly hede,
The sam lord lyst of his greet myght,
Shewyn this myracle at reverence of his knyght.
Men hav ek how in semblable caas,
As bookys olde make mencion,
How that an herte spake to seynt Eustac,
Which was first cause of his comision ;
For God hath poweer and juredyceyon
To make tongys speke of bodyes that been deed ;
Record I take of kyng Edmondys heed.
Of this miracle that Got lyst to hym shewe
Somme wept for joye, the story berith witnesse,
Upon ther chekys teerys nat a ffewe
Distillyd a don of inward kyndnesse.
They had no poweer ther sobbying to represse.

K

wooden chapel. The royal martyr lay buried in this
humble mausoleum, the best which his subjects could
raise at the time, until the ravages of war abated
and Christian piety, stimulated by frequent miracles,
translated the sacred body to a worthier shrine.

----

§ 2. THE FIRST TRANSLATION OF ST. EDMUND'S BODY TO
BEODRICSWORTH (ST. EDMUND'S BURY) BY BISHOP THEODRED
I., A.D. 903.

[*Authorities*—The Benedictine Abbo continues to narrate the history of St.
Edmund's body, but earlier records must have existed, from which later
writers copied such incidents as the cure of the blind man. The Curteys
Register and the "Liber Coenobii" place this translation 33 years after the
martyrdom.]

The Danes
invade the
rest of England.

In the early spring of 871 the Danes threw off
their winter lethargy to begin once more their destructive march through the length and breadth of the

----

> Ttween joye and sorrow he signys out shewying
> How greet entirenesse they hadde unto the kyng.
> Thus was ther weeping medlyd with gladnesse,
> And ther was gladnesse medlyd with weping,
> And hertly sobbyng meynt with ther swetnesse
> And soote compleyntes medlyd with sobbyng;
> Accord discordyng, and discoord accordyng;
> Ffor of his deth though they felte smerte,
> This sodeyn myracle rejoysshed ageyn ther herte.
> The folkys dide ther lysty dilligence
> This hooly tresour, this relyk sovereign,
> To take it up with dewe reverence
> And bar it fforth tyl they did atteyne
> Unto the body; and of thylke tweyne
> To gydre set, God by myracle a noon
> Enioyned hem, that they wer made both oon.
> Of ther departyng ther was nothyng scene
> Atween the body and this blyssed hed,
> Ffor they to gydre fastnyd wer so clene
> Except oonly wher sotilly took hed
> A space apperyed brede of a purpyl threed,
> Which God lyst shewe tokne of his suffrance,
> To put his passyon more in remembrance.

land. But they still kept a firm hold on East Anglia,
which for over thirty years they made their base of
operations against the rest of England. Little success,
however, now attended their expeditions, for the blood
of their holy victim pursued them. Hinguar died
within a year,[1] and Hubba fled the country. On entering Wessex the invaders were put to flight in Berkshire·
King Ethelred and his brother Alfred cut them to
pieces around Reading. A few days later, while
Ethelred knelt and refused to rise till the mass was
finished, Alfred, trusting to the uplifted hands of
priest and king, charged the pagans on the plain of
Ashdune and utterly routed them. Fourteen days
afterwards, however, they forced Ethelred and Alfred
to retire from Basing. Yet so conscious were they
of the change of fortune, that they sent for rein-
forcements from the mother-country. Alfred had to
contend with a newly arrived army of Danes, when
he succeeded his brother after the Easter of 871.

With the fresh hordes from Denmark success re- *The troubled
state of East
Anglia.*
turned to the heathen arms. After innumerable
skirmishes and battles by day and night, Alfred
fled before them. He was no match for an enemy
whose ranks, however thinned, were at once filled
up again. Defeat left no impression on the savages.
If thirty thousand, wrote Asser, were slain in one
day, others to double that number took their place.
When one fell, says another chronicler, ten were
ready to fill the gap. The supply from the Scandinavian wilds seemed unlimited. But in 878 Hubba
was sighted off the coast of Devon, and the return
of this man, one of the principal actors in the tragedy
of St. Edmund's murder, again brought the curse of
heaven on the arms of his countrymen. Acting on a
sudden inspiration, the Christians sallied forth from

---

[1] Ethelwerd's Chronicle, A.D. 870.

Kynwith Castle on the river Taw and slaughtered
twelve hundred of the enemy. Hubba met a miserable death and lost the sacred standard of the Raven.
Alfred and his party rallied once more; and famine,
cold and fear drove the main body of the Danes
under Gothrun to sue for peace. At last strife
ceased over St. Edmund's grave. Gothrun and
thirty of his chosen followers met Alfred at Aller
in Somersetshire and received baptism. Alfred himself stood sponsor to the Danish chief, and at the
same time acknowledged his sovereignty over East
Anglia. Thus Gothrun, or Athelstan, as he was
called in baptism, succeeded to the throne of East
Anglia without opposition. For ten years he laboured
to give tranquillity to the country and to promote
the Christian faith. Bishop Wilred,[1] the successor

The peace on Gothrun's conversion and succession to St. Edmund's throne.

---

[1] *The succession of bishops in East Anglia from the time of
St. Edmund's martyrdom to the removal of the see from Elmham
to Thetford (continued from pp. 17 and 55).*

WILRED, WYRED or WILBRED, the successor of Weremund
in the see of Dunwich, according to Wharton ("Anglia Sacra")
and Godwin, became bishop of Elmham also after the martyrdom
of St. Humbert, and, uniting the two dioceses, fixed his see at
Elmham.

THEODRED I. or TEDRED, afterwards (A.D. 926) bishop of
London.

THEODRED II., called the Good, the second witness of St.
Edmund's incorruption. He died in 962. Blomefield, vol. ii.
p. 323, gives a copy of Theodred II.'s will from the White
Register of St. Edmund's Bury Abbey.

ADULPH, ATHULF or EADULF, occurs 963.

AILFRIC I. or ALFRID, in 966. Malmesbury places Athulp and
Ailfric before the Theodreds.

ATHELSTANE or ELSTAN, was consecrated before 975.

ST. ALGAR succeeded in 1012.

AILWIN, EGELWIN or EALDWIN, succeeded in 1021. He resigned
and retired to Hulme in 1032. He was St. Edmund's "Charioteer," &c.

AILFRIC II., ELFRIC, ALURIC or ELRIC, surnamed the Black,

of the martyred Humbert, zealously seconded his efforts to repair the havoc done to learning and piety, and among other works of devotion revived the veneration of St. Edmund in the humble chapel at Heglesdune. But the efforts of both king and bishop in the cause of religion and peace proved fruitless, for a fresh danger threatened the kingdom. A new adventurer, named Hastings, with countless followers devastated the English coasts and solicited East Anglia to join him. Gothrun refused, but, on his untimely death in 890, the East Anglian Danes without hesitation declared for the new leader. They made Norfolk and Suffolk their stronghold and together with the Northumbrian Danes swelled the ranks of the last invaders in every contest. In different parts of the country Alfred drove them back broken and shattered over and over again. They returned hungry and disorganised to their wives and children, ships and treasures in East Anglia, bringing with them lawlessness and anarchy. These events kept the whole country in a state of agitation and made a translation of St. Edmund's remains impossible. Not till 901 was there a lull in the storm. In that

The death of Gothrun and fresh trouble in East Anglia.

The peace of A.D. 901.

---

died in 1038. He was a considerable benefactor to St. Edmund's monastery.

AILFRIC III., surnamed the Little. He died in 1039.

STIGAND, having obtained the see by simony, was ejected by GRIMKETEL, or GRUNKETEL, who held it together with the bishopric of the South Saxons. Malmesbury, "De. Gestis Pontif.," says, "Pro auro Grimketel electus."

STIGAND after two years was restored, succeeding Grimketel in both sees. In 1047 he took the see of Winchester and the archbishopric of Canterbury, which he held till the Conqueror's arrival. His successor at Elmham in 1047, was

EGELMAR or ETHELMAR, or AILMAR, his brother, who was deposed in 1070, and

HERFAST or ARFAST, who removed the see to Thetford, succeeded.

year Edward the Elder, Alfred the Great's son,
ascended the throne of England with all the prestige
of his father's glorious reign, and with his own in-
domitable will to strengthen his position. He awed
East Anglia as well as the rest of Danish England
into submission. At the time Eric, the successor of
Gothrun, ruled East Anglia. He was its last
king, English or Danish. With Edward's help he
kept his country quiet. The troubles which ended
in his death had not yet begun to disturb the
kingdom. Ethelwald the Rebel had not yet "enticed
the army in East Anglia to break the peace." While
tranquillity, therefore, reigned throughout the land,
Bishop Theodred I., Wilred's successor in the see of
Elmham, determined to exhume the body of the
martyr and translate it to a more suitable shrine.

The cure of a blind man draws attention to St. Edmund's grave. A great miracle stirred up the feelings of the people
and induced them to second with enthusiasm the
bishop's efforts. They had almost forgotten the martyr's
resting-place during the stormy time which followed
Gothrun's death. Frequent miracles took place there,
as St. Abbo and Malmesbury testify; some of the
faithful at times noticed a column of light hovering
over the shrine from eve-tide till dawn; but the
general apathy and neglect continued, till the following intervention of Providence roused the slumbering piety of the natives [1] to once more honour the precious remains. One night a blind man and the boy who
led him were slowly plodding through the woods
at Heglesdune. Unacquainted with the neighbourhood, apparently far distant from any house, the
boy suddenly perceived near them what seemed to
be a hovel or outhouse. Delighted to have some
refuge from the night and the prowling beasts, the

---

[1] Malmesbury speaks of the "negligent natives." St. Abbo
puts the neglect down to the unsettled times.

boy exclaimed, "Hurrah! here's a little hut to
shelter us." "Thank God!" devoutedly answered the
blind man. Boldly entering, they fell upon the
blessed martyr's grave. Though at first horrified at
finding themselves in a dead man's tomb, they preferred
it to the open unsheltered forest, and, presuming that no
one would disturb them in such a place, they fastened
the door and lay down to sleep, using the grave
for a pillow. Hardly had they closed their eyes
when a column of light illumined the whole place.
The terrified lad awoke his master. "Alas! alas!"
he cried, "our lodging is on fire." The blind man,
inspired by some divine presentiment, quieted the
boy. "Hush! hush!" he said; "our host is faithful
and generous ; no harm will befall us." At dawn to
the astonishment of his guide the blind man was the
first to announce daylight, and was able to continue
his journey without assistance. The report of the
miracle soon spread. A man blind from his birth
had received his sight. God had manifested to the
world the glory and merit of his servant Edmund.
The East Anglians lamented their past neglect and
anxiously debated the propriety of removing the
body of their martyr king to a safer and more honourable shrine.

One place especially suggested itself as suitable
for the purpose, the royal town of Beodricsworth.[1]
Formerly King Edmund's own, it had descended to the
Etheling Beodric, who now offered it back to the saint.
The Danes had destroyed its church and monastery of St. Mary, which St. Sigebert had founded;
but some priests still lived there, who would
gladly guard the shrine if it were placed in their
midst.

Bishop and people determine to translate the body to Beodricsworth.

---

[1] "Villa regia quæ lingua Anglorum Bedrices-gueord dicitur,
Latino vero Bedrici-curtis vocatur."—St. Abbo.

The first church
of Our Lady and
St. Edmund.
Accordingly clergy and people, thanes and serfs
united to construct a church at Beodricsworth which
might in some degree be worthy of their king's
remains. The uncertain future forbade delay. Even
had skilled masons been forthcoming, they could not
risk the time required for a basilica of stone. So in the
forest rather than in the quarry they sought material
for the new edifice. The stateliest oaks were felled
and their trunks sawn lengthways in halves, which
the builders made of equal height and reared aloft side
by side to form the walls of the church. The bark
or rough side was left outermost; the interstices
were filled with mud or mortar. Upon the four
walls was placed a roof of thatch. Inside this rough
but lofty and spacious structure [1] was hung the costliest
Bishop Theodred
takes up the
body,
tapestry that could be obtained. When all was
ready, Bishop Theodred and the whole clergy of
East Anglia, with great pomp of ritual and amid
an immense concourse of nobles and people, went
in procession to the place of sepulture, singing litanies
and psalms. With reverence they raised the coffin,
and, having removed the wooden lid, looked within.

And finds it
incorrupt.
A beautiful sight met their gaze. Where they had
expected to see a heap of dry bones lay the form
of their martyred king Edmund fair and peaceful,
as if resting tranquilly asleep. The crowds who
pressed forward to look at the saint saw no wound
or scar or sign of decay on the body. "The sacred
limbs," says Malmesbury, "evidenced the glory of
his unspotted soul by a surprising soundness and a
kind of milky whiteness." The head was found
miraculously united to the body. Only a purple

---

[1] A draught of this old church may be seen in the collection
of antiquities made by Mr. Martin of Palgrave in Suffolk,
together with some large pictures, manuscript books, and other
curiosities relating to the abbey of St. Edmund's Bury.

threadlike seam around the neck bore witness to
the martyrdom.[1] With tears and prayers the devout
multitude carried the body to the shrine in the new
church, there to await in the same peaceful sleep the
joys of the resurrection. In this manner took place
the first translation of St. Edmund, thirty-three years
after the burial at Heglesdune. Before another year
had passed, war[2] broke out again between the East
Anglian Danes and the West Saxons, which ended
only with the amalgamation of East Anglia with the
rest of England.

---

§ 3. OSWENE, THE FIRST WITNESS OF ST. EDMUND'S IN-
CORRUPTION. (BEFORE A.D. 925.)

[Authorities—The same as for Section 2.]

The registers of St. Edmund's Bury enumerate
with lawyer-like precision the several witnesses of
St. Edmund's incorruption. The devout woman
Oswene stands first on the list. "Oswene of happy
memory," says St. Abbo, " till almost our own days

---

[1] A legend of St. Winifride V.M. relates how she was raised
to life by St. Beuno and bore ever after, as a sign of her having
been beheaded, a red circle on her skin about the neck. Butler
regards this miracle as having no foundation in fact, and seems
to think with Muratori that many stories of the kind first took
their rise among the common people from their seeing pictures of
martyrs with red circles about their necks, by which no more
was originally meant than that they had been martyred. All these
miracles are indeed easy to Omnipotence, but must be made
credible by reasonable and convincing testimony. In the case of
St. Edmund the proofs of the miracle are overwhelming.

[2] This war fixes the date of St. Edmund's first translation, and
makes the 55 years of Herman and the 36 of Bodl. 240 improbable.
Herman gives 55 years, evidently thinking that Theodred II., and
not Theodred I., presided at this translation.

bore testimony to the sign of martyrdom around St.
Edmund's neck." She spent her days in fasting and
prayer in the martyr's church like devout Anna in
the temple; and, as no one looked after the
shrine, its custody fell to her. By divine revelation or "through excessive devotion," [1] this venerable
woman every Maundy Thursday of her life opened
the saint's coffin, and combed the dead king's hair
and pared his nails. "Truly this was a holy temerity,"
exclaims William of Malmesbury, "for a woman to
contemplate and handle limbs superior to the whole
of this world." [2] Oswene carefully collected the
combings of the saint's hair and the parings of his
nails, and preserved them as priceless relics in a little
box which she placed upon the altar of the church. [3]

---

§ 4. BISHOP THEODRED II., CALLED THE GOOD, THE SECOND
WITNESS OF ST. EDMUND'S INCORRUPTION, A.D. 945 or 950.

[*Authorities* –St. Abbo, William of Malmesbury, the "Liber Cœnobii Sti Edmundi"
and the "Vita Abbreviata" of Curteys' Register.]

*The two
Theodreds.*
The bishop, Theodred I., who removed St. Edmund's
body to Beodricsworth, was translated to the see of
London in the year 925. His namesake, Theodred II.,
called the Good, succeeded him. The Lambeth Codex
of Curteys' Register mentions only one Theodred, and
adds after his name, "postea Londiniensis." It then
relates how the same prelate opened the saint's coffin in
945, forgetting that he had left East Anglia twenty

---

[1] St. Abbo.

[2] "Chronicles of the Kings," Bohn's ed., p. 241. Malmesbury
looked upon the mere vegetable growth of the saint's hair and
nails after death as a great wonder.

[3] Where they were kept with veneration till the sixteenth
century.

years before. The copyist was evidently unaware of the existence of two Theodreds, and that it was the second who opened the shrine. St. Abbo and the compiler of the "Liber Cœnobii" fix the identity of the second Theodred by surnaming him "the Good,"[1] a title unknown in connection with Bishop Theodred of London.

After his consecration, Theodred the Good made St. Edmund's shrine his first care. Devotion to the royal martyr had again waxed cold, and his sanctuary become more or less neglected. Heaven a second time, however, roused the slumbering piety of the faithful. At night-time a column of light again rested over the shrine and enveloped the whole church in a halo of splendour.[2] Miracles, which had never ceased for long together, became more frequent. With revived enthusiasm the people brought gifts and offerings to the shrine, and a number of clerics consecrated themselves to God under the special patronage of St. Edmund, binding themselves by vow to the saint's service.[3] Four of these, Leofric, Alfric, Bomfield and Eilmund, held the dignity of priests; two, Leofric and Kenelm, were deacons.[4] Others joined in course of time, among them being Adulph, who was afterwards the bishop coadjutor and successor of Theodred. Their duties and position closely resembled those of the seven keepers of St. Cuthbert's shrine mentioned by Simeon of Durham. With the bishop's sanction they served the

The first custodians or keepers of St. Edmund's shrine, A.D. 925.

---

[1] St. Abbo speaks of him as "beatæ memoriæ," which implies that he wrote after Theodred's death in 902, though tenth century writers applied the phrase to the living.

[2] MS. Cott. Titus A. viii.

[3] Leland, "Collectanea," vol. i. p. 248, places this event in the second year of Athelstan's reign, A.D. 927. Herman implies the same. That the institution of the keepers took place as late as the reign of Ethelred (978-1016) as stated in MS. Cott. Titus A. viii. must be a mistake.

[4] So Titus A. viii. Herman says that Eilmund lived a priestly life, and that Kenelm was a levite.

church, guarded the relics and administered the property of the sanctuary. They lived on the prebends and offerings [1] which the growing fame of the saint brought to his resting-place.

Bishop Theodred desires to see the martyr's face. Out of reverence for the martyr's body and to insure its safer preservation Bishop Theodred decided to open the coffin and satisfy his pious desire of gazing upon the saint's face. A sentence of death, however, which he passed, contrary to the holy canons, upon some sacrilegious robbers made him postpone the fulfilment of his wish till the year 945 or 950. [2] St Edmund's principal biographer relates the whole incident with the minuteness and picturesqueness of a contemporary. "Though it may appear weak and trivial," says William of Malmesbury, it furnishes "proof of St. The story of the robbers. Edmund's power." The narrative runs thus: [3] Some thieves, of whom there were many infesting the country, attempted to break into the basilica in the silence and darkness of night, in order to steal the offerings of gold and silver and precious ornaments with which the faithful had enriched the shrine. They were eight in number and men lost to all sense of reverence for the holy dead. Supplied with ladders and all else necessary for their purpose, they made their way into the churchyard under cover of night. One raised a ladder in order to make an entrance by the window, another tried to force the bolt of the door with a hammer, while some commenced to dig with mattocks and spades under the wooden walls. As they thus endeavoured each in his own way to force an entrance into the

---

[1] In 945 Edmund, the successor of Athelstan, gave the first charter of lands, &c. to the "family" of St. Edmund the Martyr.

[2] 945 according to Curteys' Register ; 950 according to the "Liber Cœnobii Sti Edmundi."

[3] A similar story is told in the Life of St. Frideswide ; and also of St. Spiridion by Sozomen the historian. See Alban Butler, Dec. 14.

sanctuary, the holy martyr fixed them immoveable in their various postures and in the very places which they occupied at the moment. One stood on his ladder in mid-air; another in the act of digging held fast to his shovel and his shovel to him; another remained motionless, fastened to his blacksmith's hammer. A supernatural power transfixed them. "A pleasant spectacle enough," exclaims William of Malmesbury, "to see the plunder hold fast the thief, so that he could neither desist from the enterprise nor complete the design." Meanwhile the noise awoke one of the keepers of the shrine, sleeping inside the church,[1] but an invisible power held him speechless on his couch, and he could give no alarm. When day dawned, it revealed the robbers in the very act of sacrilege. The guardians of the sanctuary bound them with thongs and led them before the bishop's tribunal, where without more ado Theodred condemned them to be hanged.

Bishop Theodred's sin.

Here St. Abbo breaks out into a denunciation of Bishop Theodred's sin against the canons as well as against his sacred office of father of his people. He did not call to mind, says the saintly writer, our Lord's exhortation by the mouth of His prophet: "Those that are drawn to death, forbear not to deliver" from it.[2] And he did not remember the example of Eliseus, who refreshed the robbers with bread and water in Samaria and sent them back to their homes, not permitting the king to put them to death, because he had not "taken them with his sword."[3] There is also the precept of the Apostle: "If you have judgment of things pertaining to this world, set them to judge

[1] This fact, given by St. Abbo, proves conclusively the existence of the keepers of the shrine previous to 945. He mentions, moreover, the "monastery" attached to the church.

[2] Prov. xx. 11.

[3] 4 Kings vi. 22.

who are the most despised in the Church," [1] i.e. lay-
men. " So the canons forbid any bishop or any of
the clergy to fulfil the office of accuser, because it
is unbecoming for the ministers of heavenly life to
further the death of any man whatsoever."

"Theodred bitterly lamented his hasty action. He
imposed a severe penance upon himself, and for a
long time bewailed his sin. At last he earnestly

He does penance and afterwards opens the shrine. begged the people of the diocese to unite with him
in a three days' fast in order to avert the just anger
and indignation of heaven, which might otherwise
fall upon him. Our Lord, appeased by the sacrifice
of a contrite and humble spirit, granted him the
grace to dare to touch and raise the body of the
blessed martyr, who, though so glorious by his virtues,
lay buried in so poor and unworthy a sepulchre."

He examines the relics which he places in a new wooden coffin. "Thus it came to pass," about eighty years after
the saint's death, that Bishop Theodred II., called
the Good, opened the coffin and "found the body
of the most blessed king whole and incorrupt, although
it had before been gashed and bruised, and the head
severed from its trunk. He touched and washed it;
then, clothing it in new and most costly robes, laid it to
rest again in a new wooden coffin, [2] blessing God, who
is wonderful in His saints and glorious in all His works."[3]

---

§ 5. THE YOUTH LEOFSTAN, THE THIRD WITNESS OF ST.
EDMUND'S INCORRUPTION. (ABOUT A.D. 980.)

[*Authorities*—Leofstan is the last witness of St. Edmund's incorruption mentioned by St. Abbo. Spelman, in his " History of Sacrilege," dates
the punishment of Count Leofstan A.D. 880. This can hardly be correct,
considering that St. Edmund lay buried at Heglesdune in that year. More
probably 980 is the correct date.]

The proud noble Leofstan demands to see the body. With great reverence the religious of St. Edmund
watched over the precious relics committed to their

---

[1] 1 Cor. vi. 4.   [2] " Loculus."   [3] Ps. lxvii.

care. Bishop Adulph, as one of their community,
further increased their devotion by his presence and
example.[1] No one doubted the holy martyr's influence
with God, attested by that beautiful and incorrupt
form which had been so recently seen. But a youth
named Leofstan, of a noble East Anglian family,
who was not born when Bishop Theodred opened
the coffin, hearing of the saint's incorruption, demanded
to see it for himself. The keepers of the shrine refused;
the young man's attendants remonstrated. Proud
and self-willed, Leofstan insisted " on settling," as
he said, " the uncertainty of report by the testimony of
his own eyesight." Resistance to his wishes only
infuriated him, and he angrily threatened to use
force if necessary.

Fearing a disturbance in the very sanctuary from
a man of such power and insolence, the keepers of
the shrine yielded and opened the coffin.[2] Leofstan
stood and irreverently stared into the face of the
sleeping saint. At the same instant God struck him
with madness and delivered him up to a reprobate
sense.[3] His father Alfgar, a holy and religious man
and afterwards a great benefactor of St. Edmund,
terrified at his son's crime and its consequent punishment, finally disinherited him. At last, reduced by the
judgment of God to the deepest misery, Leofstan
died like Antiochus and Herod, eaten up with
worms. " Thus," concludes St. Abbo, " all recognise
the holy king and martyr Edmund to be not inferior

He sees it and is struck mad.

---

[1] Godwin, " De Præsulibus," p. 425, says Adulph was appointed
in Canterbury in 953 to be bishop of East Anglia, i.e. some years
before the death of Theodred II., whose condjutor he was, which
occurred, says Yates, in 962. He joined the brethren at Beodricsworth out of devotion to St. Edmund.

[2] Leland, " Itiner.," vol. viii. p. 82b, says that Leofstan forced
open the coffin.

[3] Rom. i. 28.

in merit to the blessed levite and martyr St.
Lawrence, whose body, as the holy father Gregory
relates, being gazed upon by some worthy or unworthy
spectators, eight of them perished on the spot
by a sudden death. Oh, how great reverence is due
to that place which guards, as it were asleep, so
illustrious a confessor of Christ!"

---

§ 6.   The Monk Ailwin, the Fourth Witness of St.
Edmund's Incorruption, A.D. 990 to 1032.

[*Authorities*—Herman, a monk of St. Edmund's Bury, fully details the events of
this and the following sections.   To his transcript, the oldest extant, of
the "Vita Sti Edmundi" by St. Abbo, Herman adds an original production on
the miracles of St. Edmund, MS. Cott. Tiber B, ii. ff 19b-84b, which is of the
highest value.   He compiled it, he says, partly from oral testimony and partly
from an old work written in a difficult and crabbed hand,—"calamo...diffi-
cillimo. et, ut ita dicam, adamantino."   Next to Herman's Chronicle ranks
the "Miracula et Translatio Sancti Edmundi Regis et Martyris," MS. Cott. Titus
A. viii. ff 83b-151b,—a compilation from Herman, Prior John and Osbert de
Clare.   Arnold in his "Memorials" ascribes the authorship of this piece
to Samson, although only four out of thirty-seven chapters are original.   Samson, however, if he be the compiler, rewrote the miracles of Herman, and added
several fresh facts.   A further account of these two authorities will be found at
the beginning of chapter xii.   In his "Speculum Historiæ" (Rolls Publ., vol.
30), Richard of Cirencester, a monk of Westminster A.D. 1850, gives the whole
history of the life of St. Edmund and of his relics at this period.   He is thus
one of the royal martyr's chief English biographers ; but he took his facts from
older annalists like Herman, and so gives no new details.   The same remark
applies to the "Liber Cœnobii" and Curteys' Register on this part of the
narrative.   Lydgate still continues to put into verse the prose of other chroniclers.]

The keepers of St. Edmund's shrine become negligent.

The clerics who first devoted their lives by a perpetual vow to the guardianship of St. Edmund's shrine
in the course of a few years increased in number
to nineteen or twenty and were constituted into a college of secular canons. [1]   After the death of Theodred
the Good they continued in their first fervour, but
only so long as Bishop Adulph lived. [2]   Under Adulph's
successors Ailfric, Athelstan and St. Algar, the ecclesiastical discipline of the secular canons of St. Edmund
gradually relaxed.   St. Abbo, who visited them about

---

[1] Probably in the reign of Ethelred the Unready.
[2] Adulph died in 966.

the year 980, and founded a school amongst them,
did not succeed in rekindling their piety and enthusiasm.   Later annalists, like Herman, justly complain of
the negligent way in which they kept the records
of miracles at this time.   Even with regard to the
shrine itself they had become careless, so that in
the year 990[1] Bishop Athelstan deprived them of its
guardianship and gave it into the charge of the Benedictine Ailwin, the fourth witness of the incorruption
of St. Edmund's body.

Ailwin[2] was the son of the Oswy and Leoflede
who gave Wisbeach to the convent of Ely, and
from his parents he inherited his love for the
supernatural.   His piety and detachment from the
world led him, while yet a layman, to St. Edmund's
sanctuary.   Feeling himself called to the ecclesiastical
state, he joined the secular canons of St. Edmund
out of love for their illustrious patron.   Afterwards,
however, won by the devout life of Wolfric and his
companions, who had restored the church of St. Benedict
and the monastic life at Hulme,[3] he petitioned for

Ailwin, out of devotion to St. Edmund, joins them for a time.

Afterwards he takes the habit of St. Benedict.

---

[1] According to the Douai MS., which dates it thirty years before
the coming in of the Benedictines.

[2] Written variously Egelwin and Alfiwinus (Herman, Hoved),
Ealwinus (Westmonaster.) Aldwin (Dunelm.) Elfwin (Text.
Roff.) Ailwin (Lydgate).

[3] St. Benedict's at Hulme or Holme at Horning in Norfolk
was a hermitage in King Edmund's time.   Suneman the anchoret
sought its marshy solitude in obedience to an angel's order.   Others
desirous of leading a penitential life resorted to him, and he built
and dedicated a chapel and hermitage in honour of the patriarch
St. Benedict, the land round about being given by the thane
Horning or Horne.   Under Hinguar and Hubba the Danes
destroyed the church and the cells of the hermits; but afterwards a holy man named Wolfric rebuilt the church, and,
gathering together seven companions, refounded the church and
monastery under the rule of St. Benedict.   Wolfric governed the
new foundation forty years as abbot or prior, and during his reign
admitted Ailwin to the habit.   Canute early in the eleventh

L

the habit of St. Benedict and became a monk. At Hulme Ailwin vied with Suneman and Wolfric in the saintliness of his life. But throughout his pious exercises he longed to see a reform among the clergy at Beodricsworth, who kept the body of the martyr king "without any honour," and instead of spending the offerings made to the saint upon the church they divided them among themselves. Ailwin at length attained the fulfilment of his desire by his own appointment to the guardianship of the shrine.

The monk Ailwin is appointed to guard the shrine.

Ailwin's tender and affectionate watchfulness over St. Edmund's body forms one of the most touching chapters in its history. To honour the earthly remains of the dead is indeed an instinct of nature. It prompts the mourner to provide the richly furnished coffin, to cover the bier with flowers and wreaths and to adorn the fresh-turfed grave. By the funeral pomp, the spacious vault, the marble monument man shows reverence for the bodies of those whom in life he loved. The Church's teaching elevates and sanctifies this instinct of nature. The body is the tabernacle of the soul, the temple of God's spirit, the resting-place of Christ's eucharistic presence. Therefore, although Mother Church allows nothing that can disparage the lesson of death, she lays the body to rest with solemn rites, because it contains the seed of immortality and shall rise again at the last day. So faith and love inspired Ailwin in his tendance of St. Edmund's body. He guarded it as the most precious of relics, once the sanctuary of a noble soul and the armour of an heroic Christian, a memento left to earth of an angel, a warrior, a king, a saint. Edmund's personality had left an indelible impression

His reverence for the dead,

And especially for St. Edmund's body.

century endowed Hulme, and from it came the colony of monks whom he put into possession of the church and abbey which he raised over St. Edmund's shrine.

on the minds and traditions of his people. His
nation held him in greater glory than modern England holds any of her heroes whose bones rest under
the dome of St. Paul's or in the consecrated aisles of
Westminster. Illustrious sanctity and his champion-
ship of the faith raised him in the eyes of Christendom
far above other defenders of their country. The
dread Lord of heaven and earth Himself glorified
the martyr and honoured his body by miracles, not
the least being its preservation from decay. Those
only who sneer at the natural and supernatural alike
can therefore wonder at Ailwin's devotion to the saint's
remains. He knew that Edmund's soul loved and
honoured its body and rewarded those who reverenced it.

Therefore, "out of devotion to the saint," writes
Herman, "Ailwin did menial service to St. Edmund."
He washes and arranges it.
He opened the coffin and, with the love of a son
arranging a dead father for his last sleep, he often
poured water on the incorrupt members of the martyr-
king's body,[1] and composed the long flowing hair of the
sacred head with a comb. Whatever hair came off
he carefully preserved in a box.[2] From this privilege of tending and waiting upon the king his
acquaintances styled him "the martyr's confidential
chamberlain;" for "in every way he did as dutiful
service to him as any man is wont to a living person." Frequently this faithful servant of St. Edmund
spent the night in mutual converse with his master.
He spoke to him as it were face to face; and whatever favour the common people sought from their
"Father Edmund" they asked for through Ailwin.

---

[1] St. Bede relates how their respective guardians washed the
incorrupt bodies of St. Ethelburga and St. Oswald, and preserved the water as holy and sacred.

[2] To treasure the hair of the dead is a common practice in our
own day.

Lydgate's des-
cription of
him.

The poet of St. Edmund's Bury has not failed to
commemorate in his epic this devoted follower of
his hero. He thus describes Ailwin's familiar inti-
macy with blessed Edmund :

> " First Ailwin that cely [celestial] creature
> Afforn [before] his shrine upon the pavement lay :
> In his praiere devoutly dyde endure,
> Scelde [seldom] or never parteden [departing] night nor day.
> For whansoever his lieges felte affraye
> The peple in him had so great beleve
> Through his request Edmund sholde hem [them] releve.
> The perfection of Allewyn was so couth [full of grace]
> So renommed his conversacioun,
> That many a tyme they spak to gidre [together] mouth by
>   mouth
> Touchynge hyh thynges off comtemplacioun,
> Expectfull oft, be revelacioun
> Off hevenly thynges, to speke in words few,
> Be gostly secretys which God lyst to him shewe. "

---

§ 7. The Second Translation of St. Edmund's Body. It is taken to London, A.D. 1010.

[Authorities—The same as for the previous section. Stowe's "Survey of London,"
edited by William J. Thoms, F.S.B., 1842, describes London at this period.
The church of St. Gregory, in which Ailwin deposited St. Edmund's body,
survived till 1645. It therefore forms, together with the chapter-house, a
marked feature in Ralph Agas' map of London. William Longman's "Three
Cathedrals dedicated to St. Paul" contains the ground-plan of St. Gregory's
church, plate 28, and a sketch of its interior, plate 14, chap. iii. Hollar's
plate shows a church of St. Gregory of a debased style, and therefore clearly
not the original one, which was Anglo-Saxon. Alban Butler dates this second
translation of St. Edmund A.D. 920, a mistake copied into the "Menology
of England and Wales," and into the inaccurate Petits Bollandistes.]

The Danes in
England at the
end of the 10th
century. ;

For twenty years Ailwin affectionately guarded
the shrine of his "lord and father Edmund" at
Beodricsworth. At the end of that time fresh troubles
overwhelmed the country, and, trembling for the
safety of his treasure, he fled with it from East
Anglia. To understand the reason of Ailwin's action
it will be necessary to take up the thread of English

and East Anglian history from the period of the
first translation in 903. Shortly after that event
King Edward annexed East Anglia to the rest of
his kingdom; and in the reign of his successor,
Athelstan, the partly independent Danish chieftains
entirely disappeared. In fact the Danes throughout
England had almost ceased to be foes. Under their
leader Anlaff they made a successful stand in
Northumbria against Athelstan's brother, King
Edmund, but it was short-lived, and after Edmund's
death they submitted to King Edred without a
struggle. After the fall of Edwy and the succession
of Edgar St. Dunstan's firm but gentle hand finally
welded Danes and English into one nation. When
the great churchman crowned St. Edward the martyr,
it seemed as if the united kingdom which he had
made could weather any storm. But the murder
of young king Edward brought endless troubles on
the hapless Ethelred, whose mother's crime gave
him his brother's throne and with it the curse of
blood. Years of scarcity, distemper among the cattle,
plague among the people combined to bring misery
on the kingdom. The Danes, getting scent of the
distracted state of the country and of the king's
unpopularity, renewed their attacks with a perti-
nacity which ended in the accession of a Danish
monarch to the English throne. At first they made
a few raids on the coasts only; then a formidable
armament reduced Ipswich. Treaties were negotiated
and thousands of pounds paid in bribes, but in vain.
Ethelred equipped armies and navies only to see
their commanders turn traitors and join the Norsemen.
In 994 Sweyn king of Denmark and Olave king of
Norway sailed up the Thames with their combined
fleets to attack London. Repulsed from the capital,
they scattered their forces over Essex, Kent, Sussex

and Hampshire, which they wasted with fire and sword. During this war or the next Sweyn invaded St. Edmund's patrimony and probably entered his town.[1] Ethelred bought off the two kings with the sum of sixteen thousand pounds. A few years later, on the feast of St. Brice, November the 13th, 1003, took place the cold-blooded slaughter of all Danes dwelling in England, known as the massacre of St. Brice. Sweyn's four years of avenging devastation and murder followed, ending with the exaction of thirty-six thousand pounds of silver as compensation. During these ferocious wars Ailwin constantly dreaded that some evil would befall St. Edmund's body. When, therefore, he heard of the landing of another Danish army under Count Turchil, he determined to seek safety in flight.

The massacre of St. Brice.

The Danish chief Turchil invaded England ostensibly to avenge the death of a brother, but really for the sake of plunder and rapine. Sweyn, who shrank from the open violation of solemn treaties, gave the expedition his secret approval. For three years England cowered terror-stricken at Turchil's feet. In the first year of his invasion (A.D. 1009) he devastated the southern counties. In the second his hordes landed at Ipswich and overran East Anglia on their way to the fens, whither thousands of the English had fled for security. But, before the invaders thus menaced St. Edmund's shrine, the blessed martyr had warned Ailwin of the approaching danger and bidden him flee with his sacred charge.

Turchil invades England, A.D. 1009.

The devoted monk hired a common cart, on which he placed the holy body, and wandered forth. He found the open country and the unfortified towns

Ailwin takes up St. Edmund's remains and wanders about with them.

---

[1] Yates says that Sweyn destroyed St. Edmund's Bury, but there is no historical proof of it.

wholly abandoned to the enemy, whose avowed object was to reduce England to a solitude. The only course left to him was to seek security in London. Repeatedly besieged even by Turchil's men, that town alone had successfully resisted attack and offered protection to its citizens. Towards the capital, then, Ailwin turned his face, stealthily avoiding the more frequented roads, and in constant fear lest the Danes should overtake him.

On reaching the borders of Essex at nightfall, he came across the quiet and secluded house of the priest Eadbright, the father of Abbot Alfwin of Ramsey.[1] There he sought shelter; but the priest, afraid to harbour strangers in those troublous times, refused admittance. With difficulty Ailwin obtained permission to rest in the adjoining yard till morning. Tired and weary he lay down to sleep under the cart in which reposed his royal master. He slept, but his heart kept watch.[2] That night a pillar of light which dimmed the very stars illumined the dome of heaven, the sole canopy over St. Edmund's body, and kept watch over the lowly shrine. Music, too, sweet as that which the shepherds heard, floated on the air.[3] At three o'clock in the morning the wheels of the cart began to move, *non hominis sed Dei motione*—not by the action of man but of God. Thus supernaturally warned, the saint's "charioteer" arose without delay and continued his flight. He had not gone far when, looking back, he beheld the priest's house enveloped in flames, in punishment, as it seemed, for his timid and inhospitable reception of the martyr's relics.

He is inhospitably received in Essex.

The priest's house consumed with fire.

Venturing at last on the wide Roman road from

---

[1] Alfwin was abbot in 1043, and ruled for thirty-six years.

[2] Herman; "Cant. of Cant.," v. 2.

[3] Gillingwater's "Account of Bury," p. 41.

Colchester to London, the faithful monk found his way barred at Stratford [1] by the swollen waters of the river Lea. Stratford is now considered part of the capital, but till half a century ago it was little more than a country village situate about four miles from St. Paul's. A slender bridge, since replaced by the solid structure connecting Stratford with Stratford-le-Bow, spanned the stream. [2] Ailwin found the bridge broken and unsafe and far too narrow for his cart to cross. He knew not what to do or whither to turn, for the ford was impassable, and the Danes—as the number of people hastening to London indicated—pressed on from behind. Ailwin saw St. Paul's and safety within reach. Putting his trust in heaven, he boldly advanced, when, behold! while the right wheel of the cart ran upon the surface of the bridge, the left, suspended between water and sky, moved along in mid-air on a level with its fellow.

> "To forme at Stratforde callyd at the horse
> His littel cane, when it should passe
> The brigge, broke the strame unknowne,
> Har we was the plawne, ther was no way but grace.
> Aloff the flood and littel wheel gan glace,
> The tother wheel glod on the boord a folfte
> And Ayllawn went afforn ful soffte. "[3]

---

[1] The Street-ford.

[2] Queen Matilda built the first bridge of stone in gratitude for her escape from drowning in the Lea. Her structure was memorable as the first bridge built in England with an arch of stone.

[3] Lydgate's verse put into modern English reads :

To a form [or plank] at Stratford called the horse [or wooden frame]
His litter came, when it came to pass that
A stream of unknown depth broke against the bridge,
How wee [small] was the plain [level] there was no way but grace.
Aloft the flood one wheel of the litter began to glance,
The other wheel glided on the board afoot
And Ailwin went before full softly.

The entry into London now became a triumphant He enters London.
procession.   Fugitives had carried the news before.
Eye-witnesses related the miraculous passage of the
Lea.   The clergy and principal citizens came forth
to welcome the royal martyr of the east and in
turns carried the coffin on their shoulders.   As the
procession entered Aldgate,[1] the crowds of spectators grew larger and lined the whole of Cheapside
as far as the Cathedral.   The name and praise of
St. Edmund were on every lip.   The defender of
his people against the Danes!   How honoured their
city to receive the visit of this illustrious guest and
powerful protector!   The sick and the lame and the
diseased pressed forward to touch the coffin.   "And Numerous miracles happen.
Edmund out of his royal clemency shed his favours
around.   To the blind he gave sight; to the deaf,
hearing; to the dumb, speech.   The crippled and
the paralysed regained the use of their limbs.   Lepers
received cleanness of body.   On the way from Aldgate to the church of Blessed Pope Gregory eighteen
miracles were wrought."

A bedridden woman of the city, with limbs con- The cure of the crippled woman.
tracted and withered from the waist downwards,
heard the commotion in the streets, as she lay in
a wicker-basket which served her for a bed.   She

---

[1] There were at this period four gates only to London :
Aldgate, or Ealsgate, for the east ; Aldersgate for the north ;
Ludgate for the west ; and Bridgegate over the Thames for the
south.   By degrees the citizens opened other gates large and
small.   Cripplesgate was at first a postern near Ealsgate, and its
vaulted passage running under the mass of the parapet and
through the rampart gave it its name of *crepel* or *cryfele* a burrow,
and *geat*, a gate.   In Agas' map Cripplesgate is given as an
important entrance conducting by Cheapside to St.   Paul's (see
Denton's "Cripplesgate, or Ealsgate Without," Appendix A.)
At Aldgate the abbot of St.   Edmund's Bury had Christ church,
the side of which bore the inscription *Bevis Marks*, a corruption
of Bury Marks.

asked the meaning of the tumult. "The innocent
St. Edmund, king of the East Angles, is passing,"
her attendants answered, "he who died for Christ by
the hands of impious men." "Oh," she exclaimed,
"that my eyes might see how great and glorious
a saint now enters our city! Could my hand
touch but the covering over his coffin, I should be
healed." That instant she felt her limbs grow strong
beneath her, and, leaping from her basket-bed, she
ran after the procession, praising God and weeping
tears of joy. This nineteenth miracle on that day
attested St. Edmund's power.

The holy body is deposited in St. Gregory's church.

So Ailwin made his way to the great basilica of
the Apostle St. Paul. The line of thoroughfare is
still the same, and busy men and women in hustling
throngs hurry to and fro over the route which eight
centuries ago the royal martyr Edmund traversed.
Under shelter of the cathedral and built close up
to its south-west wall stood the church of the blessed
Pope Gregory. [1] Within that sanctuary Ailwin deposited St. Edmund's body. He resisted all attempts

---

[1] St. Gregory's church stood at the south-west corner of St
Paul's, built close up to the wall, its façade being on a line with
the west front of the cathedral. It was not uncommon for parish
churches to be built in close proximity to a cathedral, as for instance
St. Margaret's at Westminster, but there is probably no other
instance, at least in England, of a church being erected against the
very walls of the cathedral. Three churches of St. Gregory in
turn occupied the same site : first, the Anglo-Saxon church, which
sheltered St. Edmund's body ; a second of Norman style ; and
a third, a post-reformation church of debased architecture. St.
Gregory's church stood till about 1645, and not till the great fire,
as Stowe implies. Its position was then considered to be a
mistake, and, notwithstanding a petition from the parishioners
against its demolition, it was "pulled down in regard it was
thought to be a blemish to the stately cathedral whereunto it
adjoined." (State Papers, Domestic, pp. 218-408.) The old
churchyard of St. Gregory's is probably the only vestige of the
old church. Within the parish of St. Gregory, however, was

to take it into the cathedral, suspecting that the authorities there might steal his treasure from him, —a fear not without foundation, as after events proved.

At the martyr's shrine in St. Gregory's church not only London citizens but strangers from afar paid their devotions, and the crowds of pilgrims presented gifts without number to adorn the saint's resting-place. Conspicuous among these votive offerings were two golden bracelets which a wealthy Dane gave to the saint. He had come to the church not out of devotion, but to see what attracted the people. When others knelt, he stood looking on, too proud to bend his knee. At length he stept forward and irreverently threw back the pall over the bier to see underneath, but in the act he became blind of both eyes. Overwhelmed by the suddenness and gravity of his punishment, he fell on his face on the ground and with deep sorrow acknowledged his sin. He filled the church with groans and prayers to the saint. He implored the bystanders to intercede for him, for God had touched his heart with repentance and devotion to his martyr. In answer to the people's prayers he again received his sight.

An irreverent Dane is struck blind.

erected a church of St. Edmund, whose modern substitute still exists in Lombard Street and is known as St. Edmund the Martyr's.

Perhaps the last record of St. Gregory's is the following extract from the "Times" of Friday, July 1, 1887 :

"*Union of City Benefices.*—The proposed union of the parishes of St. Gregory by St. Paul, and St. Mary Magdalen, Old Fish Street (the church of which in Knightrider Street was destroyed by fire some time since), with that of St. Martin, Ludgate, has been favourably reported on by the Commissioners who were appointed to consider the subject. The rector of the new benefice is to receive £570 per annum. The site in Knightrider Street is to be sold, and after payment of expenses, the proceeds are to go towards the erection of a new church in the metropolis."

In gratitude he took off his golden bracelets and laid them at St. Edmund's feet as a perpetual memorial of his conversion.

The three years' stay in London.

For three years the holy body rested in St. Gregory's church to the great increase of the martyr's fame throughout England. On the restoration of peace, however, Ailwin resolved to tarry there no longer, but to return to Beodricsworth.

---

§ 8. THE THIRD TRANSLATION OF ST. EDMUND'S BODY. IT IS TAKEN BACK TO BEODRICSWORTH (ST. EDMUND'S BURY), A.D. 1013.

[*Authorities*—The same as for section 6.]

Count Turchil is bought off by the English.

In the second year of St. Edmund's sojourn in London, the chief witan and clergy met to consider the best means of ridding the land of the hated invader. There was something soul-inspiring in the presence in their midst on this occasion of the body of the royal martyr, who in his day had defended his country against the Danes. But neither the presence nor the example of St. Edmund, nor the blood-stained remains of St. Elphege, archbishop of Canterbury,[1] which the faithful brought from Greenwich to St. Paul's at this juncture, could move King Ethelred and his men to a courageous resistance. Frequent treachery, defeat in the battle-field and mutual distrust inclined the English to buy off the enemy rather than risk a conflict. Accordingly they paid a bribe of eight-and-forty thousand pounds to Turchil, who, after ravaging the greater part of thirteen counties, now swore allegiance to Ethelred and sold to him his friendship and services.

---

[1] St. Elphege met his death at the hands of the Danes on refusing to allow a ransom to be paid for his release.

The attempt to keep the holy body in London.

Ailwin on the conclusion of the treaty prepared to take back to East Anglia the body of its illustrious king and patron. He had passed an anxious time in London. All his firmness had been put to the test to keep possession of the shrine or to preserve it intact. The servant of God Elphege had tried to lay hands upon the piece of the true cross which, suspended from the saint's neck, lay in a reliquary upon his breast, and only Ailwin's resistance to the archbishop's pressing entreaties had saved it. A more dangerous and ambitious foe appeared in the person of Alphun bishop of London. It was a public secret that he desired to retain the saint's body for his cathedral church. As Lydgate quaintly puts it, he "gan wishe him to translate into Pauley's cherche." Ailwin respectfully opposed the prelate's wishes. Meanwhile the "saint encourages[1] his faithful followers to go back with him again into his own territory," and with this object Ailwin appoaches the bishop for permission. It is refused, but Ailwin persists, and finally Alphun yields.

Thus

> "Aillewyn by revelacion
> Took off the bishop, upon a day, lycence
> To lead King Edmund ageyn to Bury."

Bishop Alphun finds the bier immoveable.

The parishioners, notified by the bishop of the intended departure, assembled in large numbers in the church. Alphun himself, accompanied by a considerable body of the clergy robed in albs, came in procession from the cathedral, and in a sermon, spoken amid the tears and regrets of his hearers, alluded to the great loss they were about to sustain. He hoped to rouse the populace to resistance. The sermon

[1] "Per opera mira."—Herman.

over, he and three others approached the bier as if
to bear it forth upon their shoulders out of the city,
but in reality to carry it into St. Paul's.   They
found the bier immoveable.   Four more stalwart
priests stepped forward, and then a third four, but
their efforts were in vain.   Not even twice twelve
could move it.   The bishop, feeling himself discovered,
withdrew to one side in confusion, while the assembled citizens rejoiced in the thought that St. Edmund
had chosen to remain among them.

Ailwin and his
friends easily
move it.

But there and then the faithful guardian Ailwin fell
on his knees upon the pavement, and with his whole
soul besought his master Edmund not to forsake
the country and people for whom he died, lest, like
sheep without a shepherd, they should fall a prey
to wolves.   He rose, and, to the wonder of the
spectators, himself with three companions lifted up
the coffin as though it were a light and easy burden.
They bore it forth into the open air amid the singing
of hymns, followed by a long procession.   Thus to
the great sorrow of the whole city the blessed martyr
and his servant Ailwin departed from London.

The triumphant
progress to
Beodricsworth.

It was no longer necessary to keep to lanes and
by-roads in order to avoid observation.   All along
the route the inhabitants vied with one another in
showing honour and respect to the royal martyr.[1]
On the announcement of his coming the whole population of a town or village hurried forth with shouts
of joy and welcome to meet and escort him upon
the way.   In their zeal they repaired the bridges,
strewed the streets with flowers and hung their
houses with tapestry.   God rewarded this devotion
by miraculously healing all the infirm and diseased
who invoked the intercession of St. Edmund as he
passed through their midst.

[1] Gillingwater's "Account of Bury."

Ailwin chose as his route the ancient way that The route runs from London by Chipping Ongar, Chelmsford, Braintree, and Clare and thence to St. Edmund's Bury. The first stage of his journey he made at Stapleford. The lord of the manor reverently lodged the sacred body and its guardians in his house. In By Stapleford Abbots reward St. Edmund cured him of a lingering illness, and the grateful noble presented Stapleford Manor, better known as Stapleford Abbots, as a thank-offering to the saint. The holy body next rested at Green- And Greenstead. stead within the parish of Chipping Ongar. The faithful hastily erected a church there to receive the sacred relics.[1] Chestnut trees were sawn length-ways into two, and the halves set upright in a sill and plate to form the walls. Sixteen of these half trunks and two door-posts form the south side, and twenty-three the north. In this rough edifice the body of St. Edmund remained for some days, in order to satisfy the devotion of the faithful, and then Ailwin proceeded on his way.

After the departure from Greenstead no event of importance occurred till the martyr arrived at his own town. The inhabitants of Beodricsworth, out of them- The arrival at Beodricsworth. selves with joy, gave the monk and his sacred charge a triumphant welcome and escorted them to the wooden basilica which Theodred the Good had built. Thus one hundred and forty-three years after his martyrdom their protector and patron was again laid to rest in their midst. "There," writes Richard of Ciren-cester,[2] "by the favour of God, even to this day, he ceases not to plead the cause of those who devoutly seek him." The grateful people, who had despaired

---

[1] It still stands, the oldest church in England. See Palgrave's engraving of it, and also a print in Knight's "Old England," vol. i. p. 82.

[2] And Cott. MS. Titus A. viii.

of ever seeing the saint again, loaded his shrine with
thank-offerings and prayed St. Edmund

" With them to byde
And never parte away."

---

§ 9.   THE FOURTH TRANSLATION OF ST. EDMUND.   HIS
HOLY BODY IS MOVED INTO KING CANUTE'S NEW CHURCH,
OCT. 18, A.D. 1032.

[*Authorities*—The same as for section 6.   William of Malmesbury, Matthew
of Westminster, Roger of Hovedon, Florence of Worcester and Ordericus
Vitalis corroborate the testimony of Herman and other local historians re-
garding King Sweyn's death.   Casenenve discusses that event with an historical
acumen of no mean order and decides in favour of the common tradition.
Ralph Higden in his " Polychronicon " (Rolls Publ., vol. 7, p. 96) also attributes
Canute's generosity to the royal martyr to the fact of Sweyn's tragic death by
St. Edmund's hand.]

The fourth translation of St. Edmund was made
by King Canute as an act of reparation for his father
Sweyn's irreverent conduct towards the great martyr
and his clients.   The whole incident is one of special
interest as giving an insight into the deep personal
love of the East Anglians for St. Edmund and
their unbounded confidence in his power.   At the
same time it accounts for the popularity of the saint
throughout England, the people everywhere regarding
him from this period as the saviour of the country
from further Danish invasion.

Sweyn king of Denmark.   Few tyrants have afflicted the earth more ferocious
than Sweyn, the king of Denmark at the beginning of
the eleventh century.   After murdering his own father
to obtain power, he began a career of bloodshed and
crime unparalleled in history.   Master of the whole
of Scandinavia, he ruled its wild and gigantic forces with
a skill and determination which none dared oppose.
On three occasions he invaded England: the first in
company with Olave king of Sweden; the second after

the massacre of St. Brice; and the third after Turchil's
peace with Ethelred.   Envy   at   Turchil's   success
and irritation at his subsequent engagement with
King Ethelred seem to have been the only motives for
Sweyn's third attack on the country.   He summoned all His third
invasion of
his vassals to his standard for this crowning expedition England.
and openly declared his intention of punishing his rival
subject and of conquering England for himself.   The
very year that Ailwin took back St. Edmund's body to
East Anglia, he unexpectedly set sail for Sandwich.
His fleet was equipped with plunder from every
country in Europe, and the magnificence of his own
galley astonished all who beheld it.   Foiled in his
attempt to corrupt the Danish mercenaries in Kent,
he made for the mouth of the Humber, landed his
forces and by the terror of his name subjugated
the Mercians, some of whom he enrolled among his
troops, forcing others to purchase exemption by supplying horses and provisions.   His march to the
Thames was rapid and destructive, and south of the
Thames he awed the country into submission by a
ruthless display of power.   He devastated every
foot   of   the   open   country,   demolished   towns,
villages and hamlets on the line of march and
sacked and burned to the ground churches and
monasteries.   Able-bodied men were pressed into his
service or put to the sword.   The panic-stricken
English made no resistance.   The conqueror marched
through the open gates of Oxford and Winchester, and
took hostages from both cities.   His victorious career
was only checked for a moment by Ethelred and
Turchil's brave defence of London.   The skill and
strategy of the latter baffled the tyrant, who
slowly fell back on Bath, leaving in his wake
the usual desolation and ruin.   He there proclaimed He proclaims
himself king of England and compelled the thanes himself king.

M

of Northumbria, Mercia and Wessex to acknowledge
his sovereignty.   At this juncture the Londoners,
wavering between doubt and fear, persuaded the king
and Turchil to retire, and, without further struggle,
to hand over their city to the conqueror.   In the
second week of January, 1014, Ethelred with his
queen and children fled to Normandy.   On the 2nd
of February following, Sweyn, just as he had the
whole realm in his grasp, was suddenly and mysterious-
ly struck dead.

And imposes a
tax on all the
country.
The English annalists of St. Edmund's Bury relate
the incident with careful minuteness.   Sweyn, they
say, as soon as he had established his tyranny, imposed a heavy tax on the whole country and sent
envoys throughout the length and breadth of the
land to collect it.   He exempted not even the holiest
sanctuaries.   Though he had abjured paganism, in-
fluenced by the teaching and miracles of St. Poppo,
he despised the Christian mysteries and worship
when they stood in his way.   Hence the patrimony
of St. Edmund was included in his decree.   The
canons of St. Edmund, however, and the men of his
town refused to pay the tax.   Beodric, they asserted,
had given the place to King Edmund; to him it belonged, and to him only would they pay tribute.
The tax-gatherers, filled with the traditional fear of
the royal martyr's power, dared not insist.   Mean-
The people
appeal to St.
Edmund and
Ailwin.
while, dreading the ferocious vengeance of Sweyn,
the inhabitants of the town and district came in
crowds to St. Edmund's shrine.   By prayers and
offerings and the burning of innumerable lights they
appealed to their "Father Edmund" to protect them
from the Danish tyrant, and they implored Ailwin,
the saint's "chamberlain" and intimate, to lay their
petitions before his master.

As the monk was keeping his usual night watch *St. Edmund appears in a vision to his faithful attendant,* in the silence of the church, speaking with the saint " as a friend to a friend," he fell asleep, and straightway blessed Edmund, shining and glorious, in robes white as snow and with a cheerful countenance, stood before him. " Go," spoke the saint to his faithful attendant, " go and deliver my message to King Sweyn. Ask him in my name: Why tax you the people who pay tribute to none but me ? Cease your exactions. Remove these grievous burdens or you shall know that I am a terrible defender of my own."

Next morning the pious keeper of the shrine told *Who goes to Sweyn and delivers St. Edmund's message.* the people his vision and with a light step set out for Gainsborough, where King Sweyn and his army lay encamped. [1] Admitted to the tyrant's presence, Ailwin humbly delivered his message in St. Edmund's name and implored the Dane to remit the impost out of reverence for the saint. Sweyn at first treated him with silent contempt, but, when the fearless monk upbraided him for his cruelty and threatened him with St. Edmund's anger, he broke out into a torrent of abuse. With a face livid with rage he drove the monk from his presence, swearing that, unless he departed quickly, his Edmund should receive him back a sorry sight, if indeed he left there at all alive. Ailwin, thus rudely repulsed, started for home, and the evening of the next day, " the feast of the Purification of the Blessed Virgin, St. Edmund appeared to Sweyn in a vision," says William of Malmesbury, " and remonstrated with him on the misery he was inflicting on his people. The tyrant giving an insolent reply, the saint struck him on the head, and he died of the blow immediately

---

[1] This is the second time that Sweyn is recorded to have been at Gainsborough. See Leland, "Collect.," vol. i. p. 248 ; Capgrave, apud Cressy's Church History, p. 922.

after."[1]   "The Lord," exclaims Herman, "hath broken kings in the day of His wrath. He shall crush their heads in the land of the many."[2]

Near Lincoln the saint again appears to his servant. Ailwin received the full particulars of the royal decease from eye-witnesses under the following circumstances. Downhearted at the failure of his mission, yet full of confidence in St. Edmund, he rested his weary limbs, the second night after quitting Sweyn, in the neighbourhood of Lincoln. Here the martyr ever his guide and protector, again appeared to him. "Why are you so sad and anxious?" the vision asked. "Have you forgotten my words? Arise at once and proceed on your way; before you reach home, certain news of King Sweyn shall make you and all your fellow-countrymen leap with joy." Without delay the monk arose and, though it was not yet daylight, continued his journey.

Some Danish soldiers overtake him on his way home. On taking to the high road he heard the tramp of horses and the murmur of voices behind him. As the horsemen approached, he recognised them by their dress and language as Danish soldiers. Under the guardianship of St. Edmund, however, he feared nothing, and on their overtaking him returned the customary salutations and even joined in conversation. Suddenly one of the soldiers, after observing him closely said, "Pray, friend, are you the priest whom I think I saw the day before yesterday in King Sweyn's presence boldly delivering a message from a certain Edmund?"

The monk, unable to disguise the fact, meekly answered that it was he.

They describe the manner of Sweyn's death. "Alas, alas!" exclaimed the soldier, "how heavy has fallen your threat! How true has come your

---

[1] "Chronicle of the Kings," Bohn's edit., p. 190. Leland, "Itiner.," says that this happened "in regione Flegg mari proxima."

[2] Ps. cix.

prophecy! King Sweyn's death leaves England rejoicing and Denmark mourning." With a heart throbbing betwixt fear and joy Ailwin kept silence while the soldier continued his story. It appeared that the night after Ailwin's departure King Sweyn retired to his couch as usual, secure and self-satisfied and in high spirits. And at an hour when perfect silence reigned throughout the camp, an unknown warrior of surpassing beauty and in flashing armour invaded his chamber and addressed him by name: "Do you persist," he said, "in exacting tribute from St. Edmund's territory. If so, arise now and take it." The king quickly sprang up in bed[1] as if to resist, but, affrighted by his visitor's angry countenance, he shouted vociferously, "Help, comrades, help! Behold, St. Edmund slays me!" For the "invincible" martyr had struck him with his spear.[2] Meanwhile Sweyn's followers, aroused by his shouting, rushed to his tent to find him mortally wounded and weltering in blood. He lingered long enough to tell what had happened and then miserably expired.

The Danish leaders, as far as possible, concealed the manner of their sovereign's death, not a difficult matter, seeing that few knew it, and that the body, after being embalmed in salt, was at once carried out of the country. In Denmark the truth was never wholly known. Some of its historians write as though Sweyn died religiously and gloriously. The unknown author of the "Encomium of Queen

Other historical accounts of Sweyn's death.

---

[1] Florence of Worcester (Bohn's edit., p. 123) says Sweyn was on horseback. The true account in the text is from Herman, who received it from Ailwin himself.

[2] To commemorate this incident some ancient carvings represent St. Edmund arrayed in armour and holding a spear. The Jesuit fathers preserve one of these figures in an excellent state of preservation in their church at Bury.

Emma "[1] speaks in this tone, no doubt in order to please his patroness. The Saxo-Grammaticus [2] says that he died at the acme of honour and renown. Albert Krauzius and the author of the "Abridged History of Denmark"[3] write in similar terms. He died, adds the last-named writer, beloved of God and men. These praises ill become a tyrant whose crimes include the murder of his own father, Harold Blodrand, and whose career of bloodshed shocked and terrified the whole of Europe. On the other hand, several medieval historians refer in a vague way to Sweyn's death as unnatural. Adam of Bremen, whom Henry of Huntingdon follows, states that Sweyn died suddenly. Ditmar, bishop of Mersburg,[4] who lived till 1018, and was therefore a contemporary, calls Sweyn an impious man and his children a brood of vipers; he accuses him of making a compact with the devil against God and adds that there was something supernatural in the manner of his death. One of the crude attempts to explain this mystery has found its way into the lessons for St. Edward the Confessor's feast.[5]   "Sweyn, king of the Danes," says the seventh nocturn-lesson, " was drowned in the sea, whilst embarking in a fleet for the invasion of England," and St. Edward knew of it supernaturally at the moment it happened. It is impossible to accept this explanation, for two facts to the contrary are undeniable, viz., that Sweyn died in England, and that his followers at once conveyed his body to Denmark. That St. Edward, then a boy of twelve, knew by revelation the cause of Sweyn's

---

[1] Lib. i.

[2] "Hist. Dan.," lib. x.

[3] "Hist. Compendiosa Reg. Daniæ," c. 76.

[4] Ditmarus, "Episc. Chron.," lib. vii.

[5] Benedictine Breviary, Suppl., Oct. 13.

death is doubtless true and may account for his extraordinary devotion to St. Edmund. But the truth never passed his lips. He left his biographers to draw their own conclusions, probably wishing to spare his mother's feelings, for Sweyn was her father-in-law. Local history and tradition, however, and the unanimous verdict of English chroniclers clear up the mystery. Only an unreasoning disbelief in the divine interference in the affairs of man can reject the evidence of St. Edmund's freeing England from King Sweyn.

Herman the archdeacon of Norwich, who chronicled the event when it was fresh in men's minds, relates corroborating incidents with a simplicity and minuteness that vouches for their genuineness.

Herman's proofs.

After describing the venerable Ailwin's interview with the Danish soldiers, he tells how the devoted monk on arriving in East Anglia supposed that he would be the first to announce Sweyn's death. He found, however, that it was already known, for a sick man had revealed the fact in a strange and unaccountable manner. Deprived of speech and motion, with all the appearance of a corpse save for a slight heaving of the chest, the man lay dying for three whole days. On the night of Sweyn's death he suddenly sat up in bed and, opening his eyes, turned towards those by his bedside, exclaiming in a joyful voice: "This night, at this hour, St. Edmund has pierced King Sweyn with his spear and slain him." Then he fell back in his bed and breathed his last.

A sick man in Essex announces Sweyn's death at the very instant of its happening

The people of Beodricsworth and the neighbourhood who had refused to pay the tax suffered no further molestation. Even in the rest of East Anglia the tribute was neither collected nor paid, as a certain religious woman named Alfwena, a recluse of St.

The holy woman Alfwena's testimony

Benedict's, Hulme, well remembered. For she frequently told how the simple people of the seaside district of Flegg[1] collected their quota and, in dread of the barbarians, forwarded it by her father Thurcytel to Thetford; but he did not pay it. The royal tax-gatherers sent it back, no one daring to take it, for fear St. Edmund should strike him as he had struck King Sweyn.

The carucagium granted to St. Edmund for the slaying of King Sweyn.

In thanksgiving for their singular deliverance the people of East Anglia imposed upon themselves a voluntary tax. They would pay St. Edmund annually and fore ver fourpence on every carucate of land in the diocese.[2] This gift, called the carucagium, continued to be paid to St. Edmund's monastery till the next century, when Herbert of Losinga, bishop of Norwich, first borrowed it to build his cathedral, and afterwards, with or without the monks' consent, appropriated it to his own church. A whole province thus bore witness to the fact of Sweyn's death by the hand of St. Edmund.

King Canute's reparation to St. Edmund.

King Canute, Sweyn's son and successor, shared in the popular belief. On succeeding to his father's five kingdoms, he looked upon himself as succeeding also to his responsibilities. Fearing that with the late tyrant's crown he had inherited St. Edmund's anger, or, as some say, being admonished by St. Edmund in a vision to expiate his father's crimes, he changed his whole course of life. "From a mere savage, Canute rose abruptly into a wise and temperate king," writes a modern historian.[3]

He was specially anxious to atone to the protector

---

[1] The country about Yarmouth, still known as the hundreds of East and West Flegg.

[2] Leland's "Collectanea," vol. i. p. 249. A carucate was as much land as a plough could till in a year.

[3] Green's "Short History," chap. ii.

of East Anglia for his father's ravages of that province.
Early in his reign, at a council of bishops and thanes
held in Cirencester, he adopted the suggestion of Alfwin,
bishop of East Anglia, to replace the secular canons He introduces the Benedictines to St. Edmund's Bury.
of St. Edmund by Benedictines, and commenced
at once to build a monastery for the future guardians
of St. Edmund's shrine.   Three years later, after
consulting Queen Emma and with the consent of
Earl Turchil [1] and all concerned, he brought twelve
monks from St. Benedict's, Hulme, and installed
them in the new buildings. " Over the community,"
so runs the old record, " Uvius, the first abbot, a
discreet and upright man, is appointed to rule and
most worthily to preside over that family of our Lord,
in the year from our Lord's Incarnation 1020, from
Edmund the holy king and martyr's passion the
150th year. The most pious King Canute reigning,
Turchil being earl of the East Angles, and our Lord
Jesus Christ, to whom be honour and glory for
ever, being ruler over the whole world."

Canute and his queen's costly gifts to the Canute's generosity towards St. Edmund.
new foundation exceeded any which they made
to other religious houses. According to Matthew
of Westminster, " Canute enriched the monastery
of the blessed king and martyr Edmund with such
numbers of estates and other revenues, that, as to
its temporal affairs, it is deservedly set at the head
of all other convents." At the same time he confirmed to St. Edmund the privileged franchise or
liberty which Camden states to have comprised a
third of Suffolk, and he commanded a great dyke
to be thrown up to mark and protect its boundaries.

Lastly, he raised a new church in honour of the

---

[1] Canute erected four earldoms, those of Mercia, Northumber-
land, Wessex and East Anglia, whose provincial independence
he recognized. Over the last-named he placed Turchil.

The building of Canute's church. redoubtable defender of the English against his compatriots. Ailwin, who succeeded Bishop Alfwin in the see of East Anglia, had long bemoaned the plain wooden shrine enclosing his beloved master and the plank church of St. Mary, so unworthy of the illustrious dead. With joy he laid the foundations of a more magnificent edifice of stone. The carucagium "which was granted to St. Edmund for the slaying of King Sweyn" was used by the monks to supplement Canute's generous offering, so that the people also[1] might have a share in the erection of a statelier shrine to the English champion of freedom and justice.

St. Edmund's body is enshrined in the new church Oct. 18, 1032, The new basilica took twelve years to complete, and on the feast of St. Luke, October the 18th, 1032, Agelnoth archbishop of Canterbury dedicated it to God in honour of Christ, our Lady and St. Edmund. Into its consecrated precincts a brilliant procession of prelates, priests, nobles and people bore the sleeping saint and laid him to rest in a noble shrine adorned with jewels and precious ornaments. Canute, whose example successive English sovereigns followed, himself offered his crown to the martyr, and acknowledged him conqueror and Lord of the Danish nation. Thus took place the fourth translation of St. Edmund's holy body.

And Bishop Ailwin retires to Hulme. The venerable Ailwin now saw the desire of his life fulfilled. For well nigh fifty years he had watched over the sacred body and far and wide spread devotion to the saint. As bishop he superintended the erection and dedication of the royal abbey-church. Under the auspices of his sovereign he saw his Benedictine brethren firmly established in the enjoyment of their rich and splendid possessions and invested with the guardianship of the shrine. Feeling that his work was done, he

---

[1] Malmesbury, "De Gest. Reg. Angliæ," bk. ii. c. ii., considers Canute as sole founder.

resigned his bishopric and retired to the peace and
seclusion of his monastery at Hulme, there to prepare
for death. Once afterwards, however, he left his
retreat in order to verify the sacred relics, on the
occasion of Abbot Leofstan, the fifth witness of St.
Edmund's incorruption, opening the coffin in the
reign of St. Edward the Confessor.

§ 10. ABBOT LEOFSTAN, THE FIFTH WITNESS OF ST. EDMUND'S INCORRUPTION, A.D. 1050.

[Authorities – The same as for section 6.]

On the death of the Abbot Uvius the unanimous
vote of the brethren put Leofstan in the abbatial
chair. Leofstan was a man thoroughly skilled in the
rules of monastic life. St. Edward the Confessor
held him in high esteem, and not only visited the
monastery during his rule, but munificently added
to its privileges and endowments. When Leofstan
began his reign, no one had opened the martyr's
coffin for fifty years, though all believed firmly that
the body was incorrupt. As it was likely, however,
soon to become a mere tradition, Divine Providence
brought about the verification under the following circumstances. A woman named Aelfgeth, *The cure of*
who had been dumb from her birth, came from Win- *Aelfgeth of Winchester,*
chester to seek a cure at St. Edmund's shrine. The
brethren often saw her kneeling there and making
mute gestures of prayer. One day the keepers of the
shrine found her stuttering and stammering and forming words. Finding herself cured, Aelfgeth resolved
to devote her life to the saint's service. She took
up her residence near the church and with tears

of gratitude proclaimed the miracle to all the pilgrims
to the sanctuary. She chiefly employed her time in
washing the floor of the church and adorning the
altars with flowers. One night the martyr rewarded
his humble client by appearing to her in a vision
and filling her with a supernatural sweetness. At
the same time he commissioned her to inform the
"father of the monastery" of the long neglect which
his sacred body had suffered. The coffin had become worm-eaten, the wood-dust covered the relics,
and spiders had built their webs over his very face.
Abbot Leofstan treated the woman's story next morning
as a dream and from reverence refused to touch the
royal remains. A few days later "Father Edmund"
again appeared to his handmaid, and again at his
command she delivered her message to the abbot. A
third time the saint appeared, mingling threats
with his commands. Warned so often, Leofstan
took counsel with the brethren and then determined, with certain other monks, to open the coffin
and verify the remains. On the Monday following
all the brethren began a triduum of fasting, watching
and a devout reciting of psalms in preparation for
the solemn ceremony. On the Thursday morning
the abbot, with those whom he had chosen "for
their innocent and meritorious lives," went in procession to the shrine, while the other monks by his
command sat in the cloister reciting psalms and hymns.
The coffin containing the blessed martyr was reverently
taken out of the shrine, and Bishop Ailwin, the
saint's aged servant, whom Leofstan had invited
from Hulme, approached to identify the precious relics.
Ailwin was now blind from age, but he was led
by the monks to the body, every part of which he carefully and without hesitation examined with his hands.
He found the reliquary containing a portion of

*At whose sugges-
tion Abbot Leof-
stan decides to
open the coffin
and examine the
remains.*

the true cross still suspended from the martyr's neck and lying on the breast. All remained exactly as he had left it.

The monks now lifted the body from the coffin. Under the head they found a little pillow of fine shavings, which they afterwards replaced. They laid the body, which they discovered in the state that Aelfgeth had said, upon a low wooden table or bench which they had previously prepared. For a whole day it diffused around an ineffable odour of sweetness, which filled the church, spread into the cloisters to the distraction of the monks there, and even penetrated into the interior of the monastery. For, "Blessed Edmund," writes Richard of Cirencester, "who 'offered himself a sacrifice to God in the odour of sweetness,' could say with the Apostle: 'We are the good odour of Christ unto God, in them that are saved;' and, 'Now thanks be to God, who always maketh us to triumph in Christ Jesus, and manifesteth the odour of His knowledge by us in every place.'"[1]

The body is taken from the coffin,

Carefully removing the robes or coverings of the body, they exposed to view the martyr's sleeping form, a fair and beautiful spectacle. The serene countenance, pale and almost transparent, suggested the idea of one about to rise from the dead. The blood-stained and arrow-pierced camisium or shirt and other robes, which the saint wore at the time of his martyrdom, still clothed the body. These the monks reverently took off to preserve for the veneration of the faithful. Then they wrapped the body and limbs in a linen sheet.

And exposed to view.

The monks clothe it anew.

Before replacing the remains in the coffin, Abbot Leofstan determined to ascertain that the head was firmly united to the body, as tradition and the

Abbot Leofstan tries if the head is attached to the body.

---

[1] 2 Cor. ii. 14, 15.

purple seam encircling the neck testified. For this
end he irreverently took the head in his hands and
pulled it towards him. [2] Immediately his conscience
smote him, and he shook with fear.   At the same
time his hands and fingers became strangely distorted,
and a kind of paralysis seized him.   Thus God
punished his presumption, the cramp in his hands
remaining a perpetual proof that what he had done
pleased neither God nor the saint.

He is punished with a contraction of the hands.

---

[2] Malmesbury, "De Gestis Pontif.," implies that this took
place when they drew the body from the shrine.   The following
is the account of the incident given by the author, probably Samson,
of MS. Cott. Titus A. viii., and Richard of Cirencester : Abbot
Leofstan, remembering that the martyr had been decapitated,
suggested trying whether the head really adhered to the body.
"Sight testifies to hearing, and touch should testify to the sight,"
said the abbot.   Accordingly he bade one of the monks hold the
feet while he pulled the head.   But none of the brethren dared
do it.   He reminded them of their obedience.   Still each and all
of them held back, "not from frowardness, but out of reverent
fear."   The abbot, regarding them one by one, at last singled
out Brother Turstan, whom from a boy he had educated within
the monastic precincts.   "You above all others, Brother Turstan,"
he said, "owe me obedience.   You at least have no reason to
doubt the righteousness of my commands.   Approach, then, and
confidently do my bidding."   The young monk stepped forward
and took hold of the martyr's feet, while the abbot put one hand
under the neck and the other under the chin.   Then Leofstan
hesitated.   Perhaps he was wanting in respect for the dead.
Inclining his head towards the martyr's ear, he prayed : " O
glorious St. Edmund, not out of curiosity or disbelief, as thou
knowest, do I this, but that others may know the wonders of
God in thee and proclaim them to the world.   Nevertheless,
because I am guilty of many sins and unworthy to handle thy
sacred limbs or to touch thy body, the temple of the Holy Ghost,
if this action of mine displease thee, I pray thee punish my
body now, for I would rather be marked with some bodily
deformity in this life than see my soul involved in eternal
flames."   He then pulled the head so forcibly that he dragged
the whole body and the monk who held the feet towards
himself.

Abbot Baldwin's Great Church of St. Edmund

In the 15th century.

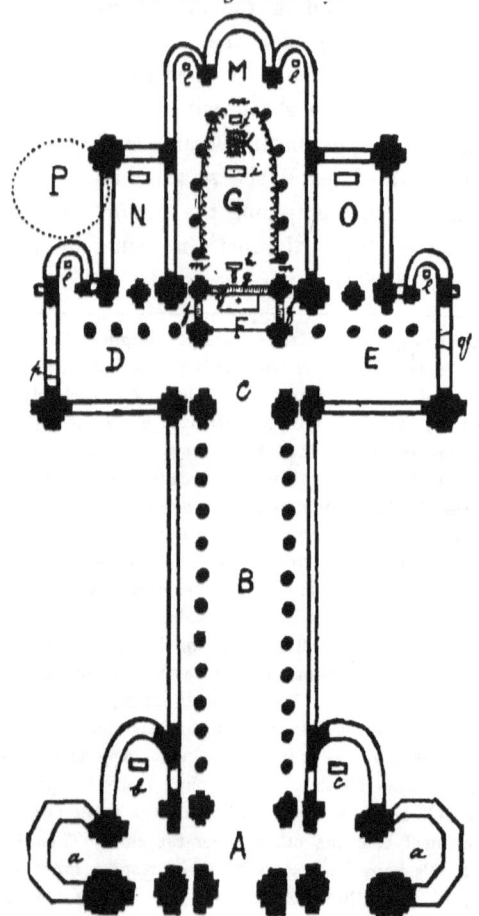

A	Western Towers.	h	Little Altar of the Choir.
a a	Octagonal Towers.	i	Altar of the Holy Cross.
B	Nave.	j	Abbot Leofstan's Shrine.
b	St. Faith's Chapel.	K	St. Edmund's Shrine.
c	St. Catharine's Chapel.	l l l l	Apsidal Chapels.
C	Central Tower.	M	Chapel of the Relics.
D	North Transept.	m m m	Entrances to Choir.
E	South Transept.	N	Lady Chapel.
F	High Altar.	O	St. Andrew's Chapel.
f f f	Altar Screen.	P	Site of the old round Chapel.
G	Choir or Presbytery.	p	Monks' entrance.
g	Abbot Baldwin's Shrine.	q	South entrance.

" For drawing of the body of the martyr
Contracted were his nerves for ever after."[1]

And now, quickly and with trembling hands, the The brethren close the coffin and put it back in its place. monks again lay the sleeping martyr in his coffin. Under the head they insert the little pillow. They cover the placid face with a veil of fine silk, and over that they spread another veil of fine linen of the same dimensions. Then they cover the whole length of the body with a linen cloth of snowy whiteness, and over that again they place a long silk veil. The relic of the true cross was not replaced, but, after the coffin was closed, and before it was sewn up in its strong linen wrapper, the aged Ailwin laid on the lid the schedule of devout prayers to St. Edmund called the "Salutacions," which Abbot Samson found there afterwards. Finally they deposited the coffin in the shrine and silently withdrew, leaving it to the custody of the appointed guardians.

---

§ 11. The Fifth Translation, by Abbot Baldwin, on Sunday, April 29, a.d. 1095.

[*Authorities*—Several special records exist of this important translation. The earliest is that of Herman, an eye-witness. Next follows the one given in the Cott. MS. Titus A. viii. The Donai MS. contains a chapter entitled "Translatio Sti Edmundi," which has the same *incipit*—"Regnante Rege Willelmo Secundo," &c.—as Bodl. 240. Both give a full narrative of the translation of St. Edmund's body "de ecclesia veteri in novam basilicam a Baldewino constructam." MS. ccc. Cant. 34, "De Translatione Sti Edmundi Regis et Martyris," and the MS. marked Cott. Julius A. vi. In Hardy's catalogue are two other records of the same translation. As the monks commemorated this "Translation of St. Edmund " in their annual round of Church festivals, a history of it forms one of the lessons in an old breviary in the library of Clare College, Cambridge, and has been used for the compilation of this section. Leland ("Collect.," vol. i. p. 247) enumerating the various translations, writes, "Quinta per Abbatem Baldwinm qui corpus Sti Edmundi a capella rotunda in novam basilicam . . . . transtulit."]

Abbot Leofstan's hands remained crippled for the rest of his life, and he sought no cure for them.

[1] Quoted from a witty monk in Gillingwater's "Account of Bury," p. 111.

When, however, other infirmities seized him, he besought St. Edward the Confessor, a devout client of St. Edmund, to send him the monk Baldwin, a well-known physician of the court. Baldwin, after receiving the Benedictine habit at St. Denis', Paris, and later on while prior of Liberaw in Alsace, had studied medicine with marked success. "Gretly expert in crafte of medycine," he acquired fame in the healing art throughout France. The Confessor invited him to England, and, on his appointment to the priorship of Deerhurst in Gloucester, a cell of St. Denis', continually had him at court. At the king's wish he now repaired to St. Edmund's abbey and succeeded in curing Leofstan of all his infirmities save the distortion of the hands. That defied his art. When, however, he heard the history of the deformity, he acknowledged his helplessness in the presence of the supernatural, and, filled with admiration of St. Edmund, desired to end his days under the shadow of the martyr's earthly presence.

Baldwin the physician.

After Leofstan's death the Confessor invited the prior and some of the monks to Windsor and recommended Baldwin to them as abbot. They adopted the king's suggestion. Baldwin was ordained priest in the royal presence on the feast of the Assumption of our Lady, 1065, and took possession of the abbatial chair. The monks found no reason to regret their choice. Baldwin proved himself a firm and able ruler. He was energetic yet prudent in his government, and continued after the Conquest to stand in high favour both at the court of the Conqueror and at that of his son.

He is elected abbot,

He gave two substantial proofs of his combined tact and energy. In an appeal to Rome he successfully vindicated the privileges of his abbey against

And builds the great church.

Bishop Herfast,[1] and he raised the grand and magnificent church over the relics of St. Edmund which until the sixteenth century ranked as the largest basilica north of the Alps after Cologne cathedral. It was the age of vast cathedrals. Baldwin had seen the huge minsters lifting themselves over the roofs of each little market-town in Normandy. Archbishop Lanfranc was building at Canterbury, and the guardians of St. Cuthbert had commenced the majestic structure of Durham. Baldwin determined to rival Canterbury and Durham. He represented to the Conqueror the inferiority of Ailwin's church[2] and proposed to raise a more stately pile over the shrine of the patron of East Anglia, the king and father of his country. Pleased with the abbot's devotion, William confirmed and extended the privileges of the monastery and thus guaranteed the necessary funds. He issued a royal mandate to the abbot of Peterborough, exhorting him to allow the abbot of St. Edmund's to take out sufficient stone from the quarries of Barnack in Northamptonshire for the erection of the new church and to exempt it from *thelonium,* or the usual toll chargeable on its carriage. Queen Matilda helped on the work by giving St. Edmund the manor of Wereketone. Stone-masons and plasterers were hired

---

[1] *Bishops of Thetford (vide note, pp. 148-9):—*

HERFAST or ARFAST, A.D. 1070, was the last bishop of Elmham. By order of a council held by Lanfranc, all bishops' sees had to be removed from villages to the most eminent cities in their dioceses. Herfast therefore removed his from Elmham to Thetford, intending afterwards, though he was hindered by Baldwin's appeal to Rome, to remove it to Bury. He was succeeded in the see of Thetford by

WILLIAM GALSAGUS, BELFOGUS or DE BELLO FAGO, Christmas day, 1085. William died in 1091.

[2] Which probably resembled St. Michael's, Oxford, or St. Benet's, Cambridge.

N

and skilled builders and sculptors brought from Italy and Normandy. For close on thirty years, under the supervision of the sacrists, Brothers Thurstan and Tolinus, a crowd of workmen laboured at the new edifice. During the course of the work the stern Conqueror passed to his rest, and, when the presbytery was finished, Baldwin applied to his suc-

The presbytery being finished, Baldwin prepares for its dedication and the translation of the saint's relics.

cessor William Rufus for his favour and that of the great men of the realm, in order that with due honour and solemnity they might dedicate the basilica and translate into it the precious body of St. Edmund. Rufus was then at Hastings attending the dedication of Battle Abbey, while he awaited a fair wind to cross to Normandy. At first he consented to both the abbot's requests. The advent of Baldwin, however, had given rise to an irreverent

Some malicious men question the saint's incorruption.

discussion among the courtiers and royal mercenaries on the continued incorruption of the martyr's body. Some contended that from the number of times on which it had been seen and touched no doubt of its integrity could be reasonably entertained. Others mocked at the tradition and suggested that, since the body must have gone to dust, the wealth lavished on the shrine should be used for payment of the king's troops. The argument so moved the red monarch that he withdrew his permission for the dedication, and left England without formally approving of the translation.

Wakelin, bishop of Winchester, and Ralph, the king's chaplain, arrive at the abbey.

But in the same year, A.D. 1095, on Wednesday, April the 25th, "at the third tax-gathering," says the old breviary, two royal commissioners arrived at the abbey on king's business, viz., Wakelin bishop of Winchester and the royal chaplain, Ralph Flambard, then "regalium provisor et exactor vectigalium," or Chancellor of the Realm. Certain influential persons now hinted that the most important "king's business"

which these royal servants could transact would be
the translation to the presbytery of the new church
of "the precious, undefiled and uncorrupted body of
the most glorious king and martyr, Saint Edmund."
Thus the conqueror had saluted it in his charter,
and the commissioners now announced that his successor had appointed them to conduct its formal
translation.   Baldwin, who all along had recom-
mended patiently waiting God's time, when notified The translation is arranged.
of this, answered, "God's will and the holy martyr's
be done." Herbert, bishop of the diocese, however,
protested that they were encroaching on his jurisdiction, but the abbot produced the bull of exemption
from episcopal control which he had obtained from
Pope Alexander II. and other decrees, and straightway invited Bishop Wakelin to preside at the
ceremony to the total exclusion of Herbert. [1]

The saintly Baldwin next exhorted all his religious Baldwin exhorts all to prepare
to make ready by greater purity of heart and by for the solem-nity.

[1] *Bishops of Norwich, (vide p. 193):—*
HERBERT DE LOSINGA, successor of William Galsagus in the
see of Thetford, at first prior of Fescamp in Normandy, and
afterwards abbot of Ramsey, is said to have procured his see
by simony in 1091, for which Rome afterwards called him to
account. He obtained leave from the Pope while at Rome, in
order to put an end to all pretensions over St. Edmund's Bury, to
fix the East Anglian see at Norwich, where he laid the foundation-
stone of his cathedral in 1096. He built his palace on the north
side and the monastery on the south. In 1101 he got together
sixty of his Benedictine brethren to serve the church. That
Norwich, however, was intended for the seat of the bishopric before
the time of Herbert of Losinga is evident from a passage in the
Domesday survey in which King William the Conqueror is expressly said to have given fourteen mansure to Ailmar towards
establishing it there. Blomefield, who took considerable pains
to collect the particulars of Herbert of Losinga's life, says :
"After he had settled his foundations thoroughly, and adorned
his church with all manner of garments and robes [by which he
probably meant vestments], books, and other necessaries, he
departed this life in the year 1119 on the 22nd day of July, and

deep and earnest devotion for the day of translation. He impressed upon the two commissioners the sacredness of the occasion as he transacted business with them, and he warned them not to incur the historical anger of St. Edmund by any arrogance or injustice towards his servants. The commissioners entered into the ceremonies with a deep sense of the responsibility of their position. The bishop put aside all secular business and on the Friday and Saturday joined the monks in fasting and prayer. He moreover spent the night previous to the translation kneeling before the body of the saint, reciting the psalter with his attendants and ardently praying to be made more worthy of his office·

The translation takes place in the presence of a great multitude of people

On Sunday, April the 29th, at the hour for terce, nine o'clock, the bishop, vested in pontificals, accompanied by Abbot Baldwin and his monks, proceeded to the old basilica. The crowds of men and women [1] who during the last three days had flocked to the town filled the church and the adjoining churchyard. The bishop first blessed the holy water and sprinkled the altars and the clergy and people. The shrine or covering was next removed, and the coffin exposed to view. In a low tone the pontiff began the antiphon "Iste sanctus," [2] and the monks around continued it :—"This saint strove for the law of his God even unto death. He feared not the gibes of the impious, for he was founded upon a strong rock."

was buried in his own cathedral before the high altar." ("Hist. of Norfolk," vol. ii. p. 333).

ROGER DE SKERING, or SCARNING, is the only other bishop of Norwich who is particularly connected with St. Edmund's Bury, to whose sanctuary he fled on Norwich being sacked by the disinherited barons, A.D. 1266. He was the 12th bishop of the see.

[1] Herman contrasts this presence of women round the shrine of St. Edmund with their absence near that of St. Cuthbert. For many years they were not allowed to enter Durham cathedral.

[2] Ant. Mag. in Communi unius Martyris.

With pious emotion the bishop incensed the coffin,
then bade the father of the monastery call forward
the six monks chosen to carry upon their shoulders
the "chest containing the precious pearl over which,
after three hundred years, nay, after a thousand
years, corruption cannot lord it." At the same time
were translated the relics of St. Botulph and St. *The bodies of other saints are*
Firminus, whose shrines the sacrists Thurstan and *also translated.*
Tolinus had newly carved, to stand sentinel on each
side of St. Edmund. Thus with great pomp they bore
the holy king and martyr to the new basilica.

When the procession came to the low and narrow *In the crush a soldier from*
south-door of the old church, the weight of the *Northampton is injured, but*
martyr's body nearly overpowered the bearers. The *miraculously cured.*
crowd rushed forward to help, and in the crush the
arm of a soldier from Northampton [1] was wedged in
between the coffin and the wall, so that the stone jamb
grazed the flesh off the bone from the wrist to the
elbow. Fearing the blood might soil the church or the
pavement of the sanctuary, the soldier wrapped the
injured arm in the soft fur of his military cloak.
Meanwhile the clergy placed the martyr's relics on the
porphyry altar which Pope Alexander had given to our
Lady and St. Edmund. A sermon followed, [2] the bishop
coming forth into the churchyard to preach to the
people on the virtues and power of St. Edmund.
While he was delivering his stirring address, the

---

[1] "Miles Hamtuniensis." The county of Northampton was gene-
rally called Hampton. Ingram remarks ("Anglo-Saxon Chronicle,"
Bohn's edition, note, p. 471) that Southampton was named
Hampton to distinguish it from Northampton town, but the
common people to this day say "Hampton" in both neighbour-
hoods. See "Chronicle of Ramsey," Rolls Publ., pp. 93-167, and
"Chronicon Petroburgense," Camden Series, vol. 47. MS. Titus
A. viii. leaves no doubt that the soldier was from Northampton.

[2] Herman implies there were two sermons, one in the church
and one in the churchyard:—"In altaris crepidine fit sermo de
sancta fide ; præsul deforis in atrio verbum facit populo."

soldier, sitting in the church, timidly examined his arm and to his astonishment found it healed, a scar alone remaining in testimony of the miracle.

The saint's body is borne outside the church, and the long drought ceases.

Bishop Wakelin's words moved his hearers to have recourse to the royal martyr to end the terrible drought which then afflicted the country. The dryness of the season "was so excessive," says the "Liber Cœnobii," "that the green corn, the grass, the early foliage, were parched for want of rain. The necessaries of human life seemed in danger of perishing." "Famine," writes another chronicler, "threatened Britain." [1] "Cannot Edmund," murmured the people, "help us in our necessity?" The general desire reached the bishop's ears. Interrupting his sermon. he caused the martyr's relics to be again carried forth in procession from the church and placed in the open air upon a heap of stones on an elevated spot. Then he again addressed the crowd on the merits of St. Edmund and the interest which he had ever taken in their welfare. The holy martyr stood in the presence of God to propitiate the Divine anger. Let them rouse their faith and call upon him for the long-needed rain. With a loud voice the bishop then thrice intoned the "Kyrie Eleison," and thrice the people repeated it "with voices discordant but with desires in harmony." And, "Behold, while they prayed to God, the saint also pleaded with Him. The heavens became overclouded, drops of grateful rain fell upon their face." [2] "A sudden fall of rain compelled those out of doors to seek shelter." [3] And, "Never in the memory of man did such abundance rejoice the heart of farmers as during that year." [4]

The bishop proclaims an indulgence, of which many avail themselves.

After the sermon the bishop gave his blessing and granted an indulgence,[5] which he extended to

---

[1] Cott. MS. Titus A. viii.   [2] Herman.   [3] Cott. MS. Titus A. viii.
[4] "Liber Cœnobii."   [5] Herman and Cott. MS. Titus A. viii.

those absent who, within a given time, should visit
the saint, a favour of which many throughout England
availed themselves. "With praise and glory the
holy martyr of God now took possession of his new
resting-place, and there the solemn mass was ponti-
fically celebrated."[1]

"While this was taking place, a man from London, A man from London has approaching the heap of stones on which the coffin his eye cured. had reposed, piously kissed it, and with the stones touched his forehead and eyes. At the same time he called upon the name of Edmund from the bottom of his heart. Straightway a growth upon his eye from which he had suffered for a long time disappeared."

"Thus," so runs the ancient lesson for the feast of
this translation of St. Edmund, "in the year—the
225th from his passion—and on the day aforesaid,
to the great joy of the people, for the perpetual
memory of the whole English nation, and for the
glory of all the saints, the incorrupt body of the
blessed martyr St. Edmund was translated, to rise in
the future to eternal happiness."

---

§ 12. TOLINUS THE SACRIST, THE SIXTH WITNESS OF ST.
EDMUND'S INCORRUPTION, WITH THREE OTHERS VERIFIES THE
SACRED BODY IN THE REIGN OF ABBOT BALDWIN, A.D.
1094-95.

[*Authorities*—The following is a digest of Section 5, Book II., of the Cottonian
Manuscript Titus A. viii. The writer, Osbert de Clare, prior of Westminster,
A.D. 1130, speaks as a contemporary of the noble lady Scietha, from whom he
heard the narrative. This event is also chronicled in Bodl. 240 f. 650.]

"Many people as well as myself know personally The recluse Scietha, a noble or by report the religious woman Scietha, who lives lady, who knew a celibate life by the shrine of St. Edmund. Now Tolinus, far advanced in years and clothed in a nun's habit,

---

[1] Herman and Cott. MS. Titus A. viii.

she had as a girl at home refused the hand of the
noblest and most illustrious Englishmen, in order to
seek a heavenly spouse. The evil tempter, as the
holy woman was wont to tell her near friends,
appeared to her in sleep and tried to move her from
her purpose. But she replied : ' My Lord Jesus Christ
have I chosen for my spouse ; to Him have I vowed
myself, to Him have I promised to preserve myself
inviolate.' Sighing after the cloistral life, she travelled
through the different counties of England, asking admission at all the convents of virgins. Everywhere
the crafty enemy prevented her entrance. Therefore
it happened that she came to St. Edmund's at Abbot
Baldwin's invitation—yea, rather at the call of Christ
—and rested there.

Relates how
St. Edmund
healed her
right hand.

"From her own lips we have heard the following
introduction to the rest of her story. ' One night,'
she used to relate, ' I went out, leaning on my companion's arm, to attend matins. On coming to the
yard through which we had to pass, I first opened
the door and held it open for my companion ; but,
although I tried to let it close gradually, the violence
of the wind slammed it to, and crushed my right
hand. The pain rendered me insensible, and I lay
prostrate on the ground, while my companion, ignorant of the accident, remained stupefied by my side.
When I recovered a little, I did not give up my
undertaking. Afterwards, however, on returning home
with the swollen hand in my breast, I found the
bone of my middle finger broken. Although in time
it grew better, a swelling about the size of a nut
remained over the place of the fracture, and per-
manently disfigured the hand. One evening, as I
kept my accustomed watch in the church, I quietly
approached the spot where I knew the holy martyr
rested, and, stretching out my deformed hand towards

the shrine, I said in all simplicity : See, my lord,
whether this swelling becomes thy handmaid. If it
be thy will, I ask thee to take it away. I then withdrew from the asylum of the saint's presence. Next
day, when I examined the finger, as I often did,
the deformity was gone.' There are many surviving
to this day who can vouch for the truth of this story,
which does not rest merely on Seietha's evidence.

"At the same time she used to add the following : Tolinus the
Sacrist was her
'Under the rule of Abbot Baldwin the venerable friend and
spiritual guide.
monk Tolinus lived in the monastery. In his life
and conversation he was an edification to many, a
mirror of innocence and a law of justice, and so he
merited to be appointed to the office of sacrist. By
word and example he endeavoured to allure all to a
love of the heavenly country. Hence if any good
can ever be in me or could have been, I owe it to
his instructions and exhortations.

"'In the same year in which the translation of The same year
as the great
our most holy Father Edmund from the old church translation took
place,
to the new basilica took place—the translation which
is yearly commemorated on April the 29th—after the
solemnity of SS. Peter and Paul, I held frequent
colloquies with Tolinus when I visited the church
for prayer and edification. One day, as he spoke to June 29, 1095,
me before the altar of St. John the Baptist on the
contempt of the world, a sweet memory of St. Edmund
which he ever cherished in his breast came to his
lips. With eyes cast down I listened, and then per-
versely asked, How is it, my father,[1] that we maintain
his incorruption, when most contend that he has
succumbed to decay ? For three days ago, as I made
my way hither to implore his intercession, a certain She had a conversation re-
specting the
knight who met me, in the course of conversation incorruption
of the martyr's
questioned the integrity of the martyr and denied it. body.

---

[1] " Domine mi."

Nay! I said to him. You err. Believe by acknowledging it, and acknowledge by believing it. Even as on the day he was crowned with martyrdom, so at the present is he incorrupt and entire. This I say in accordance with the common belief. For as yet I know no other argument to gainsay the calumnies of the incredulous. On hearing this Tolinus sighed: Alas, my most dear friend, how grievously they err who doubt on this point. They ought rather to believe the omnipotence of God and admire His clemency. Would you like them waver in your faith? I have no doubt, I replied, about the power of the Almighty, but I have never yet found the man who can satisfy me in this controversy. He answered, Will you accept my testimony in this altercation? No argument, I replied, can tear from my heart what your inviolable word has confirmed.

Tolinus assures her that he with three others had handled the incorrupt body. Then stretching forth both his hands, he said: These impure and unworthy hands have touched his sacred limbs. These irreverent eyes have gazed upon his sweet and graceful face. Remembering that some bodies embalmed with aromatic spices have subsisted incorrupt, I feared not to boldly examine that body. And even as here you see my flesh, so equally soft and yielding flesh clothes the joints of St. Edmund's body. I confess I foolishly and presumptuously did it. May He pardon me who has granted me space up to now to repent! And that there might be other witnesses I had associates in my deed, to wit, Dom William the prior, by whose authority and request I acted, and Sparawech my assistant, and Hereward the goldsmith. Shortly after hearing this, I bade farewell to the man of God, whom nevermore was I to see on earth.

The sudden death of the four witnesses. "'The three whom that venerable man mentioned as his accomplices not long after fell mortally sick and

confessed their rashness on their death-bed. None
of them lived the year out. Tolinus indeed exceeded the term allotted to the others who had
proved the martyr's incorruption, but on the feast June 17, A.D. 1096.
of St. Botulph following, whilst he walked one
early morn on the summit of the walls of the
church inspecting the work, he suddenly fell headlong off. Nevertheless the divine clemency did not
utterly desert him. For his habit caught in one of
the scaffold poles which supported the planks. Some
of the stonemasons, hoping to rescue him unhurt,
quickly mounted the ladders. But too late. For,
the hem of his habit giving way, he fell on a heap
of stones underneath. The workmen took him up
half dead and with his limbs broken in several places
by the severe collision. He lingered long enough
to confess his aforementioned presumption and to
receive the holy viaticum. Then he breathed his
last in the midst of his brethren. I was overcome
with grief on hearing the news three days after, and
I begged my father abbot to let me approach the
corpse of my dearest friend. Unwilling at first, he
at length granted my request on account of my im-
portunity and because he saw that I was prompted
only by a religious motive. While the brethren
performed the last obsequies, I busily recited the
psalter for the soul of my friend. Now at sunset one
evening, I was sitting in the church with the permission of the guardians, saying my office for his
soul, and whilst I recited the 80th psalm in which
the prophet admonishes us to exult in God, our helper,
slumber overcame me, the codex slipped from my
hand, my eyes closed and my head leaned against
the wall at my back. Suddenly some one seized me Tolinus appears to her in sleep.
by the shoulders and shook me violently, saying:
Will you sleep, while your dearest friend Tolinus

suffers bitter pains? I awoke, and the vision vanished, but the impression of his fingers remained, and I feel them now, though you can see nothing.

He reveals to a monk that his irreverent handling of the saint is the cause of his detention in purgatory.

"'About the same time and before the thirty days from his death had elapsed, Tolinus appeared in sleep to one of the brethren with whom he had been most familiar during life. By reason of their old friendship the monk ventured to address the vision: Why, my father, do I behold you darksome and bent with sorrow? Tolinus answered: Because I am not yet fit to enter into the glory of the uncircumscribed light. And why, asked the monk, since you led a blameless life here? The vision replied: I am punished because I dared to handle my lord Edmund with an unbelieving mind and to expose him to others to be handled. Therefore I beseech thy love to explain this to the brethren without delay, and to beg them to supplicate the Father of mercies and His faithful champion for me in my sufferings.

The monks pray for their dead brother and are assured afterwards that he is in glory.

"'The brother, rising early, spoke to the assembled brethren as he had been admonished. With fraternal anxiety they condoled with their departed companion and without delay made every effort to conciliate the divine justice for him. After a lapse of about six months Tolinus again appeared to his friend, this time with a cheerful countenance and clothed with snow-white garments. And on his brother-monk asking how it fared with him, he answered: I have merited to meet with my Redeemer's clemency, and the grace of my lord Edmund. I now enjoy citizenship with him in heaven, to whom I faithfully ministered on earth. I continue to wait attendance on him. I see him and I admire his glory.'"

§ 13. The Sixth Translation of St. Edmund's Body by Abbot Samson, November 23, A.D. 1198.

[*Authorities*—The events of this and of the following section immortalized by an author of some fame in English literature are probably the widest known of any in St. Edmund's history. They are taken from the "Chronica Jocelini de Brakelonda de rebus gestis Samsonis Abbatis Monasterii Sancti Edmundi," a work edited by Mr. John Rokewood for the Camden Society in 1840, and four years later translated into English by Mr. E. Tomkins as a specimen of "Social and Monastic Life in the Twelfth Century." Carlyle in his commentary upon it in "Past and Present" says : "Once written in its childlike transparency, in its innocent good humour, not without touches of ready pleasant wit, and many kinds of worth, other men liked naturally to read, whereby it failed not to be copied, to be multiplied, to be inserted in the 'Liber Albus,' and so, surviving Henry VIII., Putney Cromwell, the dissolution of Monasteries, and all accidents of malice and neglect for six centuries or so, it got into the Harleian collection, and has now, therefrom, by Mr. Rokewood of the Camden Society been deciphered into clear print, and lies before us a dainty thin quarto, to interest for a few minutes whomsoever it can." The writer of this interesting piece received the name of Brakelond from a street or quarter of old St. Edmund's Bury. In 1173 he entered the Benedictine noviciate, and later on became chaplain to Abbot Samson, his former novice-master. Jocelin was "an ingenious and ingenuous, a cheery-hearted, innocent yet withal shrewd, noticing, quick-witted man." He had in fact that wise monastic simplicity which looks from under the monk's cowl with "much natural sense." A fellow-monk speaks of him as "eximiæ religionis, potens sermone et opere." "Living beside my lord abbot, night and day for the space of six years," he became his Boswell, making him live again "visible and audible" for the benefit of moderns. Samson, who regarded himself as nothing if not the first servant and attendant of St. Edmund, after a fire in the vicinity of the shrine in 1198, translates and verifies his patron's relics. His faithful chaplain records all that happens with "a veracity which goes deeper than words." No more reliable authority can therefore be desired for this part of the great martyr's history.]

Before attaining the dignity of mitred abbot of St. Edmund's Bury, Samson of Tottingham proved himself a man of no ordinary character. After his return from studying at Paris he could preach in three languages, and no more efficient teacher could be found for the town-school. In the time of the antipopes, when business was to be done with the true pope at Rome, monk Samson was chosen to do it. Disguising himself as a Scotchman, he reached his destination in safety, and returned, though too late, with his cause won. Through no fault of his he could not always *bene stare cum abbate*—stand well with the abbot,—for time-server and flatterer he would not be. When, however, he came to be better understood, Abbot Hugo made him subsacrist, librarian, novice-master.

He had been well schooled and had learnt something of human nature, and so he discharged his
offices to perfection. But he remained all the while
unchanged. At severity he had not complained, at
kindness he did not break out into smiles and thanks.
Abbot Hugo says that he has " never seen such a
man." In this way, always right-honest, dutiful,
grave, devout, Samson reached his seven-and-fortieth
year. His make resembled his character. He was
not tall and slim, but stout-made, erect and solid
as one of the massive Norman towers of his own
church. Nearly bald, with a face neither round nor
yet long, black and slightly curly hair somewhat hoary,
a grizzled reddish beard slightly tinged with grey,
a prominent nose, thick lips, and from under bushy
but lofty eye-brows two clear and very piercing eyes,
he did not therefore present an unpleasant appearance, for kindliness of heart softened his features
and mellowed the resolution of his face. Altogether
he inspired confidence rather than fear, so that, when
Abbot Hugo was killed by a fall from his horse on
his way to the shrine of St. Thomas of Canterbury,
the monks, trying to make up their minds, flitting
from one proper person to another, seemed mostly
to revert to Brother Samson as the future abbot.

When King Henry II., still repentant for the
murder of Archbishop Thomas, decided to grant St.
Edmund's convent a free election, he summoned the
prior and his twelve to meet him at Bishop Waltham
in Hampshire. By Brother Samson's advice, before
leaving home, an electoral committee chose in secret
three names of members of their own abbey, which
they gave in a sealed paper to the prior and their
other deputies. When the king called for three
names, they broke the seal and read out the three
names. Samson's stood first. The king orders them

to nominate three others of their own community,
and they do so without hesitation. Astonished at
their expedition, the king says, "God is with them."
But for the honour of his realm he bids them add
three monks of other convents; then to strike off
three; to strike off another three, and lastly to strike
off one. Samson and the prior are left. Venerable
Brother Denis the cellarer in the name of the rest
discusses the merits of these two. He praises both
as good men, of regular life, learned, but he ever
puts Samson forward "in angulo sui sermonis"—in
the corner of his speech. The presiding bishop of
Winchester interrupts. "We see clearly what you
wish to say. It is evident you consider your prior
somewhat lax and you prefer Samson. Of two
good men you must choose the best. Speak out, do
you want Samson?" The majority answer, "Volu-
mus Samsonem"—"We want Samson." A few
keep silence, so as not to offend either candidate.
So Samson is nominated and presented at once to the
king, who accepts him: "I know him not," says
Henry; "your prior I know, and I would have accepted him; but as you wish. If your choice does
badly, per veros oculos Dei,[1] I warn you, you shall
repent of it." The prior answered the king that
Samson deserved even greater honours. The new
abbot knelt and kissed the royal feet, then, quickly
rising and quickly turning towards the altar, he
entoned in clear tenor voice the "Miserere mei Deus,"
chanting it with his brethren with head erect and
unchanged countenance. "That man," exclaimed the
king in astonishment, "believes himself fit to guard
his abbey."

Seven days later, on the 28th of February, Samson
was blessed by the bishop of Winchester. He

---

[1] A common oath of the Norman kings.

announced his intention of arriving at St. Edmund's Bury on the Palm Sunday following to take possession of his abbey. On that day the bells of St. Edmund's rent the air with their clangour, and the pealing of the organ echoed through the arches of the grand abbey. Knight and viscount, weaver and spinner, shopman and burgess, stately dame and homely housewife, chubby infants and old men, hastened out to see the lord abbot arrive. He stood at the gates, while they stripped off his sandals, and they solemnly led him barefoot to the high altar and to the shrine· On the sudden silence of bell and organ, monks and people kneel in prayer, and the lord abbot prostrates. Bell and organ again burst forth, while the "Te Deum" is chanted by all in the vast minster, and Samson is abbot.

His installation on Palm Sunday, March 21, 1182.

Without delay he attacked the difficult work before him. The dilapidated monastery needed repairing, the boundless debts clearing off. The harpy Jews and their bonds had to be banished St. Edmund's liberties, [1] and dissatisfied monks to be managed. Neither did he neglect the national duties of his high position. At one time he marched with his men to oppose John's pretensions during the absence of his brother Cœur-de-Lion ; at another he sat in parliament, making generous sacrifices for Richard's redemption, but daring peers spiritual or temporal—those who would— to lay hands on St. Edmund's shrine. Sixteen years thus passed away in earnest work. He had built and restored hospitals and schools; he had raised good dwellings for the people ; he had repaired all that was ruinous, completed churches and church-steeples, and built up anew the great tower of St. Edmund's church.

Abbot Samson's government.

One thing remained undone—the dearest to the

---

[1] This was necessary to protect them from the populace.

great abbot's heart. Long before his hair had turned
snow-white with worry and work, he had wished
to erect a new shrine for St. Edmund. For after
God did he not owe all to him who had singled
him out and saved him in his boyhood to be his
servant ? Jocelin relates a dream which he had
heard from the lips of Samson that shows the
abbot's early indebtedness to the royal martyr's
patronage. When he was a child of nine years old—so
the faithful chaplain writes,—as he lay uneasily in
his little bed at Tottingham, he dreamt that he was
standing before a noble and stately gateway, when
the arch-fiend with black-webbed wings swooped
down, and with clawed hands would have gripped
him, had not St. Edmund, who stood by, snatched
him up in his arms. Whereupon the little sleeper
shrieked out, "St. Edmund, save me !" and thus,
while he called upon him whose name he had
never heard, devil and dream passed away. His
mother, alarmed at the outcry and the accompanying
dream, took the little boy on the morrow to pray
before St. Edmund's shrine. At the sight of the
cemetery gate, [1] the Norman gate of Abbot Baldwin,
the child cried out, "See, mother, this is the place,
this is the gate which I saw in my dream, when
the devil was about to seize me." He recognised
the place, he said afterwards, just as if he had
actually seen it before with his natural eyes. His
good mother there and then dedicated him to St.
Edmund and with prayers and tears left him in
care of the monks. In after days Samson was wont
to thus interpret his dream : the demon with sable
outstretched wings foreshadowed the sin and pleasure
of this world, which would have made him their
own had not St. Edmund flung his arms around

---

[1] Which is still left standing.

O

him and made him one of his monks. From the
day of that dream Samson ever looked up to St.
Edmund as his special father and friend.

He has recourse to him in time of trial. At the time of the antipopes, when Geoffrey Ridel
laid claim to the benefice of Woolpit, Samson was
sent to the true pope, Alexander II., to defend the
rights of the abbey. He ran considerable risks, for
A.D. 1159 to 1162. the emperor's party, which supported the antipope
Octavian, waylaid all clerks carrying letters of Pope
Alexander. They would imprison or hang them, or
cut off their lips and noses and send them back to
the pope. However, by acting as a Scot,[1] and after
many sufferings and adventures, Samson saw the
pope and won his cause, and got back home with
his letter from "our lord the pope." But he found
he was too late, and he sat him down disheartened
and alone in the quiet dim apse under the shadow
of St. Edmund's shrine. "In the wide earth," asks
his eulogist, "if it be not St. Edmund, what friend
or refuge has he?" There he sat sorrowful and
silent. All his stratagems and disguises had been
in vain. His mission had failed. Woolpit church
had already been given to Geoffrey Ridel. The
abbot was angry, and therefore no monk or layman
durst speak to weary Samson or bring him food
except by stealth. Only God and St. Edmund consoled him at that moment and afterwards, when the
abbot's officers imprisoned him for his tardiness,
though it was no fault of his. When he rose to
favour later and became sub-sacrist, he did not forget
his patron, and collected money and materials to erect
something for St. Edmund, but the king's officers prohibited all spending of funds during the vacancy[2] except
for the reduction of the debt. On becoming abbot he

---

[1] The Scottish kingdom sided with Octavian.

[2] After Abbot Hugo's death.

determined to repair the church, yet twelve years passed
before, by careful management,⟨ he⟩ freed the abbey
from debt. At last he said he would stay more at
home, "for the presence of the master is the profit
of the field,"[1] and devote himself to claustral affairs.
The church needed his whole care. He had sacrificed many things for King Richard's ransom—among
other precious ornaments the silver table of the high
altar. He now resolved to construct something
which could not possibly be abstracted and where
no sacrilegious thief would venture—a new and
rich shrine over St. Edmund's body.

Accordingly he directed the preparation of a most *Samson's design for a new shrine.*
valuable outer covering, or feretry, to contain the loculus,
or coffin. He arranged that the panels should be all
of beaten gold inlaid with gems, and the roof and
gables crested with delicately worked battlements.
To support this gorgeous outer shell, he designed
a pedestal of blocks of polished marble, sculptured
into miniature pillars, and arches, and pinnacles and
crochets. Whilst the abbot planned and designed all
this, an event occurred which brought about its speedy
execution. The devout and reverential Jocelin thus
relates it:

"In the year of grace 1198, a great panic seized *The high altar aloft on which stands the shrine is damaged by fire.*
the convent, and the glorious Martyr Edmund raised
it, for he wished to make us learn to keep his
sacred body more diligently and reverently than we
had hitherto done. A wooden platform covered the
space between the shrine and the altar,[2] and upon
it the guardians of the shrine kept two tapers

---

[1] "Præsentia Domini provectus est agri." "The eye of the
master maketh the ox fat," "The eye of the master does more
work than his hands," are similar proverbs.

[2] The shrine stood behind and above the table of the altar as a
kind of reredos, and in front of it hung the golden "Majestas," or
vessel in which the Blessed Sacrament was reserved.

constantly burning, clapping new candles upon the old
in a slovenly manner. Under the platform, flax and
thread, wax ends, rags, and various utensils were
unbecomingly huddled away. In fact, whatever the
guardians of the shrine used they put there out of
the way, and concealed all behind a door with iron
gratings.

Oct. 17.

"One night, the eve of the feast of St. Etheldreda,
while the guardians were asleep, a candle which
they had carelessly fixed upon another fell, while
still alight, upon the platform. The linen cloths at
once caught fire, which soon spread to the wood-
work and the wax and rubbish underneath.   Lo !
the wrath of the Lord 'was kindled,'[1] but not without
mercy, according to that, 'In wrath He remembered
mercy.'[2] For just then the clock struck the hour
for matins, though it was not yet time, and when
the master of the vestiary got up, he noticed the
unusual glare of fire around the shrine and ran to
strike the gong as if for the dead. At the same
time he cried at the top of his voice that the shrine
was on fire. We rushed to the church, where we
found that the fire was burning fiercely, the
flames actually encircling the whole shrine, and
mounting almost to the beams of the church-roof.
Our juniors ran for water, some to the well, some
to the clock ;[3] others with great difficulty smothered
the flames with their cowls or rescued from destruction the sanctuary furniture. When they threw the
cold water upon the heated stones, it crumbled them
to dust ; the wood underneath the plates of silver
was charred to the thickness of my finger, leaving

The feretry or
shrine itself
narrowly es-
caped destruc-
tion,

---

[1] Numb. xi. 33.   [2] Habac. iii. 2.

[3] This little incident shows that the abbey-clock was worked by
water.

the nails standing out, and the plates themselves
hung loose, having lost the support of the nails
that fastened them. The golden majestas in front
of the shrine, with some of the stone-work, remained
undamaged. If anything, the majestas, being all of
gold, looked brighter than before. Providentially *And the rood
the great beam behind the altar had been removed *and relics.*
for fresh carving. It supported the crucifix and our
Lady and St. John, and on it rested other sacred
and precious objects. The chest containing St.
Edmund's *camisia*, and some other reliquaries and
relics generally hung from the beam. All, however,
had been previously removed, otherwise they would
have been burnt like the tapestry, which hung in
the place of the beam. What would it have been,
had the church been curtained? Having made sure
that the fire had not penetrated to the sacred coffin,
we next carefully examined if there were any chinks
or cracks.

"When all had cooled, and our anxiety had in a *St. Edmund's
great measure subsided, behold! some of the brethren *cup is found
exclaimed with plaintive voice that St. Edmund's *uninjured.*
cup was destroyed. A search amongst the débris of
stones and cinders brought to light the cup uninjured and perfect, lying amongst pieces of charred
wood, and wrapped up in a half-burnt linen cloth.
The fire had burnt to ashes the oaken box which
had enclosed it, leaving only the iron band and iron
lock. We wept for joy at the marvellous preservation of the cup.

"We now saw that the greater number of the metal *The damage
plates which faced the shrine were stripped off. *to the shrine
While therefore we blamed the disgraceful sloven- *is repaired.*
liness of the keepers, we all agreed to secretly call
in the goldsmith to our assistance, and to make him
join together the metal plates and fix them again

to the shrine, in order to avoid scandal. . At the
same time we removed all traces of the fire. But,
as the evangelist bears witness: 'There is nothing
covered that shall not be revealed.'[1]   Very early
in the morning some pilgrims came to make their
offerings, and, although they could perceive no vestige
of the fire, yet some of them, peering about, asked
where it had broken out, for the news had already
spread. Since we could not altogether conceal the
fact, we answered these prying folk that a candle
had fallen down and burnt three napkins, and that
the heat of the flames had damaged the stone-work
in front of the shrine. Yet some spread the rumour
that the saint's head was burnt, while others said
that the hair only was singed. The truth afterwards became known, and the mouth was stopped of
them that spoke wicked things. [2] All this happened
by the providence of God, in order to teach us to
keep more becomingly the shrine and its surroundings; and also to enable our lord abbot to more
speedily and thoroughly fulfil his desire of placing
the holy martyr's body in security and honour in a
more prominent position. Already before this unfortunate accident, the golden crest-work was half
completed, and the marble blocks on which the
feretry was to be raised were nearly all prepared
and polished.

The shrine or feretry is transferred to the high altar, Nov. 20, 1198.

" By the feast of St. Edmund everything was ready.
The feast fell on Friday. On the Sunday following[3]
a three days' fast was proclaimed to the people
and its object explained to them. The abbot himself
exhorted the brethren to prepare themselves for the
removal of the shrine to the high altar, on which it
was to stand, while the masons erected its base of

---

[1] St. Luke xii. 2.   [2] Ps. lxii. 12.

[3] I.e., the Sunday within the Octave.

marble. The abbot arranged the time and manner
of carrying out the work. That night, when we
came to matins, we found the large feretry standing
upon the altar. It was empty and lined with white
doe-skins fixed to the wood with silver nails, and
one panel was removed and placed on one side
against a pillar. The holy body lay in its usual
place at the back of the altar.

"After chanting lauds we took our disciplines. The coverings
are taken off the
coffin or loculus.
Then the lord abbot with some of the brethren
vested in albs, approached the coffin with becoming
reverence, and proceeded to uncover it. An outer
linen cloth enveloped all. We found this tied on
the upper side with strings of its own. A silken
cloth was next folded round the coffin, then another
linen cloth, and then a third, after which
the coffin stood exposed. It rested upon a little
wooden tray to prevent injury from the marble.
Affixed to the outside over the martyr's breast lay
a golden angel about the length of a man's foot,
holding in one hand a golden sword and in the other
a banner; under this we saw the hole in the lid
through which the ancient keepers put their hands
for the purpose of touching the sacred body. Over
the figure of the angel ran this superscription:

Martiris ecce ʒoma servat Michaelis agalma. [1]

"Near the figure of the angel we found the silk
bag wherein Ailwin, the bishop and monk,
deposited the schedule written in English, which
contained certain salutations or devout praises of
St. Edmund.

"Now iron rings projected from the ends of the
coffin in Norman fashion. [2] The brethren in white

---

[1] "Behold, the Martyr's body St. Michael's image keeps." See
Leland's "Collect.," vol. i. p. 267, the *zoma* is more correctly
spelt with an *s*.

[2] "In cistâ Norensi."

The coffin with
the sacred body
s placed within
the shrine. albs, taking hold of these, carried the coffin to the altar. And I lent thereto my sinful hand, although the abbot had commanded that none should come nigh unless called. The coffin was placed within the shrine, the panel put back and fastened, and for the present the shrine closed. We all thought that the abbot would show the coffin to the people, and some time during the octave of the feast bring forth the sacred body before us all. In this, however, we were woefully mistaken, as the following will show."

§ 14. ABBOT SAMSON, THE SEVENTH WITNESS OF ST. EDMUND'S INCORRUPTION, NOV. 26, 1198.

[Authorities—The same as for the previous section.]

Samson desires
to look upon St.
Edmund's face. " On Wednesday while the community sang compline, the abbot consulted in private with the sacrist and Walter the physician regarding the appointment against midnight of twelve brethren strong enough to carry the panels of the shrine, and skilful[1] in unfixing and refixing them. Moreover the abbot said that he desired to look upon the face of his master and to associate with him in that act the sacrist and Walter the physician. To be present on the occasion he selected his two chaplains, the two keepers of the shrine, the two masters of the vestiary and six others, Hugo the sacrist, Walter the physician, Augustine, William of Diss, Robert and Richard.

Attended by
twelve of the
brethren, he
opens the coffin. " When the convent was asleep, these twelve, clothed in white albs, removed a panel of the shrine,

_____

[1] 1 Paralipomenon xxii. 15.

and drew out the coffin, which they laid upon a
table prepared for it near the site of the old shrine.
Then they began to take off the lid, which proved
a difficult task, for sixteen long iron nails held it
to the coffin. When this was accomplished, the abbot
motioned all except his two aforenamed associates
to retire a little. Now the sacred body so filled the
coffin, both in length and width, that between the
head and the wood, and between the feet and the
wood, hardly space to put a needle remained. The
head lay united to the body somewhat raised on a
little pillow. The abbot straightway examined the
sacred relics. He found them protected by a silk
cloth over a linen cloth spotlessly white. On the
face rested a small linen cloth over one of very fine
silk, like a nun's veil. The body itself was wrapped
in a linen sheet, under which its outlines were visible.

"Here the abbot paused, and said that he durst
not proceed further and look upon the sacred flesh
uncovered. But, taking the head between his hands,
he murmured: 'O glorious martyr St. Edmund, blessed
be the hour wherein thou wast born. O glorious
martyr, turn not to my perdition my boldness in
touching thee, sinful and miserable as I am. Thou
knowest my devotion and my intention.' And proceeding he passed his hands over the eyes and the
very massive and prominent nose; he touched the
breast and arms, and, raising the left hand, put his
fingers between the fingers of the saint. He found
the feet standing stiff upright, like the feet of a man
who had died that day, and he touched the toes
and counted them. [1]

The holy body exposed to view.

---

[1] The following occurred in the Life of St. Thomas of Canterbury and is quoted by F. Morris, S.J., in his history of the archbishop, page 576 :

"When he raised from the earth to his shrine the Blessed

Twenty-two
other monks
see the body.
"And now it was proposed to call the other ten
forward to see the marvel, and also six others, while
six more stole in without the abbot's leave, viz.,
Walter of St. Alban's, Hugh the infirmarian, Gilbert
the brother of the prior, Richard of Hingham, Jocell
the cellarer, and Thurstan the Little. All these
looked upon the saint, but Thurstan alone put forth
his hand and touched the feet and knees.

John of Diss and
others look down
from the roof.
"In order that there might be an abundance of
witnesses the Most High disposed that John of
Diss, sitting in the roof of the church with the
servants of the vestiary, should look down and see
the proceedings."

The solemness
of the scene.
A strange and solemn scene! The monastery
silent! The world asleep! The darkness of night
outside, and a gloom in the long nave of the
church! One spot alone luminous! and Brother
John and his assistants, peering down from the roof,
see it,—the flicker of tapers and lamps illumining
a group of white-albed and black-cowled men reverently gathered round and bending over the pale
and placid form of the martyr Edmund.

"Let the modern eye look earnestly on that old
midnight hour in St. Edmund's Bury church, shining
yet on us, ruddy bright, through the depths of

Cuthbert, the bishop beloved of God and venerable amongst men,
and touched each of his limbs and his face and all the members
of the saint which had suffered no corruption though 600 years
had passed, for he had lived a virgin from his childhood, famou
for holiness and miracles, the king asked the archbishop how he
presumed to touch all the members of so great a saint; on which
the man of God replied—'Do not wonder, sire, at this, that with
my consecrated hands I have touched him, for far higher is that
sacrament which day by day I, as other priests, handle on the
altar, the blessed Body of Christ, which is committed to three
orders of priests, deacons and subdeacons.'" ("Anecdota Bedæ,"
&c., edit. Giles, Caxton Soc., 1851, p. 234.)

seven hundred years; and consider mournfully what
our hero worship once was, and what it now is.   .   .   ·
On the whole who knows how to reverence the
body of a man? It is the most reverend phenomenon
under the sun."[1] Yet the modern world often worships
those whose moral life has been questionable and whose
deeds have not always resulted in unmixed good.   Not
so Abbot Samson and his monks in the great church
over the dead martyr endued with Christ's incorruption.
No questionable reverence theirs.   If men may worship
any mortal relics, surely they may worship here.

After the abbot and his monks, Jocelin continues,
had indentified the sacred body and satisfied their
reverence, they replaced the silken and linen cloths
and fastened the lid down again with its sixteen
ancient nails.   Then placing the coffin on its wooden
tray, they conveyed it to its ordinary place.   On the
lid, close to the figure of the angel, they again deposited
the silk bag containing the monk Ailwin's parchment.
By the abbot's order another document, couched
in the following terms, was penned there and then,
and enclosed in the same packet: *The body is covered up again.*

"Anno ab incarnatione Domini M°C. nonagesimo octavo,
abbas Samson, tractus devotione, corpus Sancti Aedmundi
vidit et tetigit, nocte proxima post festum Sanctæ Kather=
inæ bis testibus:"[2] *Nov. 26.*

Then followed the signatures of eighteen monks.
The brethren now enveloped the whole coffin in a
linen wrapper, and over the linen wrapper they
threw a new and costly covering of silk, which
Hubert archbishop of Canterbury gave as an offering
to St. Edmund that very year.   They doubled
lengthways on the stone a linen cloth to keep

---

[1] Carlyle, "Past and Present," pp. 105-107, edit. 1872.

[2] "In the year from the Lord's Incarnation MCXCVIII.,
Abbot Samson upon an impulse of devotion saw and touched
the body of St. Edmund on the night immediately following the
feast of St. Catherine, in presence of these witnesses :—"

the coffin or tray from damp. Then they lifted

Midnight.

the panels of the shrine into their place and fastened them together before the convent assembled for matins.[1]

The grief of the monks who were not present.

On perceiving what had taken place those who had been absent were filled with grief, each saying to himself, "Alas! I was deceived!" Matins over, the abbot called the brethren around him at the foot of the high altar and briefly explained what he had done, alleging that he ought not to and could not invite them all to be present on such an occasion.

The abbot deposes the former keepers and draws up new rules.

Four days later the abbot deposed the keepers of the shrine and the keeper of St. Botulph's, at the same time appointing others and issuing new regulations for the more careful and becoming guardianship of the holy places. The high altar, which had hitherto been used as a receptacle for the irreverent storage of miscellaneous articles, the abbot ordered to be made solid with stone and cement, as well as the space between the shrine

---

[1] The new shrine which Abbot Samson constructed lasted till the sixteenth century, when the desecrators under Henry VIII. described it as "most comberous to efface." The print no. 463 in Knight's "Old England," vol. i., gives some idea of it, and the limning in Lydgate's MS. Harl. 2267 depicts it "as of gold standing on a pedestal of gothic stonework," and sculptured with miniature pillars and arches and pinnacles and crochets. Since the style of both shrine and pedestal was not generally known at the end of the 12th century, Abbot Samson's workmen must have been among the most skilful of their time and the pioneers of the decorated gothic so common fifty years later. After ages, however, may have added the elaborate sculpture and other embellishments. Jocelin confirms this supposition when he tells us, in speaking of the punishment of Geoffrey Rufus, that Abbot Samson laid hold of 200 marks and set them aside for the front of St. Edmund's shrine. This evidently implies further improvements. In fact, Abbot Samson's structure lent itself to any amount of adornment. The gold-plated panels were so thick and massive that they required several strong men to lift them into place, and the base was formed of large solid blocks of marble. Thus substantial foundations existed for goldsmith and sculptor to work upon.

and the altar, so that henceforth he averted any danger from fire through the negligence of the keepers, according to that wise saw :

" Happy is the man whom the peril of others makes wary." [1]

---

§ 15. The Seventh Translation of St. Edmund's Body to France by Louis the Dauphin, Sept. 11, a.d. 1217.

[*Authorities*—Abbot Samson's translation of St. Edmund's glorious and incorrupt body was the sixth, and his verification of it the seventh. The longest interval between any of these translations or verifications was 103 years. The monastic records minutely describe them up to 1198, but after that period they are ominously silent. To pursue the history of the saint it is necessary to turn to French authorities, and principally to Pierre de Caseneuve and the traditions of the church Saint-Sernin at Toulouse. The "Propre de la Basilique Saint-Sernin, publié en 1672 avec trois approbations," distinctly states that the body of St. Edmund "translatum fuit in Gallias a rege Ludovico Octavo," and the approved nocturn lessons now in use at Toulouse assert the same fact. A pamphlet on "The Relics of St. Edmund" by Lord Francis Hervey, printed at the "Standard" office, Bury-St.-Edmund's, 1886, discusses the whole question whether Louis the Dauphin, afterwards Louis VIII., stole the body of St. Edmund and carried it to France. The "monks" of St. Sernin's, whom the learned lord mentions, were really Augustinian canons, and the "certain devout exercises in Latin," the nocturn lessons of the saint's office. Apart from these inaccuracies the pamphlet is interesting as a summary of the French tradition. The history of King John's last days fully bears out the statements of Caseneuve and the tradition of Toulouse. See Hollinshed, edit. of 1577, vol. ii. p. 597 ; Matthew of Paris, Rolls Series, ii. 655 ; Roger of Wendover, Bohn's ed. vol. ii. p. 385 ; Yates' "Hist. of Bury-St.-Edmund's," p. 147, etc.]

In the stirring times of the great struggle for Magna Charta St. Edmund's Bury played a conspicuous part. The tradition of the abbey prompted the monks to side with the king. The ever present body of their royal patron without doubt fostered a feeling of loyalty. In the late reign Abbot Samson had put on his helmet and led his men in person to the siege of Windsor, in order to oppose John's plot to supplant his brother Richard the Lion-Heart. He even excommunicated all in his jurisdiction who favoured the would-be usurper and proclaimed himself ready to go in disguise or in any other way

St. Edmund's Bury and the struggle for Magna Charta.

. [1] Erasmus, referring to Samson, quotes this old monastic saw, "Felix quem faciunt aliena pericula cautum." (" Adag.," 616.)

to search for his rightful sovereign. Abbot and monks just as readily espoused John Lackland's cause when that prince lawfully ascended the throne. In return John confirmed their liberties in the first year of his reign, frequently paid them friendly visits,[1] and, when the monks granted him for life the valuable jewels which his mother Queen Eleanor had bequeathed to the abbey, exempted them from taxation.

The first meeting of the barons at the shrine of St. Edmund, A.D. 1205. But the monks' loyalty did not prevent the barons from assembling in the abbey church in 1205 at the commencement of their constitutional struggle with John. One king in his day had ruled wisely and died manfully in defence of the liberty and religion of his people. Could they have a more fitting patron? Under his protection the primate Hubert and the Earl Marshal could unite the nation against a tyrannical king and show the new spirit of national freedom which the hitherto humbled Church and baronage had assumed.

John's unconstitutional action. The death of Archbishop Hubert of Canterbury, the election of two rival successors, the putting aside of both by Pope Innocent III. and the appointment of Stephen Cardinal Langton followed in quick succession. John defiantly refused to receive the new primate and thus brought the struggle to a head. Innocent was not a pontiff to be thwarted in his government of the Church by a king notorious for faithlessness, tyranny, shamelessness and utter selfishness. He laid the country under an interdict. The churches were closed, the bells silenced; the solemn round of services ceased; chant and organ were hushed throughout the length and breadth of the land. The sacraments were administered privately;

---

[1] Jocelin says: "King John, immediately after his coronation, setting aside all other affairs, came down to St. Edmund, drawn thither by his vow and by devotion." (A.D. 1199.)

the dead received burial without mass or dirge.
Like other churches, St. Edmund's was closed,
the lights around the shrine were extinguished, and
the frequent pilgrimages discontinued.   During the
four years of interdict the disaffection of the king's
subjects grew.   The outraged leaders banded together
in secret conspiracy and at length proclaimed a
crusade under the generalship of Philip of France.
John, in order to gain breathing time, submitted to
the papal legate.   He hoped with the alliance of the
Emperor and the Flemings to crush France and
have clergy and baronage at his mercy.   But France
was victorious in the battle of Bouvines, and John
returned to England to find the barons strongly
united in defence of law and liberty.

A second time St. Edmund figures in the scene. *The second meeting of the Barons at St. Edmund's shrine.*
"The time is favourable," they said, "the feast of
St. Edmund approaches.   Amidst the crowds that
resort to his shrine we may assemble without suspicion."   The undertaking was hazardous.   Some
would perhaps waver, unless their resolution were
clenched by an oath and by the example of Martyr
Edmund.   On the saint's feast, therefore, Nov. 20, *Nov. 20, A.D. 1214.*
1214, the primate met the barons at the shrine, and
in the soft quiet glimmer of the relighted tapers
they, one by one, with slow and measured step,
approached the high altar, and, laying their hand
upon it, vowed to heaven never to sheath the sword
till the king granted the charter which they saw
held unfolded before them. [1]

Seven months later John signed the Magna Charta
on an island in the Thames, in the face of a nation
under arms encamped in the neighbouring meadow
of Runnymede.

---

[1] Abbot Samson had passed to his reward two years previous, and
Hugh of Northwold ruled the abbey.

The war around St. Edmund.

That day, however, did not bring the long-wished-for peace. The war soon broke out again, and the East of England became the field, and St. Edmund's Bury the centre of conflict between John and the barons, and afterwards between the English and French. In the consequent turmoil and confusion St. Edmund's body disappeared. At the beginning of hostilities the barons fortified the saint's town and abbey, an action which John deeply resented in a letter to the monks dated St. Alban's, the 18th day of December, 1215. Yet, when he let loose his foreign hordes under the Earl of Salisbury to burn and destroy Norfolk and Suffolk, he reverently spared both town and abbey.

The French invasion.

The barons, driven to despair by the king's dogged resistance, a second time sought the aid of France. Philip Augustus, glad of an opportunity of punishing John for his repeated treachery and crimes, quickly despatched Louis the Dauphin with a considerable army to their help. While in England this Louis, the father of St. Louis, and afterwards King Louis VIII., surnamed Le Gros, robbed the nation of Edmund's body. Before the war brought him to East Anglia, Louis received the homage of the barons in St. Paul's, and with it the support of the country. But his soldiers proved a greater scourge than John's mercenaries; and a reported design on the part of the French to supplant the English nobles took the soul out of Louis' cause. At the same time occurred John's disaster in crossing the Wash, his sudden death and the coronation at Gloucester of his son Henry III., then only ten years old. The whole sympathy of the nation went out towards the innocent boy-king, and even Louis was induced to make a short truce. On his return from France at Easter time, 1217, hostilities recommenced with the march of the confederates from London to the relief of Montsorel.

The French soldiers rob the churches of their relics.

In this expedition the French freely indulged in their well-known propensity for stealing the relics of saints from churches.[1] Roger of Wendover[2] thus describes their conduct: "On Monday the 30th of April, the wicked French robbers, sparing neither churches nor cemeteries, came to St. Alban's. They spared the abbey except from supplying food and drink, because the abbot, on a former occasion, paid Louis eighty marks to save it. At the town of Redbourn they pillaged the church of the body of St. Amphibalus. They also dared to take the relics of the saints from above the high altar. One among them seized on a silver and gold ornamented cross, which contained a piece of our Lord's cross, and he hid it in his wicked bosom. Louis with his army arrived at Dunstable,[3] and there passed the night, and next day went on to Montsorel, where he raised the siege." From Montsorel an army of 600 knights and 20,000 Frenchmen under the Count of Perche made for Lincoln. According to their custom they pillaged all the churches and cemeteries on the march.

They purloin the body of St. Amphibalus.

Louis himself did not go to Lincoln, but "with a powerful host," says Matthew of Paris,[4] "he rode

[1] The relics of saints have always been regarded as the common property of the faithful. Hence they do not fall under the vow of poverty in religious orders, and, apart from their reliquaries, it has not been considered a sin to purloin them. On this principle St. Benedict's body was taken, it is said, from Monte Cassino in troublous days, and carried to Fleury on the Loire. The crusaders, no doubt with the laudable intention of rescuing what was holy from infidel hands, robbed saints' shrines without remorse and enriched the West with the bodies of the most illustrious saints of the East. The French in the middle ages were notorious relic-stealers.

[2] Bohn's edition, vol. ii. p. 385.

[3] In Bedfordshire.

[4] Rolls Series, ii. 655.

Louis le Gros
makes for East
Anglia and St.
Edmund's
shrine.

towards the East coast, and miserably despoiled the towns and villages of Essex, Suffolk and Norfolk." The two former ravages by the Earl of Salisbury and by King John, just before his death, left the French prince very little spoil. The patrimony of St. Edmund, however, remained untouched, and both curiosity and devotion attracted him to the spot most memorable throughout the struggle. It is said that, warned by the example of the abbot of St. Alban's, Hugh of Northwold [1] saved his monastery and the shrine of the martyr by a bribe, but the Dauphin, fearful of the fate of the sacrilegious and filled with the traditional dread of St. Edmund's anger, had no intention of violating either. No scruple, however, withheld him from taking away the sacred body of the martyr himself. On the contrary, every motive urged him to it. The monks had returned among the first to their allegiance to John. They had always secretly favoured his cause. They now showed the deepest pity for his young son and successor. Why should he not punish them by exacting the relics of their patron as his price for sparing the abbey? The nation, too, after inviting him to the kingdom and throne, had withdrawn its adherence. He had no hesitation in avenging himself by taking away to France the most precious national treasure, the traditional protector of the people's rights.

He abstracts the
martyr's body
from the shrine,

The monks, eighty only in number, were helpless to resist save by protest. Probably none, or a few only, knew of the intended spoliation. The soldiery held the town at their mercy, so that the burgesses could make no defence even if they became aware

---

[1] Hugh became bishop of Ely. At the foot of his tomb in Ely cathedral is carved the history of St. Edmund, a sad and loving testimony to the loss which the abbey sustained under his reign

of the robbery. Louis found it a comparatively easy task to raise the "crest," or slanting roof-like covering, to take out a panel of the shrine and thus abstract the coffin, which as so much plunder his men carried out of the church without creating surprise. "Crest" and panel were carefully replaced, and the shrine left apparently as before. Not an offering to the saint was touched.

Meanwhile William the earl marshal had defeated the united army of Frenchmen and confederate barons and driven them from Lincoln. The Count of Perche fell in battle, and his followers fled. The English only pretended to pursue[1] and allowed them to make their way to London with their plunder, which included the body of St. Gilbert. Louis marched from St. Edmund's Bury to cover their retreat, and the joint armies gathered within the walls of London which received a second time the body of St. Edmund. Almost at once the treaty of Lambeth was negociated, and the grand marshal conducted the strangers out of the country. With them they carried into France much spoil and the relics of many saints, but of all their treasures they held none more precious than the body of St. Edmund the king and martyr. Little did they dream, however, that they were fulfilling the prophecy of the widow of Rome by spreading devotion to his name far and wide.

And carries it to France.

---

[1] Roger of Wendover, Bohn's edit.

§ 16.   The Eighth Translation of St. Edmund's Body
to the Basilica of Saint-Sernin, Toulouse, A.D. 1219.

[*Authorities*—The learned Chanoine le Douais, Professeur à l'école supérieure de
Théologie de Toulouse, edited in 1886 the "Inventaire de Saint Sernin de
Toulouse, 1489," (Paris: Alphonse Picard, Rue Bonaparte), referred to by
Caseneuve. This "Inventaire" contains the following passage : "Item in
tribus vasis lapideis marmoris, unum supra aliud, sunt corpora quatuor
coronatorum et Sancti Aymundi regis Angliæ quondam. Quorum in vase
inferiore sunt corpora Claudii et Nicostrati, in secundo vase sunt corpora
Simphoriani et Castoris, et in superiore vase corpus dicti beati Aymundi."
"Likewise in three marble sepulchres one above the other, lie the bodies of
the four coronati and of St. Edmund formerly king of England. The lowest
contains the bodies of Claudius and Nicostratus ; the second the bodies of
Simphorian and Castor, the top one the body of the said blessed Edmund."
A second "Inventaire," brought to light by the same learned canon and
drawn up as early as 1246, names only the moveables and immoveables in the
basilica, and therefore omits all mention of the body of St. Edmund or of any
other saint. De la Faille's "Annales de Toulouse" contain no information
on the subject. Rapin (Hist., edit. 1724, vol. i. p. 299) merely notices the
finding of the body at Toulouse and no more. The cathedral of Seville
possesses inexhaustible MSS. from which might probably be collected the full
history of St. Edmund's translation to Toulouse, but they are unarranged,
and the necessary search would take a life-time. The prefecture of Toulouse
possesses many ancient maps, bulls and parchments taken from Saint-
Sernin's, but Sir Antoine du Bourg, the highest authority on the history of
the great basilica, in a letter on St. Edmund's relics to the author, says
that in his researches he has found no stronger evidence past or present than
the records now in the archives of Saint-Sernin itself, copies of which have
been obtained for the compilation of the following sections.]

St Edmund's
body saved from
desecration.

With the scenes of the so-called reformation before
our eyes, the presence of St. Edmund's body in
France [1] is a subject of congratulation.   Better far

---

[1] *The French Tradition.*—Caseneuve in his "Vie de St. Edmond,"
speaks of the translation of the body of St. Edmund to France
and its possession by the Church of Toulouse as follows :

"The church of Saint-Sernin for many centuries has possessed
the precious relics of the glorious martyr St. Edmund, precious
even among those of so many apostles, martyrs, confessors, and
virgins which have acquired for it the glory of being one of the
most holy places on the earth.   We understand that these relics of
St. Edmund the king were presented to this venerable church by
Louis VIII., the father of St. Louis.

"Divine Providence, foreseeing that heresy would within a few
centuries separate England from the unity of the Church, as
nature has separated it from the rest of the world, deigned to save
the bones of this illustrious martyr from the profanation to which
those of so many other saints were exposed.

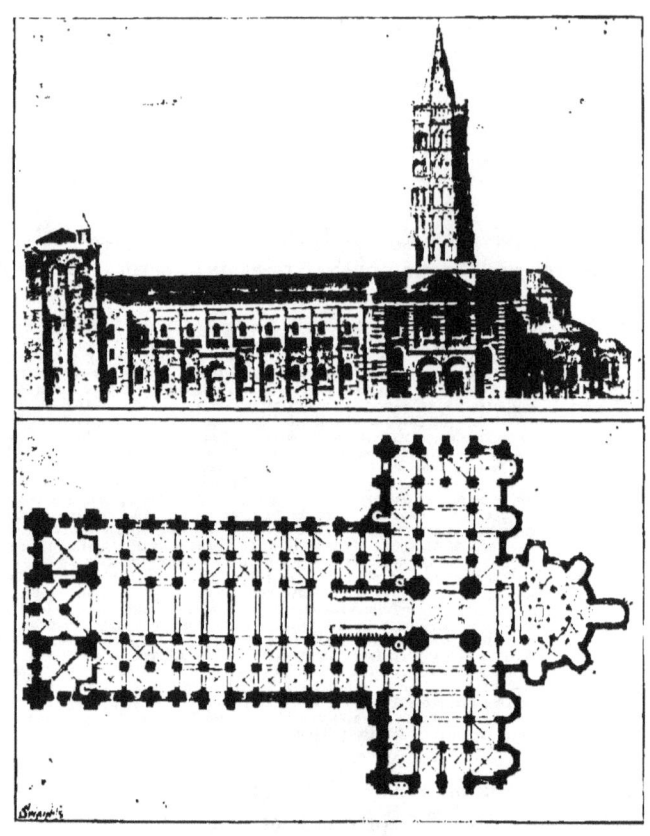

The Basilica of Saint Sernin

AT TOULOUSE.

that his bones should be held in honour and respect
in a foreign land, than be in his own, hidden away
unknown and unworshipped, like St. Cuthbert's in

"Louis VIII., having been elected king of England on the
deposition of King John, nicknamed Lackland, was for some time
engaged in war in that kingdom, and Matthew Paris states
that his army pillaged all the churches of the county of Suffolk.
Among them, as I have before remarked, was the abbey church
in which rested the body of St. Edmund. In those days Christian
soldiers gloried in committing the pious theft of taking away the
relics of the saints and transporting them to their own country,
and it was in consequence of this custom that we have acquired
part of the relics formerly belonging to the churches of the Levant.
It is probable that the French obtained the body of St. Edmund in
this way, and Louis VIII., on coming to besiege the town of
Toulouse a short time after his return from England (as everybody
knows), presented the relics of St. Edmund to the church Saint-
Sernin, where he lodged during the siege, it being at that time
outside the walls. . . .

"As a matter of fact the body of the martyr St. Edmund, king
of England, is mentioned in the inventories of the relics of Saint-
Sernin about 200 years ago, and, from the time when the army of
Louis VIII. plundered the church of St. Edmund, the English
chroniclers, who never lost an opportunity of signalising the
miracles wrought by that saint in his own church, make no
further mention of them, and by their silence, as I am convinced,
tacitly allow that his body had been taken away and translated
elsewhere." This statement is confirmed by the "Procès Verbal,"
1644 (Cahier G, Folio 70) of the Archives of Saint-Sernin ; by the
"Propre de la Basilique Saint-Sernin," published in 1672 with
three approbations ; and by the "Proper" now used at Saint-
Sernin for the feast of St. Edmund with the approval of the Holy
See. Mr. Yates, an author thoroughly acquainted with monastic
records, in his "History of Bury" admits the tradition, though he
states it inaccurately. The "Monasticon" follows Casencuve and
Yates. Rapin in his History of England (edit. 1724, vol. i. p. 290),
while unable to account for the presence of the body at
Toulouse, acknowledges it in the following words : "Je ne sai par
quelle avanture ce corps a été transporté à Toulouse, où on prétend
l'avoir découvert en 1667."—"I know not by what accident this
body (of St. Edmund) was translated to Toulouse, where it is
alleged to have been discovered in 1667." (Correctly 1644).

The following works contain no reference to the body of St.

Durham, or cast to the winds like St. Thomas of
Canterbury's, or left silent and cold, with no lighted
taper or kneeling pilgrim to do them reverence, like

Edmund : "Histoire Générale de Languedoc," &c., par Dom
Claude de Vic et Dom Vaissete, O.S.B. ; "Hist. Générale de
l'Eglise de Toulouse," &c., par M. l'Abbé Salvan ; "Histoire des
Institutions, &c., de Toulouse," par M. le Chevalier Du Mège ;
"Hist. des Evêques et Archevêques de Toulouse," par M. l'Abbé
Cayre ; "Hist. de la ville de Toulouse," &c., par M. J. Raynal,
1759 ; "Hist. des Comtes de Tolose," par M. Guillaume Catel, 1623 ;
"Histoire Tolosaine," par Antoine Noguier Tolosain, 1559, which
only goes to 1218. M. Raymond Daydé (Tolose, 1661), in his
"Histoire de St.-Sernin, ou l'incomparable trésor de son Eglise
Abbatiale de Tolose," 1661, gives on p. 83, "Le corps et Teste de S.
Edmond Roy d'Angleterre, Martyr." "Les Gestes des Tolosains
et d'autres nations," &c., composées, &c., par Nicolas Bertrand
(Tolose, 1555), contains in the list of the bodies of saints : "Item, le
corps de Sainct Aymōd cōfesseur du Roy d' Angleterre, item
le corps de Sainct Gilbert, Abbé."

The evidence in support of the Toulouse tradition is to most minds
conclusive. First, the whole history of the period between 1205
and 1219 accords with it. The prominence of St. Edmund's Bury
in the dispute ; the friendly feeling which always existed between
John and the monks ; their known sympathy for his son, marked
the abbey as a fit object of spoil. Matthew Paris' testimony as
to the pillage of the churches of Norfolk and Suffolk, and Roger of
Wendover's as to the practice of the French soldiery of stealing
the bodies and relics of saints, a practice extensively carried on
in the East, amount to all but a definite statement that they
purloined St. Edmund's body. The date of Louis' quitting
England and his sojourn in the abbey Saint-Sernin, and the fame
of that basilica as a sanctuary for relics perfectly fit in with the
received tradition. Secondly, the ancient inventories mentioned
by Caseneuve, and especially the one of 1489 which is still extant,
are proof positive of the authenticity of the Toulouse relics.
Probably the latter inventory was a copy of an earlier one. In
any case the body of St. Edmund must have been in the crypt
before the inventory was made. Thirdly, the chain of evidence
from 1489 is unbroken : the inscription on the stone sepulchre ; the
cessation of the plague in 1631 ; the translation of the relics in
1644 ; the authentication in 1807 ; the opening of the shrine by
Cardinal Desprez in 1867, bring us to our own times. Fourthly, the
silence meanwhile of the chronicles and registers of St. Edmund's

St. Edward's in the now uncatholic and desolate sanctuary of Westminster.

Little more than a year had elapsed after the

abbey strongly argues that the body was not there. From the saint's martyrdom to 1198 no period of one hundred years elapsed without some verification or translation of the incorrupt body being chronicled, but, although according to the "Monasticon" the existing chartularies of St. Edmund's Abbey are probably more numerous than those of any other in England, all researches up to the present have failed to discover any record of the martyr's body having been seen or moved from Abbot Samson's time to the dissolution of the monastery in 1539, a period of 341 years. At the dissolution Cromwell's commissioners found the body absent, as we may judge by their silence concerning it in the following extracts from their letters, the originals of which are preserved in the Cottonian Library (see Dugdale's "Mon.," Nums. xliv. xlv. under St. Edmundsbury). The first is signed

John Williams.
Richard Pollard.
Phylyp Parys.
John Smyth,

and reads :

"Pleaseth it your Lordship to be advertised that we have been at Saynt Edmondsbury, where we found a riche shryne which was very comberous to deface. We have taken in the seyd monastery in golde and silver 5000 markes and above, besyds as well a riche crosse with emeralds, as also dyvers and sundry stones of grete value," &c., &c.

The second is from a letter by John ap Rice : "Amongst the relics we founde moche vanitie and supersticion, as the coles that S. Lawrence was tosted withal, the parings of St. Edmund's naylls," &c. Weever likewise in his enumeration of the relics of the abbey church observes absolute silence with regard to St. Edmund's body. This two-fold negative evidence proves that it was not at St Edmund's Bury at the time of the dissolution.

Fifthly, a story in the "Registrum Rubrum" and an extract from an old MS. positively imply the absence of the body. The story of the monk's dream is given in the "Registrum Rubrum" as occurring in Abbot Bernham's time (1335-1361). A certain monk dreamt that he saw St. Edmund leave his shrine and then return to it. The story itself is of trifling consequence, but the conclusion drawn from it by the monk is not so. He was terrified for fear of a speedy fulfilment

removal of St. Edmund's body from its English shrine when political events called Louis the Dauphin to the south of France. For a long time the fanatical and

---

of an old prophecy that St. Edmund, after returning to Beodricsworth a third time, would abandon it for Hoxne. "Post quam tertio Beatus Edmundus cornu suum flaverit, relinquens Boedericsworth rediret ad Hoxne."—"After Blessed Edmund shall thrice have blown his horn, leaving Bury he will return to Hoxne." The monks evidently knew the prophecy and its reference to a third return of St. Edmund to Bury, where it is implied he was not then. St. Edmund first entered Bury in 903, and a second time, when Ailwin brought the holy body back from London in 1013. Both entrances were celebrated by a concourse of people and with great pomp, or in other words, "with sound of trumpet." But a third blowing of trumpets was expected, that is, a triumphant return from Toulouse, where his body in the time of Abbot Bernham had rested for 114 years.

In the quotation in the "Monasticon" (vol. iii. p. 135) from a MS. of a date say not earlier than Abbot Curteys' time (1429-1446), the words "incorruptum ipsius corpus requiescit humatum "—"*his body rests entombed without decay*,"—can only indicate the stone sepulchre at Toulouse, for the word "humatum" would never be used of the shrine at St. Edmund's Bury. In fact, considering that in 1400 Abbot Cratfield took £30 from the shrine to defray the expenses of his papal election, a few, at least, knew, forty years before, that St. Edmund's body was not there.

Sixthly and lastly, the verification of the relics at Toulouse confirms all previous evidence. When the body was authenticated, the flesh had indeed decayed, but the bones of the entire skeleton remained, except one, viz., the radius, a bone of the fore-arm. Now this bone is the only relic of St. Edmund's body which the later records of his abbey mention. It was preserved by the monks and publicly venerated, notably at the visit of Henry VI. to the abbey in 1433. Its recorded and unchallenged existence in England establishes the authenticity of the rest of the body in France.

It is objected that in the first place the diplomas of aggregation and other documents refer to the presence of the body, although there is no actual record of it. The Benedictines from the time of the holy Patriarch St. Benedict have had the practice of giving the habit, with letters of aggregation or fraternity, to distinguished benefactors lay and cleric, and thus admitting them to the order and to a community of prayers. For instance, John Duke of

immoral sect of the Albigenses had agitated that portion of the kingdom, and their violent attitude now actually threatened its dismemberment.

Lancaster in 1392 and the Earl of March and Ulster in 1415 were so received. The diplomas or forms in use at St. Edmund's Bury for affiliating members to the order still exist. In one of the time of Abbot Curteys the letter of fraternity accorded to William Paston contains the following words : " For the devotion which you have to God and to our monastery, in which the most glorious king and martyr St. Edmund *reposes in the body and without decay*, we receive you," etc. (Yates, p. 157). This evidence would be very strong did it not rest merely on the wording of an old formula which was probably retained unchanged after 1219 on account of its antiquity.

In Pat. 41, Henry III. (A.D. 1257), a charter granting custody of the barony of the abbot of St. Edmund, occur the words : "Cujus corpus requiescit ibidem "—" *whose body rests in the same place.*" ("Monasticon," vol. iii. p. 160).

Again (ibid. p. 162) we read the directions regarding the tapers to be burnt on St. Edmund's feast "circa corpus "—" *round his body.*" No doubt phrases like these were used in isolated cases from custom or by an individual ignorant of the actual fact.

In "Bury Wills and Inventories," Caxton Publ., p. 13, vol. 49, occurs the bequest : "Item lego feretro Sti Edmundi monile aureum cum figura cerui ipssima," by which Lady Sharedelowe (A.D. 1457) bequeaths to the shrine of St. Edmund a golden necklace with its valuable pendant of lapis-lazuli, but no deduction can be drawn from this except that the testatrix knew not of the absence of the body, or probably knowing it, willed to honour the place in which it had lain.

Referring to Ailwin's return to St. Edmondsbury, Richard of Cirencester writes (A.D. 1337): " Then with the greatest honour he [St. Edmund] is laid in his old resting place, Bury-St.-Edmund's, where by the favour of God even to this day he ceases not to plead the cause of those who devoutly seek him." Here mention is distinctly made of the " power of St. Edmund's intercession at St. Edmund's Bury " even " *to this day ;* " but the fact of the body being there is markedly omitted, so that the passage rather favours the French tradition than militates against it.

Secondly, pilgrimages and even royal visits continued to be made to the shrine during the whole period of the supposed absence of St. Edmund's body. Thus King Henry III., Edward I. and Queen Eleanor, Edward II., Edward III., Richard II. and

Prince Louis hastened southwards to quell the rebel-
lion and particularly to dislodge the enemy from
Toulouse. He carried with him the relics of many

Henry VI. paid their devotions at the shrine. Lydgate's magnificent manuscript depicts the last-named king kneeling before the
shrine. Was not the body there? The pilgrimages continued
until the dissolution, and at the close of the last century Cook
Row (now Abbey-gate-street), where the pilgrims used to take
their meals, still retained signs of its original character. Did the
nation worship at an empty shrine?

It is answered that the absence of the body would not affect the
devotion of the people to St. Edmund. That devotion had become
ingrafted in the habits of the nation. The pilgrimage was so
ancient and traditional, the shrine itself so renowned, the venerable
abbey-church so full of memorials of the saint and of the shrines of
other servants of God, that the custom of journeying to St.
Edmund's Bury continued unchanged. In a similar manner
Hoxne was a favourite pilgrimage for centuries after St. Edmund's
body was removed from it, just as Becket's Crown, Durham
Cathedral, Lindisfarne or Iona now-a-days, although the bones of
their saints are gone. A higher example is the sepulchre of our
Lord, or the spot where the cross was found, for Catholic devotion
honours not only the holy but the spots hallowed by the holy.

Thirdly, the decay of the body found at Toulouse seems to tell
against the French tradition. St. Edmund's was one of the five
well-known incorrupt bodies of Catholic England. "There are
altogether five which I have known of," writes Malmesbury,
"though the residents in many places boast of more; Saints
Etheldreda and Werburga, virgins; King Edmund; Archbishop
Elphege; Cuthbert the ancient father; these with skin and flesh
unwasted and their joints flexile appear to have a certain vital
warmth about them and to be merely sleeping." In our own day
St. Catherine at Bologna, St. John of Prague in Bohemia, St.
Zita at Lucca, St. Teresa at Avignon, St. Francis Xavier at
Goa, and nearer home the hand of Father Arrowsmith, are
instances of incorruption similar to St. Edmund's. In the
year 1198, three hundred and twenty-eight years after the
royal martyr's death, Abbot Samson found the body perfect and
undecayed. That is an incontestable fact. Abbot Samson's
"robust and upright character" would not have stooped to decep-
tion. Honest Jocelin wrote of what he saw without suspicion of
imposture. Mr. Rokewood, the editor of the Latin text of
Jocelin's Chronicle, and blunt Carlyle, who read it and wrote

saints, and notably the bodies of St. Edmund and St.
Gilbert, that through their intercession the God of
armies might bless his enterprise.   On arriving

---

of it with undisguised admiration, believed the historical evidence
before them.   Only the translator of Jocelin's Chronicle, a certain
Mr. Tomkins, with an impudent curtness and without producing
any evidence to support his case, denies probability, possibility and
continuous tradition, gives the lie direct to abbot, chronicler, editor
and commentator, and peremptorily asserts : " There is not the
slightest doubt but that this body was a supposititious corpse and
perhaps not the first " (p. 47, note).

The difficulty however still remains.   When the archbishop of
Toulouse, Charles de Montchal, opened the stone sepulchre upon
which St. Edmund the martyr's name was inscribed, he found a
skeleton only.   The possession of the radius or arm-bone at old
St. Edmund's Bury points to the decay taking place years before
the dissolution, but not even Caseneuve attempts to explain
it.   The incorruption of the soulless body is, however, only
an extraordinary manifestation of the Divine Wisdom and
Omnipotence, and like other miracles its continuance or cessation surpasses human calculation.   But who can say that the
decay of St. Edmund's body is not a lesser evil than its total
destruction, or that there is not a certain congruity in its being
deprived of its prerogative of incorruption at a time when it was
deprived of its honour by being taken to a strange country and laid
in a neglected tomb ?   Again, if Mr. Raine's contention is true, and
the skeleton which he discovered in May, 1827, in Durham cathedral
was St. Cuthbert's and not that of Bishop Frithestan or some
other bishop, then we have another instance of an undoubtedly
incorrupt body decaying.   Could the bodies of St. Etheldreda or
Archbishop Elphege be exhumed, perhaps further light might be
thrown upon this question.   The hand of St. Etheldreda, which
is reverently preserved at St. Dominic's Convent, Stone, Staffs., is
still incorrupt, but the flesh is gradually perishing.   Nature is
thus allowed by Divine Providence to reassert itself.   St. Edmund's
body, preserved at Bury with care and reverence, likewise remained incorrupt for the glory of the saint and the edification of
the faithful, and yet was afterwards allowed to crumble to dust
after exposure to a long march over rough roads, in a rumbling
thirteenth century military waggon, and after years of comparative neglect, for its incorruption was no longer necessary for its
special glory and renown, since there were no more pilgrims as
of old, and no longer a nation's reverence and homage.

before the gates of Toulouse he took up his quarters in the cloisters of the basilica of Saint Saturninus, or Sernin, which at that time stood outside the walls, and the body of St. Edmund was placed for the time being within its sacred precincts.

The basilica which thus providentially received St. Edmund's remains was renowned throughout Christendom for its treasures and antiquity. From the earliest times it has enjoyed the name and rights of a basilica. Two early bishops of Toulouse, St. Sylvus and St. Exuperus, erected it in the fourth century to receive the body of the martyred prelate St. Saturninus. It was rebuilt in the eleventh century in the full majesty of the Roman style, with a vastness of conception and a simplicity of detail which inspires a feeling rather of awe than of admiration. Pope Urban II. consecrated it in 1096. Its abbots, who presided over a chapter of Augustinian canons, became by royal decree the hereditary protectors of the university of Toulouse and ranked amongst the highest prelates of the land. In the war with the Albigenses they often stepped in as mediators between the two parties. By their permission Count Raymund VI. held the common assembly of citizens of Toulouse within the impregnable basilica, at the foot of whose walls the redoubtable Simon de Montfort was slain on June the 25th, 1218.

The basilica was still more famous for its numerous relics of saints. Over its portals stands the inscription: "Non est in toto sanctior orbe locus"—" *There is no spot more holy in the whole earth,*"—for it is the third richest church in the world for relics. Two holy bishops raised it over the grave of their predecessor. Afterwards Charlemagne, desiring to repair the injury which he had inflicted by the temporary removal of the body of St. Saturninus, promised to give it a court as numerous and as illustrious as that of St. Denis at Paris. He kept his promise, and the basilica received the bodies of six apostles which Pope Leo III. had presented to him. On an old tapestry which represents this benefaction a distich runs as follows :

> "Sex vexit hæc rediens Hispanis magnus ab oris
>   Carlus apostolici corpora sancta gregis." [1]

In the course of ages the crusaders from the town further enriched the great church with the bodies and relics of saints brought from the East, and popes and kings vied with each other in adding to its treasury, till the bones of sixty saints seemed to satisfy even the proverbial love of the Toulousians for pious relics.

Prince Louis, emulous of Charlemagne, and grateful to the canons for their hospitality and prayers, now offered to the basilica the bodies of St. Edmund and St. Gilbert. He knew no church more worthy by its sanctity and age to receive the body of the royal martyr or to replace the stately abbey church from which he had taken it. Accordingly the Augustinians laid St. Edmund to rest in the crypt beneath the great basilica where Pope St. Urban had preached the first crusade and St. Bernard the second, under the vaulted roof which was ringing with the burning words of St. Dominic, in the company of the apostles, near St. Agatha and St. Lucy, to be numbered in future with the martyrs St. Stephen and St. George, St. Blasius and St. Christopher, in the calendar of Saint-Sernin.

It receives the body of St. Edmund.

---

[1] "Charles the Great, returning from the borders of Spain, brought hither these sacred relics, six bodies of the Apostolic band."

The crypt of
Saint-Sernin. The crypt which received the English martyr was
rich in the bodies of saints, but they were hidden
away in unrecognised tombs. The invasions of the
Vandals, of the Alans, Sueves and Visigoths prevented the exhuming of the bodies in the early
centuries, so that even the remains of St. Saturninus
and the precious relics brought thither by Charlemagne lay buried for generations, marked indeed
with their names, but so hastily put away that only
the tradition of their presence remained. The Albi-
A.D. 1258. gensian troubles caused St. Edmund's body to be
treated in a similar manner. Forty years later, however, the crypt of the basilica became too small to
contain all the relics of saints which had accumulated in the course of centuries, and the canons
commenced the present crypt. As the work proceeded, they searched for, exhumed and translated
the sacred bodies, in some instances enshrining them
in jewelled reliquaries of gold or silver,[1] in others
merely verifying the bodies, and then placing them
in sepulchres of stone or marble. They seem to have
St. Edmund's
tomb, A.D., 1489. taken this latter course with the body of our saint, for
according to the inventory of 1489 the body of
"Saint Edmund once king of England" rested in a

---

[1] Thus on the 6th of September, 1258, the body of St. Satur-
ninus was searched for and found in the vault in which St.
Exuperus had placed it. It was removed tomb and all to the
spot in the east apse where the marble shrine now canopies it.
About the same time the bodies of SS. Sylvus, Hilary and
Honoratus were merely exhumed. In 1386 the relics of St.
James the Greater were translated to a rich reliquary. Those of
St. Jude and St. Susanna of Babylon were exhumed on the 25th
of January, 1511; those of St. Papoul, St. Philip, St. James the
Less, and St. Gilbert of Sempringham on the 24th of March,
1507; those of St. Exuperus on the 13th of April, 1586, and those
of St. Barnabas, St. Edmund, and St. Raymond of Toulouse in
1607, 1644, and 1656. By the end of the 17th century all the
relics had been thus translated and enshrined.

plain marble tomb, the uppermost of three, all similar
in character, the lowest of which contained the bones
of SS. Claudius and Nicostratus, and the second those
of SS. Simphorian and Castor.

---

§ 17.   The Ninth Translation of St. Edmund's Body.

[*Authorities*—The archives of Saint-Sernin, Toulouse contain—Cahier G, folio 70—
the " Procès Verbal (A.D. 1644) sur l'élévation du corps et saints reliques du
glorieux Saint Edmond martyr Roi d'Angleterre," etc., which incidentally
refers to a ninth translation or removal of St. Edmund's relics between 1489
and 1644.   For the contemporary history of the great church see the " Monographie de la Basilique Saint-Sernin de Toulouse," par S. Manant ; Toulouse :
Imprimerie Vialelle et Cie., 1879.]

The enlargement of the crypt of Saint-Sernin and
the gradual exhuming and translating of the bodies
of the saints made room for the more reverent keeping of St. Edmund's remains.   Accordingly they were
removed before the seventeenth century into a small
arched and vaulted recess, in the west corner of which
the sarcophagus was erected and covered with a large
stone like an altar-stone.   On the front of this tomb
an inscription was cut in big thick letters which
ran thus ·

St. Edmund's
second tomb
at Saint-Sernin.

ICI REPOSE LE VENERABLE CORPS DE SAINT-EDMOND
ROY D'ANGLETERRE.[1]

---

[1] " Here reposes the venerable body of Saint Edmund King of
England."

---

§ 18. THE TENTH TRANSLATION OF ST. EDMUND'S BODY
BY HIS GRACE CHARLES DE MONTCHAL, ARCHBISHOP OF
TOULOUSE, A.D. 1644.

[*Authorities*—A paper from the archives of Saint-Sernin on the "Translations de
    ces Reliques" in Nov., 1644, supplements the authorities referred to in the
    last section and gives a full description of this gorgeous and solemn ceremony
    connected with St. Edmund's memory. The late Father Lazenby, S.J., of
    Bury-St.-Edmund's, kindly supplied copies of the "Procès Verbal" and of the
    "Translation de ces Reliques" for this work, which he obtained through the
    kindness of the late Father Ramière, S.J. Further details may be gathered from
    a small volume entitled "L'élévation des reliques du glorieux martyr Saint
    Edmond roy d'Angleterre, etc., etc., ... faite par messire Charles de
    Montchal archevesque de Toulouse, . . . pour l'accomplissement d'un
    vœu de ladite ville.   Ensemble l'extrait des sermons du dit archevesque et de
    Mgr. l'evesque de S. Papoul."   Toulouse, 1645, 4to. The "Livre de prières
    à l'usage de ceux qui ont la dévotion de visiter les sacrées reliques dans
    l'insigne Basilique de Saint-Sernin, &c.," printed in 1762, gives an engraving, on
    p. 7 of the preface, representing the altar on which St. Edmund's body rested
    during the octave of the translation, and, on p. 82, an account of their transla-
    tion itself. See also the small brochure, "Les Corps Saints de l'insigne Basili-
    que Saint-Saturnin de Toulouse," Toulouse: Imprimerie Saint-Cyprien, 1881.]

The plague at
Toulouse in 1631.
During the four years 1628,-29,-30,-31, the justice
and mercy of God afflicted the city of Toulouse with
a plague which raged so virulently that the streets
of the large and populous city soon became silent
and forsaken and the majority of the houses unin-
habited. All those human succours which proved
efficacious on former occasion failed on this, and
the people in despair looked about for some Moses
to stand between them and the anger of God. They
had ever regarded the relics of the saints treasured
up in their great basilica as pledges of God's favour.
Carried in procession through the streets, they had
more than once stayed the avenging Hand. The
Toulousians now determined to appeal to the Almighty in the name of His servant Edmund to help
them, as He had helped the people of old for the
sake of Abraham and Isaac and Jacob.

For this end the capitouls or consuls [1] of Toulouse, *The vow of the Toulousians to St. Edmund, August 12, 1631.* on the 12th of August, 1631, publicly vowed in the name of the people to bring forth St. Edmund's body from the obscurity in which it had lain for years and, at the expense of the town, to present for its enshrinement a silver reliquary richly enchased, as a memorial to posterity of the cessation of the plague, for which they petitioned through the intercession of the blessed king and martyr of England. The plague suddenly ceased its ravages, the saint renewing in a strange land the miracles discontinued in his own. Thus it pleased God to glorify once more his royal champion.

For thirteen years the desolation and poverty of *The fulfilment of the vow in 1644.* the town delayed the fulfilment of the citizens' vow. In 1644, however, the lord abbot of Saint-Sernin, Monseigneur Défiat, authorised his vicar-general, John Jerome Duthil, to call the attention of the chapter as well as of the principal citizens to the subject of the vow. On the 22nd of April the canons of *April 22.* the basilica unanimously resolved on the translation.

They undertook to make the ceremony as solemn and imposing as possible, and one of their number, Pierre de Caseneuve, wrote a life of the saint in preparation for it. On the 10th of July the canons *July 10.* invited the archbishop of Toulouse, Monseigneur Charles de Montchal, to preside at the translation, saving the rights of their abbot. The archbishop consented, and a document with the saving clause inserted was drawn up and signed. His Grace further arranged to enter upon the examination of the martyr's relics after vespers on the following Saturday, July the 16th. The register in the archives of Saint-Sernin describes the opening of the tomb as follows:

---

[1] A title held by the magistrates of Toulouse, and a reminiscence of the connection of their city with ancient Rome.

Q

The opening of
St. Edmund's
tomb, July 16.

"When the said 16th day of the above-mentioned month of July arrived in the year one thousand six hundred and forty-four, the above-mentioned chapter deputed two canons, Monsieur de Mervilla and Monsieur de Parade, to attend upon the archbishop in his archiepiscopal palace and to conduct him to our church. On his approach, Messieurs the Canons d'Armaing and de Cambolas de Touzin and de Lassur offered him holy water at the door of the basilica and led him to the sacristy of the Holy Bodies. There we found assembled M. Jean de Bertier, lord of Montrabé, the king's councillor and first president of the Toulouse parliament; M. Jacques de Maussac, councillor and dean of the said parliament; M. Jean George de Caulis, king's councillor and chief judge in the seneschal's court at Toulouse; MM. Antoine de l'Aquavigne, George Falaire, barristers; Jean Virazil, Valive Toulé, Rollaund Fauré and d'Oubiea, citizens of Toulouse, and capitouls for the current year; M. Bartholomew Sixte, priest and sacristan of the Holy Bodies, together with the regent-treasurers and officials entrusted with the care of the Holy Bodies.

"Word was given to the sacristan to lead the way to the place in which the body of blessed Edmund, king of England, rested.

"Descending into the crypt of the said Holy Bodies, we proceeded to conduct his Grace the archbishop to a small arched and vaulted recess, in the west corner of which stood a sarcophagus covered with a large stone like an altar-stone. On the front of this tomb an inscription in big thick letters ran thus:

HERE REPOSES THE VENERABLE BODY OF SAINT
EDMUND KING OF ENGLAND.

"For the opening of the tomb, William Bagilet, custodian of the Holy Bodies, now presented a hammer decked with flowers, which we handed to the archbishop, requesting him in the name of our lord abbot Défiat and of the venerable chapter of the basilica, to deign to proceed with the authentication. Then his Grace, taking the hammer, struck the stone three different times; whereupon, by our orders, the masons set to work to open the tomb.

"Under an archway let into the wall on the other side of the same recess, we now took the opportunity of pointing out to the archbishop the two stone sepulchres containing the bodies of SS. Claudius, Nicostratus and others.

"By this time the masons had raised the stone slab which covered St. Edmund's tomb. At once Messieurs the Canons Doberal, Mervilla and de Parade placed themselves near the coffin, so as to prevent any one touching the holy relics. The opened tomb disclosed a quantity of bones and topmost a human skull. We called to our aid Sieur André Lubio, chief surgeon of Toulouse, and requested him to make a list of the bones in order to insert it in this document." ^{The verification of the martyr's relics.}

Here follows the catalogue of bones, each technically named. None were missing,[1] except the small bone of the fore-arm which St. Edmund's own abbey had preserved. Each bone was reverently taken from the stone coffin, classified and then carefully placed in a wooden chest, which was lined inside and out with yellow satin. The chest was finally

---

[1] The catalogue of bones contained in the "Procès Verbal," having been submitted to an M.D. and Fellow of the Royal College of Surgeons, Edin., s reported to contain all those bones which constitute the skeleton except the radius, a bone of the forearm. The skull, however, contained only seven teeth in the lower jaw and three in the upper. For the question of the decay of the sacred body see note, p. 234.

locked up in the safe of the relic of the Holy Thorn, which an iron grating fastened with a padlock made doubly secure. The archbishop put his seal on the padlock; the key was taken away, and so ended the first part of the ceremony of the royal martyr's tenth translation. [1]

The preparation for the great ceremony.

The final solemnities were appointed to take place in connection with St. Edmund's feast in the November following. The register of Saint-Sernin relates with almost wearisome minuteness the preparations for the occasion. On October the 17th, the greater number of the shrines of the basilica were cleaned and got in order. On the 25th, "according to ancient custom," certain canons in the name of the lord abbot and of the chapter invited the city-parliament to attend, and the president answered that all the members would be present in their scarlet robes to add what solemnity they could to the occasion. About the same time criers proclaimed the coming event in the neighbouring villages.

Oct. 17.

Oct. 25.

In the interior of the basilica.

In the basilica itself the noise of hammer and saw told of more material preparations. In the midst of the nave a lofty flight of steps covered with carpet mounted to a wooden platform, on which three altars were erected to receive the shrines of St. Edmund and of the other saints. Rich hangings covered the long double line of columns on each side of the basilica. Afar off at the end of the vista of columns, and under the great chancel arch, in front of which lay the choir, stood the high altar with a reredos of inestimable value, consisting of the shrines and reliquaries of the church each with its halo of tapers, and arranged in storeys which reached from floor to

[1] The verification of the five bodies of martyrs which lay near to St. Edmund's tomb was deferred to the following Monday, July 18.

roof. The workmen had removed the choir-screen, in order that all might see the relics. The archbishop's throne stood on one side, and on the other were arranged seats for the assistant bishops. In the aisles at the side of the choir the carpenters built a temporary gallery for a full band. All these preparations were complete by Saturday, November the 12th.

On that day the archbishop descended into the crypt in order to bring to the upper church the bodies of the saints. He wore his pontifical robes; the archiepiscopal cross and the crozier were borne before him, it being provised that this should be done without prejudice to the immunities or privileges of the basilica and its canons—a proviso which recalls similar precautions in St. Edmund's abbey in England. The canons of Saint-Sernin attended the archbishop. In the dull eventide, about four o'clock, the procession wended its way through the passages of the dimly lighted crypt. The first and second presidents and the members of the Toulouse parliament; the municipal authorities in their red robes; the seventy-two custodians of the bodies of the saints and their assistants, and a crowd of other distinguished citizens followed in the procession. All carried lighted tapers. The prelate incensed the relics, then paused for a few moments in prayer. Next two canons took up the chest containing the relics of SS. Claudius and Nicostratus, and two others that containing the bones of SS. Simplex, Symphorian and Castor, in order to carry them to the church. Lastly, the vicar-general and Canon de Foudeyre raised to their shoulders the coffin enclosing the body of St. Edmund and carried it in the procession under a canopy supported by the mayor and three senators. The bearers deposited the three chests on the altars in the nave

The commencement of the ceremony, November 12.

of the basilica each near its silver shrine. The archbishop again incensed the relics and prayed in
silence; then he descended the platform to officiate
at solemn vespers. Outside in the streets and squares
the citizens lighted bonfires and illuminated the
windows of their houses with torches.

The tenth trans-
lation of St.
Edmund's relics,
Sunday, Nov. 13,
1644.

Next day at eight o'clock in the morning the
archbishop returned to the basilica to sing the solemn
mass and preside at the translation of St. Edmund's
body and of the bodies of the other holy martyrs.
The church presented a scene of unusual magnificence. The background of glittering shrines and
lights closed the vista of the tapestried lines of pillars.

The brilliant
assembly.

Around the altar the archbishop on his throne
and his eight mitred brethren, the assistant priests
and deacons and the other sacred ministers were
grouped, while the robed canons and the privileged
doctors of the university filled the rest of the
sanctuary. In the choir the members of the Toulouse
parliament had assembled in their red robes; and
also the treasurers of France, the city magistrates,
proud of their imperial title, and the mayor and
aldermen. The various trades of the city filled the
nave between the choir and the platform of the relics.
The platform itself with its three altars rose gloriously
above the heads of the crowd in the centre of the
church and displayed the coffins and shrines of the
newly exhumed relics and the vicar-general and two
canons religiously guarding them, while, upon the steps,
the custodians, superintendents, treasurers, and officers
of the Holy Bodies stood with lighted white tapers in
their hands. An immense multitude of people crowded
the nave and double aisles. Never had the old city
seen so joyous and magnificent a pageant; never had
there been a more glorious translation of St.
Edmund's relics, even in his old abbey-church.

After the gospel the archbishop ascended a pulpit <small>The archbishop preaches.</small> which stood opposite the platform of the relics, and preached on the virtues of East Anglia's king and martyr,[1] as Bishop Wakelin had done on a similar occasion six hundred years before. The mass over, vested in cope, he ascends the platform of the relics accompanied by the members of the chapter.   He incenses the relics and blesses the silver shrines. The vicar-general opens the wooden chests, and, taking out the bones one by one, presents them to the arch-bishop, who, showing each in turn to the people, places them with religious care in their silver shrines. "Meanwhile," says the register, "the band of musi-cians continued to stir up devotion in the hearts of the audience, and salvoes of artillery proclaimed far and wide the piety and religious joy of the inhabi-tants." At the end of the ceremony the archbishop retired, to return later for the solemn vespers.

For a whole week the relics of St. Edmund and <small>The pilgrimages to St. Edmund.</small> of the other holy martyrs remained exposed for the veneration of the faithful. Every two hours the vicar-general presented those of St. Edmund to the people to kiss, and two canons presented those of the other saints. Every day processions, each headed by its priests, flocked in from the neighbouring parishes. The pious associations of the city and of the towns in the vicinity also came, each in its turn, so that fifty pilgrimages were made to the basilica during the week, and God blessed the faith of the people by numerous miracles.

The solemnities on the festival itself surpassed if <small>The feast of St. Edmund, Nov. 20</small> possible those of the first day of the translation.   On Sunday, the 20th of November, the 744th anniver-sary of St. Edmund's martyrdom, by proclamation

---

[1] This sermon, as well as one preached a few days later by the bishop of Papoul, was printed in 1645 in a 4to volume.

The gorgeous procession.

of parliament a procession passed through the streets of the city. Starting from the basilica, it wended its way to the cathedral of St. Stephen, to conduct thence the Blessed Sacrament. All the relics of the basilica were carried in this procession, some by religious in their various habits, others by craft-guilds decorated with their distinctive badges. Canopy after canopy, forty-two in number, prepared with rival magnificence by the various trades, were borne over the shrines. The heads of the five martyrs SS. Symphorian, Castor, Claudius, Nicostra-tus and Simplex, surrounded by surpliced priests and master-tradesmen, were followed respectively by the shrines which enclosed their sacred bodies.

Crowned by St. Edmund's relics.

Last of all in the procession the principal group came, made up of the highest dignitaries of church and city, who attended that day to do honour to St. Edmund the king. First amongst them the manda-tory of the holy relics walked, in his robes of purple cloth and red taffety with head-piece of red velvet and the emblem of the Holy Ghost suspended from his neck. The custodians of the holy relics of the basilica, carrying lighted tapers and engravings of St. Edmund, next led the way before four priests,

The royal martyr's head.

who carried upon their shoulders the head of the royal martyr under a canopy trimmed with cloth of silver and covered with embroidered gold and silver crowns to represent royalty and martyrdom. The

His shrine.

venerable chapter of the basilica followed, carrying in their midst, on a portable stand hung with crim-son, the shrine in which rested the bones of the martyr-king of England.[1] Four magistrates of the

---

[1] It is worthy of remark that Pierre de Casenueve, St. Edmund's French biographer, was one of the four canons who carried the royal martyr's shrine.

city held over it a rich canopy, and the treasurers past and present of the holy relics, holding lighted tapers, formed a body-guard on each side. The vicar-general with his master of ceremonies, the sacristan of the crypt and the confessor of the pilgrims closed the procession. Thus the citizens of Toulouse bore St. Edmund through their streets to the cathedral church.

They passed along the Rues du Tour, de Sénéchal, Rivals and the Square de Capitole to the church of St. Antony, where they paused awhile before proceeding by the Rue de la Pomme and Rue Boulbonne to the cathedral, at the western door of which the greater and more honourable procession of the Blessed Sacrament awaited them. *The route of the procession.*

The archbishop held aloft the sacred Host under a canopy of cloth of silver; the cathedral chapter stood around, as also the magistrates and officials of the city according to their rank; the parliament of Toulouse headed by its two presidents; and the king's lieutenant, the viceroy of Languedoc. The procession thus completed returned through the gaily decked streets, in the midst of music and singing, to the church of St. Antony and thence to the great basilica. The bishop of Saint-Papoul preached, vespers was chanted, and, when all was over inside the church, the lofty pyramid which had been erected outside in the square was set on fire. The canons of the basilica and the magistrates of the city stood and watched the flames rising to the sky and signalling to the whole town the commencement of rejoicings and illuminations. *The procession of the Blessed Sacrament.* *The sermon by the bishop of St.-Papoul.*

As the feast was to be solemnized with an octave, the archbishop, the chapter, the magistrates and the parliament again assembled next morning for mass at the altar of the relics in the middle of the nave. *The octave of the feast.* *Nov. 21.*

Afterwards they carried St. Edmund's shrine to the chapel of the Holy Ghost, where for eight days citizens and strangers alike came to see and pray before it.

Thus exposed to public view, all could examine its rare workmanship. It was a masterpiece of the silver-smith's skill. At each corner stood figures of the saint-bishops of Toulouse, and, under a portico in the front centre, one of St. Edmund in massive silver. Four Corinthian columns supported an exquisitely wrought balcony, from which rose a dome surmounted by a cross. All was made of solid silver.

After the octave the custodians took the shrine and its precious contents back to the crypt. As a record to posterity the register from which this account is taken was drawn up and signed by witnesses, and then enclosed in a phial and placed within the shrine. Thus concluded the tenth translation of St. Edmund.

———

§ 19. St. Edmund's Body and its present Resting-place. A.D. 1644 to 1892.

[*Authorities*—"La vérification des Reliques en 1807," the original of which is preserved in the archiepiscopal archives at Toulouse, and also the "Monographie de la Basilique," etc., which has been already referred to under Section 17.]

From 1644 to the French Revolution the history of St. Edmund's body is uneventful. His shrine was annually exposed, like those of other saints, on

the feast of Relics in Whit-week, and at the cen-
tenary celebration of 1762, one of the most magni- ^{A.D. 1762.}
ficent on record, his relics were carried in the great
procession. Beyond this the annals of Saint-Sernin's
record nothing.

Before the end of the century the hurricane of the ^{The French Revolution.}
French Revolution broke over the city, overturning
everything sacred and profane. In 1790 it suppressed
the abbey of Saint-Sernin.[1] Nevertheless, the traditional
love and respect of the Toulousians for their saints
saved the relics of the basilica. Previous to the
storm the Abbé du Bourg removed some to a place
of safety, and on the institution of the civil clergy
Père Hubert, formerly provincial of the Minims,
who was appointed to Saint-Sernin, though he could
not hinder the spoliation of the shrines and reliquaries, ^{Feb. 27, 1794.}
watched over their contents with jealous care, and
within eighteen months placed them all with reverence
and order in less costly reliquaries.

In June and August, 1807, in eleven long sittings ^{A commission verifies the}
presided over by Monsieur de Barbazan, vicar-general ^{relics, June and August, 1807,}
of the archbishop of Toulouse, and Monseigneur du
Bourg, then bishop of Limoges, an ecclesiastical commission examined all the relics of the basilica.
Monseigneur du Bourg and the commissioners who
had assisted at the removal of the relics when the
shrines were confiscated in 1794, gave evidence as to
their identity, and eighteen witnesses signed the
document which enumerated and authenticated them.

Since that day the reliquaries and their priceless ^{And the city still carefully}
contents have been kept under three locks, the keys ^{guards them.}
of which are held by the archbishop, the parish-
priest of Saint-Sernin, and the town council, and so
strictly are the relics guarded that in 1822 the

---

[1] It numbered 24 canons, 10 prebendaries and 10 choir priests.
A line of 34 abbots had ruled the abbey.

municipal council refused Cardinal de Clermont-
Tonnerre, archbishop of Toulouse, any portion of them
for himself or other churches. They were gifts, they
pleaded, of popes and kings; the inhabitants of the
city set a high value upon them; strangers came from
afar to visit them; to scatter them broadcast would
inflict an irreparable loss on Toulouse. Only for a
special reason, and that to repair a past injury, did
they permit the present Cardinal Archbishop of
Toulouse to open St. Edmund's shrine in 1867, and
to abstract a bone in order to present relics of the
saint to his abbey-town and to the monastery which
still glories in his patronage.

St. Edmund's present resting-place. The rest of St. Edmund's earthly remains still
repose in the crypt of Saint-Sernin, which vies with
that of St. Peter's at Rome in sacred treasures. Its
subterranean chambers, excavated behind the high
altar, correspond with the apse above, in which the
shrine of St. Saturninus stands overshadowed by its
The crypt of Saint-Sernin. marble baldachin. After wandering round the vast
basilica, the pilgrim approaches, with a feeling of
awe, this place renowned throughout Christendom,
in which the bones of apostles and of the most
illustrious martyrs, confessors and virgins repose,
the pious objects of veneration for generations
past.

Its entrance. The inscription "Non est in toto sanctior orbe
locus" distinguishes the handsome doorway known as
the "Pilgrims'," by the side of which is a second
doorway, inscribed with the words, "Hic sunt vigiles
qui custodiunt civitatem,"—"Here are the watchers
who keep the city." This second doorway opens upon
The inscriptions on the walls. the flight of steps descending to the crypts. On
entering, the stranger first pauses to read from the
two white marble tablets let into the walls on

each side, these simple but soul-stirring words:

D.O.M. [1] Under the auspices and by the pious munificence of the Emperor Charlemagne, Louis le Debonnaire, and Charles the Bald, the illustrious basilica of St. Saturninus received the precious remains of several Apostles and of a great number of Martyrs, Virgins and Confessors of the faith. The Dukes of Aquitaine and the Counts of Toulouse added to their number. The magistrates of this city have assiduously guarded them. Here Religion preserves for the perpetual edification of the faithful a portion of the cross of our Saviour; a thorn of His crown, a gift of Count Alphonsus, the brother of St. Louis; a fragment of the stone of the Holy Sepulchre, the glorious spoil of the crusaders of Toulouse; and a portion of one of the robes of the Mother of God.

Under these vaults, O pious pilgrim, are venerated relics of the Apostles St. Peter, St. Paul, St. James the Greater, St. James the Less, St. Philip, St. Simon, St. Jude, St. Barnabas, St. Bartholomew—and of St. Claudius, St. Crescentius, St. Nicostratus, St. Simplex, St. Castor, St. Christopher, St. Julian, St. Cyr, St. Ascisclus, St. Cyril, St. Blasius, St. George.

Here rest the first bishops of Toulouse, whose line begins in the third century—St. Saturninus, St. Honorius, St. Hilary, St. Sylvus, St. Exuperus. Not far from their venerated remains repose those of St. Papoul, St. Honestus, St. William Duke of Aquitaine, St. Edmund King of England, St. Giles, St. Gilbert, St. Thomas Aquinas, St. Vincent of Paul, St. Raymund, Pope St. Pius V., St. Susanna, St. Julitta, St. Marguerita, St. Catharine, St. Lucy, St. Agatha.

The second inscription runs as follows: The second tablet.

D.O.M. Pope Urban II., after having assembled at Clermont, in the year of our Lord 1096, the faithful destined to deliver the Holy Sepulchre, deigned to consecrate with his own hands this basilica, one of the most precious monuments of Christian art. This Sovereign Pontiff was attended by Raymund IV. Count of Toulouse and Saint-Gilles, the illustrious prince who first of all adorned his standards and his arms with the holy cross of our Saviour. The supreme Pontiffs Clement VII., Paul V., Urban V. and Pius IV. have granted numerous privileges to this abbatial church. Those who visit its seven principal altars may gain the same

---

[1] Domino optime Maximo.

indulgences as by praying before the seven altars of St. Peter's at Rome. The kings of France Charles VI., Louis XI., Francis I., Charles IX., Louis XIII., and Louis XVI. have visited these holy catacombs and offered up their prayers before these shrines. To this spot the pious inhabitants of this country, when public calamity befalls them, hasten to beg the powerful intercession of the Saints, the protectors of this ancient and religious city.

The descent into the first crypt. After passing the marble tablets the pilgrim descends a flight of five steps, which abut upon the upper part of the crypt. Thence three steps, and again eleven steps wind down to the part excavated *The first crypt,* under the high altar and the adjacent aisles. Here, each in a niche or upon an altar, the numerous reliquaries are kept, which in Whit-week every year are carried in procession and exposed for the veneration of the faithful. The head of St. Thomas Aquinas in a magnificent silver reliquary, the relics of St. Francis of Paula in a shrine of marvellous workmanship, the relics of St. Pius V., of St. Gregory the *In which is the head of St. Edmund.* Great and of thirty other saints rest there, and among them the head of St. Edmund in a simple reliquary of gilt wood.

The inner crypt, The lower and inner part of the crypt lies under the apse of the basilica. The gilded statues of the emperors Constantine and Charlemagne stand sentinel at the entrance. In the eight chapels around and in the six intermediate niches the bodies of saints repose in shrines more or less precious. The bodies of St. Raymund, St. Honoratus, St. Exuperus, St. Hilary, St. Gilbert, and St. Giles fill the niches. Of the two chapels at the end one contains the Holy Thorn in a silver reliquary in the form of a baldachin, the other a notable part of the body of St. James the Greater. In four other chapels the bodies of SS. Simon and Jude, St. Philip and St. James the Less, St. Papoul and the collected relics of several less known saints are preserved. Lastly the two chapels on the left of the entrance are occupied, Which contains St. Edmund's body. the first by the body of St. Barnabas, and the second by a wooden shrine plated with copper gilt, which encloses the body of St. Edmund, the martyr-king of East Anglia.

---

§ 20. MINOR RELICS OF ST. EDMUND IN ANCIENT AND MODERN TIMES.

[*Authorities*—Herman, and Osbert de Clare and Samson, the joint authors of MS. Cott. Titus A. viii., relate several incidents in connection with the relics of the royal martyr. Weever in his "Funeral Monuments," pp. 463-4, gives a list of relics of St. Edmund found at the abbey at the dissolution, and Dugdale's "Monasticon," edit. 1846, mentions various relics ; see vol. ii. p. 235, vol. iii. p. 124 and vol. v. p. 148. The work "L'Eglise Métropolitaine et primatiale Saint-André de Bordeaux," par M. Hierosme Lopes (Bordeaux, 1668) p. 37, vouches for the existence of the Bordeaux relic, but inquiries made both at Bordeaux and Lucca have failed to trace the relics in either city.]

At the opening of St. Edmund's tomb in 1644 the Ex ossibus Sancti Edmundi, radius, a small bone of the fore-arm, was found missing. The monks of St. Edmundsbury possessed this relic, which they carried in procession on great festivals, as we learn from the record of King Henry VI.'s visit to the abbey in 1433. Weever At old St. Edmund's Bury. enumerates it among the relics of the abbey as a "sinew" of St. Edmund's arm. No record, however, exists of the time or circumstances under which it was separated from the body.

The Toulouse "Procès Verbal" also notices the absence of all but seven teeth in the lower jaw and three in the upper. The martyr may have lost some of these during his passion from the brutality of the Danes. Others may have been taken as relics at any time. If so, what became of them ? No register of St. Edmund's Bury or known inventory of

any other abbey or church mentions them. Dugdale [1]
enumerates among the treasures of St. Alban's a relic

At St. Alban's. "De Sancto Edmundo Rege et Martyre," which was
evidently distinct from the relic "de camisia" which
he also mentions, but he gives no particulars, and
therefore it is quite uncertain what it consisted of.

At Bordeaux. The cathedral of Bordeaux possessed a relic of St.
Edmund in its treasury in 1668; so also did the
city of Dijon. These two relics were probably given

At Dijon. away in 1644 at the time of the translation of the
martyr's body. The great Revolution destroyed all
authentications in both places, and, although Bordeaux
possesses a box full of the relics of saints, no tradition
exists to prove that any portion of St. Edmund's
bones is there.

At St. Edmund's Douai. In 1867 Cardinal Desprez, the present archbishop
of Toulouse, opened the shrine of St. Edmund and
abstracted some of the relics, of which he presented
a bone an inch long, and probably the largest out of
the shrine, to St. Edmund's, Douai, with which he
had been connected from a child. The monastery and
college of St. Edmund at Douai possesses a second portion of the royal martyr's bones, which the same cardinal
archbishop gave to the late Father Ring of Waltham-
stow, who bequeathed it and its reliquary to the
present owners. The cardinal presented a third
portion to an English bishop, [2] who wears it in his
pectoral cross, the most precious memorial of his patron
saint which he could possess. Lastly the noble and

At modern Bury. generous cardinal gave the only portion which remained to St. Edmund's church, Bury-St.-Edmund's,
where it is kept in a silver and gold reliquary, on
a stand set with emeralds and chased with designs
emblematic of martyrdom. The inscription, " From

---

[1] "Monasticon," vol. ii. p. 232.

[2] The Right Rev. Edmund Knight, D. D., bishop of Shrewsbury.

the bones of St. Edmund the Martyr, king of East
England," encircles it, and yearly on the feast of St.
Edmund this relic, in the midst of flowers and lighted
tapers, is exposed upon the saint's altar for the
veneration of the faithful.

The holy woman Oswene, the devout keeper of *The martyr's nails and hair.*
the martyr's body in the early church at Beodrics-
worth, preserved the fragments of St. Edmund's nails
in a little box upon the altar. In the days of Matthew
of Westminster the monks still treasured these curious
relics, and at the dissolution of the monastery Cromwell's commissioners wrote of the "paryngs of St.
Edmund's naylls" as among the treasures of the
abbey. The monk Ailwin, when guardian of the holy
body, also kept with care the combings of the martyr's
hair, which the monks afterwards preserved with
other mementoes of their patron in the "Chapel of
the Relics," which was built east of the shrine
purposely to receive such sacred treasures.

The most precious, however, of all the mementoes *St. Edmund's garments.*
of the royal martyr were the garments which he
wore at his passion. Abbot Leofstan had removed
them, torn and blood-stained, from the holy body
and laid them up in a crystal case for the veneration
of pilgrims. In speaking of relics of St. Edmund
Herman states that he refers only to pieces of these
robes. St. Alban's possessed a portion of the martyr's *At St. Alban's.*
camisia, or under-tunic, which it esteemed among
its most valuable treasures. And Abbot Baldwin, in
his personal appeal to Alexander II. against Bishop
Herfast's attempt to fix his see at St. Edmund's Bury
and to degrade the abbey to a cathedral priory, took
pieces of them with him, in order to spread devotion
to the protector of his abbey. He bestowed a part
on the cathedral church of St. Martin at Lucca,[1] *At Lucca.*

---

[1] Consecrated A.D. 1070. Abbot Leofstan also had visited

R

where an altar under the invocation of the martyr
Edmund was erected at the entrance of the church
to receive it.[1] Not long after Baldwin's return home,
Prior Edfric and the priest Siward went on a
pilgrimage to Rome and lodged at Lucca at the house
of a man named Peter, who gave them the following
explanation of the devotion to St. Edmund which they
had remarked in the city. A wealthy man and his wife
living in the suburbs had an only son, a little boy,
whom they passionately loved. When they saw the
child growing up weak and feeble, they were overwhelmed with grief. Physicians could give no cure,
so they carried the boy to the shrines of saints;
they burnt lights in many sanctuaries; they gave
abundant alms to the poor and to the Church. The
child only grew weaker and weaker, till it hovered
between life and death. At this juncture a certain
venerable priest unexpectedly visited them and put
the question, " Whether they knew of the holy King
Edmund, who rested incorrupt in England, and
through whom the Lord did wonderful things ? "
A miracle there. They answered that they had never heard of him.
Then he commanded them to carry the child at once
into the city to the church of blessed Martin and
to lay it upon the steps of the altar of the martyr
Edmund, and to keep vigil there. Hastening to the
church, they lighted tapers to the saint; they knelt
through the livelong day in prayer. As darkness
came on, wearied out with watching, they fell asleep.

Lucca on his way to Rome, and he brought thence a fac-simile
of the renowned crucifix *Volto Santo* of Lucca, the work of St.
Nicodemus, which was venerated for centuries n St. Edmund's
abbey church. To Leofstan and Baldwin Lucca probably owes its
two valuable medieval MSS. of St. Abbo's " Vita et Passio Sti
Edmundi." See Battely, p. 42.

[1] " In porticu ecclesiæ."

When they awoke at break of day, they found the child alive and well, sitting up and playing with the leaves of thyme with which in those days they carpeted the floor of the church. The host Peter affirmed to the two English pilgrims that he had seen the boy sick and dying and just afterwards full of health. Other people saw the miracle, so that when an annual feast in honour of St. Edmund was instituted, crowds from all parts flocked to its celebration.[1]

Herman relates two other stories connected with relics of the "exuviæ Sti Edmundi." It appears by the first that Warner, the devout abbot of Rebaix in Hainault, a man of extraordinary literary and musical powers, visited St. Edmund's. The monks received him with their customary ceremonies and hospitality, and he composed for them four antiphons in honour of St. Edmund, which he put to the sweetest music. He became a great favourite with the monks, and at his departure Abbot Baldwin gave him a relic in order that he might spread devotion to the royal martyr in foreign parts.[2] After crossing the sea and while passing through Ponthieu on his way to St.-Riquier, he fell into the hands of bandits, who stripped him of everything. Gerwin, abbot of St.-Riquier, who was universally feared and respected, distressed at his brother's mishap, at once sought out the robbers, and by threats and persuasions forced them to give up their spoil. The relic of St. Edmund,

A relic possessed by the abbot of Rebaix.

---

[1] At the present day there is no trace of this relic at Lucca. A lot of relics in confusion exist, but that of St. Edmund is not among them. Being of silk or linen only, it has probably long since fallen to dust. Cardinal Franciotti, a native of Lucca, A.D. 1570, in his "Lives of the Saints" connected with the city, makes no mention of a relic of St. Edmund in the list of the treasures at San Martino.

[2] "In exteras regiones."

however, which the pious Warner valued more than
all his goods, was lost. All that night till about
dawn he lay awake lamenting it. When he fell
asleep, it seemed to him as if St. Edmund came and
laid his hand upon his breast and with reassuring
words told him that the relic was there. Next
morning he found it as the vision said, and he laid it
afterwards upon the altar in his abbey church.

Abbot Baldwin's relic.

Herman's second story relates how Abbot Baldwin
being in Normandy at the court of William and
Matilda, with whom he was often in request both
as counsellor and physician, sent a soldier named
Norman to his abbey for news and medicine and
other necessaries, and above all for a phylactery of
St. Edmund.[1] Norman, desirous of returning without
delay, took passage on a boat which was just setting
sail, with sixty passengers, thirty-six head of cattle,
sixteen horses and a heavy cargo. When out at sea a
storm arose which threatened the utter destruction of the
vessel. Then Norman, who was sleeping by the side of
his horse, saw St. Edmund approach him, who bade him
rise and not forget his relic. Norman awoke, and,
raising aloft in his hand the reliquary which hung
from his neck, he called upon captain and men to
pray to God and St. Edmund to save them. As they
knelt in prayer the storm abated, and they reached
port in safety. On the same journey Baldwin's
messenger ascribed his safe passage of a perilous ford to the like protection of the saint's phylactery.

Other portions.

A heading in the Bodleian MS. 240 f. 646, entitled
"De Mantica cum reliquiis Sti Edmundi furata et
postea miraculose inventa,"[2] shows that other relics

---

[1] Phylacterium (see Ducange) was a case containing a relic.

[2] About a wallet containing relics of St. Edmund which was
stolen and afterwards miraculously found.

of the saint existed, and probably they also consisted
of pieces of his robes.

These relics, however, judging from the custom of
the church, were in most instances very small. The
greater portion of the martyr's robes lay in their
crystal case in the "Chapel of the Relics," as the
following interesting story proves :[1] Brother Herman,
a monk of St. Edmund's and a friend of Tolinus,
frequently preached to the people. One Whit-Sunday,
moved by the crowds of people, and carried away
by his fervour, he summarily brought out the chest
of relics and displayed the martyr's robes to the
faithful, who, giving praise to God, approached and
reverenced them. Three weeks after, some nobles
who heard of the incident devoutly begged the favour
which had been accorded to the common people.
The brethren assented and privately presented the
relics to be kissed in the crypt. The news soon
spread, and an immense multitude of both sexes
flocked to the abbey and refused to leave without
seeing the relics. To allay the excitement, the coffer
containing them was placed on a wooden stand in
the middle of the apse, and Herman exposed them
for veneration. He even took the camisia, or under-
garment, purple with the martyr's blood, from the
casket, pointed out the blood-stains and arrow-rents
and even unfolded it for the people to kiss. The
devout virgin Seietha, with soul magnifying God,
looked on, while the holy robe diffused a fragrance
surpassing anything earthly, as the crowd bore witness.

That same day Herman fell sick, and the following
night Tolinus, appearing to Brother Edwin with a
severe countenance, strongly blamed him and the
other brethren for their irreverence. "The camisia
of St. Edmund," he said, "for the sake of vulgar

*The monk Her-
man displays the
martyr's robes to
the people.*

*He is punished
for his irrever-
ence.*

---

[1] Cott. MS. Titus A. viii.

applause has been carelessly taken from its casket
and still more carelessly unfolded, so that the martyr's
blood which clung to it has fallen to the ground and
perished." Edwin gave the message to the brethren,
and on the third day at sunset Herman died,—a severe
lesson to those who treat the relics of saints without care.

St. Edmund's Psalter. Besides his garments the monks religiously preserved the psalter from which St. Edmund in his
younger days studied the outpourings of the royal
Prophet's soul. According to Blomefield and Butler
this priceless volume found its way after the dissolution of the abbey to the library of St. James' church
at Bury.

St. Edmund's sword. St. Edmund's abbey possessed another memento of
its illustrious protector in his sword, which lay in
its scabbard among the other relics.[1] The "Registrum Rubrum" relates the following dream in connection with this sword:[2] When William Bateman,
bishop of Norwich, attempted to subject the abbey
to his visitation and jurisdiction (A.D. 1345), William
of Hengham, a monk of devout and religious life and
keeper of the shrine, while asleep upon a bench[3] to
the right of the high altar, saw the martyr clothed
in royal robes, crowned and armed, rise from the
shrine and go towards the chapel of the relics, where
Ailwin, his chamberlain, drew the sword from its
Brother William's dream. scabbard and respectfully presented it to his master,
who, taking it from the monk's hand, proceeded with
an animated but placid countenance through the
church into the open air, the doors opening to him

---

[1] From two instances at least in which St. Edmund appeared
and pointed to his sword with such words as "Hæc est victoria
qua mundum vicit Ædmundus," we may imply that the sword in
the Chapel of the Relics was at least emblematic of the sword of
martyrdom, if not the actual instrument.

[2] Yates' "History of Bury," p. 110.

[3] "Super bancum."

with a great noise but without any human assistance.
The vision distressed the sleeping monk, who thought
that the saint was abandoning his abbey. The return
of the martyr, however, after a short absence comforted him.   He saw him deliver the sword now
covered with blood to his faithful Ailwin, who, after
cleansing and sheathing it, restored it to its place
and disappeared. Then blessed Edmund laid himself
to rest again in his shrine. The bishop lost his suit
the very next day, and afterwards, prosecuting it in
the pope's court, he suddenly expired, exclaiming with
his last breath, as many in the Roman court bear
witness : " Bury ! Bury ! Saint Edmund ! Saint Edmund ! " This failure of the bishop's claim and the
previous vision of Brother William naturally caused
the monks to attribute their victory to their royal
patron.   The incident is mentioned here, however,
merely as a record of the existence of St. Edmund's
sword. [1]

The next relic of the saint, his drinking-cup, was St. Edmund's
kept in Abbot Samson's time on the rood-beam near cup.
the shrine. An oaken box bound with iron bands and
fastened with an iron lock enclosed it. At the fire
in 1198 the monks showed the deepest anxiety for this
precious relic, till they found it in its singed linen
cloth among some pieces of charred wood. An indulgence of five hundred days " toties quoties " was
granted to pilgrims who drank from it " in the wor-
shippe of God and Saint Edmund," and hence its name
of " Pardon Bowl." The Books of Miracles [2] recount

---

[1] Osbert de Clare in his second book of St. Edmund's Miracles,
no. xviii. (Cott. MS. Titus A. viii.) mentions the cure of a
monk of Shrewsbury, to whom the martyr appeared with a sword
on which was inscribed, " This is the victory by which Edmund
overcame the world."

[2] Osbert de Clare, Cott. MS. Titus A. viii., bk. ii. nos. xiii.
xiv. xix. See also Bodl. MS. 240 fol. 656-658-659 for miracles
" De Cipho Sti Edmundi."

several instances of sick persons regaining their health on drinking from St. Edmund's cup, notably a rich lady after long suffering from fever; a Dunwich man with dropsy; and Gervasius, a Cluniac monk of St. Saviour's, Southwark, who himself related it to the writer of the miracle. This same Gervasius, meeting with a fresh malady almost immediately afterwards, was carried by the monks to their infirmary. There he begged to drink again from the martyr's cup, and the seniors brought it to him from the treasury. That night he recovered, and next day, the feast of St. Edmund, he went to the church to give thanks, "Thus," concludes the narrator, "mayest thou work. O Edmund, venerated and illustrious king in Christ, that God may magnify thy glory through the ages and by the fulness of thy virtues exalt His own name everywhere upon earth." [1]

Miracles by drinking from it.

St. Edmund's banner.

Among the relics of St. Edmund his banner or standard holds an historic position. Lydgate describes two banners. The first, merely symbolic of the martyr's virtues, is depicted in the poet's richly illuminated work with the device of three gold crowns on an azure ground :

> " Which (banneret)   .   .   .   .
> .   .   .   King Edmund bar certeyn,
> When he was sent be grace of Goddis hond,
> At Geyneburuk for to slew Kyng Sweyn."

The other standard, [2] which went before King Edmund in his royal progresses and overshadowed

---

[1] A second cup of St. Edmund seems to have belonged to Henry, last Earl of Lincoln of that name, who gave it to the abbey about the reign of Henry VI. This cup had a bowl of silver gilt, and altogether was a piece of rare workmanship. The earl's chaplain, wearing a surplice, on great feasts offered his patron's most dignified guests to drink from this bowl.

[2] See the print of it in the Camden edition of Jocelin's Chronicle, vol. 13, p. 183, and also the magnificent illumination of it which forms the frontispiece of the Harleian MS. 2278.

his armies in the battle-field, represented on a bright red ground the tree of knowledge embroidered in gold with silver fruit. The horizontal branches of the tree Its workman-
ship. divided the banner into two. In the lower part, on either side, worked in silver, Adam and Eve stood about to eat the forbidden fruit, which the serpent, twined round the trunk and represented with a human shape down to the middle, handed to the woman. In the centre of the upper part a circle of gold surrounded the Agnus Dei or Holy Lamb in silver with a gold glory around the head, its right foot bearing up a golden cross *fleurée fitchée*. The red ground of the upper part was powdered with golden crescents within the circle and with stars of gold outside. Gold stars also bespangled the tree. The Benedictine poet of St. Edmund's abbey thus describes this ancient and venerable piece of East Anglian workmanship:

> " Blyssyd Edmund, kyng, martir and vyrgyne, Lydg te's de-
scription of it.
> Hadde, in thre vertues, by grace of soveryn prys
> Be which he venquysshed all venymes serpentyne.
> Adam ba serpent banysshed fro paradys ;
> Eva also, because she was not wys,
> Eet off an appyl off flesshly fals plesance.
> Which thre figures, Edmund, by gret avys,
> Bar in his baner, for a remembrance,
> Lyk a wys kyng peeplys to governe.
> Ay unto reson he gaff the sovereynte,
> Figur off Adam wysly to dyscerne
> T' oppresse in Eva sensualite.
> A Lamb off gold hyh upon a tre,
> An hevenly signe, a tokne off most vertu
> To declare how that humylite
> Above alle vertues pleseth most Jesu.
> Off Adamys synne was wasshe a way the rust
> Be vertu only off thys lambys blood.
> The serpentys venym and al flesshly lust
> Sathan outraied a geyn man, most wood,
> Tyme whan this lamb was offred on the rood

> For our redempcioun, to which havyng reward,
> This hooly martir, this blyssyd kyng so good,
> Bar this lamb hiest a loffte in his standard.
> The feeld of Gowlys was tokne off his suffrance
> Whan cruel Danys were with hym at werre ;
> And for a signe off royal suffisance
> That no vices never maad hym erre,
> The feeld powdryd with many hevenly sterre,
> And half cressantis off gold, ful bryht and cleer.
> And wher that evere he journeyde nyh or ferre
> Ay in the feeld with hym was this baneer."[1]

Its efficacy against fires. The poet next describes its miraculous efficacy against fires and conflagrations. Those who wish, he remarks, can easily verify the cases in which it is said to have extinguished devouring flames.

The battle of St. Edmund's Standard. An historical instance of the use of St. Edmund's banner occurred in 1173, when the battle of Fornham, on which the fate of king and kingdom depended, was fought and won under its protection. Henry II.'s three sons, Henry (who had been crowned king in 1170), Richard and Geoffrey, with the support of the kings of France and Scotland, the Count of Flanders and several powerful nobles, formed against their father as formidable a combination as ever opposed English or European sovereign. The civil war broke out in England in the summer of 1173, and at the same time the Scots began their raids on the northern borders. While the royal forces battled with the insurgents in the north, Robert Earl of Leicester with a **The invasion of East Anglia.** large force of Flemings landed at Walton-le-Naze in Suffolk on the 29th of September, and Earl Bigot received him with open arms at Framlingham Castle, twenty miles inland. The people of the neighbouring district anxiously assembled in considerable force under the Earls of Cornwall, Gloucester, and Arundel,

---

[1] This extract from the beginning of the Harl. MS. 2278 has been printed by Sir Harris Nicholas in the "Retrospective Review," N.S., vol. i. pp. 98-100.

to repel the insurgents and save their homes from destruction. Meanwhile the news of this fresh incursion filled the royal leaders in the north with dismay. Concealing the intelligence from the Scots, they patched up a hasty truce and marched southwards to St. Edmund's Bury. They had scarcely entered the town when the Earl of Leicester, not aware of their presence, in forcing his way to his own county, passed Fornham-St.-Geneviève within four miles of the north gate. The king and his adherents committed their cause to St. Edmund. They begged for the royal martyr's standard from the hands of Abbot Hugh, and with it unfurled at the head of their force they marched to meet the invaders on the right bank of the Larke. Imitating the Northerners with the improvised standard of St. Cuthbert's corporal, they placed their sacred banner in a conspicuous position and attacked the insurgents, whom they routed in a few hours. Ten thousand of the enemy were left dead on the field. The victors returned to the abbey to restore the sacred standard, now more precious than ever in the eyes of the people east of the fens, and to sing the "Te Deum" at St. Edmund's shrine. For centuries after this English victory, the greatest nobles contended for the right of carrying St. Edmund's banner.

The royal army at St. Edmund's Bury.

Fornham-St.-Geneviève, Oct. 13, 1173.

The following narrative from the Bodleian MS. 240 indicates the existence of a relic, in the shape of an arrow, at St. Edmund's church in London in the 14th or 15th century. A rector of that church, wishing to exchange benefices with a country vicar, stipulated to take with him from the church an arrow, said to be one of the instruments of St. Edmund's martyrdom, and which he therefore valued more than gold. On entering a barge at Billingsgate to proceed by water to his vicarage, the barge remained immovable in the water. Only after

An arrow at St. Edmund the Martyr's in London.

he had returned to shore with the relic could the boatman proceed. Resolving to go by land, some invisible power stopped him on the bridge, and against his will he at last restored the arrow to its former resting-place.

Pieces of St. Edmund's coffin.

The last ancient relics of St. Edmund of which there is record are some pieces of his coffin which the Cluniacs of Thetford kept among their treasures.[1] They perhaps belonged to the old coffin which Theodred the Good replaced by a new one in 950. No history, however, exists of these pieces of wood, or how they were obtained, and, like the martyr's garment, arrow, psalter, sword, cup and standard, they are probably lost forever.

The oak of the martyrdom

One memento, however, of the royal martyr survived in his own land to the present century. A tradition unbroken for generations pointed out in Hoxne or Heglesdune wood the oak-tree to which King Edmund was bound by his executioners, and which our Catholic forefathers venerated as a priceless memorial of the saint's martyrdom. Langtoft thus commemorates it :

"Where he was shot a noble chapel standes,
And somwhat of that tree that thei bond untill his handes."[2]

Fell in August, 1848.

On a calm summer's evening in the August of 1848, this venerable witness of the Christian Edmund's victory, wrinkled and gnarled with the storms of a thousand winters, fell by its own weight. On splitting up the trunk the saw grated on a hard substance in the heart of the tree, which proved on examination to be a delicate little arrow-head firmly embedded in a

---

[1] Thetford Priory, "Monasticon," vol. v. p. 148, edit. 1821.

[2] An old legend says that wolves from the country round, when wounded or worn out with age, crawled to the foot of this sacred tree to die.

black knot that had grown round it, a fact which the *An arrow-head was found embedded in it.*
Antiquarian Society of London considered as an un-
questionable confirmation of the ancient tradition.
Sir Edward Kerrison, on whose estate the oak stood,
preserved the piece of wood with the arrow adhering to
it, and exhibited it for some time in the museum of
the Athenæum at St. Edmund's Bury.[1]

The English Benedictines of St. Edmund's monastery *Some portions are preserved at St. Edmund's, Douai,*
at Douai in France obtained possession of a large piece
of the oak[2] in December, 1848, which they now
preserve on the high altar of their chapel. The
Jesuit fathers at Bury-St.-Edmund's also possess a *And at Bury.*
piece of the hallowed tree in their church in the
martyr's own town.

At the end of this chapter on the sacred body and *The return of St. Edmund to England.*
relics of St. Edmund, the question naturally comes to
the lips, when will the royal martyr, according to the
old prophecy, return to his own land ? England is the
natural home of St. Edmund as it is of every English
saint. When the hour of doom came for Jerusalem,
a voice was heard through the streets proclaiming that
the saints were departing from the city. The besieged
then knew that God had given up His favoured city
to vengeance and would not be appeased. The banishment of our holy ones from the eyes and hearts of the
people signalled England's fate, and their removal in
body and in spirit foreboded its evil day. May their
return to honour and veneration proclaim that the
time of vengeance is passed and the hour of recon-
ciliation at hand !

---

[1] Lady Bateman of Hoxne Hall—recently named Oakley Park
—is its present happy owner, and other pieces of the oak are still
in the hands of her agent.

[2] Through the united kindness of Rev. L. F. Page, of Woolpit
Parsonage, Suffolk, the Rev. R. Cobbold, Rector of Wostham, and
Mr. C. Smythies, agent of Sir Edward Kerrison, by whose
permission he made the gift.

CHAPTER X.

The Miracles of St. Edmund.

[*Authorities.*—Special records of the miracles of St. Edmund were kept by the guardians of the shrine at least from the time of the translation of the sacred body to Beodricsworth in 903. These earliest registers have perished, however, and their contents only partially reach us through other sources, of which St. Abbo's "Vita" is the first. The next and oldest register of miracles properly so called is the fine eleventh century MS. in the Cottonian collection. Tiber B. ii., entitled "Miracula B. Edmundi Regis," auctore Hermanno archidiacono. Its age and style seem to denote it as the author's autograph. It is also probably the "Book of Miracles" referred to by Matthew of Westminster (vol. i. p. 509, Bohn's edit.) The writer has first transcribed St. Abbo's "Vita." The record of miracles follows, fol. 19, and continues to fol. 84, where the narrative ends abruptly shortly after the description of the translation of the relics into the new church in 1095. St. Edmund's name at first is written in emerald and gold, but after a few pages the spaces for it are left blank, the illuminator not having completed his work. "There is considerable doubt," writes Hardy, "as to the identity of the individual here styled Herman the archdeacon." In the opening lines the illuminator neglected to fill in the author's name, but a 15th century hand has written at the foot of fol. 19, "Incipiunt miracula scripta ab Hermano Archidiacono tempore Baldeweni circa annum Christi 1070." A 14th century note records the same fact in Bodl. 240. The author in his preface writes that not "his own presumption, but the command of Abbot Baldwin of happy memory, led him to compile his work," partly from oral testimony and partly from an old register then in the abbey library. Again in the body of the MS., in narrating the punishment of Bishop Herfast, he speaks of himself as one of that prelate's officials. There can be little doubt, then, that Herman was archdeacon of Norwich, and in later life a monk of St. Edmund's Bury, to which he shows an enthusiastic attachment in every page of his work. Several copies of Herman's "Miracula" exist. A complete copy, made by Father Augustine Baker, the Benedictine, in the 17th century, and entitled by Butler the "Liber Feretrariorum," is in the library of Jesus College, Oxford, 75. 30. The Bodleian Library possesses another copy in the small 11th century MS., Digby, no. 39, fol. 24-39, which once belonged to the monastery of St. Mary, Abingdon. The 13th century MS., "Liber Miraculorum S. Edmundi Orientalium Anglorum Regis, auctore anonymo," of the Bibl. du Roi, 2621, is merely an abridgement of Herman's work, ending with the cure of the crippled woman. Dom Martène has printed this piece in his "Amplissima Collectio." tom. vi. p. 821, the MS. being at the time in the library of the king of France. Herman's compilation has lately been edited in full by von F. Lieberman in "Ungedruckte-Anglo-Normannische Geschichtsquellen" (Trübner and Co., Strasburg and London), and also by Arnold in his "Memorials of St. Edmund's Abbey," I., Rolls Series.

The beautifully written volume Titus A. viii. in the Cottonian collection, a MS. of the 13th century, contains after the Life of St. Abbo, which Butler inadvertently ascribes to Osbert of Clare, prior of Westminster, two books "on the Miracles of St. Edmund." The prologue to Book I. begins by saying that, as the deeds of worldlings are lauded to the skies, so the marvels of God in His saints should be proclaimed without fear. Edmund as a shining light placed upon a candlestick, "ut luceat omnibus qui in domo sunt,"—"*that he may shine to all that are in the house,*"—is illustrious not only in Britain but beyond the seas by his miracles, sixteen of which the author proceeds to relate. Book II. begins with a eulogistic prologue on the royal martyr, the conclusion of which compares his virtue to the precious stones in Aaron's breastplate. A description of Abbot Baldwin's translation and of nineteen miracles follows. A fifteenth century hand has added, "Here is found wanting the miracle wrought by St. Edmund on Henry of Essex, also innumerable others." In the margin a 14th century hand has written, "Expliciunt miracula scripta per Osbertum de Clare Priorem Westmonasteriensem,"—"*Here end the miracles written by Osbert de Clare, prior of Westminster.*" The cure of Robert of Hasley, a canon of Hereford, is added, signed "*Per Willelmum Heyhorn. Amen.*" The name is in the same hand-writing as the main part of the MS. and is probably that of the scribe who wrote it. The authorship of this collection of thirty-seven miracles is twofold. Osbert of Clare in Essex, prior of Westminster, A.D. 1108-1140, was the original compiler; but his work, says Bale, began "Cum laureatus Dei Martyr Edmundus." If so, as a complete work, it is lost. The present MS. is an adapted and partly rewritten copy by an author whose identity the Bodl. MS. 240 firmly establishes by placing opposite to extracts from it the marginal notes, "Ex libro de miraculis ejus, Sampson;" "Sampson abbas Sancti Edmundi;" "Ex libro primo miraculorum Sampsonis Abbatis," and the like. Samson, however, must be regarded rather as a compiler than as an original author. To the first book he prefixed a preface of his own, and then rewrote the miracles of Herman and others in his own grave and earnest style. In the second book he begins with Osbert de Clare's prologue, distinguishable by its florid but not unpleasant style; then he gives eight chapters from unknown sources and copies the rest to no. xx. from Prior Osbert. No. xxi. was added after Samson's death. MS. Bodl. 240, described at length in Chap. II., after ninety miracles extracted from Herman, Osbert de Clare and others, gives on fol. 661 the "miracula excerpta de parvo quodam antiquo quaternio ad feretrum,"—"*miracles extracted from a quaint little register kept at the shrine;*"—on fol. 667, other miracles from another old register kept at the shrine; fol. 672, the "miracula xvii. facta apud Wainflete, 1374-75,"—"*the xvii. miracles wrought at Wainfleet, 1374-75,*"—and fol. 674, the "miracula seu in capella sci Edmundi de Lynge,"—"*the miracles in the sanctuary of St. Edmund at Lyng.*" These extracts from the most authentic sources are extremely valuable and interesting in any account of the supernatural manifestations of the royal martyr.

Of other MSS. bearing on the miracles of St. Edmund, Ashmole 463, ff. 70-79, holds the first place. It was written by Lydgate for presentation to Edward IV., as Harl. 2278 was for presentation to Henry VI. After the "Life and Acts of St. Edmund" the poet describes his banner and records his miracles, of which the last took place April 28, 1441. Gerald Cambrensis relates a curious incident which happened at St. Edmund's Bury in his time, and the annals of Toulouse refer to more recent ones.]

A history of St. Edmund would be incomplete without some further mention of the "Miracles" which generations of records attribute to him. It is not intended to write a vindication of them here. Their possibility to the Creator and Ruler of the universe cannot be a subject of discussion among His children and believers. Whether He uses supernatural or unfathomed natural forces to bring about those extraordinary results which we call miraculous, is of little moment. God can manifest divine power in whichever way He wills. That He has done so times without number is beyond reasonable dispute. The history of the patriarchs and prophets in the old dispensation and of the apostles and saints in the new affords overwhelming evidence of the fact. Indeed, not only His own glory, the honour of His servants and the spread of His kingdom demand it, but the soul of man unconsciously looks for these displays of God's existence

General view of the miraculous.

and provident watchfulness over the interests of
His creatures. The invisible world surrounds man so
closely that it would be the strangest of phenomena
if it did not sometimes visibly affect his material
being. Apart from these general principles a wide
field is still left open for the discussion of evidence
for and against any miracle in particular. To be accepted each must rest on testimony which no historian
can reject or impartial judge refuse. Some of St.
Edmund's miracles hardly deserve the name: his
clients saw in them the supernatural, where others
would see only the natural; but all of them are interesting pictures of the customs and habit of thought
of the times.

The chroniclers
of St. Edmund's
miracles.
    The keepers of the shrine from a very early date
inscribed them as they happened in the *libri feretrari-*
orum, or registers of the feretry. The priests and
clerics who devoted themselves to the service of St.
Edmund soon after the translation of his body to
Beodricsworth wrote them in the small and crabbed
hand which Herman found so difficult to decipher.
With a simplicity all its own later writers copied them
into the monastic chronicles and added other marvels
which they had seen themselves or heard from eye-
witnesses. Of these writers St. Abbo stands first for
his learning and culture; then come Gaufridus, bishop
of Ely; Herman, the archdeacon of Norwich, who had
conversed with the holy bishop Ailwin, the saint's
"chamberlain;" Osbert de Clare, prior of Westminster, whose refined taste is noticeable in every line of
his picturesque Latin; and William of Malmesbury
and Abbot Samson, both historical for common sense.
The honesty of such men is unimpeachable, and to the
modern criticism of their narratives they would probably reply in the words of Venerable Bede: "Is it to
be wondered at that the sick should be healed in that

place where he died? for, whilst he lived, he never
ceased to provide for the poor and infirm, and to
bestow alms on them and to assist them." [1] Nevertheless in this sceptical age an account of St. Edmund's
miracles would perhaps be ill-timed, if they did not
fill so important a page in the royal martyr and the
nation's history.

"On the death of St. Edmund, the purity of his past A retrospect of
life," writes William of Malmesbury, [2] "was evidenced the earlier
miracles.
by unheard-of miracles.   The lifeless head uttered a
voice inviting all who were in search of it to approach;
a wolf, a beast accustomed to prey upon dead carcases,
was holding it in its paws, and guarding it intact,
which animal also, after the manner of a tame creature,
gently followed the bearers to the tomb and neither did
nor received injury." The people committed the sacred
body to the earth, turfed over the grave, and sheltered it
with a wooden chapel of mean and slight construction.
"The negligent natives, however, were soon made sen-
sible of the virtue of the martyr by the miracles which
he performed." At night a column of heavenly light
hovered over the spot; a blind man received his sight
there.   At last Theodred I. exhumed the body, to find
"the sacred limbs evidencing the glory of his unspotted
soul by surprising soundness and a milk-like whiteness.
The head, which was formerly divided from the neck,
was again united to the rest of the body, showing only
the sign of martyrdom by a purple seam." [3] So bishop
and clergy and people translated it to the comparatively handsome structure at Beodricsworth, "where," says
St. Abbo, "in him such glorious powers shine forth and
are recounted far and wide, as were never before heard
of among the English people."

[1] Bede's "Ecclesiastical History," Bohn's edit., p. 124.
[2] "Chronicle of the Kings," Bohn's edit., pp. 240-241.
[3] William of Malmesbury, ibid.

S

St. Edmund
makes the un-
just fear him,
Of all these manifestations of the supernatural the most striking class comprises those punishments inflicted on the invaders of St. Edmund's rights or sanctuary. They were so well known and believed in as to create a traditional fear of St. Edmund throughout the nation. "He was felt capable of doing now, what he used to do before," remarks William of Malmesbury; "that is,

> "'To spare the suppliant, but confound the proud,'

by which means he so completely attached the inhabitants of all Britain to him, that every person looked upon himself as particularly happy in contributing either money or gifts to St. Edmund's monastery; even kings themselves, who rule others, boasted of being his servants and sent him their royal crown, redeeming it, if they required to wear it, at a great price. The exactors of taxes also, who, in other places, gave loose to injustice, were there suppliant, and ceased their cavilling at St. Edmund's boundary, admonished thereto by the punishment of others who had presumed to overpass it."[1] The monks doubtless gave prominence to those miracles by which their patron defended his own with such power. They could not repel force by force. Providence, therefore, gave them this means of keeping at bay the unbridled power of kings and barons. So, when King Richard was in captivity and the royal justiciaries drew on the treasuries of every abbey and church in the land, St. Edmund's shrine remained untouched. The gold could be pealed off, they said, at least in parts, and afterwards replaced; but Abbot Samson, starting up, answered them: "Know ye for certain that I will in no wise do this thing, nor is there any man who could force me to consent thereto. But I will open the doors of the church; let him that

A.D. 1193,

---

[1] "Chronicle of Kings," Bohn's edit., p. 242; see also "De Gestis Pontif.," lib. ii. f. 136, b, edit. Lond.

likes enter; let him that dares come forward!" The justiciaries were afraid to move in the matter. With oath, each for himself, they answered, "I will not come forward for my share;" "Nor will I! Nor I! The distant and the absent who offend him, St. Edmund has been known to punish fearfully: much more will he those who close by lay violent hands on his coat, and would strip it off!" The shrine was left untouched; "for," adds the modern eulogist of those times, "Lords of the Treasury have in all times their impassable limits, be it by 'force of public opinion' or otherwise; and in those days a heavenly awe over-shadowed and encompassed, as it still ought and must, all earthly business whatsoever."[1]

The historical punishments which inspired this wholesome fear begin with the robbers who were trans-fixed in their sacrilegious attempt to enter Beodrics-worth church and plunder the shrine. The slaying of King Sweyn years afterwards made a still deeper impression, and the event was everywhere perpetuated along the east coast in stone and window, the royal martyr being represented with spear in hand and the Danish tyrant dead at his feet. *By miraculously punishing the sacrilegious invaders of his rights.*

The case of Llafford Leofstan[2] still further illustrates this class of miracle. It probably happened after the induction of the Benedictines. A poor woman, the chronicler relates, one 1st of May, fled to the shrine of the martyr to escape the notorious severity of the "king's man," Sheriff Leofstan, who was holding his court on the moot-hill, Thinghogo, near the sanctuary. On hearing of the criminal's flight the judge, scoffing at St. Edmund's protection, sent his men to apprehend her; when Bomfild, the priest, *The instance of Llafford Leofstan,*

---

[1] Carlyle, "Past and Present," p. 92, edit. 1843.

[2] A different person from young Count Leofstan or Abbot Leofstan.

Who causes a woman to be dragged from the shrine.

and Leofric, the levite, met them at the church-door and forbade them entrance; for "whom the saint receives in sanctuary," they said, "can by no means be delivered up for condemnation." Thus the church protected the oppressed and ensured mercy as well as justice. The men persisted and threatened force. Whereupon the guardians of the shrine fell on their knees and began reciting the seven penitential psalms and the litanies. Meanwhile Leofstan, enraged at the delay in the execution of his orders, hastened to support his men; but he got no farther than the tomb of Bundus the priest. There he was seized with mad-

For his impiety he is seized with madness and expires.

ness, and rolled on the ground in a fit, foaming at the mouth and gnashing his teeth. Finally he expired, and his body was thrown into a stagnant pool, while the poor woman escaped.[1]

One of William the Conqueror's followers seizes a manor belonging to St. Edmund,

On another occasion one of the Conqueror's Norman followers, expecting the same impunity for lawlessness as his comrades in the rest of England, unjustly annexed a manor which belonged to St. Edmund. The abbot and monks protested. "With unbridled tongue," the insolent Norman answers "that he knows not what the sleeping Edmund will do with the land; that it will be far more useful to him than to monk or martyr." A few days after a white tumour of the

And misfortune falls upon him

size of a pea suddenly grew on the pupil of his right eye, and there it remained. At the instance of his friends rather than of his own free will, he sent a large wax candle as an offering to the martyr.

His votive candle breaks into pieces.

But the saints by the power of God sometimes see the inmost heart of man, and God and St. Edmund refused the light which an evil mind and an unrepentant heart had lighted. The taper, an eyewitness relates, fell to the ground and broke into

---

[1] Samson adds that his ghost troubled the neighbourhood and was with difficulty laid.

niue pieces. " Iniquorum dona non probat Altissimus,"
concludes Herman ;—" The Most High approveth not
the gifts of the wicked." [1]

An incident of a similar kind is related to have *The attempt of Robert de Curzun, A.D. 1087,* occurred in the first year of the reign of William
Rufus.[2] Robert de Curzuu prevailed on Roger Bigot,
sheriff of Norfolk, to let him seize upon the saint's
manor of Southwold,[3] which, he said, was in the centre
of his domain. When, however, he rode with his *To seize the saint's manor of Southwold.* followers to take possession, a storm of wind and hail
accompanied by thunder and lightning raged with
such violence that he believed it to be supernatural,
and, dreading what might happen, he desisted. But
two of his men, Turold, his *dapifer*, and Gyrenew de *Two followers persevering are struck mad.* Mouneyn, persevered in the unjust proceeding and lost
their reason.[4] So far Herman ; Samson adds that
William de Curzuu, a successor of Robert, in the *William de Curzun, a successor of Robert, renews the attempt, A.D. 1168.* fourteenth year of the reign of Henry II., renewed
the claim on Southwold, through Richard, archdeacon
of Poicticrs,[5] at whose representation the king granted
a mandate for its surrender. William at once proceeded to the abbey armed with the royal letters, and
demanded their execution. Abbot Hugh naturally
requested a short delay. Then we have a picture of
the baffled noble hurrying to London to recount how
another priest, like Archbishop Thomas, is defying
the royal will, and of the prior despatched to court

---

[1] Ecclus. xxxiv. 23.   [2] The Bodl. MS. dates this incident 1087.
[3] On the coast of Suffolk.   Its church is named after St. Edmund
to this day.
[4] The Bodleian MS. 240 adds that Roger Bigot about the year
1107, claiming another farm of St. Edmund's, and being about
to bring an action against Abbot Roger, died very suddenly, his
body being afterwards taken to Norwich and buried by Bishop
Herfast.
[5] One of the most astute supporters of Henry II. against St.
Thomas à Becket, by whom he was excommunicated in 1166.

by the abbot to represent the monks' side. Archdeacon Richard tries the case and, *mirabile dictu!*
grants a delay till the Nativity of St. John the
Baptist; it was then Whitweek. The prior returns
home, and on the same day William leaves London to
be ready to seize Southwold. But at the hospice at

He is suddenly taken ill. Chelmsford he was suddenly taken ill. He prosecuted
his journey on the morrow as far as Colchester Abbey,
where the monks received him a raving maniac. His
attendants and even his own wife, horror-struck,

At Colchester he is raving mad. abandoned him. So he remained "panno involutus"—
bound and bandaged,—yet kept under restraint with
the greatest difficulty. On the news reaching the
abbot's ears, he sent the prior to exhort the wretched
man to desist from his robbery; but he had lost all
memory. Then straightway Richard, one of his
attendants, stepped forward and promised to go bail
for his master, if only St. Edmund would take pity
on him. That night the madman's rabies subsided,

He returns to his right mind and abandons his claim. and, before the prior left next day, he had returned
to his right mind, abandoned his claim and vowed
himself a devout servant of St. Edmund for the
remainder of his life.

Prince Eustace despoils the martyr's lands, A.D. 1153. The example of Eustace, son of King Stephen, is
more striking and better known than any of the above
narratives. In the time of Abbot Ording, A.D. 1153,
just after the succession to the throne had been settled
in favour of Prince Henry, and peace at last established,
Eustace came to St. Edmund's Bury. "He was angry
with his father," writes Stowe, who summarises the
incident, "for agreeing to this peace, and therefore in
a rage he departed from the court towards Cambridge,
to destroy that country. Coming to St. Edmund's
Bury, he was there honourably received and feasted,
but when he could not have such money as he
demanded to bestow among his men of war, he went

away in a rage, spoiling the corn in the fields belonging to the abbey, and carrying it into the castles thereby; but, as he sat down to dinner, he fell mad upon receiv- ing the first morsel, and miserably died, and was buried at Feversham." [1]

He is struck mad and expires.

Here is a curious story of a thief told by Gerald Cambrensis, who affirms that it happened in his own day, about ten years before the death of Abbot Samson. A wretched woman was wont to visit the shrine of St. Edmund, not to make offerings herself, but to steal what was offered by others. With pretence of great devotion she would bow down and kiss the iron plate before the shrine on which devout persons usually placed silver and gold, and while kissing would take up the offerings with her mouth and carry them away. She committed this sacri- lege once too often, for her lips and tongue one day stuck firm and fast to the table, while the money she had licked up fell out of her mouth. Christians and Jews ran to witness this spectacle, for through the whole day the woman continued with her lips fastened to the table—a wholesome punishment and indeed a kindness, for the saint thus put an end to the poor woman's propensity for stealing. [2]

A story by Gerald Cam- brensis

Of a woman who stole at the shrine

And was fixed to the place.

The anger of the martyr at the invasion of his rights was not only incurred by rough warriors and silly women, but by pious ecclesiastics. The punish- ment of Bishop Herfast supplies an interesting and

Bishop Herfast impugns the jurisdiction of the abbey, A.D. 1070.

---

[1] Quoted by Cressy.

[2] The Bodl. MS. 297 mentions the similar case of a Fleming ap- proaching the feretry under pretext of devotion and trying to bite away a gold piece attached to it. His teeth are glued to the coin, and he cannot stir. He confesses his act and is set free. (See Appendix B of "Memorials of St. Edmund's Abbey," vol. i.) MS. Bodl. 240 has also a paragraph "De ultione capta super quendam prædatorem, rapientem pavonem de dominio S. Ed- mundi."

historical illustration. He was a "major persona
nostris temporibus"—a rather important personage in
our time,—writes his archdeacon, Herman. Herfast
was elevated to the see of Elmham in 1070, but
removed it to Thetford, and further announced his
intention of finally establishing it at St. Edmund's
Bury. This transfer would have ruined the immunities and privileges of the abbey, and the alarmed
monks at once took speedy and energetic measures
to hinder the bishop from carrying out his design.
To give colour to his pretensions Herfast obtained
the king's licence to claim an old crozier kept in
the monastery, and, unable to obtain it by other means,
he bribed some one to bring it to him. He considered

He takes a crozier from it.

the presence of the crozier in the abbey sufficient
proof that his predecessors exercised jurisdiction over
the monks of St. Edmund. Abbot Baldwin at once
applied for protection to Pope Alexander II., who
received him honourably and ordained him priest.
Lanfranc and Thomas of York were then in Rome,
which gave greater weight to the decision of the
Apostolic See confirming all the privileges and exemptions granted to the monastery by Bishop Ailwin
and King Canute. On Baldwin's return from Rome
Herfast refused to submit to the papal decree on
the plea that the appeal had been made without his
permission, and he still more strenuously prosecuted
his design, directing his archdeacon to write letters
for him to king and Pope. But one day, "as the
bishop was riding through a wood," writes his
archdeacon, "and conversing on the injury which

His chastise-
ment.

he meditated against the monastery, a branch struck
him in the face so violently that the eyes were suffused
with blood and eventually became sightless: *Sancti
effectualis ultio* — an effectual punishment from the
saint." "One morning," continues Herman, "seeing

him depressed and wretched, for his blindness affected
his whole body, out of pity I boldly said to him:
'My Lord Bishop, all your remedies are in vain.
No collyrium avails; not even Hippocrates or Gal-
lienus could help you, unless God have compassion
on you.   Seek the favour of God through St. Edmund.
Go at once to Abbot Baldwin in humility and peace,
that God through him may heal you.'   He rejected
this counsel at first, but when we all advised him
to follow it, he consented.   That same day, the feast
of SS. Simon and Jude, by his commission, I set out
for the abbey.   Abbot Baldwin benignly received me, *He repents and abandons his claim,*
and by his leave the sick bishop came with his
retinue to the abbey.   And first the abbot admonished
him to reflect if he had given any offence to God
or St. Edmund, for he should get forgiveness of his
sins before thinking of the application of other
remedies.   In chapter, therefore, which was then held
in the vestiary of the monastery, in the presence of
the elder brethren and of the royal barons, Hugh
de Montfort, Roger Bigot, Richard, son of Count
Gislebert, Turold of Lincoln,[1] Alvered the Spaniard
and others, the prelate declared the cause of his
misfortune, confessed his sin and anathematized his
conduct and all who counselled it.   He then advanced
with sighs and groans to the great altar, laid thereon
the crozier, which he had caused to be brought from
Thetford, and, prostrate on the steps of the altar,
begged pardon of God and St. Edmund.   The abbot
and monks recited over him the seven penitential
psalms and absolved him."   After these spiritual
remedies the abbot applied those temporal medicines
in the preparation of which he was so skilled.   "By
frequent   fomentations,   cauteries   and   collyriums, *And receives back his sight and health.*
supplemented by the prayers of the monks to God

---

[1] For Turold of Lincoln see Lingard, vol. i. p. 235, edit. 1854.

and his martyr Edmund, I saw the bishop regaining
his health, and at last only a slight obscurity remained on the pupil of one eye for a sign of his
audacity. So that on the martyr's feast he preached
the panegyric." [1]

Afterwards, persuaded by evil counsellors, Herfast
renewed his claim, but when Archbishop Lanfranc
came down to enquire into it, the aged Abbot Ælfwin
gave testimony to the exemptions granted by King
Canute and Bishop Ailwin and at the same time
was able to corroborate the story of the burning of
the house of his father, Eadbright, on occasion of his
refusing Ailwin and St. Edmund the shelter of a roof,—
a warning to all to take care how they treat St. Edmund
and his servants. But in spite of evidence to the
contrary the bishop stubbornly persevered. Abbot
Baldwin refuted all his assertions in a great court
of enquiry convened for the purpose in 1181. It
was all of no use. At last, in a regular trial held
by the king's order, judgment was given for the
abbot. The bishop refused to submit and was there-

upon forced to give up ring and crozier, which
amounted to his practical deposition. He returned
to his diocese to end his days, a disgraced and disappointed man. [2]

Akin to these chastisements of the invaders of
the royal martyr's privileges and possessions are
those inflicted on the irreverent. The impetuous
youth Count Leofstan was struck with madness for
looking profanely on the saint's face; a presumptuous
Dane became blind in St. Gregory's church in London;
Abbot Leofstan for disrespectfully handling the holy
body suffered a contraction of the hands to the day

---

[1] Besides Herman, see "Regist. Rub.," Collect. Buriens.,
p. 330.

[2] Compare the history of Bishop Bateman, p. 262.

of his death; Tolinus and his associates died pre-
maturely for rashly opening the coffin and touching
the martyr's limbs; Herman the monk fell sick and
died after carelessly exhibiting the martyr's garments.

The case of Osgod-Clapa is a further illustration
of irreverent conduct towards the saint and its
penalty. It occurred early one summer when St.
Edward the Confessor was on a visit to the abbey.
The most conspicuous figure in the royal train both
by his haughty bearing and gorgeous dress was
Osgod-Clapa, the master of the horse.[1] On the
"Finding of the Holy Cross," which that year
fell on a Sunday, Osgod, decked out in barbaric
finery, with golden bracelets on both arms and a
gilded axe flung over his shoulder, indevoutly entered
the martyr's church. The bystanders cried out to
him to lay aside his axe at the door, but he took
no heed and insolently passed on through the choir
to the very Holy of Holies! There he began to
unfasten his axe, not from reverence, but to lean
on it, while he considered what to do next, when
the mighty hand of the saint struck him with madness and dashed him against the wall of the basilica
as one possessed. The people, hearing an uproar,
crowded to the spot to see this man, "sæculo famosissi-
mus, sed rebus martyris infestissimus"—famous in the
eyes of the world, but abominable[2] to St. Edmund,—
humiliated in the sight of all. King Edward and

The story of
Osgod-Clapa,
who is chastised
for his pride,
A.D. 1044.

---

[1] The Worcester Chronicle calls him "Stallere," or master
of the horse. The sudden death of Hardacnut occurred at the
feast given by Osgod after the marriage of his daughter Gytha to
the Danish chieftain Tovi, surnamed the Proud (see Florence of
Worcester, A.D. 1042). Osgod was a benefactor of the monastery of
Waltham. In reputation and power, says Samson, he was next to
the king. He was outlawed in 1046, but returned to England and
died according to the Saxon Chronicle in 1054.

[2] "Every proud man is an abomination to the Lord."—*Prov.*
vi. 5.

He is cured and repents, the monks assembled with him in chapter heard the uproar, and on learning its' cause made their way to the church. There the king turned to Abbot Leofstan and said, "Father, it is your duty with your monks to supplicate the saint to restore this unfortunate man, so that, corrected by this punishment, he may confess his sins and amend his life." Thereupon the monks commenced to recite the psalms and litanies, and the abbot read the exorcisms and sprinkled the maniac with holy water: but with no effect. Thereupon Ailwin, the saint's "chamberlain," recommended that he should be brought to the martyr's tomb. There the brethren, vested in white albs, again chant the seven psalms and the litanies over him; and the Dane, coming to himself, acknowledged his profanity and in his fervour embraced the shrine. "The king and the crowd glorified God, who is wonderful in His saints and through them works wonderful things." Osgod repented and corrected his life, but his hands remained withered as a perpetual reminder that God will not permit any irreverence towards His champion Edmund—Athleta Edmundus.

But his hands remain withered.

A summary. The Bodleian compilation gives the above and several additional " miracles " of the same character, [1] showing

---

[1] Thus fol. 633 : "De muliere liberata et vicecomite punito. De quodam Leofstano punito, &c. Qualiter Theodredus epō. fecit suspendi latronès,"&c. ; fol. 634 : "De Daco cæcitate punito," &c. ; fol. 636 : "De interfectione regis Swani per sētum Edm̄. ; " fol. 640 : "Qualiter Osgothi Daci superbia punita sit ; " fol. 643 : " De ultione facta in Erfastum epē. per sanctum Edmundum ; " fol. 645 : " De quodam milite demoniaco rapiente quoddam manerium de Sōto Edm̄. ; " fol. 646 : " De ultione facta in pervasores rerum suarum ; " fol. 650 : " De incorruptione Scī Edm̄. et de ultione facta in Tolinum monachum palpantem et videntem corpus Scī Edm̄. incorruptum ; " fol. 651 : " De ultione facta in Hermanum monachum explicantem camisiam Scī Edm̄. et ostendentem populo ad osculandum ; " fol. 653 : "De ultione facta in latronem rapientem de feretro Scī Edm̄. ; " fol. 654 : "De ultione sumpta in

that kings like Sweyn and Edward I., petty thieves
and great barons, soldiers and civilians, judges and
royal justiciaries were punished without distinction for
sacrilegious attempts against St. Edmund's church,
so that all classes feared to wrongfully attack its
privileges and possessions, or to treat with irreverence
the martyr and his servants.

The punishments inflicted on evil-doers are more
than counterbalanced by the graces and blessings
which the royal saint gained for devout suppliants.
Scattered over a period of a thousand years, these
favours have continued to the present day and may
be said to be countless. The records of some hundreds
still exist, having survived the sixteenth century wreck
of the monastic libraries and their invaluable treasures.
The Wainflete Register brings the miracles down to
1374-75. Lydgate recounts one as happening on
April 20, 1441. The archives of Toulouse chronicle
the cessation of the plague and the cure of the
fever-stricken in 1631, while at St. Edmund's Wells
at Hunstanton an extraordinary if not miraculous cure
in 1864 rewarded the faith of a young girl who
bathed there. The miracles of which the details exist
are, however, few compared with the period over
which they extend, and of these few only the following
selections in addition to those related in the body of
the work will be given to illustrate their general
characteristics.

Continuity of the miracles.

Eustachium filium Regis Stephani, &c. De ultione sumpta in
Henricum de Essexia. De ultione sumpta in Willielmum de
Curzun;" fol. 661: "De ultione facta pro festo Sci Edm̄. non
observato;" fol. 663: "De ultione facta super quendam prædi-
torem rapientem pavonem de dominio Sci Edm̄.;" fol. 667: "De
quodam blasphemo punito;" fol. 668: "Quomodo S. Edm̄.
terruit comitem Lincolnie, &c.;" fol. 669: "De ultione facta
super Dominum Johannem de Bello monte, militem. De ultione
facta super Willielnium de Gillingham justiciarium regis."

The glory of
St. Edmund
attested by
miracles
wrought at
his tomb.

The cures wrought under the very shadow of the
shrine naturally hold the first rank. Within the holy
and mellowed light which the ever burning tapers for
seven hundred years shed around that hallowed
sepulchre, the crippled and maimed left their
crutches, the blind received their sight, the dumb
learned to speak, the sick recovered health, the dead
were restored to life. Wherever St. Edmund's body
went, its miraculous power followed it. When Ailwin
entered London, nineteen cures took place. They were
of daily occurrence in St. Gregory's church, and the
cure of the Lord of Stapleford is only one of many
which happened on the way back to Beodricsworth.
Once the holy body was in its own church, the guardians of the shrine could commit to writing the circum-
stantial details which made such miracles a picture
of the times. They could describe for instance the
dumb woman, Ælfgeth of Winchester, who, in the
time of Abbot Leofstan, received the gift of speech,
and would never afterwards leave St. Edmund's shrine,
but spent her life cleaning the church and tending the
altars.

A dumb girl
cured about
A.D. 1095.

In the same manner through the monk Tolinus,
a " vir bonus et religiosus," who ascertained the facts,
they could chronicle the cure of a poor girl, the
servant of a lady in Essex, who had been dumb
for three years. Her mistress brought her at last
on a pilgrimage to the shrine, and, while praying
there, the girl suddenly exclaimed: "My lady! my
lady! behold I can speak." This cure took place on
the eve of the feast of the Seven Martyrs.

The blind son of
Knight Yvo,
A.D. 1088,

Edmund, the son of Yvo, one of the knights of
William Rufus, had been struck with blindness for
using profane language, it appears, regarding the
saint. " Verrucæ concretæ, rufæ atque pillosæ,"—red
warty substances covered with hair had strangely

grown about the eyes. Before starting for the Scotch war, Yvo ordered his son to be taken to the saint's shrine. For fifteen days the boy tarried at the church of Binneham with the monk Herman, [1] whose acolyte and scholar he was. Then in spite of the boy's un- willingness and his tutor's protest the uncle and step- mother took him to St. Edmund's shrine, where they arrived on the eve of the martyr's feast. As they keep watch near the holy body, the boy falls asleep, and in that sweet sleep, before the bells for matins chime, the heavenly power of St. Edmund heals him, by mercifully drawing from his eyes the blinding excrescence, and on waking he sees the lights around the shrine. The news of the miracle soon spread, and after the gospel of the high mass a sermon was preached, and thanksgiving made to God and St. Edmund by the multitude with the boy standing in their midst.

In spite of the monk Herman, his tutor, is taken to the shrine,

And receives his sight.

On the Nativity of the ever glorious Virgin, William of Colchester's little girl was similarly cured. On the eve of the festival her father sent the child, who had been blind for five weeks, in charge of its nurse, to St. Edmund, and the next day it recovered its sight. After the solemn mass the monks sang the "Te Deum" with the child standing before the altar.

A child of three years old is cured of blind- ness, A.D. 1088.

On the feast of St. John the Baptist in the year of Abbot Baldwin's translation a poor lame girl on crutches came to the saint with her relations, and she left her crutches with him for a testimony of her cure.

The cure of a lame girl, A.D. 1095.

On the martyr's festival the same year a blind girl named Lyeveva received her sight, which she had lost a year before by an accident. Her relatives and fellow-townsmen came with her on pilgrimage. "We saw her prostrate in the new presbytery on the eve

A blind girl named Lyeveva has her sight restored.

---

[1] A different personage from Archdeacon Herman, who relates the incident after hearing the evidence of his repentant namesake.

of the feast, when at the 'Magnificat' we proceeded
with our venerable Abbot Baldwin to incense the
Holy of Holies." She spent the night in prayer, and
the evening of the feast during vespers she regained
her sight. She assisted at high mass the next day,
and after a sermon the "Te Deum" was sung.

A woman who
had been blind
thirty-two years
is cured.

Another woman from Winchester, who had been
thirty-two years blind, hearing of the glorious series
of miracles at St. Edmund's Bury, begged her daughter
to lead her thither. After keeping vigil, she was, next
morning, between matins and lauds, blessed with
sight.

Brichtiva, the
housekeeper of
Odo the priest,

A priest named Odo had in his service a housekeeper, by name Brichtiva, who looked after his
scholars with all the devotion of a mother. After
many years' service she became bedridden through

Bedridden for
seven years,

a contraction of the nerves of both legs. For seven
years she lay in this state, till, seized by a sudden
inspiration, she said to her master: "Sir, remember
the long and devoted service of thy handmaid, and in
thy charity grant me this favour. Have me placed
on some vehicle and carried to St. Edmund's basilica,
for surely the gate of mercy which admits all will not
be shut to me if I knock." Accordingly she was
carried to the church, and crept to the altar, to which
she held fast with her hands. It was the vigil of the

On June 23rd,

Precursor of Christ, at whose nativity, according to
the inspired prophecy, "many shall rejoice." [1] While
the alternate choirs sang the "Magnificat" at vespers,
the prior ascended the altar to incense it, when to his
astonishment he saw the woman, whom a little time

Recovers in St.
Edmund's
church,

before he had condoled with in her affliction, standing
erect with a crowd of people round her. The prior,
to ascertain the truth, with a loud voice asked if any
one knew her. Not one or two, but many who knew

---

[1] St. Luke i. 14.

her master, testified to her previous helpless condition. As many testify.
But Brichtiva ever cherished in her heart the memory
of St. Edmund, and never ceased to praise him to the
end of her days.

In the reign of Henry I. a girl from Clare in Essex, A girl from Clare
is cured, A.D.
born without the use of arms or legs, was brought by 1100-1135.
her relations to the church "pretiosi regis Ædmundi,'
and was restored whole and sound to her parents.
" Radulf the monk [1] saw it with his own eyes," writes
the chronicler; " he who devoutly guarded the royal
tomb—mausoleum regis—for years, and accurately
narrated the wonders which he saw." " Sic operatur
dilectus noster et princeps Ædmundus, candidus et
rubicundus; quem et nivea integritas induit virginei
corporis, et rosea circumdat laurea pretiosæ passionis."
—"*So worketh our beloved prince Edmund, the fair and
ruddy one; whose robe is the snow-white integrity of
his virginal body, whose crown is the rose-wreath of
his precious passion.*"

From every part of the country sick of both Other miracles
at the tomb.
sexes and of every age visited the shrine and received
their health. At one time a girl from Spalding is
healed. At another, a paralytic farmer from Rutland
in the diocese of Lincoln, who in his days of health
was a frequent and devout pilgrim to the martyr's
church, is brought there by his friends and returns
home upright and whole, after giving the animal which
carried him to the monks. Now a monk of Shrewsbury
gets his health. Now an old blind man from Northum-
berland joins a party of pilgrims, and, coming within
sight of the high bell-tower of the abbey-church, kneels
down to pray with the rest; he thereupon recovers his
sight and leads the pilgrimage into the town. Again,
a certain Matilda belonging to London lays her little
dying son at the foot of the shrine, and he recovers.

---

[1] For the history of this Radulf, see note, p. 302.

T

Miracles at a
distance from
the shrine.

At Lucca ;

Hereford ;

Canterbury ;

Acre, 1190 ;

Chichester ;

Evesham ;

Shimpling ;

Northampton ;

Swineshead :

From these graphic and touching scenes around the shrine we turn to others at a distance, in England or abroad. For instance, at Lucca a rich man's little boy is cured; at Hereford Robert of Haseley, a canon, recovers from a quartan ague. In another part of the country a soldier and his wife vow their dying boy to God and St. Edmund, and he revives and lives. The same happens in the case of the son of one Henry, a knight of Canterbury, and also in that of the son of William de Bealver. A soldier at the siege of Acre during the crusade of Richard I., afflicted with all the symptoms of black death, begs the intercession of the glorious martyr and suddenly grows better. A cleric at Chichester, working in the roof of the cathedral, falls from a height of forty-seven feet to the ground. He calls upon St. Edmund, whose feast it is, and receives but little hurt. An Evesham monk, on seeking the intercession of the martyr, is marvellously cured of a painful disease. A young man from Shimpling taken in war, tortured and loaded with chains, on invoking St. Edmund and St. Nicholas is set free. A miller at Warkton,[1] unjustly thrown into the dungeons of Northampton Castle with nineteen others, cries to St. Edmund; the shackles fall from his feet, and, rising up, he makes for the church of St. Edmund in that town, the four guards, helpless, allowing him to pass. Similarly the bailiff of Robert de Gresley, whom his master had thrown into prison at Swineshead, with tears and groans implores St. Edmund and St. Etheldreda to deliver him from his bonds; and St. Edmund, appearing to him, sets

---

[1] Or Wereketon, a village near Kettering in Northamptonshire. Queen Matilda, the wife of the Conqueror, gave its manor to St. Edmund's Abbey towards the building of the great church.

him free.   Whereupon he makes a pilgrimage to
the shrine to return thanks.

Among the miracles which thus took place outside *The Wainfleet miracles.*
the precincts of the martyr's sanctuary, come the
seventeen recorded in the Wainfleet register.   After
the narration of "How the ruined chapel of Wainfleet was repaired by reason of a revelation from
St. Edmund," the chronicler describes among other
incidents the restoration to life of a dead girl and
of two drowned children; the cure of four cripples
and two blind persons; several rescues from shipwreck, and the release of six pilgrims in Spain from
prison and chains.

Similar miracles were registered in a certain chapel *The Lynn miracles.*
of St. Edmund at Lynn.   Special interest centres
round King's Lynn.   According to Camden, St.
Edmund landed there before proceeding to Hunstanton.   No doubt its connection with the gentle
and saintly king dates from an early period, as
its name, its ancient and venerable chapel to his
memory, and the miracles which took place there,
testify.   In this sanctuary, among other favours granted
through the intercession of St. Edmund, it is averred
that three dead men were raised to life, and several
blind and dumb people, as well as cripples, were cured.

Instances of the protection afforded to St. Edmund's *On the high seas St. Edmund protects his suppliants.*
suppliants on the high seas are strikingly numerous
in all the lists of miracles.   They were of the utmost
interest to seafaring Englishmen generally, and
especially to the men of Norfolk and Suffolk with
their long sea-board.   Hence the careful registry
of them in the monastic books.   Herman's Book
of Miracles breaks off abruptly in the midst of a
narrative of this kind, in which he describes some
pilgrims returning by sea from Rome on the Friday *Some pilgrims returning by sea from Rome, A.D. 1095,*
before the Rogation days, May 15, 1095.   Samson

finishes the story. The ship had sixty-four souls on board and a cargo of precious objects from the Are in danger of shipwreck. Eternal City. In mid-ocean the vessel sprang a leak, and the hold quickly filled with water, which rose higher and higher in spite of energetic and continuous pumping. In despair sailors and passengers prepared for death. Then Wulfward, the priest, and Robert, both of St. Edmund's, remembering the great power of their patron, asking for silence, thus addressed their comrades: "Men, brethren! Why give way to despair? Who does not know our St. Edmund? The fame of his virtues extends over land and sea. Who has ever sought protection under They invoke St. Edmund, his wings and been repulsed? Let us each and all call upon him in this hour of danger after first making an offering for his shrine." The advice was taken. Then from the silent ocean the cry went up to heaven: "Sancte Ædmunde, libera nos." To the joy and astonishment of all, the water in the hold suddenly began to subside, and the sails began to fill with wind; and "felix carina feliciter And are saved. cepit velificare,"—the ship, happily saved from destruction, began once more to merrily plough the billows. On reaching port, Wulfward and Robert, commissioned by their fellow-passengers, carried the offering to St. Edmund's monastery, and there related the history of their marvellous preservation.

The narrative of Lambert, an Angevin abbot,[1] Lambert, abbot of St. Nicholas,' Angers, used to relate how on one of his many visits to the tomb of the renowned king and martyr the community asked him the reason of his singular devotion to St. Edmund, and he answered them: "Beloved brethren, St. Edmund king and martyr is deservedly considered our father as well as patron of England, as the following story will testify:

---

[1] "Relatio Domni Lamberti Abbatis."

"One winter, although we had most pressing business to transact, the intense cold and the tempestuous sea delayed us several days at Barfleur. Most earnestly we prayed to many saints, not forgetting our own St. Nicholas. One afternoon, as we spoke of the merits and powers of different saints, Natalis, an old monk of ours, who had honourably worn the religious habit for well nigh fifty years, asked if we would take his advice in order to get a secure and speedy voyage. We eagerly professed our willingness to do so. 'Promise,' he said, 'to the glorious and blessed Edmund, the martyr-king of the English, that, your request granted, you will go and return thanks in his church and in future regard him as his own household does.'[1] To our criticisms on this he answered: To pray to St. Edmund, known to be so powerful in England, would spread his glory in Europe, and be no disparagement to our patron, St. Nicholas, whom all the world invokes in danger and distress. Thereupon we earnestly besought St. Edmund, and, confidently embarking that evening, reached Southampton harbour at nine o'clock next day, having crossed the channel in the incredible space of ten hours. Not unmindful of our promise, we came to blessed Edmund's church to fulfil our vows. This was the beginning of our love and devotion towards the most holy Edmund."

While Abbot Lambert told his story, three men from London, Hervey, Yvo, and another, were paying their devotions at the shrine. They afterwards described how, being wind-bound on a voyage to St. Gilles,[2] they implored the martyr's help, and a pleasant breeze quickly brought them to port. The

Margin notes: Who, being wind-bound at Barfleur, / Made a vow to St. Edmund, / And afterwards safely reached port. / Three pilgrims in the church tell a similar story.

---

[1] "Familia."

[2] St. Gilles, on the Little Rhone below Arles. Its abbey-church even in its present ruin is a work of great splendour.

chronicler, admiring their faith, promised to put
their tale on record, and so it reaches us.

Radulph the monk, while assiduously performing
his duties at the shrine, saw three other men
prostrate before it and fervently kissing the very
stones on which it rested. Rising from their prayers,

they told him how their ship was nearly foundering
in a violent storm which lasted three days, till
they all cried to St. Edmund, " O sancte rex et
martyr Ædmunde! O potens et benigne princeps,
nobis auxilium tuæ pietatis porrige! insignis tri-
umphator Ædmunde!"—" O holy king and martyr Edmund! O mighty and benignant prince, stretch forth
thy kind helping hand! O triumphant Edmund!"
And behold the storm abated, and they reached port
in safety.

A cleric from
Lichfield tells
how St. Edmund
saved him from
drowning.

A cleric from Lichfield, coming to return thanks
to St. Edmund, declared to the monks in chapter
that, on his going to Jerusalem, the ship in which
he sailed was wrecked in a great storm. Struggling
for life in the boiling sea, he invoked St. Edmund,
and, as it is recorded of the blessed confessor St.
Nicholas that he is present to sailors who call upon
him, so the glorious martyr Edmund came to him, and,
seizing him by the hair, brought him to land. With
grateful tears the cleric asked his rescuer's name.
" I am Edmund, whose help you implored," answered
the vision and disappeared.

On another occasion some Dunwich fishermen
came to hang up an anchor of wax before the
shrine in thanksgiving to St. Edmund, whom they
had invoked in a storm. Again, three men cast on
a sand-bank in a wreck were marvellously saved
after invoking the royal martyr. So also were a
Norfolk man and his wife.

Conspicuous among these and many other instances

of St. Edmund's protection of the shipwrecked and *The story of King Henry I.* drowning is the case of Henry I. In 1132 Henry, after his interview with Pope Innocent II., left Chartres for England. On the passage a violent storm arose, which threatened the utter destruction of vessel and crew. The king, fearing with reason that it was a visitation of God upon him, made solemn vows of reformation and amendment, at the same time calling upon St. Edmund to help him. On the ship's arriving safe in port, Henry set out on a pilgrimage of thanksgiving to St. Edmund's shrine.

Passing to another class of favours, we find St. *St. Edmund the St. Antony of England.* Edmund invoked by our forefathers, very much as St. Antony of Padua is to-day, for things that are lost. For instance, Abbot Baldwin's messenger, Norman, when his luggage had been stolen at Barfleur, recovered it in a surprising manner after praying to St. Edmund. The martyr restored to Warner, abbot of Rebaix, a relic which he had lost. Some horses taken away from the monastery were miraculously brought back, an incident which the monks carved over the abbot's stall in the choir of the great church, giving its history underneath in four lines of verse. [1]

Again one 20th of November, the festival of St. *Deorman, a London merchant,* Edmund, Deorman, a rich London merchant, who exposed his silks and spices in the town for sale, went into the basilica to pray at the shrine. While prostrate there, a woman cut away the bag which *Is robbed at the shrine.* contained his money and jewels, so that when he prepared to make his offering he found nothing to give. Then, turning to the saint, he expostulated: "I came, holy prince," he said, "into your house to pray; and why have you allowed impious hands

---

[1] Bodl. MS. 240 f. 667.

to rob me? Surely my possessions ought to be
secure here!" Going out at the church-door, he
unawares put his hands on a woman in the crowd,
who at once fell on her knees, and, handing back
his bag and its untouched contents, begged him not
to expose her. Letting the thief go free, he re-entered
the church to give thanks to God and St. Edmund,
Afterwards he became a monk and lived holily many
years in the monastery.

After expostulating with the saint, he recovers his money.

Again, a knight of Copeland beyond York, who
owned farms in East Anglia, sent his servant to
collect the rents. The servant lost the money, but
after invoking St. Edmund found it again. Some
fishermen, having lost their nets, prayed to St. Edmund
and they miraculously recovered them.

Two other examples.

These temporal favours are eclipsed by the spiritual
graces which the royal martyr dispensed with lavish
hand. Often he gave them as well as corporal
health, as in the case of William de Curzun, Bishop
Herfast and others, but still more frequently by
themselves. A wicked squire, moved by the healing
of a rich lady whom he had accompanied to St.
Edmund's church, confessed his sins and received
from the martyr health of soul and body. A wealthy
knight, in despair of salvation by reason of a vice
which had enslaved him, resorted to St. Edmund,
prayed before the shrine, and, confessing his guilt,
was freed from temptation. A licentious ecclesiastic
from the diocese of Chichester was likewise converted
through the invocation of St. Edmund.

Spiritual graces.

Both spiritual and temporal graces were sometimes
accompanied by a vision of the saint. In their
invocations our ancestors coupled St. Edmund with
St. Nicholas, St. Etheldreda, or St. Thomas of Canterbury, and on two occasions, at least, the royal
martyr is related to have appeared in company

Visions of the saint,

In company with St. Thomas of Canterbury.

with St. Thomas: once after the battle of Fornham
in the reign of Henry II., when the two martyrs
liberated some prisoners of war; and again to a
certain Earl Simon, their devout client, to console
him for the death of an only son, whom they
pointed out to him in heaven.[1]

These apparitions show the sympathy which *Their meaning.*
medieval writers believed the saint to have with
those on earth in sorrow and difficulty. Unbelievers
may consider them dreams only; yet they prove
what a reality the martyr's power and presence
were in the minds of the people. And while re-
vealing our ancestors' deep sense of St. Edmund's
solicitude for their welfare,[2] they throw a special
heavenly and supernatural light over the history
of many of the royal martyr's devoted servants, like
Ailwin and Abbot Samson.

The most beautiful and touching scenes are por- *The vision of St.*
trayed in connection with these visions. The cure *Edmund,*
of the poor crippled woman who, in the reign of
the Confessor, sat begging at the porch of the great
church, is a case in point. Her legs hung withered
and useless on her body. Sitting on a little stool
and with smaller stools in her hands, she moved
about with great exertion, and thus often approached
the shrine asking for her cure. Night and day
she remained in the church, for, like the infirm
man at the pool at Bethsaida, she had no one to
take care of her. At eventide, when others went

---

[1] Bodl. 240 f. 663.

[2] E.g. St. Edmund appears to a peasant of Exming, a village on
the Suffolk border of Cambridgeshire, and reveals his wish to see
a road made for the benefit of pilgrims from St. Etheldreda's, Ely,
to St. Edmund's Bury; and the monks constructed Soham cause-
way in consequence (Bodl. 240 f. 662). "Hæc magna et mirabilia
dignatus est in parvis facere Maximus in S. Edmundi favorem, ut
ostendat qualis gratiæ sit apud eum etiam in magnis."

away, she, poor and neglected, slept inside the western

And the cure of
the crippled
woman.

door. One night a pious matron of Essex named Ælfweve, keeping vigil at the shrine, praying out the candle which she held in her hand, saw a man venerable of countenance and clothed in dazzling and shining robes issue from the precincts of the shrine, and glide through the lines of stalls in the choir and down the long nave, his brightness throwing the shadows of the lines of pillars into the aisles. Arriving at the western doors, the vision paused, benignly regarded the sleeping cripple, as SS. Peter and John did the beggar at the Beautiful Gate of the Temple, and, standing, signed the sleeping woman with the sign of the cross from head to foot. Then the heavenly visitor returned whence he came, shining like the sun in the darkness. But by that saving sign he had restored to the crippled woman the nerves and members lost for so many years. Ælfweve looked on in ecstasy. The infirm

The matron
Ælfweve from
Essex

woman, waking up, made the vast and silent church echo with her cries. She skipped and danced and and wept, praising God. Meanwhile the "faithful monk," Brunstan, the keeper of the shrine, who slept in the church, thinking that robbers had broken in, ran to the *cortina*,[1] only to find its gates locked as he left them, and the woman whom he had seen a cripple praising God and St. Edmund. Just then the bells rang to assemble the monks for matins. After matins the miracle

And the monk
Brunstan confirm it.

became public. Brother Brunstan gave evidence, as did the matron Ælfweve and the crippled woman. So the bells were rung, and the alternate choirs sang lauds to Him "who is wonderful in His saints, and renders them wonderful on earth, that all may know how great glory they enjoy in heaven."

---

[1] A railing round the shrine.

St. Edmund, luminous in the darkness, traversing
the long nave, healing the crippled beggar lying in
poverty and loneliness at the church-porch—the sleeping
keeper—the watching matron—and, matins over, the
monks crowding round the cured woman—the bells
ringing and the thanksgiving sung—behold a picture
earthly yet unearthly!

One of these visions, glimpses of heaven, accom- ^{William Fitz}
panied the cure of the Frenchman William, son of ^{Asketil,} consumed with
Asketil, of the county of Hereford. Fever and racking ^{fever,}
pains had already deprived him of the use of his
limbs, when he heard of the fame of St. Edmund
and asked to be carried to his tomb. There he made
his offering and prayed to the saint for a cure.
When his attendants carried him on his litter from
the church back to the hospice, they momentarily
expected him to breathe his last. A thousand fevers
seemed to consume him, his eyes stood fixed and
staring as if he was in the last agony.

About mid-day the bystanders heard him conversing ^{Is cured in a}
with some one. As he related afterwards, he spoke to a ^{vision of the saint.}
man of medium stature, in the bloom of youth, very
noble in appearance and of kingly dignity and attire,
who stood at his side and, touching him with a rod,
asked why he lay there. The sick man answered,
"Consumed with fever and loaded with infirmity,
I am seeking a cure from St. Edmund." His attendants
thought him delirious. The heavenly visitor asked,
"Do you believe that he can give what you ask?"
"Without doubt, I believe," the dying man replied.
"Arise then safe and sound," the vision commanded,
"and rejoicing, mount your horse and return home."
The sick man enquired who thus, like to our Saviour
in the gospel, bade him arise and walk. "I am
Edmund, the servant of Jesus Christ," the saint
replied. "Get up, and hastening home with your

servants, tell what great things the Almighty has
done for you." Those around during all this time
heard but saw nothing. The sick man, at once rising
up, ate and drank at a banquet with his friends,
and after making a suitable thank-offering in the
church, returned home, proclaiming the name and
power of St. Edmund in town and country, affirming
that he had seen him and spoken with him face
to face.

The story of
Wulmar,

A similar and not less graphic incident, " which,"
says Herman, " we know to be true, because it
came under our own observation," is told of Wulmar,
an honest burgess of the town, who after a pilgrimage
to Rome placed an offering on the " marble and crystal altar " in thanksgiving for a safe return. Leaving
the church one Sunday evening, Wulmar fell down
in a fit and was carried home insensible. For four
days he lay paralysed and helpless. On Friday his
friends summoned Goding the parish-priest, who,
" coming with his scholars," administered the Viaticum.
All that day and the three following, the sick man
lay with eyes closed and limbs cold and stiff, as though
dead, except for his breathing. The next day, Tuesday,
was a festival—the translation of blessed Edmund
by Abbot Leofstan,—and our protector chose that
day to manifest his power. After midnight, as the
bells chimed for the matins of the feast, the dying
man fell into a sweet sleep, in which he saw as
though with his real eyes the door of his room open

Who sees a
vision of the
saint,

and a bright cloud like a dove enter, which,
approaching, grew larger as he gazed, till the vision
of a man of fair and dazzling form stood beside
him. The vision touched his eyes as if to open them,
saying, " Fear nothing ; you shall know the great mercy
of God. Now you are whole, go to the festival in
the church and give thanks to your Saviour." " But

who art thou ? " asked the sick man. " I am Edmund,
the servant of the Eternal King," answered the vision,
gradually fading away as it had come. Wulmar, to
the amazement of his attendants, arose at once, clothed
himself and walked to church, where he offered to And recovers
his health.
the martyr four crystals which he had brought
from Rome, as a perpetual memorial of his vision
and cure. Then, calling Brother Tolinus, he told
him all. Abbot Baldwin, informed of the incident,
summoned the priests Siward and Goding and many
others, and took their evidence and the oath of the
cured man. When the miracle could not be gain-
said, assembling the people in the church, the abbot
caused a sermon to be preached, and, with the pealing
of the bells, the " Te Deum " to be sung.

Of these visions of mercy not the least striking Ranulf, a
Norman knight
are those in which St. Edmund is said to have con-
verted sinners and inspired them to dedicate their
lives to God. The conversion of Ranulf is a case
in point. Ranulf, " vitæ religiosæ monachus," the
monk of religious life, the assiduous keeper of the
shrine for many years, the witness and narrator of
miracles, had been a courtier of the Conqueror's, a
knight " militari perversus in opere," the comrade
of Chichester.[1] Struck down by fever in one of his
foraging expeditions, he lay tossing on his bed of
sickness for eight days, unable to eat, drink or sleep.

" On the eighth day God deigned to visit him Sees St.
Edmund,
through his martyr, who desired to show him mercy,
and whom the sick man had ever remembered."
For, falling asleep, he dreamt of St. Edmund, saw
the saint on horseback in glittering armour pursuing
him, felt his lance strike him in the back and throw

---

[1] Probably Robert, the unworthy son of the noble Roger de
Montgomeri, Earl of Chichester and Shrewsbury, who died in 1094.
(See Ordericus Vit., v. 14.)

him prostrate from his horse into a hedged enclosure
full of flowers, and saw him standing over him threatening death. He pitifully begged for mercy and life.
Edmund kindly laid his open right hand upon the
soldier's head, and making the sign of the cross
Who cures him, upon him, answered, " If you would but do what
will bring them to you, you can be free." In answer
to the knight's request Edmund revealed his name and
disappeared. When the sick man awoke, he found
himself well, and in the morning explained his
miraculous cure to the ecclesiastics of the court, to
Samson, [1] and to others who knew of his sickness.
Unable to throw off the impression which that dream
And he becomes had made, Knight Ranulf asked for the tonsure, and
a monk. shortly after took the religious habit in St. Edmund's
abbey. [2] He had been a " literatus " and had abandoned the schools for a military life. Now we see
him a priest and monk, " Deum laudans in martyrem

---

[1] Not necessarily Abbot Samson.

[2] It is not clear whether the monk Ranulf is the same as
Radulph of whom the following is related in Bodl. 240 f. 663 :

" *The Vision of the Monk Radulph.*—We have seen a religious man
named Radulph, a monk of St. Edmund's, who fell sick, after he
had persevered from youth to old age in the religious life, and by
the command of Abbot Hugh had built the altars of St. Thomas the
Martyr, St. Botulph, and St. Jurminus, and collected the relics of
St. Thomas and of as many others as possible in gold and jewelled
shrines. One Sunday night, when his sickness had become
very grave, he saw approach him in most sweet vision our
Lord Jesus Christ, Edmund also with Thomas, and St. Botulph
with St. Jurminus and St. Nicholas. They spoke to him in melli-
fluous colloquy, saying: ' Adorn the chamber of thy heart, and
come to us ; is there aught beyond? You shall come to rest and
eternal glory.' The holy vision passed ; he asked for his confessor
to be summoned and related all to him. Then he made his confession, and when he had received the body of the Lord, commending his soul to God, to Blessed Mary and St. Edmund, and
to the others mentioned above, and to all the saints, he fell asleep
in peace."

Eadmundum, et ipsum martyrem pretiosum venerans in Omnipotentem Deum,"—"praising God in His martyr Edmund and venerating the precious martyr himself in Almighty God."

The apparition of Edmund which changed " the once proud Henry Earl of Essex " into " the tonsured, mournful, penitent monk " of Reading Abbey, has been described by Carlyle with more than his usual force and beauty of language. Abbot Samson, being on a visit to Reading, heard the particulars from Henry's own mouth and charged one of his attendant monks to commit it to writing. Hence it found its way as an episode into a copy of Jocelin's Chronicle and gets commented upon in the pages of " Past and Present." *The story of Henry of Essex.*

Henry Earl of Essex, standard-bearer of England, held high rank among the barons of Henry II. and filled important offices in the state during that monarch's reign. Haughty and imperious, however, he thought little of the laws of right and justice. He threw Gilbert of Cereville into prison and with chains and torments gradually wore out his life, although his only crime was that of the innocent Joseph. He showed no reverence for St. Edmund, as all others did who respected the " heavenly in man." While the people of the eastern counties endowed King Edmund the martyr's resting-place with rich gifts, Henry by violence defrauded it of five *solidi* yearly and converted the said sum to his own uses. Again for his own profit he questioned the right of St. Edmund's court to try a certain cause, saying that it belonged to his in Lailand Hundred, and thus " involved us in travellings and innumerable expenses, vexing the servants of St. Edmund for a long period." But all this time he did but weave his own evil destiny. For in the year 1157, attending *His character.* *He defrauds St. Edmund's ;*

King Henry in the Welsh wars as hereditary standard-bearer, when the enemy made a sudden attack on the English in the difficult pass of Coleshill, he dropped the standard and shrieked out that the king was slain and all was lost. The utmost confusion ensued, and destruction threatened king and army, till the brave Count Roger of Clare came dashing up with his men, and, raising the royal standard from the ground, rallied the fugitives and drove back the Welshmen.[1] Once they were home again, the incident was not forgotten, and Earl Robert de Montfort, the standard-bearer's kinsman and match in strength, rising up in the assembly of the great barons, declared him unfit for standard-bearer and branded him traitor and coward.

Is charged with treachery by Robert de Montfort.

A duel in consequence on a Thames Eyot near Reading, A.D. 1163.

Henry answers in a recriminatory speech. A challenge is offered and accepted, and a duel appointed to be fought on an island of the Thames near Reading, within a short distance of the abbey. King, peers and a great multitude of people on scaffoldings and hillocks assemble to see the issue. "And it came to pass," writes the scribe, "while Robert thundered on him with hard and frequent strokes, and a bold beginning promised the fruit of victory, Henry, fainting a little, looked around; and lo! on the confines of river and land he discerned, as if hovering in the air, the glorious king and martyr in shining armour, and with austere countenance nodding his head towards him in an angry and threatening manner. At St. Edmund's side stood another knight, Gilbert de Cereville, in armour less splendid, in stature smaller, but casting indignant and revengeful looks at him. Startled and trembling, he saw them and that old remembered crime brings new shame. And

---

[1] See Gervase, Rolls Series, i. 165 ; Diceto, " Ymag Hist.," Rolls Series, i. p. 310.

now wholly desperate, instead of using his reason
in skilled defence he begins a wild and blind
attack. But while he struck fiercely, he was more
fiercely struck, and while he fought manfully, he
was more manfully fought; and so he fell down Essex is taken
for dead and
carried into
Reading abbey,
vanquished and, as it was thought, slain. As he
lay there for dead, his kinsmen, magnates of England,
besought the king that the monks of Reading might
have leave to bury him. However, he proved not
to be dead, and got well again among them, and,
restored to health, he strove in the regular habit to
wipe out the stain of his former life, and to redeem
the long week of his dissolute history by at least an
edifying sabbath, cultivating virtue into the fruit of Where he be-
comes a monk.
eternal felicity.'

Thus St. Edmund was believed to influence the
minds and hearts of men, whether by real visions
"on the rim of the horizon," or by silent presence
in the tomb, teaching generations of Englishmen to
be just and reverent, and reminding them of the
other world to which he and they belonged.

St. Abbo supplies the final comment on these St. Abbo's
commentary on
the miracles.
scenes so old yet so actual, and in their meaning so
beautiful, great and true, which are now left to the
scepticism or faith of moderns. " Desirous of being
brief," writes the saintly abbot, " I pass over many
of the glorious virtues which shine forth from St.
Edmund, lest I offend the over-fastidious by my
lengthiness. Besides I think that what I have related
will be sufficient for the fervour and devotion of
those who after the protection of God desire nothing
so much as the patronage of this great martyr. Of
him it is evident, as it is of other saints reigning
with Christ, that, though his soul is in heavenly
glory, still it is not far distant, either by day or
night, from the body in whose company it merited

U

those joys of blessed immortality which it now possesses. Until they are joined in the eternal kingdom, where they shall be forever together, he has indeed whatever he can have or wish to have, except only that he desires with unwearied desire that by the resurrection he may be surrounded with the robe of flesh. When by the bounteousness of Christ that shall come to be, then shall the happiness of the saints be complete."

King Henry vi. at St. Edmund's Shrine.

(From Dom Lydgate's "Life and Acts of St. Edmund."

Harleian MSS. 2478.)

307

CHAPTER XI.

Devotion to St. Edmund.

[*Authorities*—Most of the authorities referred to at the beginning of previous chapters illustrate one or other phase of devotion to the great martyr of England, and are therefore spoken of when necessary in the body of this chapter. Several pieces of which no mention has been made before, and notably the epic by Denis Piramus and the "Vita sti Edmundi" by William of Ramsey, are specially noticed. The Bodl. MS. Digby 109, which contains the ancient office of the royal martyr, is fully described among the authorities at the beginning of Chapter IV.]

A MAN's personality is sometimes more vividly felt in his absence than in his presence. When the changeable and disturbing elements of appearance, mannerisms and faults have passed away, his genuine character, power and influence are more fully realized. Thus great men often exercise more influence over their followers after death than during life, for their admirers keep fresh the memory of what attracted them and forget what repelled them. The personality of St. Edmund, more markedly than in an ordinary hero, won the affection and loyalty of all with whom he came into contact during life, but it stood revealed in all its force and beauty only after his death. He was indelibly fixed in the minds not only of his subjects but of future kings and people, English and Danes, clergy and laity, as the model of a ruler, a saintly high-souled Christian, an unflinching champion of the faith, and a valiant defender of people and country against a national enemy. This high idea of his nobleness resulted in an extraordinary devotion to his memory. No sooner

Inspires the early devotion.
did the people issue from their hiding-places than, unmindful of their own troubles, they sought with tears and prayers for the remains of their king, in order to bury them with deepest reverence and love. Other leaders who had fallen in conflict with the Danes had been covered with a simple mound of earth hastily constructed, and had soon been forgotten. But the East Anglians could not easily forget their "good shepherd," their "loving father," their "heavenly intercessor," so close to the throne of the Lamb. His grave was sacred, a holy spot, and they erected to perpetuate their martyr's memory a chapel over it.

Divine Providence kept alive the devotion,
Almighty God in His Providence, in order to signalize the saintly king's distinctive character and to glorify the Christian faith, assisted the devotion of the faithful by special graces and miracles, and the Church by enrolling the martyr amongst her saints proclaimed far and wide the grandeur of his life and deeds.

Which found expression
The consequent outward expressions of enthusiastic love and admiration for the holy king are scarcely surpassed in the annals of the saints of God. Again and again, bishop and abbot, clergy and people assembled, with all the ceremony and display that reverence and affection could suggest, to translate his relics, and each time to a richer shrine and a more magnificent

In personal service;
basilica. Devout women, like Oswene, elected to spend their life in attendance at the martyr's tomb and to minister with motherly care to the incorrupt body. Faithful guardians, like Ailwin, dedicated their lives to perform "menial service" at his tomb, or, like Herman and Radulph, to solemnly attestate and register the miracles which shed a lustre

In written eulogies;
on his name. Chroniclers took delight in recording the martyr's exploits and in sounding his eulogies; poets selected his deeds for the theme of

their verses, and made him the hero of their devout
epics; liturgists composed in his honour antiphons and
hymns, lessons and prayers for the mass and divine
office. Men of faith, emulous of his service, sought _{In external}
for the religious habit in his monastery, and even _{worship;}
monks of other abbeys resigned their dignities to
live under the shadow of his shrine. In distant towns and villages devout clients invoked his
intercession, and from every county a ceaseless stream
of pilgrims came to his tomb to return thanks or to _{In pilgrimages;}
offer homage. The Church inserted his name in her
martyrologies, instituted festivals in his honour and
specially solemnized the day of his martyrdom.
Churches and chapels were dedicated under his
invocation not only in England but throughout _{In churches and}
Christendom. Lastly, the accumulated worship of ages _{chapels;}
took a material and tangible form in the magnificent
memorial known as St. Edmund's patrimony, in whose _{In the building}
centre lay the incorrupt body of the saint, peacefully _{up of St. Edmund's patrimony;}
reposing in the golden shrine, which glittered with
jewels, and which was surmounted by the stone canopy
of Baldwin's mighty basilica. Around, the gables and
turrets of the vast pile of monastic buildings
formed a sacred rampart of defence garrisoned by
the Benedictine guardians of the sanctuary. On
all sides clustered the roofs and spires of the town
peopled by the martyr's own subjects, and adorned
with churches and libraries, hospitals and free
schools, while far away beyond extended the wide
possessions which generations of devoted clients,
kings and freemen, nobles and burgesses, had humbly
offered to that saintly form sleeping in their midst.

The devotion of the people was fostered by the _{Literary tributes}
literary tribute to the royal martyr, his life written _{to the saint.}
by various pens, the poems in his honour, the
liturgical hymns, the accounts of his miracles and

the translations of his body, the references and
records in monastic chronicles of the details of his
life. Among them all, the Life of the martyr by
St. Abbo holds the chief place, by reason of its
origin and the touching piety of its style. St. Abbo
wrote at the request of St. Dunstan, then archbishop of Canterbury, supplementing the story of
the old armour-bearer, as he had received it from
the archbishop, with the information which he
picked up from the keepers of the shrine when he
visited Beodricsworth ; and he produced a history of
the Judas Machabeus of East Anglia, the Aloysius
of the ninth century, the Sebastian of English legend,
which was transcribed and multiplied until it found
its way into all the important abbeys of Europe.
Herman and Osbert de Clare made it the preface of
their Books of the Miracles of St. Edmund; Abbots
Leofstan and Baldwin took copies to Italy. In old
illuminated manuscripts it survived the destruction
of much else around it and found its way into the
great modern libraries of Copenhagen, Gotha, Lucca,
Vienna, Paris, London and Oxford. Surius printed
it among his Lives of the Saints, and others followed
his example, so that now all who wish can read it.[1]

Other monks as devout as Abbo, like the authors
of the Harleian Life[2] and the Bodleian compilation,[3]
made the writing of St. Edmund's Life a labour of
love. Many of these Lives, long since perished,
were much fuller than Abbo's, notably the " Prolixa
Vita " abbreviated in Curteys' Register, and the
" Acts," from which Gaufridus drew his account of
the saint's childhood. Monastic scribes multiplied
copies in the vernacular, so that the people might

St. Abbo's tribute.

Other Lives of the saint.

Lives in the vernacular.

---

[1] For a full notice of St. Abbo and his work see Authorities, Chapter IV.

[2] MS. 802 f. 226b.   [3] MS. 240. See Authorities, Chapter II.

read them. Five such in the East Anglian dialect
are extant in the libraries of Oxford, Cambridge and
the British Museum. The devotion of the people
called too for the history of the Passion of St.
Edmund in their own tongue, and five copies in
East Anglian dialect survive in ancient manuscript
and one in modern print.[1]

The religious houses of England almost without *The homage of the religious* exception rendered homage to the martyr of the *houses.* East by recording his life and deeds in their annals. William, the monk of Ramsey Abbey, in the thirteenth century wrote the Life now extant in the public library of Cambridge.[2] He confesses that he did so from zeal, not because he considered himself worthy—"Plus volo quam valeo regis memorando triumphos." Westminster, Malmesbury, Croyland, Durham, Ely, Peterborough, Gloucester, and other convents great and small, followed his example, for no chronicler thought his work complete without the history of the Royal Edmund.

This universal homage frequently took the form *The tribute of verse.* of verse. A poet of Rufford Abbey conceived the lines which fixed St. Edmund as a national patron. Monk William of Ramsey adds to his Life of the saint the two hymns beginning "Stupet caro, stupet mundus" and "Profitendo fidem solam," each of thirty leonine lines. Samson invokes the muse, "Martyris ut laudes digne narrare,"—that he may worthily speak of the martyr. An unknown poet sings the elegy, "Salve festa dies toto," found in the old manuscript Bodl. 832, and Robert of

---

[1] The text of the MS. on the Passion of St. Edmund, Bodl. N. E. f. 4, has been printed in Mr. Thorpe's "Analecta Anglo-Saxonica," pp. 119-126, as an interesting specimen of the dialect of East Anglia.

[2] MS. D. d. ii. ff. 125b-136b.

Gloucester writes in his native tongue the poetical
life, beginning

"Edmund, ye holi holi king, of whom we make great feste,"

and ending

"Now God for ye love of Saint Edmund that was so noble a king,
Grant ous ye joy yat he is inne, after oure ending.
                                                            Amen."[1]

which the martyr's scribes multiplied for the people
to read.

Two epics.   With St. Edmund as the hero, the two epics, one
by the courtier Denis Piramus and the other by the
monk Lydgate, surpass all minor poems in depth of
devotion and poetic language. Even the laudatory
and beautiful epithets lavished on the royal martyr
by Herman, Osbert de Clare, and Samson, do not
express more enthusiastically the piety of contemporaries.

The French one by Denis Piramus.   Denis Piramus, the French author of the first
epic, passed the greater part of his life in the court
of Henry III. and composed his poem, he says, to
entertain the king and his nobles with holy thoughts
on a sea-voyage. The poet begins his " Vie S.
Edmund le Rey "[2] with an act of sorrow for his
Its prologue.   ill-spent life :

> "Mult ay use, cum pechere,
> Ma vie en trop foli manere
> E trop ay use ma vie
> En peche e en folie."

---

[1] Harl. MS. 2277. Printed for the Philological Society by Mr.
F. J. Furnivall in his volume of " Early English Poems and Lives
of the Saints," 8vo, 1862. Five copies of this poet's Life of
St. Edmund are extant.

[2] " La Vie de S. Edmund le Rey en vers," MS. Cott. Domit.
A xi. ff. 1-24.

He then laments the time spent in making profane rhymes, of which he now expresses his repentance, and resolves to use his talents for a nobler end. "Jes ay noun Deñis Piramus"—"I am named Denis Piramus,"[1] he says, as he proceeds to comment on the popularity with the nobility of the author of the "Parthonopeus" and Marie de France, and to beg his audience to listen to his song, if they wish to hear something a thousand times sweeter and worthier of their notice than the compositions of either versifier, and what moreover will do good to their souls. The prologue finished, he begins the Life: The Life.

> " Ore oyez, Cristiene gent,
> Vus qui en Dieu Omnipotent
> Anez et fey e esperance
> E de salvaciun fiance."

The Life extends to 3,286 verses and ends:

> " La teste unt pur ces desevre
> Loinz del cors que nel trouassent
> Cristiens, ne al cors la justassent
> E que en honeste sepulture
> Ne meissent, par aventure,
> Le chief et le cors ensement
> Del martir Dieu Omnipotent. "

---

[1] See the article "Denis Piramus" in the "Histoire Littéraire de la France," vol. xix. 629, where special mention is made of his MS. Life of St. Edmund. In this article Piramus' reference to the "Parthonopeus" (whose author is unknown) is taken as an acknowledgment of himself as the author, but really Denis does no more than contrast himself with the writer of the "Parthonopeus de Blois" and of Marie de France. "The Abbé de la Rue," says Hardy, "in his 'Essais historiques sur les Bardes' (vol. iii. p. 101), makes no suggestion as to Denis being the author of the 'Parthonopeus.' He had the MS. before him, and he would, I think, have noticed the fact, had he interpreted the sentence as M. Francique Michael, the author of the article in 'Histoire Littéraire,' had done."

The third part. After the Life come 714 verses or lines on the "Miracles,"[1] but the work is incomplete and ends abruptly. As an historical piece Denis Piramus' poem has much in common with the works of St. Abbo, Gaufridus, Gaimar and Simeon of Durham;[2] but it is fuller, and excels them all as a fervent eulogy of St. Edmund.

The English epic by the Benedictine Lydgate. Two hundred years after the death of Denis Piramus, the monk-poet of St. Edmund's Bury and the disciple of Chaucer composed his famous epic in English :

> "The noble story to putte in remembraunce
> Off Sancte Edmond, mayde, Martyr and Kyng."[3]

With the united love of a son for his father, of a loyal subject for his king, of a devout client for his saintly patron, John Lydgate sang of St. Edmund. Nine copies of his work live in manuscript, some with the addition of the "Miracles" or other rhythmic pieces in honour of the martyr, but all rich in language and pathos. The devout poet, while adhering strictly to historical fact, ever and anon breaks forth into hymns and prayers and invocations. One copy[4] begins with a Latin poem, another[5] ends with "a requeste of the translatour unto seynt Edmond in conservacion of his franchyse," commencing the prayer, "Now let us alle with hertly confydense," &c. The preface of the Ashmole MS. 46 i. is followed by the invocation, "O precious Charbouncle of Martirs alle," placed at the beginning

---

[1] Fol. 16.

[2] Both Gaimar and Simeon of Durham have written at length on St. Edmund, but it is impossible to notice every chronicler of the royal martyr's life and passion.

[3] See Authorities Chapter II. for a full account of Dom Lydgate.

[4] MS. Harl. 4826.

[5] MS. Bodl. Tanner 347 f. 98.

of this volume, and in Ashmole 463 the eighty-seventh stanza is followed by the invocation to the saint and prayer for the king, " O Glorious Martir, which of devout humblesse," &c. These are samples of the outpourings of the learned Benedictine's heart towards the grand patron of his abbey and country. Royal hands did not disdain to accept his poem, and Henry VI. and Edward IV. set high value on the copies which the monks presented to them.

One of these copies illustrates the labour and skill which the monastic illuminators and scribes bestowed on all manuscripts treating of their martyr patron. The highest order of workmanship distinguishes most of those extant. In some the love of the scribe has specially lavished itself on the name "Edmund." Herman would write it in gold wherever it occurred; others, like Prior Osbert or Samson, made it to stand out from their pages in crimson or in emerald and gold. But "The Life and Acts of St. Edmund the King and Martyr" by John Lydgate, presented to King Henry VI., surpassed them all in brilliant colouring, thick gold, blackest lettering, whitest vellum and beautiful pictures. This, the richest illuminated manuscript in the world, is a standing record of the devotion of transcriber and painter to St. Edmund.[1]

The scribes' tribute.

No generation of chroniclers from the century of the saint's birth failed in its literary tribute to his memory. His contemporary Asser began the series. Each succeeding age produced its conspicuous biographer and a host of minor ones. Thus St. Abbo wrote in the tenth century; Herman the archdeacon and Gaufridus de Fontibus in the eleventh;[2] William

The homage of the centuries.

---

[1] For a description of it see the Harleian Catalogue, vol. ii. pp. 639, 640.

[2] The MS. Bodl. Digby 109 speaks, so it appears from a note taken in reading it, of Gaufridus as living in the 11th century.

of Malmesbury, Osbert de Clare[1] and Samson in the
twelfth; William of Ramsey, Denis Piramus and
Roger of Wendover in the thirteenth; Matthew of
Westminster and the copious Richard of Cirencester
in the fourteenth; Lydgate and Capgrave[2] in the
fifteenth; Polydorus Vergil, and Harpsfield in the
sixteenth, and the second French biographer, Pierre
de Caseneuve, in the seventeenth. All these and a
hundred others, impressed by the charm and nobleness of Edmund's character, committed their thoughts
and knowledge to writing, in order to hand down
from age to age an unbroken record of devotion to
one of the most popular English saints.

he pilgrimage
to St. Edmund's
Court. It is not surprising that this wide-spread knowledge and admiration of St. Edmund, and the
noble and unique individuality which his name
implied, should attract pilgrims from every part of
Christendom. Pilgrimages in the middle ages, unlike
modern excursions, were prompted by feelings of
piety and reverence. The pilgrimage to the
"seven incorrupt" was a favourite devotion with
our Catholic forefathers, and St. Edmund's Bury or
Its popularity. Court was the most favoured among the seven. Round
his shrine the devout female sex—*specialis Eadmundi
gloria*[3]—had an honourable place, which contrasted
favourably with their reception when visiting St.
Cuthbert, from whose church at Durham they were
for a long time excluded.[4] St. Edmund's was, moreover, one of the three great pilgrimages of England,
determined every year by the "lasting out" of the
votive candles lighted for that purpose. No one can

---

[1] A.D. 1136. Bale (i. 189) states that Prior Osbert flourished
in the time of Innocent II., A.D. 1130, and wrote a Life of St.
Edward the Confessor, which he presented to that pontiff's legate.

[2] Capgrave's is the first *printed* life and in black letter.

[3] Herman.

[4] Simeon of Durham, ii. 7, Rolls ed.

fail to be struck with the pictures of the times which these pilgrimages ever and anon unveil. Whole villages full of Christian sympathy would accompany their blind or sick or lame to seek a cure; at the first sight of the abbey-towers all knelt to salute St. Edmund, and on arriving within a mile of the city completed the journey barefoot; bishops, nobles, and people joined in the pilgrimage, and, as the numerous parties approached the gates of the town, the concourse increased to thousands, especially about the 20th of November. The great barons of the realm and their numerous retainers could there meet without creating surprise in 1205 and again in 1214. Large accommodation was needed for the pilgrims ever coming and going, and till lately Cook Row, Abbey Gate Street, in which they took their meals, bore traces of the kind supplied. Thus the foot-sore and disappointed, like Abbot Samson "when his soul was struck with sorrow," the poor and the weary the happy and the fortunate, came to sit down under the shadow of St. Edmund's shrine, feeling that no resting-place could be sweeter or more peaceful.

St. Edmund's fame like Solomon's brought his *Royal pilgrims.* fellow-monarchs to worship at his shrine. "Even kings themselves, who rule others," wrote William of Malmesbury, "used to boast of being St. Edmund's servants." From the time of Canute it was usual for our kings to send their crown to his church and afterwards to redeem it at a great price, and even to be crowned there anew. Some showed a special love for St. Edmund. St. Edward the Confessor delighted to call him his cousin and kinsman, and frequently visited his sanctuary, within a mile of which he would alight from his horse and make the remainder of the journey on foot, "giving this open testimony

of his humility and devotion," and of his acknowledgment of King Edmund's more exalted sovereignty.
Henry I. made a special pilgrimage of thanksgiving
for his preservation from shipwreck. Henry II. after
the martyrdom of St. Thomas came to St. Edmund
in penitential garb, to beg his protection against his
sons, and to make his confession to Abbot Samson.
Richard the Lion-Heart, before starting for the Holy
Land, in person recommended his crusade to the
prayers of the soldier Edmund. "King John, immediately after his coronation, setting aside all other
affairs," says Jocelin, "came down to St. Edmund,
drawn thither by his vow and devotion." Edward
I. and his queen visited the abbey and shrine
thirteen times. Henry VII. was the last Catholic
king to visit St. Edmund's, and Mary, queen dowager
of France and sister of Henry VIII., the last Catholic
queen.[1]

The pilgrimage
of King Henry
VI.

Nov. 1, 1433.

The preparation.

The pilgrimage of Henry VI. described in Abbot
Curteys' Register will give some idea of the character
of these royal visits.[2] On All Saint's Day, 1433, the
young king announced in parliament his intention of
making a visit to St. Edmund's Bury. The news
reached Abbot Curteys while he was staying at his
manor of Elmswell six miles from the abbey. Without delay he returned to the monastery to prepare
for the royal visit;—no slight undertaking, for house
and board had to be provided for a king, a court and
all the numerous attendants, from the lords and
knights to the lowest valets. At once he engaged

---

[1] When the abbey was in ruins, Elizabeth came to gloat over
its destruction.

[2] This account was communicated to the Society of Antiquaries
in 1803 by Craven Ord, Esq., who took it from Abbot Curteys'
Register, which then belonged to him. It is printed in the "Archæo-
logia," vol. xv. pp. 65-71; see also Yates' account and the supplement to the "Tablet," Dec. 26, 1891.

eighty workmen to repair his house or "palace" and
to decorate and beautify it, and appointed one hundred
officers of every rank to attend on Henry during
his stay. He summoned the aldermen and chief
burgesses to discuss how they might best receive
their prince and in what dress, and it was agreed
that the aldermen should wear scarlet, and their
inferiors red cloth gowns and hoods of blood colour.
At daybreak on Christmas eve, the day fixed for the *Christmas eve 1433.*
king's arrival, these gaily dressed burgesses, five
hundred in number, started from the town on horseback, in open ranks stretching a mile along the
road, to meet the king and his brilliant retinue at
Newmarket Heath.   Crowds of spectators from the
town and villages of St. Edmund's franchise, eager to
catch a glimpse of their sovereign, filled the streets
and the vast abbey-courts.   Henry and his gay
cavalcade entered the precincts by the great gateway
of the cemetery [1] into the full view of the western
front of the basilica with its Norman towers and *The reception.*
unbroken width of 250 feet.   Its huge doors of
bronze, cunningly chiselled by Brother Hugh, were
thrown open at his approach, and the community
to the number of seventy or eighty issued forth, all
vested in precious copes, headed by cross and candles
and followed by the abbot in full pontificals, with
Bishop Alnwich of Norwich by his side, whom the
monks had invited to join them as host.   The
brilliant procession divided, so as to allow the
abbot and bishop to pass through their ranks,
while the Earl of Warwick, alighting from his
horse, offered his arm to the king to assist him

---

[1] This gateway was not in ruins at this or any other time, as the
writer in the "Tablet" of December 26, 1891, implies. The central
tower of the church was, however, at this time in ruins, but afterwards rebuilt by Abbot Curteys.

to dismount. Henry advanced towards the procession, and, as he knelt upon the silken carpet spread out on the ground, the abbot, approaching, sprinkled him with holy water and presented the crucifix, which the king devoutly kissed. Then the procession

The king approaches the shrine.

turned and re-entered the stately church, the whole of the varied crowd following. An unbroken length of 500 feet stretched before them, guarded on either side by ranks of massive Norman columns and illuminated by painted roof and coloured glass. The organ burst forth in jubilant strains of music, and the vaulting of the vast basilica rang with the anthem of the martyred king, "Ave Rex gentis Anglorum," which the whole body of monks chanted in unison as they led the boy-king to the high altar. Then Henry, having prayed before the Blessed Sacrament, which hung over the altar in a cup of pure gold presented by Henry III. for that purpose, passed through one of the side doors in the painted altar-screen into the feretory beyond, to pay his

The feretory itself.

devotions to the shrine of the martyr. This masterpiece of art had grown richer since the days of Abbot Samson. A precious sapphire and a ruby of great price, the special gifts of King John, now sparkled among the other jewels, countless in number, which were set in the plates of solid gold. On the right side again, among other additions, a golden cross, surmounted by a flaming carbuncle and set thick with jewels, glistened in the work, and a second golden cross, weighing sixty-six shillings, the gift of the same benefactor, Henry Lacy, the last Earl of Lincoln of that name, crowned one apex of the shrine. At the four corners four great waxen candles burned day and night, the cost of which was defrayed by the rent of a Norfolk manor, a legacy of King Richard I. Above the whole stretched a

canopy adorned with painted pictures. Here then,
upon a cloth spread over the marble step, the boy-king
knelt to pay his devotions to St. Edmund, and having
finished his prayers, he turned to the abbot, thanked
him for the reception given him and passed with
his suite into the abbot's palace. Henry spent
Christmastide at the abbey, being present at all the
Church solemnities. After the Epiphany celebrations
he moved into the prior's house to enjoy the special
hospitality of the monks, and to have easier access
through the "vineyard" to the far-stretching wood
beyond, in which king and court could indulge in
the healthy pastime of the chase. During Henry's stay *Dom John Lydgate presents his poem.*
at the abbey the aged Dom John Lydgate, at the
time prior of Hatfield, Broadoak, the poet of his day
and without a rival in England, presented to him
a neatly written and gorgeously illuminated poem of
"St. Edmund's Acts and Life" which has now become one of our national treasures. The young
king spent Lent with the monks, joined in the
celebrations of Easter and then prepared to leave.
But first he petitioned to be received into the
fraternity of the family of St. Edmund.[1] The Earl *The king is admitted to fraternity.*
of Warwick and his countess had already petitioned
for and received the favour; other courtiers had
followed their example, notably Humphrey Duke of
Gloucester, the king's uncle. Henry would not leave
the monastery and the many friends he had made

---

[1] The ancient and present Benedictine system of admission to
fraternity differs from the third orders which had their rise in the
thirteenth century. In the Benedictine fraternity the bond of
union is not to the order but to a particular house, to which henceforth the *confrater* holds a distinct and personal relation. He
receives a share in the prayers and good works of the monastery,
and himself engages to make its interests his own. He becomes
one of the members of the monastic family who have received him.

there without suing for a like privilege. Having
prostrated himself before the shrine of the saint he
went to the chapter-house with Gloucester and other
nobles, and sent to inform the abbot of his desire.
Abbot Curteys and the whole convent at once
assembled in chapter and granted the young king's
petition.   The usual solemnities took place, and the
sovereign and all the new *confratres* received the
kiss of peace.   Then the Duke of Gloucester, kneeling, reminded the king to thank the abbot for his
kindness.   Taking the prelate by the hand, Henry
thanked him again and again, bade farewell to the
assembled monks, and touchingly commended himself
to God, to St. Edmund and to them.   The king

The royal departure.

and his train then passed out of the abbey precincts,
the five hundred good and true men of Bury, in
their scarlet robes and red cloth gowns with blood-
red hoods, escorting him the first stage of his journey
to London.   As the years of his troubled reign
flowed on, Henry looked back with regret to those
peaceful days at St. Edmund's, till again at the
shrine, weighed down with sorrow, he mourned the
murder of his uncle the good Duke of Gloucester.

Distinguished prelates visit the tomb.

Besides royalty the highest ecclesiastical dignities
visited the martyr's tomb to reverence the saint and
show their admiration for his principles.   Cardinals
and legates, archbishops, bishops and abbots knelt
at the shrine to beg the intercession of St. Edmund,
and afterwards to make him their offerings.   The
monks delighted to recall the names of such pilgrims
as Blessed Lanfranc and St. Anselm, St. Thomas à
Becket and Cardinal Langton.

Archbishop Arundel, A.D. 1400.

The description [1] of Archbishop Arundel's pilgrimage in the year 1400 illustrates the nature of

---

[1] Given by Yates.

these visits, always made, as the abbey registers have
it, "saving the rights of the monastery." The prior
and convent met him in the nave of the basilica,
and after the usual sprinkling with holy water and
kissing of the crucifix, all advanced to the high
altar, and thence through the choir to the shrine of
St. Edmund beyond.   After his prayer, the archbishop expressed his admiration of the painting and
decoration of the feretory.   Then withdrawing to the
abbot's palace, he took some refreshment, and afterwards returned to the church for vespers.   Next
day being Sunday, the archbishop heard two masses
in the Chapel of the Relics, himself celebrated a third,
and then heard two more.   After this he devoutly
approached the shrine to make his oblation.   From
the church the monks conducted the illustrious
prelate through the great cemetery to the chapel of
St. Andrew and thence into the vineyard.   The party
returned by the infirmary, visited the hall and
chamber of the prior, and, passing through the
cloisters, came to the refectory.   Leaving the refectory,
they reached the "palace" about eleven o'clock, and
there the lord abbot sumptuously entertained the
archbishop and the Earl of Suffolk and their
attendants.   The clergy and squires of the archbishop
declared that never had they been entertained in so
honourable and splendid a manner.   When the time
came for the prelate to bid farewell to his hosts, the
abbot, the Earl of Suffolk, Lord Maubray, the prior,
sacrist, cellerarius, and a great multitude of people
attended him to Rysby on his road to Newmarket.

The road to Newmarket was only one of the *The pilgrims'*
pilgrims' ways which converged towards St. Edmund's *way.*
Bury.   Crowds entered by all the ways, but pilgrims
from the south had a special devotion for the route
by which Ailwin travelled with the saint's body on

his return to Beodricsworth. For five centuries they remembered the highway which, as they said, St. Edmund himself had traversed, and towns, like Braintree, on the main road from London to Suffolk gained their importance from the concourse of pilgrims who tarried at their inns.

Neither did the lovers of St. Edmund forget the little chapel at Heglesdune, the martyr's first resting-place, which continued to be a favourite place of pilgrimage for many centuries. It belonged to the Benedictines of Norwich, who rebuilt it as the cell or chapel of St. Edmund King and Martyr, dependent on their cathedral priory. Langtoft sings of it:

"Where he was shot, a noble chapel stands."

Near by, the monks built Heglesdune or Hoxne Priory, and thither the bishops of Norwich often came to rest and pray. Thomas Brown, the 27th bishop, and William Lyhert or Hart, the 29th, breathed their last there. Those who visited St. Edmund's Bury generally made the pilgrimage to the scene of the martyrdom also, thereby gaining an indulgence of forty days.[1]

It is not surprising that the feelings inspired by a visit to the martyr's shrine bore fruit in the erection of churches and altars under his invocation at home and abroad. Christian art adorned these with paintings and sculptures, which appealed to the hearts and intellects of a Catholic people, while they illustrated the legend of the Martyr's life. "So," writes Green, "his figure gleamed from the pictured windows of every church along the eastern coast."

Fifty-five of these old churches are still left standing,[2] of which Southwold church, St. Edmund the

---

[1] Which can still be gained on the same conditions.

[2] There are fifteen remaining in Norfolk and seven in Suffolk.

Martyr's, Lombard Street, London, St. Edmund's,
Northampton, Dunwich church, and the chapel at
Dereham in Norfolk, where the poet Cowper lies
buried, are examples. In great English abbey and
cathedral churches, as at Chichester and Tewkesbury,
devout clients also raised chapels or altars in honour
of the martyr. The chapel of St. Edmund behind
the high altar of Tewkesbury abbey church still
retains the sculptured history of its royal patron.
Not only in England but even abroad St. Edmund _{And abroad.}
received special honour. A church and hospice of
St. Edmund the king and martyr existed in Rome
in the middle ages.[1] A church of St. Edmund
was built at Damietta, and existed there in the
twelfth century. Robillet, bishop of Avesnes and
suffragan bishop of Autun, on Sept. 22, 1489, consecrated an altar to the martyr kings SS. Edmund
and Oswald in the priory church of Bar-le-Regulier.
St. Edmund's altar stood in the portico of St. Martin's
cathedral church at Lucca in the eleventh century,
and his chapel in St. John's church at Dijon in the
eighteenth. The English Benedictines in the seventeenth century dedicated their church at Paris under
his name. And if these ancient memorials of St.
Edmund have perished or are forgotten, modern
devotion, at least in the eastern counties, still commemorates by new churches and windows and
sculptures the saint who for seven centuries was the
exemplar of our sovereigns, the model of our youth, the
patron of our knights, and a tutelar saint of our country.[2]

---

[1] See Appendix.

[2] For example, the church at Bungay, the monastery at Douai,
and the church at Bury hold St. Edmund as their patron, and his
figure and arms may be seen in modern sculpture and painted
glass, not only in his own city, but in places as wide apart as
Cheltenham and Blyth, Cambridge and Douai.

The feast of St. Edmund, November, 20.

In parish-church and humble chapel, in abbey and cathedral, the martyr's two annual festivals were kept with unusual solemnity. The day of the martyrdom had never been forgotten. The Roman and several other Martyrologies recorded it on the 20th of November in these words: "*In England the commemoration of St. Edmund, king and martyr.*" At his own monastery the monks doubtless celebrated the day with as

The ringing in of the feast.

great solemnity as Christmas or Easter. On the previous evening four successive changes of the great bells, subject, like everything else in an orderly house, to rule, announced to monks, townspeople and pilgrims the quality of the festival. The two Londons, the greater and the Holy-water bell, clanged out the first peal. The bells of the cemetery, including the Gabriel or thunderstorm bell, and the chimes of St. Mary's, St. James' and St. Margaret's rang out the second and third peal. Lastly, the younger monks, sounding the chimes in the great lantern-tower, gave the signal to all the bells of the monastery to take up the music. The united peals from far and wide, with the well-known *Haut-et-Cler* bell, ringing high and clear above the others, produced the fourth peal, or *Le Glas*, as the citizens called it.

Preparation for Vespers.

At the first peal the monks hastened from the dormitory to the lavatory to wash, and thence to the choir to put on the albs there laid out for them, in preparation for vespers, while the abbot, prior, cantors and other ministers put on copes in the sacristy.

The lighting of the church.

Meantime torches and candles were lighted throughout the church. The four huge candles, never extinguished, burnt at the angles of the shrine, twenty-four of a pound weight, round the walls of the feretory, and seventeen in the windows of the presbytery; before the high altar, four large torches

of four pounds weight with the great candle, and
the seven of the same size which continued burning till
second vespers in the branch candlestick with gold
reflectors. In the church twelve great torches were
ablaze in the choir and rood, twelve in the lantern-
tower, twenty-six in each transept, twenty-four under
the arches of the nave, several before each of the
twenty-four altars, and twelve each of eight pounds
weight before the Lady altar.

At the fourth peal of the bells, the grand procession ^{1st Vespers.}
of prelates and cantors in cope, and assistant ministers
and priests and clerics from many parts, marched
into the choir. Vespers commenced with the single
antiphon, "Ave rex gentis Anglorum," sung by
the whole body of monks and people. Now a few
picked voices, now all together, sang the other parts
of the office. At the "Magnificat" took place the The incensing at
the Magnificat.
elaborate incensing. The prior, who had been waiting either in the vestry or before the altar of St.
Saba, entered the choir and joined the abbot, sub-
prior, sacrist, the abbot's chaplains and the vestiarius,
preceded by two acolytes and two thurifers. The
abbot, having put incense into both thuribles, took
one, the prior the other; then they jointly incensed
the Blessed Sacrament hanging over the altar in the
majestas. Next, passing through the doors of the
altar screen, the abbot by the south door, preceded
by two acolytes, and the sub-prior carrying the thurible
the prior by the north, each with his part of the
procession, they perform the same ceremony at the
shrines of St. Edmund, SS. Botulph, Thomas, and
Firminus, and Abbot Baldwin, as well as at the little
altar of the choir in front of the last. Returning
they incense the monks. Lastly the prior proceeds
to incense the altar of the holy cross at the feet
of St. Edmund's shrine, and the altar in the Lady

chapel. The prolonged and solemn "Magnificat" finished, the prayer chanted and the "Benedicamus" sung, the brilliant procession passed out of the choir, and the throng of pilgrims and burgesses dispersed to their lodgings and homes to talk of St. Edmund and the festivities of the morrow.

Matins and Lauds.

When the bells rang out again in the silence of the night for matins, the same scene was repeated with longer and more magnificent ceremonial. An expectant multitude of pilgrims again thronged the vast building, for religion was interwoven with the life of the people, and they delighted in the solemn worship of God. The shadows of the night magnified the spacious structure and added a deeper brilliancy to the religious light. The disposition of the candles and torches purposely left the nave in comparative darkness, while the transept arms shone bright, and from the strong lantern-tower fell rays of brilliant light upon the Rood and the attendant figures of our Lady and St. John. Again the choir was dimly illuminated, while the altar and the feretory blazed with light. The monks sang the long matins and the lauds which followed. At the closing of each nocturn at matins, an increased number of cantors in cope sang the responsory, standing around Prior Brundish's gorgeous antiphonal. As on other principal feasts, two picked voices would with thrilling effect send their clear and resonant tones through the vaulted roof of the basilica in such antiphons as "Gloriosus Dei Athleta Ædmundus." The same elaborate incensing as at vespers marked the end of each nocturn and the "Benedictus" of lauds, so that before the end of the office the church was fragrant with a cloud of incense.

The procession before the high mass

The great mass of St. Edmund would be preceded by the procession. Servers with holy water

and two thuribles led the way; next two cross-
bearers in copes, each accompanied by two torch-
bearers; then two secular chaplains in albs and
copes bore the shrine containing St. Edmund's *camisia;*
three sub-deacons followed, of whom one—the epis-
tolar of the mass—reverently carried the great
gospel-book, the sumptuous gift of Abbot Samson,
and the other two "texts" of lesser price; three
deacons walked next carrying relics, the middle
one—the gospeller—having the reliquary with *Ave*
at the top. Following them a priest, a grave and
ancient senior, carried the arm of St. Edmund, and
after him two by two the whole convent, with the
precentor and the succentor regulating the chant,
the former with the seniors, the latter with the juniors.
The abbot in full pontificals closed the procession,
followed by as many of the burgesses and pilgrims as
chose to join. The procession passed along the Around the
cloisters.
west cloister by the statue of Anselm, the first mitred
abbot, and so through the south cloister to the east,
from which it entered the *crypt* under the eastern part Into the crypt.
of the church, which was occupied above by the shrine
of St. Edmund. Twenty-four columns supported this
subterranean church, dedicated, like that at Canterbury, to the Blessed Virgin. When all had entered,
the clerics placed the relics upon the altar, and the
ministers ranging themselves within the altar-rails,
the prior and sub-prior incensed the altar and the
dignitaries, and the thurifers the community. Six
voices sang a prose in honour of the martyr, and
the prayer of the Station being said, the procession
returned through the cloister to the church, singing
hymns in praise of St. Edmund.[1] Arrived in the

[1] I am indebted to the supplement to the "Tablet" of Dec. 26,
1891, for this beautiful description of a St. Edmund's Bury procession and for many of the details of this part of the chapter.

choir, the convent venerated the relics, and then the mass began. The precentor and succentor, assisted

The great mass. by four companions, sang the Introit. Into the "Kyrie" they inserted one of the two *fansuræ* or antiphons allowed by the old use of the house. The whole choir of monks sang the "Gloria in excelsis," their trained voices making the mighty roof of the basilica re-echo with the chant. A jubilant peal of bells from the great tower prefaced the singing of the Sequence, and when the mass was over, the joy-bells rang out again, and priests and monks and people left the church to assemble again later for vespers.

St. Edmund's monks kept a second feast of their

The feast of the Translation, April 29. patron on April 29, the anniversary of the translation of his sacred body by Abbot Baldwin from the old round chapel to the new church. Both festivals were kept in the refectory also, the old "Liber Cœnobii," or customary of St. Edmund's Bury, allowing a third *ferculum* or dish in the *aula* or dining-hall at the principal meal on the feast of St. Edmund, and also on its *dies octava* and on the *dies translationis*. [1]

Both feasts were observed beyond the limits of

The feasts kept throughout England, St. Edmund's franchise. A decree of the Council of Oxford in 1222 made the 20th of November a holyday of obligation for the whole of England, and in 1298 the feast of the translation was extended to every diocese in the kingdom. [2] After the break-up of religion in this country, the English Benedictines of St. Edmund's monastery at Paris still continued to

And in France. solemnize the greater festival, and the annalist of

---

[1] They also seem to have annually kept a feast of the translation of St. Edmund by Abbot Leofstan on June 20.

[2] The feast of St. Edmund was also observed at Lucca from a very early date.

the house, Dom Bennet Weldon, records the plenary
indulgence to be annually gained on the martyr's
feast in his Paris church, and informs us that, besides
the Augustinians at Toulouse, the monks of the
noble abbey of Fécamp in Normandy and the Benedictines of St.-Maur observed St. Edmund's day
with solemnity. At the present time the Church in
England keeps it as a double major, and the Benedictines at Douai and the Catholics in the martyr's
own town as a feast of the first class.

With what antiphons and prayers, lessons and *The liturgy of the martyr's*
responsories, hymns and canticles ancient England *feast.*
celebrated St. Edmund's memory, may be seen from
the old liturgies or fragments of them which have
survived the sixteenth century wreck. Of these the
office written by St. Abbo and found at the end of
his "Vita Sti Edmundi" in the Bodleian Library [1] is
the most interesting and beautiful. The lessons have
been copied into the exquisitely written and illuminated manuscript on St. Edmund in the Public
Library of Copenhagen. [2] Hardy, ignorant of the arrangement and terminology of the breviary, speaks
of the lessons and responsories as "short pieces of
prose and hymns alternately occurring." St. Abbo
really divides them into nocturns, and heads the
"Lectiones," or lessons, according to present custom.
In the arrangement of this old tenth-century office
and the recurrence in it of the familiar hymns "Deus
tuorum militum" and "Martyr Dei qui unicum," it
is gratifying to trace our continuity with the past.
In the original all the antiphons and responsories

---

[1] MS. Digby 109, a small folio volume of 13th century penman-
ship.

[2] MS. 1588, an 8vo volume in vellum in a 12th century hand. The
lessons for the day of St. Edmund come after a copy of St. Abbo's
"Vita."

are put to chant. The wording of them is so exceedingly beautiful that no apology is needed for transcribing them here.

The first Vespers. The single Antiphon.

The single antiphon for vespers resembles the " Ave Regina cœlorum " of our Lady.

Ave   rex gentis An- glor -um, mi-les re-gis an-ge - lo - rum.

O Æd-mun-de flos mar - ty - rum, ve- lut rosa   vel li - li-

um, fun-de   pre - ces ad Do - minum, pro sa - lu   e

fi - de - li - um.   (P n e u m a.)

King Edmund, hail! East Anglians' king,
Hail, soldier of the Angels, sing!
Thy valour's bright beyond compare,
Thy virtues rose and lily share;
Pour forth thy prayers at Jesus' feet,
That we with thee in heaven may meet. [1]

Psalm. Dixit Dominus.

Hymn. Deus tuorum militum.

---

[1] Translation by the late Father Lazenby, S.J., a devout client of St. Edmund. St. Catharine of Sienna made a similar reference to the red rose of martyrdom : "In His mercy," she says, " He has granted me the white rose of virginity, and I had hoped He would add the red rose of martyrdom, but I am disappointed of my hope, and doubtless it is my innumerable sins that are the cause." (Life of St. Catharine of Sienna, p. 416, 1st edit.)

The Antiphon for the " Magnificat " is a soul-moving call to Englishmen to glory in the possession of so noble a hero:

Ad Magnificat Ant. Exulta sancta ecclesia totius gentis Anglice;[1] ecce in manibus est laudatio Ædmundi, regis incliti, et martyris invictissimi, qui triumphato mundi principe celos ascendit victoriossime. Sancte Pater Ædmunde, tuis supplicibus intende.

Antiphon at the Magnificat. Exult, O holy Church of the entire English nation; behold to thee it is given to praise Edmund, the illustrious king and the most invincible martyr, who, triumphing over the prince of this world, most victoriously ascended into heaven. Holy Father Edmund, hearken to thy suppliants.

The invitatory of matins runs thus:

Invitatorium. Regem regum adoremus in milite suo Ædmundo gloriosum: * per quem ecclesiam snam mirificavit et celi senatum letificavit.

Invitatory. Let us adore the King of kings, glorious in His soldier Edmund; * through whom He has made wonderful His Church and given joy to the court of heaven.

Hymn. Martyr Dei, qui unicum.

THE FIRST NOCTURN.

Ant. Sanctus Ædmundus clarissimus natalibus oriundus a primevo juventutis tempore Christum toto secutus est pectore.

Ant. Saint Edmund, flower of an illustrious line, from his earliest youth followed Christ with his whole heart.

Ps. Beatus vir.

Ant. Cumque inventus adolesceret cum gratia, cum in regni solio Dei sublimavit providentia, ecclesiæ suæ statuens defensorem pro qua usque ad sanguinem decertaret.

Ant. And when found to have grown up to youth in grace, God's Providence raised him to the throne of a kingdom, and established him a defender of His Church, for which he strove even to the shedding of his blood.

Ps. Quare fremuerunt gentes.

Ant. Legem dedit rex crudelis Inguar, ut Ædmundum

Ant. The cruel king Inguar gave command to force Edmund

---

[1] The *e* in place of the *æ* or *œ* is common among medieval writers.

exilio relegarent, aut capite potius detruncarent, si eum suis legibus inclinare aut subdere non possent.

into exile, or rather to cut off his head, if they could not bend him to their laws or subdue him.

Ps. Domine quid.

The Responsories of the first Nocturn lessons.

The nine lessons of this beautiful office are omitted here for fear of wearying the reader, but the responsories after each are given as they occur.

I. R̰. Sancte indolis puer, Ædmundus ex antiquorum personis regum nativitatis sumpsit exordium. Informavit Rex celestis : * Ut sibi coheredem transferret in celis. V̰. Cujus infantiam illustravit Spiritus Sancti gratia, quoniam complacuit sibi in illo anima Domini Jesu.* Ut sibi.

I. R̰. Edmund, a boy of saintly character, was descended from an ancient race of kings. The heavenly King fashioned him,* that he might translate him to heaven as his coheir. The grace of the Holy Ghost illumined his childhood, for the spirit of Jesus Christ in him was pleasing to Him. That he might, &c.

II. R̰. Egregium decus et salus magna fuit, quod in solio regni princeps Dei Ædmundus surrexit : * Cum in templo Dei ut columna lucis et fulsit. V̰. Vita ejus gloriosa virtutibus, distincta fuit sanctitate et pietate decora. * Cum in templo.

II. R̰. Transcendant was our glory, great our security, because the prince of God, Edmund, ascended the throne of our kingdom. * Since in God's temple even as a column of light he shone. V̰. His life, glorious by its virtues, was conspicuous for holiness, and beautiful with piety. * Since in God's temple, &c.

III. R̰. Miles Christi sanctus, Ædmundus, Spiritu Sancto plenus dixit ad regem : Non me tue incurvant amicitie, nec tormenta terrent mine. *Gloriosum est enim mori pro Domino. V̰. Ignis et ferrum super mel et favum michi est jocundum. * Gloriosum. Gloria. Gloriosum.

III. R̰. The holy soldier of Christ, Edmund, full of the Holy Ghost, spoke to the king : Thy friendship does not make me deviate, nor thy threats and torments frighten me. * For it is glorious to die for the Lord. V̰. Fire and sword are sweet to me above honey and the honeycomb. * For it is glorious, &c. Glory be to the Father, &c. For it is glorious &c.

THE SECOND NOCTURN.

Ant. Ait autem Ædmundus, sed et Spiritus Sanctus per os ejus : Non me terrent exilii mine, nec inclinant regis amicitie ; jocundum est pro Deo mori ; ecce contingat me Deo sacrificium fieri.

Ant. Edmund indeed spoke, but it was even the Holy Ghost speaking by his mouth : Threats of banishment do not frighten me, nor a king's offer of friendship move me. It is pleasant to die for God ; behold let it be given to me to become a sacrifice to God.

The Antiphons of the second Nocturn.

Ps. Cum invocarem.

Ant. Vinctus ferro lamentabilibus illuditur modis ; atque stipite religatus, flagris exuritur ; tum varias mortis species pro Christo letus amplectitur.

Ant. Bound with chains, he is piteously mocked ; and tied to a tree, he is branded by scourges ; then he joyfully embraces death in many forms for Christ's sake.

Ps. Verba mea.

Ant. Quo amplior esset mercedis gloria, accrevit et pena ; ad signum positus telis obruitur ; et mille mortis species amplectitur ; Christumque sereno vultu precatur.

Ant. In proportion to the glory of the reward, the pain also increased ; as a target is he set up, and covered over with darts ; and he embraces a thousand deaths, while he beseeches Christ with a countenance unmoved.

Ps. Domine Dominus noster.

IV. ℟. Crescit ad penam sanctus Dei ; positus ad signum confoditur nimbo verberum. * Et per omnia manet martyr invictus et miles emeritus. ℣. Rivus sanguinis membratim decurrit, nec jam super est locus vulneris. * Et per omnia.

IV. ℟. The holy one of God grows braver at the pain ; set up as a target, he is buried under a shower of arrows.* And through all the martyr stands unconquered and the soldier victorious. ℣. Streams of blood flow from limb to limb, nor is there now any more place for a wound. * And through all, &c.

The Responsories of the second Nocturn lessons.

V. ℟. Martyri adhuc palpitanti, sed Christum confitenti, jussit Inguar caput auferri :* sicque Ædmundus martyrium consummavit, et ad Deum exul-

V. ℟. The martyr still breathing, but confessing Christ, is ordered by Inguar to be beheaded.* And so Edmund consummates his martyrdom, and

tans vadit. [1] ℣. Caput sanctitate plenum decollatum resiliit
inter verba orationis. * Sicque.

rejoicing goes to God. ℣. The
head, full holy, severed from the
body, rebounds uttering words of
prayer. * And so, &c.

VI. ℞. Refectum ergo de
corpore caput plebs devota Deo
requisitum pergit illacrimans et
dicens :* Heu pastor bone ; heu
pater pie Eadmunde, ubi es?
℣. Exaudivit Dominus cla-
morem pauperum, et suscepit
gemitum servorum.* Heu.
Gloria. Heu.

℞. A people devoted to God
set out to seek the head then
apart from the body but living
again. They shed tears and
said : Alas, good shepherd, alas,
kind father Edmund, where art
thou? ℣. The Lord has heard
the cry of the poor, and He has
received the groans of His servants.* Alas ! &c. Glory be to
the Father, &c. Alas ! &c.

THE THIRD NOCTURN.

The Antiphons
of the third
Nocturn.

Ant. Misso spiculatore, de-
crevit tyrannus Dei athletam
Ædmundum capite detruncari :
sicque hymnum Deo præsonuit
et animam celo gaudens intulit.

Ant. The guard dismissed,
the tyrant decreed that God's
champion Edmund should be beheaded : and so he sounded forth
his hymn to God, and rejoicing
brought his soul to heaven.

Ps. In Domino confido.

Ant. O martyr invincibilis,
O Ædmunde, testis indomabilis !
hic te dies terris exemit, et cum
triumpho in senatu celi recondidit : intercede pro nobis in
celis, qui post te suspiramus in
terris.

Ant. O invincible martyr !
O Edmund, unconquerable witness ! This day released thee
from the earth, and triumphantly ushered thee into the
court of heaven ; intercede in
heaven for us who sigh after
thee on earth.

Ps. Domine quis habitabit.

Ant. Refectum ergo de corpore caput plebs devota requisitum pergit illacrimans et dicens :
Heu pastor bone, heu pater pie
Ædmunde, ubi es ?

Ant. A people devoted to
God set out to seek the head,
then apart from the body but
living again. They shed tears
and said : Alas ! good shepherd,
alas, kind father Edmund,
where art thou ?

Ps. Posuisti Domine.

The Responsories
of the third
Nocturn lessons.

VII. ℞. Caput martyris verba

VII. ℞. The martyr's head

[1] This ℞. and its chant may be found in Jocelin, Caxton
pub., vol. 13, p. 115.

edidit ; ecce quem queritis, inquit. Assum, filii.* Ecce me regem quondam vestrum, ecce me nunc patronum vobis ad Deum. ℣. Condoluit pater pius caris suis, quos benigno confortabat alloquio. * Ecce me.

uttered words : Behold whom you seek, it says. I am here, children. * Behold me, heretofore your king, behold me now your advocate with God. ℣. The kind father condoled with his beloved ones, whom he consoled with benevolent words. * Behold me, &c.

VIII. ℟. Admirabilis fuit et in illo digitus Dei. *Quia ad excubias martyris lupus procubuit, fovit ac doluit. ℣. Ex jocunditate signi in lacrimas proruperunt corda populi. * Quia.

VIII. ℟. Admirable was the finger of God upon him. * For a couching wolf mournfully watched over the martyr. ℣. From joy at the wonder, the hearts of the people burst forth into tears. * For, &c.

IX. ℟. O martyr invincibilis ! O Eadmunde testis indomabilis ! hic te dies terris exemit, et cum triumpho in celestis curiæ senatu recondidit : * intercede pro nobis in celis qui post te suspiramus in terris. ℣. Collucens ante thronum Dei stola insigni, oramus, pater pie. * Intercede. Gloria. O martyr, suspirat anima nostra malis afflicta. ℟. Lugensque peracta crimina plangit delicta. O Ædmunde rex martyr spes nostra. ℟. Suscipe famulorum libens vota. Da nobis in celis gaudia. ℟. Qui tibi longa suspiria damus in terris.

IX. ℟. O invincible martyr ! O Edmund, unconquerable witness ! This day released thee from earth, and triumphantly ushered thee into the court of heaven. * Intercede in heaven for us who send up our sighs to thee on earth. ℣. Shining before the throne of God in thy illustrious robe, we pray thee, O loving father, * intercede, &c. Glory be to the Father, &c. O martyr, our soul soars up to thee in our affliction. ℟. Groaning over past offences, it mourns for its sins. O Edmund, king and martyr, our hope. ℟. Receive graciously the vows of thy servants. Give to us joys in heaven. ℟. Who on earth send forth deep sighs to thee.

Te Deum laudamus, &c.

LAUDS.

Ant. Quidam maligne mentis homines aggressi sunt nocturno tempore infringere Sancti basilicam ; sed eos in ipso conatu

Ant. Certain evil-minded men approached under cover of night and attempted to break into the saint's church ; but the martyr's

The Antiphons at Lauds.

Y

operis ligavit virtus martyris.

power bound them fast in the very act.

2. *Ant.* Facto autem mane alius cum scala sua eminus pependit, alius tortis brachiis diriguit, quidam incurvus fossor stupuit, et ita quod quisque incepti habuit versa vice sibi pena fuit.

2. *Ant.* In the morning one man hung aloft on his ladder, another stood immovable with his arms bent for work, a digger remained stupefied over his spade, and so what each one had undertaken turned against him and became a punishment.

3. *Ant.* Quidam magne potentie vir Leofstanus, dum juvenilis non refrenavit impetum animi, in temeritatem incidit, accedens ad tumbam sci, jussit sibi ossa martyris ostendi.

3. *Ant.* One Leofstan, a man of great power, from not curbing his violent nature in youth became reckless, and approaching the tomb of the saint, demanded that the bones of the martyr should be shown to him.

4. *Ant.* Reserato ergo locello, astitit, aspexit, et aspectu nequam, mox vexari cepit, tandemque judicio perculsus divino interiit.

4. *Ant.* The coffin was therefore opened ; he stood and gazed therein, and by that wicked glance he began straightway to be tormented, and at last, stricken by the divine judgment, he perished.

5. *Ant.* O martyr magni meriti, qui virtutibus ita efflornisti, intercede pro nobis.

5. *Ant.* O martyr of great merit, who so flourished in all virtues, intercede for us.

Hymn.

Hymn. Deus tuorum militum.

The Antiphon for the "Benedictus."

Ad Benedictus Ant. Gloriosus Dei Athleta, Edmundus, per regiam dignitatem, insignem obtinuit victoriæ palmam ; unde nunc fruitur societate angelorum, senatu apostolorum, contubernio martyrum, cujus ergo precibus adjuvari Rex Christe deposcimus. Alle. Alle. Alle.

Antiphon at the Benedictus. Edmund, the glorious champion of God, through the royal dignity, won the glorious palm of victory ; whence he now enjoys the society of the angels, the senatorial council of the apostles, the fellowship of the martyrs, by whose prayers therefore we ask to be helped, O Christ our King. Alleluia. Alle. Alle.

Second Vespers.

The antiphons and hymn of lauds were sung again at the second vespers. But the following

glorious invocation of the martyr formed the antiphon
at the "Magnificat:"

<table>
<tr><td>

Ad Magnificat Ant. O Sanc-
tissimi Patris Edmundi, incliti
regis et martyris, sancta pre-
conia, qui factus victima Deo
pro populo suo hodie assumptus
est sacrificium laudis in odorem
suavitatis; hinc laus et gloria
Deo et Christo suo atque Spiritui
Sancto. Alleluia.

</td><td>

Ant. at the Magnificat. O
saintly renown of our holy father
Edmund, glorious king and mar-
tyr, who, having become a victim
to God for his people, was to-day
assumed into heaven, a sacrifice
of praise in the odour of sweet-
ness: hence praise and glory to
God and to his Christ, and to the
Holy Ghost. Alleluia.

</td></tr>
</table>

The Antiphon at the "Magnificat."

Besides the lections or lessons of the above office *The Lessons of the feast.*
at least four other sets are extant. Those formerly
used in the Basilica Saint-Sernin were compiled from
the narratives of St. Abbo, William of Malmesbury,
and Matthew of Westminster, the tradition of St.
Edmund's translation to Toulouse forming the sixth
lesson. In the "Propre actuel" of Saint-Sernin, the
lessons are the same as those in the supplement of
the English-Benedictine breviary, with the addition
of the Toulouse tradition. The lessons of the York
breviary, which the Surtees Society has published,
are of an ordinary type. The lessons of the Sarum *The "Sarum Lessons."*
breviary, compiled by St. Osmund, are probably the
most interesting of all those which were in use in
the medieval Church, and will form a fair specimen of
the style and tone of the rest. The old annalist of
St. Edmund's, Paris, in copying them into his
Chronicle remarks that, "though no more in use,
yet they show what veneration antiquity held St.
Edmund in." They run as follows:

<table>
<tr><td>

Lectio I.
Provinciæ,quæ et Anglia nun-
cupatur, præfuit S. Edmundus
ex antiquorum Saxonum nobili

</td><td>

Lesson I.
Edmund, born of noble and
ancient Saxon stock, ruled over
the province which is called

</td></tr>
</table>

prosapia oriundus, qui a prim-
ævo ætatis tempore cultor
veracissimus fidei extitit chris-
tianæ. Eodem tempore impius
Hinguar cum altero, Hubba
nomine, conatus est in extermi-
nium adducere omnes fines
Britanniæ.

Anglia. From his very childhood he was a most sincere
observer of the Christian faith.
At the same time the impious
Hinguar and with him another
named Hubba endeavoured to
bring destruction and ruin
through all the confines of
Britain.

Lectio II.

Idem vero Hinguar post mul-
torum interfectionem evocans
quosdam plebeios quos suo gladio
credidit esse indignos, sciscita-
tus est ab eis ubi eorum Rex
tunc vitam degeret : Audivit
enim quod rex Edmundus
florenti ætate et robustus viribus
bello per omnia strenuus esset.
Qui eo tempore morabatur in
villa quæ Eglisdone nominatur.

Lesson II.

This same Hinguar after the
slaughter of many, calling to
him some of the common people
whom he deemed unworthy of
his sword, asked where their
king was tarrying. For he had
heard that King Edmund, then
in the flower of his age and in
fulness of strength, was in every
way vigorous in war. Edmund
at that time was halting at his
castle called Eglisdone.

Lectio III.

Consuevit enim eadem Dan-
orum natio nunquam palam cum
hoste contendere nisi insidiis
prævento. Quapropter unum de
commilitonibus dirigit ad Edmundum qui exploretur quæ sit
ei summa rei familiaris. Ipse
autem cum multo comitatu sub-
sequitur, ut improvisum facilius
suis legibus subjugaret. Manda-
verat autem iniquæ legationis
bajulo tyrannus iniquior ut in-
cautum taliter alloquatur :

Lesson III.

This same Danish nation would
never contend with an enemy in
the open field unless waylaid by
stratagem. Therefore he sent
one of his soldiers to Edmund's camp, to find out the
greatest force at his command.
Hinguar himself with a numerous
retinue follows, in order the more
easily to subject him, if unpre-
pared, to accept his terms. The
bearer of the iniquitous message
was commanded by the more
iniquitous tyrant to address the
unsuspecting king in these words:

Lectio IV.

Terræ marisque metuendus
Dominus noster Hinguar terras
subjugando sibi armis, sed hujus
provinciæ optatum littus cum

Lesson IV.

Our lord Hinguar, terrible on
land and sea by the subjugation
of the nations by his arms, is now
about to winter with many ships

multis navibus hyematurus applicuit, mandans ut cum eo antiquos thesauros et paternas divitias sub eo regnaturus dividas vel morte morieris.

on the pleasant shores of this province, and he sends, demanding that you reign under him, dividing with him your ancient treasures and ancestral riches, or die the death.

Lectio V.

Audito nuntio rex ingemuit, consulens unum de episcopis suis quid super his respondere deberet. Qui timens pro vita regis ad consentiendum plurimis exhortabatur exemplis. Rex paululum conticuit, et sic demum post multa devota verba nuntio respondebat. Hoc dicas Dño tuo : Noveris quod amore vitæ temporalis, Christianus rex Edmundus se non subdet pagano duci, nisi prius compos effectus fuerit nostræ religionis.

Lesson V.

At this message the king groaned within himself, as he asked advice of one of his bishops what he should reply. Fearing for the life of his sovereign, the bishop urged him to bend like most others to the storm. For a little while the king was silent. At length, after much devout prayer, he replied to the messenger : Tell this to your master : Know that the Christian king Edmund will not subject himself for love of earthly life to any pagan ruler, who has not first become a follower of our religion.

Lectio VI.

Vix egresso nuntio, ecce Hinguar obvius illi jubet breviloquio uti. Quo verba Regis referente, imperat tyrannus circumfundi omnem turbam servorum, ut interius solumque Regem teneant, quem suis iniquis legibus cognoverat jam rebellem. Tunc S. Edmundus capitur, et vinculis constrictus sistitur ante ducem.

Lesson VI.

Scarcely had the messenger appeared, when Hinguar met him, and ordered him to be brief, On the report of the king's words the tyrant commands all his horde of followers to surround the place and to keep the king only inside, who, he knew, had rejected his iniquitous terms. Then St. Edmund is taken prisoner, and bound with chains, and brought before the chief.

Lectio VII.

Tandem fatigatus acri instantia, perducitur ad arborem vicinam, ad quam adversarii eum ligantes, sagittis confodiunt, in quo vulnera vulneribus locum dabant, dum jacula jaculis imprimebantur. Cumque

Lesson VII.

At length, worn out by their bitter persistence, he is led to a neighbouring tree, to which his enemies bind him : and they transfix him with arrows. Wounds gave way to wounds, while arrow pressed arrow. And

nec sic a laude Dei cessaret inter verba orationis capita truncatus est.

when, even in these straits, he would not cease from the praise of God, his head was struck from the body amid words of prayer.

Lectio VIII.

Dani vero relinquentes corpus, caput in silvam recedentes asportaverunt, atque inter densa veprium fruteta occultarunt; quibus abeuntibus, Christiani corpus invenientes, caput quæsierunt: atque Ubi es? aliis ad alios in silva clamantibus, caput respondit: Her, Her, Her, quod est, Hic, Hic, Hic, nec ea repetere destitit, donec omnes ad se perduxit.

Lesson VIII.

The Danes leaving the body, carried the head into the depths of the wood, where they hid it in the thick undergrowth of briars. When they had gone away, the Christians finding the body, began to search for the head. And while they cried to one another in the wood saying: Where art thou? the head answered: Here, Here, Here,— nor did it cease to repeat that word until it had brought them all to itself.

Lectio IX.

Huic etiam miraculo Dominus addidit aliud, dum cœlesti thesauro insolitum custodem dedit. Immanis siquidem lupus caput sanctum inter brachia complectens ab omnibus feris et avibus intactum custodivit, et deferentes illud ad corpus usque ad locum sepulchri, humiliter sequebatur. Quo cum corpore sepulto, lupus nullum lædens ad silvam rediit festinanter.

Lesson IX.

To this miracle the Lord added even another, by placing an unusual guardian over the heavenly treasure. A savage wolf holding the sacred head within its forefeet, guarded it untouched from all wild beasts and birds, and afterwards it tamely followed those who bore it to the body, even to the place of sepulchre. When the body was buried, the wolf, without hurting any one, speedily returned to the forest.

Lesson for the feast of St. Edmund's translation. The following lesson for the feast of St. Edmund's translation occurs in an old breviary in Clare College Library, Oxford:

Anno ab incarnatione Domini millesimo nonagesimo quinto, a passione Sancti Edmundi Regis et Martyris ducentesimo vicesimo

In the year 1095 from our Lord's Incarnation, and the 225th from St. Edmund the King and Martyr's passion, in

quinto, indictione tertia, regnante rege Willelmo in Anglia secundo, venerabili viro Herberto apud Norwicam pontificante, et Abbate Baldewyno ecclesiam Sancti Edmundi tenente, Wakelinus Wintoniensis Episcopus cum his et aliis viris religiosis et honestis apud Edmundisberi, tertio calendas Maii, die Dominica, hora jam tertia, intrans ecclesiam, more pontificali, aquam consecravit benedixit et aspersit. Deinde detegitur locellus ligneus post longam orationem a circumstantibus factam, in quo incontaminatum ac venerabile quiescit corpus. Sic dictus pontifex humili voce inchoans et psalmodians, Iste Sanctus pro lege Dei sui certavit usque ad mortem et a verbis impiorum non timuit; fundatus enim erat supra firmam petram. Aperto monumento, tanta ex eo odoris suavissimi fragrantia emanavit, ut qui aderunt in paradisi deliciis se constitutos existimarent. Transfertur itaque corpus incorruptum beati Edmundi Martyris anno et die supradictis, ad magnam populi lætitiam, totius gentis Anglicanæ perpetuam memoriam, omniumque sanctorum gloriam, in futuro resurrecturum ad beatitudinem sempiternam.

the third indiction, during the reign of William II. in England and the pontificate of the venerable Herbert at Norwich, while Abbot Baldwin presided over the church of St. Edmund, Wakelin bishop of Winchester, with his attendants and other religious and noble men of Edmundsbury, at the hour of terce, entering the church, in pontifical array, consecrated and blessed water, and sprinkled it, it being Sunday, the third of the calends of May. Then after long prayer offered up by those standing around, he uncovers the wooden coffin in which the incorrupt and venerable body rests. At this point the said bishop began the chant: This saint strove for the law of his God even to death and feared not the gibes of the impious; for he was founded upon a firm rock. When the shrine was opened so great a fragrance of most sweet odour issued from it that those present thought themselves transported to paradise. And thus took place the translation of Blessed Edmund the martyr's body in the year and day above mentioned, to the great joy of the people, for a perpetual memorial to the whole English nation and to the glory of all the saints, to rise in time to come to everlasting bliss.

An eleventh century manuscript in the Lambeth Library [1] gives an addition to the rest of the office

Liturgical hymns in honour of St. Edmund.

---

[1] MS. 362, fol. 11.

in the form of the following hymns for St. Edmund's feast, which the Surtees Society has printed in its collection of Latin hymns of the Anglo-Saxon Church.[1]

Hymn for
Vespers.

Ad Vesperas.

Eadmundus martyr inclytus,
Anglorum rex sanctissimus,
Hac luce palmam nobilem
Triumphans celos intulit.

Tulit jubar hoc splendidum
Opima tellus Anglica,
Quo splendet omne seculum
Et celis crescit gaudium.

Quorum murmur pauperum
Exaudiat sacrarium
Et ad celestis perferat
Regis pius causidicus.

Favorem Christi celitus
Nostris piaclis impetret,
Orbs ut gravata sentiat
Donativum indulgentie.

Precantum votis annuat
Pater Deus cum Filio,
Simul cum Sancto Spiritu
Per seculorum secula.
                    Amen.

At Vespers.

Edmund, renowned martyr,
Most holy king of the English,
At this hour of even, the noble
    palm of victory
Into heaven with triumph bore.

This brilliant radiance
The fertile land of England bore;
By it each epoch shines resplen-
    dent,
And the joys of heaven increase.

The plaints of all the poor
May he our loving advocate
    graciously hear   [of Holies
And convey them into the Holy
Of our celestial King.

May he in heaven beseech
Christ's favour for our sins,
That the burdened world may
    feel
The Lord's indulgent pardon.
                    [pray,
Grant the vows of those who
O God the Father, with the Son,
Together with the Holy Spirit,
Through the eternal ages.
                    Amen.

Hymn for
Matins.

Ad Matutinum.

Laurea regni redimitus olim,
Rex Eadmundus, decus orbis
    hujus,
Nunc suis adsit famulis precamur
    Supplici voto.

At Matins.

Once crowned with the wreath
    of earthly power,   [world,
King Edmund, glory of this
Now to be present with his ser-
    vants we beseech
By suppliant vows.

---

[1] Vol. 23. The editor has used MS. Cott. Vesp. D. fol. 116, a twelfth century copy, instead of the Lambeth MS. The version in the text has been collated with the older and more correct copy. The ancient spelling has been retained.

Hac die celi fruitur secretis
Qua triumphalem meruit coronam,
Nactus ex Dani gladiis tyranni
    Sanguine palmam.

This day he enjoys the secrets
  of heaven ;   [umphal crown,
This day he merited the tri-
Having won from the swords of
    the tyrant Dane
By his blood the palm of victory.

Cujus exsectum caput ore prono
Trux lupus fovit famulatus illi,
Donec ad ustum rediit cadaver
    Vulneris expers.

His head, severed while his face
    was bent,
A grim wolf attendant guarded,
Until it returned to the bereav-
    ed body,
Then free from wound.

Unde Rex martyr tibi magnus
    heres,   [purus,
Integer   membris   maculæque
Fungeris digno meritis honore
    Talibus hymnis.

Whence, martyr king, our great
    master   [from stain,
Whole in all thy limbs, and free
Thou deservedly holdest honour
    worthy of such hymns
As we now sing to thee.

Sit honor Patri jugis et perhennis,
Qui tuos signis decorat triumphos,
Cujus obtentu pius ipse pascat
    Trinus et unus.
          Amen.

Honour to the Father, always
  and for ever,   [triumphs.
Who by miracles adorns thy
At thy request may He Him
  self most loving feed us,
He who is one and three. Amen.

Ad Laudes.

Laus et corona militum,
Jesu, tibi certantium,
Hujus triumpho subditis
Intende regis martyris.

At Lauds.

O Jesus, glory and crown
Of those soldiers who strive for
    thee,   [martyr
By the triumph of this royal
Bend thine ear to his subjects'
    prayer.

Hymn for Lauds.

Hac rex Eadmundus die
Raptus cruento scammate,
Sese flagrorum stigmati
Celo receptus exuit.

On this day King Edmund,
Snatched away from the blood-
    stained arena,
Rid himself of the lash's stigma
And was received by the hea-
    venly court.

Devinctus acri stipite,
Loris cruentis undique,

Fastened to the galling tree
On all sides bound by the blood-
    stained thongs,

Danis tribunal execrat Ac numen ejus improbat.	He execrates the Danish court And rejects its favour.
Qui terebratus spiculis Regis cruorem combibit, Quem pro suis fidelibus Velle mori conjicimus.	Now pierced with arrow-points, He drinks the chalice with that King Who, we preach, willed to die For his faithful people.
Nos hac Eadmundus die Rex Martyr optet gratie, Qua perfruamur celitum Bonis per omne seculum. Amen.	May Edmund king and martyr On this day choose for us the grace [things By which we may enjoy good Through all the heavenly ages. Amen.

The ancient "Mass."

The ancient "Mass" for St. Edmund's feast had its own collect, secret and postcommunion, the same as those still in use among the English Benedictines with the exception of the few verbal differences which are here noticed :

The Collect.

Collect.

Deus ineffabilis misericordiae, qui beatissimo regi Edmundo (beatissimum regem Edmundum —*Sarum, Lambeth, St. Abbo ;* beato regi Edmundo— *Propre Saint-Sernin, 1672*) tribuisti inimicum pro tuo nomine (pro tuo nomine inimicum—*Sarum, Lambeth and St. Abbo*) moriendo vincere ; concede propitius huic (huic omitted, *Lambeth, St. Abbo, Propre Saint-Sernin, 1672*) familiæ tuæ ut eo interveniente mereatur in se antiqui hostis incitamenta superando extinguere (incitamenta superare— *Propre Saint-Sernin, 1672*). Per Dominum.

Collect.

O God of unspeakable mercy, who hath granted to the most blessed king Edmund, by dying for Thy name, to conquer the enemy, graciously give to this Thy family, by his intercession, the grace to overcome and extinguish in ourselves the incitements to evil of our ancient enemy, through our Lord Jesus Christ, &c.

The Secret.

Secret.

Hoc sacrificium redemptionis (devotionis—*St. Abbo and Lambeth*) nostræ quæsumus Omni-

Secret.

Translation. In Thy clemency, O omnipotent God, regard this sacrifice of our redemption, and

potens Deus, clementer respice, et intercedente beato Edmundo rege et martyre (tuo—*St. Abbo*) pro hac familia tua placatus assume (per hoc nobis salutem mentis et corporis benignus impende—*St. Abbo*).

through the intercession of the blessed king and martyr, Edmund, favourably accept it in behalf of this Thy family.

Postcommunion.

Sint tibi Omnipotens Deus grata nostrae servitutis obsequia, et hæc sancta quæ sumpsimus, intercedente beato Edmundo rege et martyre tuo, prosint nobis ad capessenda premia vitæ perpetuæ.

Postcommunion.

Translation. May the homage of our service be pleasing to thee, Almighty God, and may these holy oblations which we have received, by the intercession of Blessed Edmund king and martyr, be profitable to us for the gaining of the rewards of eternal life.

The Post-communion.

The Church of Toulouse now uses this collect :

Deus, qui Beatum Edmundum, per martyrii palmam, a terreno principatu ad celestem gloriam transtulisti, concede propitius, ut quod ipsi præstitit inter tormenta constantiam adversus hostis antiqui incitamenta nos fortes efficiat nomen Domini nostri Jesu Christi Filii tui, qui tecum vivit.

Translation. O God, who hath translated Blessed Edmund, by the victory of martyrdom, from earthly sovereignty to heavenly glory ; mercifully grant that the name of Thy Son Jesus Christ, which gave him constancy in his torments, may make us strong against the incitements of our old enemy. Who with Thee, &c.

The following sequence, the composition of Monk William of Ramsey, is from the old breviary of Clare College Library, Cambridge :

A Sequence.

Profitendo fidem solam
Rex Edmundus suam stolam
  Lavit Agni sanguine.
Signum factus ad sagittam
Penam necis exquisitam
  Fert pro Christi nomine.

By professing the only faith,
King Edmund washed his stole
  In the blood of the Lamb.
Made a mark for their arrows
He bore the searching pain of
  death
  For the name of Christ.

Perforatur mille telis,
Decollatur rex fidelis,
    Pro grege fidelium.
Caput exit in loquelam,
Cui lupus dat tutelam ;
    Prædo patrocinium.

Sepelitur caro cæsa,
Laniata sed illæsa,
    De sepulchro tollitur.
Sed pro nece sic allata
Vena quasi deaurata
    Collo circumducitur.

Ungues ejus et capillos
Tondet anus ; stupet illos
    Tot annis recrescere.
Opus furum inanitur ;
Judex perit ; rex punitur ;
    Rota fertur aere.

Domus ardet sacerdotis ;
Claudi saltant, et ægrotis
    Præstantur remedia.
Qui sic fecit et medetur
Promoveri nos dignetur
    Ad æterna gaudia.

He is pierced with a thousand
    darts,
The faithful king is beheaded
For the fold of the faithful.
His head breaks out into speech,
Over it a wolf stands guard,
A prowling beast its protection.

The slain flesh is buried,
Torn but unhurt,
    It is taken from the tomb.
But for death so borne,
A vein like to a chain of gold
    Is thrown around his neck.

His nails and his hair an aged
    woman trims ;
She wonders that they grow again
    So many years.
An attempt of robbers comes to
    nought ;   [punished ;
A judge perishes ; a king is
A wheel is held in mid-air.

The priest's house is consumed
    with flames ;
The lame dance, and to the sick
    Cures are granted.
May He who so works and cures,
    Deign to advance us
    To everlasting joys.

Amen.   Amen.

Two Prefaces. St. Abbo and the Lambeth manuscript give proper prefaces for St. Edmund's day, the former a long the latter a shorter one. These prefaces, in no way inferior in sublimity and feeling to other compositions of a similar nature, worthily complete the ancient liturgical honours of the saint.

Surviving memorials of St. Edmund. Besides these pious records a few other memorials of a devotion now rare have also survived. Hunstanton perpetuates in its very name the gentleness and valour of St. Edmund and his followers,[1] and the tradition

----

[1] See p. 50.

of their landing even now surrounds it. The miraculous wells may still be seen bubbling from the earth near St. Mary's in Old Hunstanton; the promontory sheltering the creek is called to this day St. Edmund's Point, and near the light-house which crowns it the foundations of St. Edmund's chapel and retreat still remain. In many parts of the eastern counties, other traditions more or less *Traditions.* vague exist, confirming and supplementing chronicle and record, though possessing no tangible memorial of the martyr beyond his name, like Caistor St. Edmund's, and the carved invocation "Ste Edmunde, ora pro nobis," around the west-door of the old church at Southwold. More interesting and definite, however, are the ancient portraits of the saint, not- *Portraits.* ably in the initial letter of one of the Lucca manu- scripts,[1] in an old glass-painted window in Hardwick House, near Bury, in the quatre-foil of the south chancel window of St. James' church at Bury itself, and among the saints in the frontispiece of Capgrave's " Nova Legenda Angliæ." Four busts of the saint are also visible, carved on the helves of the panels of the roof in St. Mary's church at Bury. One holds a scroll or psalter; another a sceptre in the right hand; the third has a sword in the right hand, and a sceptre in the left; the fourth holds an arrow in the right hand and a sceptre in the left. Yates writes that in one of the south windows of Merton church St. Edmund is also represented in his regalia, arrow in hand, with the kneeling form of Sir Robert Clifton, Knt., at his feet, from whose mouth waves a scroll having on it, " Sancte Edmunde, ora pro nobis."[2]

---

[1] MS. Bibl., Canon., Pl. ix. F. p. 102.

[2] Yates' History of St. Edmund's Bury contains numerous plates of other memorials of St. Edmund which existed in his day, A.D. 1805, and among them two carved heads.

Sculptures and
pictures of the
legend of
St. Edmund.

The scene of the saint's martyrdom is found sculptured at the foot of Hugh of Northwold's tomb in Ely cathedral, which he in a great measure built during his episcopate,[1] and the fretwork roof of St. Edmund's chapel behind the high altar of Tewkesbury abbey church represents the same event.[2] The wolf guarding the martyr's head, which formed the seal of the sacrist, Walter de Banham,[3] is sculptured under one of the perpendicular windows of Moyse's Hall at Bury St. Edmund's, and in Hoxne church is a fine old poppy head carved with the same legend,[4] while the Jesuits at Bury possess an antique sculpture of the saint, with armour and spear, as he appeared to King Sweyn. The hundred and twenty pictures in Lydgate's famous poem[5] represent with the richness of mediaval illumination all the principal scenes in the saint's history, together with a coloured frontispiece of St. Edmund's banner,[6] the arms, three crowns d'or on azure ground,[7] the shrine with King Henry VI. kneeling at it,[8] the early miracles, the building of the great church, and the translation of

The 120 pictures
in Lydgate's
poem.

---

[1] Hugh was Abbot of St. Edmund's Bury, but died Bishop of Ely in 1254.

[2] Yates, p. 44. See also the seal of the friars of Norwich in the same work, Pl. vi.

[3] Ibid. In this seal the wolf is under a tree, holding in its paws St. Edmund's head.

[4] Ibid., Pl. i. and Pl. ii.

[5] Harl. MS. 2278.

[6] See also the Camden edition of Jocelin's Chronicle, vol. 13, p. 183.

[7] See also the initial letter in Dugdale's "Monasticon," vol. iii. edit. 1821, p. 98, and Bloomfield's "Norfolk," p. 387, where the author says that the arms which he gives are sketches from the windows of Winfarthing church in Norfolk and were seen there in 1600, although all others except those relating to St. Edmund had been defaced.

[8] See also Dugdale's "Monasticon," vol. iii. edit. 1821, under St. Edmund's Bury; Knight's "Old England," vol. i. no. 463.

the incorrupt body. Part of the device of St. Edmund's banner may also be seen carved on one of the bosses in the north aisle of St. Mary's church at Bury.

Among all these relics of a past history the little wooden church at Greenstead in Essex stands unique. *Greenstead church.* In antiquity it surpasses St.-Sernin, the martyr's modern resting-place. Built of wooden planks in the year 1013 to shelter St. Edmund's body on its way from London, it was preserved with care and reverence till the sixteenth century. Then, being considered valueless, it escaped the destruction which befell so many venerable sanctuaries and has survived to the present day,[1] more happy in that respect than the grander patrimony of St. Edmund, whose growth and magnificence as a record of devotion to a hero are treated of in the following chapter.

Lastly, the history of the devotion of ages to St. Edmund carries pilgrim and antiquarian back to the *Hoxne.* place of martyrdom. On the spot where the oak grew to which the royal martyr was bound, rises a memorial in the shape of a stone cross, on one side of which is the inscription:

St. Edmund King and Martyr, Nov. 20, a.d. 870. Oak tree fell Aug., 1848, by its own weight.

On the other side is inscribed:

The tree which stood here is said by tradition to have been the one against which King Edmund was shot.[2]

---

[1] See Knight's "Old England," vol. i. print no. 306 ; Palgrave's "Antiquities of Norfolk and Suffolk," vol. i. p. 82 ; Suckling's "Antiquities and Architecture of Essex," p. 4.

[2] The late Sir Edward Kerrison, who erected this monument, was not so happy in rebuilding the bridge over the *Gold Brook,* as it is called, to perpetuate the fable that St. Edmund fled before his martyrdom and hid under the arch of a former bridge, under which he was discovered by his golden spurs.

CHAPTER XII.

St. Edmund's Patrimony.

[*Authorities*—In the 16th century the so-called Reformers wrecked all the great libraries of England, and among them that of St. Edmund's Bury, and destroyed or scattered their literary and historical treasures. Many of the chartularies of St. Edmund's abbey, however, were saved and are now the most numerous extant of any old religious house of England. Dugdale ("Monasticon Anglicanum," vol. iii. p. 98, edit. 1821) devotes seventy-eight folio pages to their enumeration and a digest of their contents. They supply abundant material for a valuable and authentic history of St. Edmund's patrimony, of which this chapter is intended to be only a sketch. Much useful information is also contained in the "Antiquitates S. Edmundi Burgi," Joannis Battely, S.T.D., Archidiaconi Cantuariensis, Opera Posthuma, &c., Oxoniae: E. Theatro Sheldoniano, A.D. MDCCXLV., which is printed and published as a supplement to the "Antiquitates Rutupinae" (Richborough) of the same author. The "Illustration of the Monastic History and Antiquities of the Town and Abbey of St. Edmundsbury," by the Rev. Richard Yates, F.S.A., of Jesus College, Cambridge, &c., &c., London, 1805, is also a work of great antiquarian value. Both Battely and Yates illustrate their pages with plans and sketches of the monastic buildings and their remains. Gillingwater's "Historical and Descriptive Account of St. Edmund's Bury," published in 1804, and now a rare book, contains many interesting notes on the old abbey. Sir James Borrough's "History of Bury," Morant's "History of the Abbey of Bury St. Edmund's," and Green's "Description of the Ancient and Present State of the Town and Abbey of Bury St. Edmund's," supplement other authors. William of Worcester, a native of Bristol, gives the various dimensions of the abbey and its buildings, which he took himself when on a visit to the abbey in the reign of the Sixth Henry (A.D. 1479.) The "Annals" of Dom Bennet Weldon, O.S.B., preserved at the English College, Douai, the "Chronological Notes" by the same author, edited by a monk of Downside, the "Downside Review" of July, 1887, and the useful history of the "Établissements Religieux Britanniques Fondés a Donai, &c.," (Douai: Lucien Crepin, éditeur, 1880) supply most of the information required respecting the modern patrimony of St. Edmund.]

Modern Bury. THE town of Bury in Suffolk is the modern representative of the abbey and town which rose over and around the shrine of East England's martyr king. It stands in the centre of that western division of the county which was called the liberty, franchise or patrimony of St. Edmund. Now, though only a shadow of the magnificent past, having rejected even the name of the saint to whom it owes its existence, Bury is a bright and cheerful town, looking out right smilingly towards the eastern sun from the

grassy slope along which it stretches for a mile and
a half, and whose base is washed by the rivers
Linnet and Lark.   Around, the alternate green and,
in autumn, the famous yellow barley frame its clean
brick houses and its ancient streets in emerald and
gold.   The taste and feeling of the inhabitants have
considerably improved the natural beauty of the
town's position, and municipal enterprise has paved,
lighted and drained its wide streets and its numerous
and   spacious   squares.   These advantages, enhanced
by the dry and invigorating air, the vicinity of the
University of Cambridge, the numerous schools and
civil and polite institutions, have combined to make
it a favourite resort for the refined and educated.
Only one feature casts a gloom over the scene.   In
the midst of botanic gardens, bowling greens, private
lawns, fields and a few houses and public buildings, The site of the
dark reefs of broken walls rise mournfully here and abbey.
there, to tell of the destruction of the abbey which
once towered to heaven on this spot.

On the east, the neighbouring waters reflect a The ruins
fringe of sable and mouldering ruins on their banks;
over the juncture of the two streams the dismantled
arches of the abbot's bridge stretch their grim and
moss-covered masonry; on the western slope, some
pieces of broken sculpture, a solitary pier or grass-
grown mound repeat the sad history of destruction
and sacrilege.   Here a wall or window marks the
refectory, dormitory or guest house; there the rising
ground the cloisters or chapter house of the second
largest abbey in England.[1]   Part of the old embattled
walls, two lofty sculptured and storied gateways,

---

[1] For views of the ruins in 1745, see Battely's "Antiquitates S.
Edmundi Burgi" and Knight's "Old England," vol. i. prints 691,
692, 693.   The "Antiquarian and Topographical Cabinet" also
gives three views of St. Edmund's Bury.

two of the three magnificent churches which stood attendant on the abbey church, still define the western boundary of the monastic precincts.[1]

The remains of the great church.

But amid these faint rays of a glorious past, the stranger looks in vain for the great basilica which canopied St. Edmund's shrine. A few straggling ruins alone remain. A dilapidated tower converted into a stable, and three defaced archways, originally the portals of the church and now filled in with houses, alone mark the western front. Eastwards in a private garden, the bases of a line of pillars tell of the transepts and their columned chapels; and one broken group of the stately piers, which supported the central tower, stands solitary, hiding its grief under weeds of sable ivy. These are the last remnant of the high altar, the choir, the presbytery, and the "Holy of Holies," where the martyr's body reposed for centuries. No memory of the saint is perpetuated in the place, but the great event in the history of England due to his influence and that of the religious house which guarded his tomb is recorded on one

A memento of the past.

of three tablets of stone. The *sacrarium regis* is forgotten, but the *cunabula legis*[2] is commemorated in the following lines:

NEAR THIS SPOT,
ON THE 20TH OF NOVEMBER, A.D. 1215,
CARDINAL LANGTON AND THE BARONS
SWORE AT ST. EDMUND'S ALTAR
THAT THEY WOULD OBTAIN FROM
KING JOHN
THE RATIFICATION OF
MAGNA CHARTA.

---

[1] See Willis' "Parliamentary Abbeys," vol. i. p. 8.

[2] "The shrine of the king, the cradle of the law," the motto of Bury town.

" Where the rude buttress totters to its fall,
    And ivy mantles o'er the crumbled wall,
    Where e'en the skilful eye can scarcely trace
    The once High Altar's lowly resting-place—
    Let patriotic fancy muse awhile
    Amid the ruins of this ancient pile.
    Six weary centuries have passed away,
    Palace and Abbey moulder in decay ;
    Cold death enshrouds the learned and the brave ;
    LANGTON, FITZWALTER, slumber in the grave.
    But still we read in deathless records how
    The high soul'd priest confirmed the Barons' vow ;
    And FREEDOM unforgetful still recites
    This second birthplace of our native Rights."

" Ruina splendida," exclaimed Leland, just after the dissolution, " quam quicunque intueatur, et admiretur et simul commiseretur."—" Splendid ruin ! whoever sees it admires and pities."

" This abbey, the owner and indeed the creator of St. Edmund's town, itself owner of wide lands and revenues,"[1] at the beginning of the sixteenth century " stood proudly eminent, surpassing almost all the monasteries of England."[2] The old antiquary Leland, on seeing its far-spreading cloisters and its countless towers and spires rising to the sky, was unable to contain his admiration. " The sun," he wrote, " hath not shone on a town more delightfully situated on a gradual and easy descent with a small river flowing on the eastern part, or a monastery more illustrious, whether we consider its wealth, extent, or its incomparable magnificence. You might, indeed, say that the monastery itself is a town, so many gates there are, some of them of brass, so many towers, and a stately church, than which none can be more magnificent, upon which attend three others also, standing gloriously in one and the same church-yard, all splendidly adorned with curious

The abbey immediately before the dissolution.

Its extent and magnificence.

---

[1] Carlyle.   [2] William of Malmesbury.

workmanship." These buildings covered twenty-three acres of ground, not including the vineyard of six acres and the "Walnut-tree yard" on the eastern bank of the river Lark. A lofty embattled wall [1] *Its boundaries.* and a deep ditch [2] bounded this area on three sides, the two rivers on the fourth. Towering above the walls rose the four majestic gates which led into the precincts. The western boundary measured 1,100 feet, and presented a glorious frontage embellished by two superb and stately gates and the façades of St. James' and St. Mary's churches. The abbey-gate,[3] 62 feet high, 50 long and 41 broad, led into the *The abbey entrance.* great northern courtyard of the abbey. Ornamented with carved device, canopied niche and heaven-aspiring pinnacle, it ranked as one of the most beautiful gateways in England.[4] Just within its archway an outer portcullis, and 15 feet farther inwards gates of massive iron and polished brass, defended the entrance. Beyond the inner gates, in the inside wall to the right, a doorway opened into the lodge, where the brother porter and his deputy attended to receive strangers and announce them to the abbot;[5] and two staircases in

---

[1] Built by Hervey the sacrist at the beginning of the 12th century.

[2] Several instances occur of drowning in this ditch, which was filled up about the year 1750.

[3] The original gate was destroyed by rioters in 1327, and afterwards re-erected by them in reparation for their offence.

[4] This gateway has been well illustrated by Britton in his "Architectural Antiquities," vol. iii. p. 88 et seq.; Morant and others have minutely described it.

[5] According to the regulations for the reception of guests, the abbot, when at home, received all guests, whatsoever their condition, except religious and priests of secular habit and their men. In the absence of the abbot, the cellarer received all guests of whatsoever condition up to 13 horses. If a layman or a cleric came with more than 13 horses, the abbot's servants entertained them either within the guest-house or without at the abbot's expense. All religious men, even bishops who were not monks, were charged upon the

octagon corner-turrets led to the spacious chamber above, where abbot or monks gave audience to illustrious guests.[1] The guest-house, 25 yards long, with its store-rooms, almonry and chapel of St. Lawrence, extended along the western wall on the right of the gateway.[2] A magnificent spectacle met the eye from the flat roof of the abbey tower, or from its audience-chamber, as it ranged towards the east. Below lay the "Great Court" of the abbey, four acres in extent; on the north of which the stables and offices, 500 feet in length and 30 wide, stretched east and west, cut off from

The guest-house.

The great court-yard.

The stables and offices on the north.

cellary at the expense of the convent, unless the abbot wished to do them special honour and entertain them in his own palace at his own expense.

[1] This reception room or audience-chamber is 50 feet by 30, lighted on three sides by windows; on the fourth side is a fire-place and garde-robe.

[2] During Samson's abbacy Hugh the sacrist replaced the wooden guest-house by one of stone, covering an area 25 yards by 11 in extent, the expense being defrayed by "much of what Brother Walter the physician had acquired by his practice of physic." In this building was the large store-room, which the guest-master was bound to keep well supplied with beds, seats, tables, towels and similar articles ready for strangers and pilgrims, and also with bread, beer and other necessary viands. The monk in charge of the gates and the adjoining spacious and roomy guest-house introduced all visitors to the abbot and convent, conducted them to the refectory, church and cloisters, and procured for them every accommodation according to their rank and character. The almonry was attended by the almoner, who distributed the alms and charitable donations of the convent to pilgrims, travellers and the poor, who came to the abbey gate. On founders' days and other *obits* and anniversaries he gave out the *gifts*, and he and his servants attended the dinner of the abbot and monks to receive from them whatever they handed him from their portions. After their departure he could collect what they left of their charity. He purchased annually before Christmas cloth and shoes for widows and orphans and the poor clergy. He renewed the mats in the choir cloister, &c., and made other small provisions.

the court by an embattled wall. Here the abbot
lodged the horses up to 100, and the retainers
of any nobleman or prelate who visited the town,[1]
for at least one night without remuneration. The
north gate rose in the midst of, and above, the
offices, with the prison and hall of pleas at its side;

The cellarer's
premises
beyond.

the store-houses, bakery, brewery and the cellarer's
house adjoined. Farther on lay the cellarer's yard
formerly the manse of Beodric, at whose north-east
corner the abbot's bridge spanned the united rivers.

The abbot's
palace on the
east.

The abbot's "palace," 240 feet in length, occupied the east end of the abbey court, communi-
cating with the offices on the north and the
conventual buildings on the south.[2] In the centre
a high turret facing the spectator contained the
staircase, which led from a lower chamber supported
by ten pillars to the abbot's dining-hall above. At
the back of the "palace" the abbot's two "garners"
stood, and a wall, which separated the abbot's garden
from the cellarer's yard, ran down to the "dovecote,"

The view
beyond.

or summer-house on the banks of the river. The
view on the east side of the abbot's palace carried
the eye over the abbot's garden down the river
Linnet, beyond which flowed the Lark. In the narrow

---

[1] Part of the north wall of these offices remains, and their south
wall, which forms the northern enclosure of the *court*, is nearly entire.
Three entrances and seven windows may still (1872) be seen therein.
The stables and offices were thatched until Abbot Samson's time, but
with the assistance of Hugh the sacrist he stone-roofed them, "so
all peril and danger of fire was prevented."

[2] The abbot's palace, built by Geoffrey the sacrist in the reign
of Henry I., having been consumed by fire, was rebuilt by Hugh
the sacrist in 1155. From 1685 to 1688 the Jesuits seem to have
had a chapel and residence in it. It was used as a dwelling house
till 1720. On the southern side the crypt of the abbot's dining-hall
may still be seen. It is 55 feet long and 48 broad, including walls
5 feet in thickness. Ten pillars of an octagon form decorate the
inside. The base of the north-west turret may still be seen.

space between the two streams lay the six serpentine fish-ponds, called the "Crankles." Across the Lark and east of the cellarer's yard, the "Walnut-tree yard" was situated, and to its right the vineyard,[1] laid out in regular walks and parterres. Each was protected by its walls and the river Lark.

Along the south side of the great abbey court, The south-side of the great court. from the guest-house to the "palace" and beyond, clustered a multitude of noble but irregular buildings, turreted, pinnacled and carved, and presenting all the appearance of a miniature medieval city. The "Mint," The "Mint." where the monks had the right of coining from the time of the Confessor, began this gorgeous line of buildings, and ran contiguous to the western wall at the right of the guest-house.

The monastery, "the magnificent and peaceful The monastery. abode of religion," as Dr. Yates proclaims it, extended eastward from the mint to the very banks of the river. First, the lesser monastery with its grassy enclosure[2] lay, like the mint, in the protecting

---

[1] Bought by the sacrist Robert de Gravel "ad solatium infirmorum et amicorum," A.D. 1221. A wall 22 feet high, and a hill gently sloping to the height of 70 feet, sheltered it from the north, and houses from the east, while to the south-west it is open to the genial sun. In 1875 Mr. J. Darkin here grew to perfection in the open air several varieties of foreign grapes.

[2] Now known as the bowling green. As the "Lesser Monastery" stood on the site of the chamberer's office mentioned in the deed of grant to John Eyre, Esq., temp. Eliz., and described by Jocelyn (Gage's edit., p. 70) as a large hall with dormitories on the upper storey, there can be no doubt about its position. The foundations shown in old maps of a spacious edifice behind the east wall and northern wall of the bowling green prove that a monastery existed there. The old monastery in which Bishop Ailwin placed the Benedictines was south-east of this, and removed by Abbot Baldwin to make room for the nave and façade of the abbey church. To replace the old monastery Baldwin built the "Lesser Monastery" in stone, and probably also first built the great refectory. Abbot Robert II. seems to have continued the refectory wing as a scriptorium and in-

shade of St. James' church. The new or greater monastery came next in one long sweep which ran parallel
to the nave of the great basilica. Its west wing con-
The refectory. tained the monk's "aula," or dining-hall, 171 feet in
length and 40 feet in breadth,[1] surmounted by the dormitory or cells. The east wing contained the scriptorium,
The infirmary the infirmary and the infirmary chapel of St. Michael.
Between the greater monastery and the basilica the
kitchens and offices lay to the west, and to the east
The cloisters. the quadrangle of monastic cloisters.[2] The chapter-
house,[3] the vestry[4] and the north transept of the

---

firmary. In process of time these two wings were rebuilt, probably by
Geoffrey the sacrist, temp. Henry I., and they were called the New or
Greater Monastery. From Battely's mention of the New Monastery,
p. 27, and of the Greater Monastery, p. 63, they were evidently
one and the same. The great refectory adjoined the east end of the
Lesser Monastery and not the west end of the palace. When it
was burnt down by the great fire, Helyas the sacrist rebuilt it and
the other parts which had been destroyed in 1155, on the same
site. Many facts bear out this assignment of the refectory to
the west and the infirmary to the east. In building the refectory,
the kitchens which stood on part of the site of Ailwin's old monastery would be retained, there being no signs or record of any others.
The position of the infirmary cloisters equally proves that the infirmary was in the vicinity of the abbot's palace.

[1] In this great refectory the parliament of 1446 sat, whose object,
it is said, was to compass the death of Humphrey Duke of Gloucester.

[2] These cloisters were built by Prior John Gosford.

[3] The chapter-house was originally the work of Geoffrey the
sacrist. After the great fire, Hugh the sacrist rebuilt it, A.D. 1155.
In 1156 Abbot Anselm was buried in it. See Knight's "Old
England" for an ideal view of it, vol. i. print 696.

[4] A writer in the "Tablet" of December 26, 1891, has tried to
give a description of the vestry of this great abbey and of its presses
and strong chests with their treasures of vestments, jewels and
objects of gold and silver. No inventory of them, however, exists,
and only from fragmentary notices can they be conceived. Yet
their value was so great that Walter of Diss, overwhelmed with
the responsibility of their guardianship, four days after his appointment to the office of sacrist, petitioned Abbot Samson to relieve him
from it, since he had not closed his eyes, nor could he rest or sleep

basilica adjoined the eastern cloister. The chapter- The chapter-house and library.
house, which measured 100 feet in length and 40 in
breadth, was surmounted by the library, which Hervey,
the brother of Prior Talbot, enriched with valuable

from anxiety. As the monks of St. Edmund carried out the
ceremonial of the Church with extraordinary splendour, they
required many "sets" of copes and other vestments. At times
eighty of the monks wore copes. On certain feasts a crowd of
priests and clerics joined the religious, and at the great offices, like
mass and vespers, were all clad in sacred vestments. From fifty to
a hundred masses were daily celebrated in the basilica, and for
these, the vestry presses supplied all the necessary sets of vestments
in every one of the church colours. To read of sets of ten, thirty,
or sixty copes is not then extraordinary. "The fragmentary
notices which remain," says the writer referred to, "afford at all
events some idea of that of which all exact record is now lost.
Here, for example, is the cope woven with gold, and the precious
chasuble given by Abbot Samson ; here the chasuble adorned with
gold and precious stones and a cope of the like set given to the
house by Abbot Hugh II., afterwards bishop of Ely. Then in this
press are kept the precious copes and silken hangings, and other
most noble ornaments provided by Abbot Richard I. (A.D. 1229-
1234) ; and in this other the set of fifty copes and things belonging
thereto like albs, apparels, hoods and morses, which Prior John
Gosford had done so much to acquire. Then, to mention one or two
more instances, there were the vestments obtained at the cost of
£200 by John Lavenham ; the vestment *broden cum botterflies de
satyn* given by Dom Edmund Bokenham, chaplain to King Edward
III. ; the embroidered cope of Prior William de Rokeland ; the
precious cope bought for over £40 (£400 of our money) by Prior
Edmund de Brundish ; the sumptuously embroidered cope given by
Henry Lacy, Earl of Lincoln."

The following is an example of the kind of plate the vestry kept :
the great chalice of gold, weighing nearly fourteen marks, the gift of
Eleanor, queen of Henry II. The convent had given it as a contri-
bution towards the ransom of Richard I. The queen-mother,
however, paid its value and restored it to the abbey on condition—
so the charter runs—that never again should it be alienated, but
kept as a perpetual memorial of her son ; a chalice of fine gold
weighing five marks, procured by the sacrist Hugh ; the cross of
gold given by Abbot Samson ; the third golden cross, one of the
presents of Henry Lacy, which sparkled with precious stones
and contained a relic of the true cross ; a second cup of St. Edmund

manuscripts and Master Hugh ornamented most gorgeously with his own hand. The cloisters led to the "Abbot's Palace," which an open ambulatory also connected with the main building, so that easy access might be had to and from all parts of the monastery. The infirmary cloister, 175 feet square, joined the north-eastern corner of the chapter-house, and contained the lavatory,[1] a splendid work of art, adorned with statuary and coloured windows. The infirmary northern cloister bounded the abbot's garden, while between its southern cloister and the basilica lay the brethren's cemetery.[2] The "Prior's House"[3] and offices joined the infirmary cloisters and stood east of the great church. Beyond, to the south-east, lay the bath,[4]

The infirmary cloister.

The prior's house.

The bath.

with a bowl of silver gilt and marvellous workmanship, which the same Henry Lacy, Earl of Lincoln, gave to the monks, asserting that it once belonged to the royal martyr; a pastoral staff of Abbot Curteys, a work of art which did honour to John Horwell, goldsmith, of London, who made it in 1430 in time for the feast of All Saints. In the crook itself were two figured scenes, on one side the Assumption, and on the other the Annunciation; below the springing of the curve a richly ornamented niche enshrined the figure of St. Edmund, whilst below this again and forming the summit of the staff, were twelve similar canopied niches, each containing a figure of one of the apostles. This precious pastoral staff weighed 12lbs. 9½ oz., and the abbot paid £40 (£400) for it. This mere glance at the vestry of a single monastery affords some idea of the devastation which took place a few years later.

[1] It was begun by Walter de Banham (Battely, p. 154), and finished by Prior John of Gosford.

[2] The monk's cemetery also extended to the south-eastern side of the basilica. Here skeletons buried without coffins have been frequently found, with small crosses of lead of divers form, most of them inscribed "Crux Xti pellit hostem" on one side, and, "Crux Xti triūphat," on the other.

[3] Part of the foundations of this house was laid open a few years since by the Suffolk Archæological Society, and an accurate plan of them was taken by Mr. John Darkin.

[4] Excavated by Helyas the sacrist, about 1150, and filled up by reformers about 150 years ago.

20 yards square, divided into apartments and fed
by the river Linnet. The strong wall, now in ruins,
with its buttresses diversely shaped to resist and
break the flow of water, here flanked the river for
some distance and thus protected the eastern buildings from the floods. The whole length of this
stately pile of monastic buildings, was overshadowed by
the massive towers, the spires and stretch of roof of
the abbey church. This church which stood guardian
over St. Edmund's shrine, was a vast Norman basilica The abbey church.
dedicated to Christ, St. Mary and St. Edmund, came
next in capacity to Cologne cathedral, and ranked with
Amiens and York among the greater churches of Europe.
It was entered from the abbey by the east and west
cloisters which reposed under its shade. [1] The townsmen
and pilgrims approached by the Norman tower or "great The great gate of St. Edmund's church.
gate of the church-yard," [2] which immediately fronted
the western doors of the basilica and rose in three
storeys to the height of 90 feet over the wide and
lofty archway. In stately grandeur, in refinement
of decoration and proportion of parts, no Romanesque
work in England surpasses this Norman gateway.
On its western side, and projecting five feet from
the face of the tower, a porch of unique Norman
work rises to the height of 30 feet, and consists of a
decorated pediment covering an arch which springs
from three pillars. Two square and storeyed turrets

---

[1] For ground plan and dimensions of the abbey church, see
Battely and Yates.

[2] Abbot Baldwin erected this tower, which was the one that the
boy Samson saw in his dream. It still remains, and is 86 feet
high and 36 feet square, the walls being six feet in thickness, built
of rubble and faced with hewn Barnack stone. As usual with highly
finished Norman buildings, the stones are of a size which a labourer
could easily carry on his back to the top. The storeys are marked by
three string courses and arcades of arches, each line of arcading varying with each storey. It is now the bell-tower of St. James' church.

flank the porch on each side. A sculpture representing our Saviour in an elliptic aureole filled the great arch.[1] In the archway a square-headed doorway in the south wall marks the postern or porter's gate. Here again gates of bronze and iron, opening outwards, guarded the entrance. A newel stone staircase in the north-west turret ascended to a gallery above, which connected the small doors on the north and south sides, and enabled the warders to enter on the embattled walls which surrounded the whole abbey and its grounds.

St. Edmund's cemetery or church-yard

Passing through this majestic entrance, the pilgrim saw before and around him the great cemetery or church-yard of St. Edmund, acres in extent, reaching from his feet to the gardens and orchards which lay at the far east on the banks of the river Linnet, surrounded and dotted over with countless edifices, churches, chapels, schools and residences for priests, chaplains and abbey officials—the great cross of the cemetery rising in the midst of all. Chapels dedicated to St. Edmund, St. Andrew, St. John ad Montem, and one called the Chapel of the Charnel, as well as three churches, besides the vast abbey church, and the houses and gardens attached to each chapel, found abundant room within this extensive enclosure.[2]

With its church of St. Mary.

The eye, wandering to the right, passed the line of buildings adjacent to the western wall, to light on the church of St. Mary, standing at the south corner, in all its perfection and freshness; for it was only built at the commencement of the fifteenth century

---

[1] It was removed in 1789 to provide freer access for "loads of hay and straw"—fit simile of the destruction of the old religion.

[2] Up to the time of Abbot Samson the mystery plays, which were the delight of the common people, and shows, wrestling and other sports took place in the church-yard. In 1197 the famous abbot stopped them, because of the broils and bickerings between the townspeople and the abbey servants.

in its present perfect perpendicular style, vast proportions and beautiful delicate minuteness of parts.
On its north-west rose the tower.   Inside the church a
long vista of slender columns, lofty, storeyed and
coloured windows, far-stretching aisles and nave, distant
chapels, and open timber roof elaborately carved and
gilded, would have met the gaze as it wandered
from St. Peter's aisle on the north to St. Mary's on
the south, and up the nave for 200 feet and more to
the Jesus aisle or chancel at the east, the great
west window all the while shedding its mellowed
light over the whole scene.[1]

At the east of St. Mary's church the buildings
and residences of the clergy, who served it, clustered
and extended to the south gate, called St. Margaret's,[2]
beyond which stood St. Margaret's church,[3] the largest
of the churches, and described by Leland as of
curious workmanship and remarkable for large and
beautiful traceried windows.

At the east of St. Margaret's church stood Abbot

St. Margaret's or the south gate.

St. Margaret's church.

Abbot Samson's schools.

---

[1] Tymns' "Handbook of Bury-St.-Edmund's" gives a full description of this grand church. It still remains, though robbed of brasses
and tombs and much else that made it magnificent. It is altogether
213½ feet in length, 68 feet in breadth and 60 feet in height. Its
roof is perfect, and probably the finest specimen in the world of
an open timber roof. Its west window is said to be the largest in
any parochial church in England and measures 35½ feet high and
18½ broad, clear dimensions. It would take the curious visitor
many days to inspect Jankyn Smith's chantry of St. John the
Baptist (A.D. 1480), his friend John Baret's Lady chapel, John
of Nottingham's porch (A.D. 1437), the countless helves, cornices,
corbels, bosses, spandrels, which are carved with the emblems of
the passion, legends and arms of St. Edmund and of the saints,
and the shields and mottoes of all England's highest nobility.

[2] Removed in 1760.

[3] St. Margaret's was not a parish church, and hence is sometimes
called a chapel. It existed in Leland's time, but no trace on record
survives to back up the traditions concerning it. It was built by
Abbot Anselm.

Samson's schools,[1] built in the early English style with a Norman arched gateway, ornamented on each side with niches with chevron moulding. The school bordered on the abbey gardens.

Of the chapels within the area of the cemetery, that of the "Charnel" with "the pardoned grave" by its side [2] held the most conspicuous place. Abbot John of Northwold founded it [3] in 1301, the year of his own death. The charter of foundation recites that, "lately passing over the cemetery allotted for the burial of the common people," the abbot had observed, "not without sorrow of heart and pressure of vehement grief," how very many of the graves had been violated by the multiplied burials of bodies, and the bones of the buried "indecently cast forth and left." He therefore directed this chapel to be built, "paved with stone competently, that the exposed bones may be laid in the cavity beneath reverently and decently." And he decrees "that the place shall happily be rendered most famous by the perpetual celebration of the masses of two chaplains," [4] one of whom was to

---

[1] In a deed of 1579 described as "the late gramer schole hall, nowe the shire-house."

[2] In this part of the cemetery seem to have been laid those who had received the plenary indulgence at the hour of death, or, as non-Catholics writers put it, who had purchased remission of purgatorial punishments. It seems to have been similar to the "Pardon churchyard" on the north side of the charnel of old St. Paul's cathedral in London.

[3] The chapel was rated £6 for first fruits temp. Henry VIII. It was a "common ale-house" in 1637, and complained of as being also a "common nuisance." It was afterwards a blacksmith's shop. Last it was designed for a family mausoleum by Mr. Alderman Spink, who put up iron palisades round its ivy-covered walls and planted the enclosure with shrubs. The entrance to the crypt was discovered in 1844. The stairs had disappeared, but the floor was found paved with Barnack stone and covered to a depth of two feet with bones.

[*] These two chaplains were endowed "with the whole profit of

carry the pastoral staff before the lord abbot on public occasions and in processions.[1] Prior William of Rokelond provided a third chaplain [2] to say mass in the venerable Chapel of the Charnel.

The spectator still standing within the great gate of the cemetery, having made a survey of the southern precincts, now turns to the left to view St. James' church, which stretches from the great gate 193 feet eastwards. Most exquisite tracery and delicate sculpture ornamented the windows and walls of this beautiful edifice. Altars to St. Anne, St. John, St. Lawrence, St. Mary, St. Michael, St. Peter, St. Stephen and St. Thomas à Becket stood in all their rich carving under its open cinque-foiled and decorated timber-roof. [3] At the west of its south aisle, called St. Mary's, was situated the popular altar and chapel of the Holy Name of Jesus, and in the south porch our Lady's chapel with its doors of brass. Statues and pictures adorned the walls, like that of St. John the Evangelist in the chancel, and of St. James and the Virgin Mother and the picture of the " Salutation " in the north aisle, where the guilds of St. Botulph and of

St. James' church.

the ministry or office of the clerk serving with us of our pastoral staff, which is called the Staphacres," *i.e.*, the crop of an acre of corn in various manors around the town ; and the number of chaplains were to be increased as the amount of alms and legacies of the faithful would admit. They were only removable "for incurable infirmity or evident honest cause," and then to be maintained in the hospital of St. Saviour, unless "overspread with such a contagious disease, that among other men he or they cannot decently keep company, and then in the hospital of St. Peter or St. Nicholas."

[1] The charters appointing the principal chaplain or *custos*, " to the free chapel called Le Charnell," provided that "he or his honest deputy should carry before the lord abbot his pastoral staff, on the usual occasions and according to ancient custom."

[2] A house in Bernewell Street, now College Street, was assigne to the three chaplains for residence.

[-] The roof was extremely similar to that of Burwell, Cambs.

Jesus held their meetings, under the bright and coloured light of the saints of the old and new testament, who looked down from the storied windows.
St. James' church [1] with its many chapels and altars stood in the shadow of the west front of the abbey church, which rose straight in front of the great gate, and surpassed in glory and magnificence all that existed in the other churches.

The great church.

> " For if the servants we so much commend,
> What was the mistress whom they did attend ! "

The lofty roof, massive towers and tapering pinnacles of this " Great Church " rose high above all other buildings and formed a conspicuous landmark to all the country round, being the very centre of the far-spreading lands and houses.   All other churches, chapels, and chantries, cloisters, halls and gates perforce paid it lowly homage.   Its west front, 250 feet wide, with three lofty arched portals and two lower ones, rivalled that of Peterborough.   A high and massive bell-tower, supported by two lateral towers, as in present Ely cathedral, stood majestically in the centre of the façade, and western transepts, also imitated at Ely, flanked by low octagonal towers 30 feet wide inside, completed the broad and imposing frontage.   At the end of the nave-roof a lofty chancel tower and two lower towers rose to the sky, massive and solid, from which the transepts to the north and south, and the apse to the east branched out, completing with the nave the church's cruciform shape.   From contemplating the exterior, the pilgrim passed under one of the sublimely

Its façade.

Its western towers.

Its eastern towers.

---

[1] The church of St. James still stands, and in one of its aisle windows some of the old glass, containing figures of David, Abia and other scripture kings, may be seen.

arched and pointed[1] doorways through the skilfully The Interior.
chiselled gates of beaten bronze within the basilica
itself. The long western transepts lay on his right
and left, the two apsidal chapels of St. Catherine and
St. Faith being at their eastern corners. Before him
the dim and columned nave, the largest of any church
north of the Alps except old St. Paul's, stretched in
an unbroken length of 500 feet.[2] A scene of unexam-
pled beauty and solemness broke upon the vision.
Between the twelve bays formed by the huge Norman
columns, in transept and apse glimmered the lights
at altars and in chapels too numerous to name, for The numerous
eighty priests of the abbey, as well as those who came altars.
in pilgrimage, required altars on which each might
daily offer the great Christian Sacrifice. The painted
vaulting—that of the choir by "Dom John Wodecroft,
the king's painter,"[3] and that of the nave, to match,
by the sacrist John Lavenham[4]—relieved the massive
Norman architecture, while the clerestory and aisle
windows and the distant windows of choir and apse,
filled with painted glass, the gifts of kings and nobles,
brought the court and glory as it were of heaven into the

---

[1] They were originally three great Norman archways, but
seem to have been changed for pointed ones before the 14th
century.

[2] See letter of E. B. Denison, Esq., in the "Times," Sept. 1,
1871. Its length was 505 feet, the nave was 33 feet broad, the
upper transepts 246½ feet from north to south. It thus surpassed any
other church or cathedral at the time of its erection. The following are the lengths of some of its rivals, after additions had been
made to them : Durham, 414 feet ; Winchester, 545 ; Canterbury,
514 ; Salisbury, 474 ; Westminster, 489 ; York and Lincoln, 498 ;
Ely, 517 ; St. Alban's, 600. Norwich cathedral, including the Lady
chapel at the east end, could have been placed within St. Edmund's
church with many feet to spare all round it.

[3] A.D. 1279-1301, in the days of Abbot John I. de Northwold.

[4] A.D. 1370. John Lavenham spent £50,000 of our money in
beautifying the church.

scene.   Six clusters of pillars,[1] springing from the tiled
pavement, soaring aloft, upheld the chancel lantern
tower, which cast down rays of light upon the high

The high altar.   altar with its silver base and porphyry table,
presented by Pope Alexander III. to Abbot Baldwin.
The altar screen with side doors leading beyond, and
all adorned with paintings by Prior Edmund Brundish,

The choir and presbytery.   surrounded the altar.   The choir and presbytery
extended behind the altar, and was so magnificent,
so glorious, so gorgeously rich even in Herman's
time, that he compared it to Solomon's temple and
testified that many pronounced it the most costly
temple to God they had seen.   The oak carved stalls
of the monks extended from pillar to pillar, and in
their midst, in the centre of the apse,[2] stood the price-

The martyr's shrine.   less shrine of the martyr on its gothic stonework base,
glittering with gold and gems and lighted tapers, and
surmounted by a coloured and pictured baldachin.
On the east, at the head of the saint, two small
columns supported a smaller shrine containing the
relics of Abbot Leofstan and others, whilst at the feet
of the saint were the shrine of Abbot Baldwin and
the altar of the Holy Cross.   "Oh, how worthy was
this spot, in which so great a witness of Christ reposed,

The east end.   apparently asleep!"[3]   An opening at the most eastern
point of the choir brought the pilgrim face to face
with the three apsidal chapels of the east end.
The centre one was the chapel of the relics; the other
two had been built in honour of St. Thomas and to

---

[1] Abbot Baldwin originally intended the two easternmost piers
to support that side of the central tower, but Abbot Robert, his
successor, deciding to lengthen the choir one bay, left the intended
tower piers standing, and built four others towards the west.

[2] It was placed there by Abbot Baldwin in 1095, and never afterwards removed, except to a new stone base in 1198.

[3] St. Abbo.

receive the shrines of St. Firminus and St. Botulph, which once stood attendant on St. Edmund's shrine.

The stranger, passing by many a sculptured chapel, screened chantry and recumbent tomb of holy and illustrious dead,[1] next visits the transepts, 246 *The eastern transepts.* feet from north to south, and crossing the nave under the chancel tower. A single row of columns on the east side of each formed aisles, and divided the main part from the side-chapels. Apsidal chapels projected eastwards at the extreme corners, and the "pity rood" or "ruby rood," a copy of the "Santo Volto" which Abbot Leofstan brought from Lucca, adorned that near the south door. The Lady chapel, 80 feet long and 42 broad, adjoined the north transept, and ran eastwards parallel to the choir aisle, while the chapel of St. Andrew corresponded with it in the south transept. By a side-door in the north transept the visitor entered the east cloister of the monastery, and thence descended to the crypt—St. Mary *in cryptis*,—which extended *The crypt.* under that eastern limb of the church which was occupied by the shrine of St. Edmund and its magnificent surroundings. The crypt was a veritable underground church, 100 feet long and 80 broad, its vaulted roof being supported by 24 polished marble pillars.[2] In its centre welled up a fountain of crystal water.[3] Three apsidal chapels [4] corresponded

---

[1] The bare enumeration, says Tymms, of the royal and noble persons who found their last resting-place within these walls would occupy many pages. He then proceeds to give a few names of earls, dukes and princes buried there, ending with Mary Tudor, sister of Henry VIII. and queen of Louis XII. of France.

[2] Probably Purbeck marble.

[3] There seems to have been a baptismal font connected with this spring. The font with its lofty canopy is now in Worlingworth church.

[4] The foundations of these chapels were laid open in 1849, during

with those in the church above, the centre one
being dedicated to St. Mary, that to the south
to the Holy Cross and that to the north to St. Saba.
Chapels to St. Anne, St. Botulph, Abbot of Ramsey,
and St. Lawrence also adorned the undercrofts. The
pilgrim ascends once more to the abbey cloister,
having finished his tour of what an ancient writer
describes as "the magnificent pile of many kings, built
of hewn stone by masterly hands of many ages, and
elevated with lofty columns ornamented with marble:
shewing in the texture of its vaulted roof, under the
mortal image, the countenance of heaven. Why
should I recount the walls terminated with battlements? Why should I extol the towers with folding
doors, and in their turn the many interior buildings,
rearing with united roofs their pinnacles to the
clouds? You might call it a beautiful city within
a small space." [1]

St. Edmund's
town.

Around this majestic pile, St. Edmund's town
clustered. In the course of ages many circumstances
had contributed to the growth of the borough. What
were plough-lands, for instance, in Edward the
Confessor's reign, were covered with houses under the
Norman rule, when the building of the great church
drew craftsmen and masons to the place and mingled
them with the plough-men and reapers of the abbey
domains. Serfs, traders, Jews and fugitives from justice,
or their lord, sought protection in rough times under
the strong hand of St. Edmund,[2] and having found it,
settled down under the convent rule, so that long

some excavations undertaken by the Suffolk Archæological Institute.
The northern one had some fragments of encaustic tile pavement
and the lateral supports of a stone altar. The sedilia for the
officiating priests were still observable.

[1] Quoted by Yates, p. 176.

[2] Green's "Short History of the English People," edit. 1877, p. 90.

before the fifteenth century the space within the walls was filled with the houses of the burgesses. And judging from the size and number of the parish churches and the pious bequests made to them, and from the reception accorded to kings and high functionaries, the population was not only large but well-to-do. At every step wealthy homes, hospitals, halls, convents and schools met the wayfarer. A wall guarded by five gates surrounded the town. At each gate a canopied niche enclosed a statue of our Lady, before which lamp or candle constantly burnt. Near each gate a hospice or religious house, for the entertainment of pilgrims, had also been established, and a chapel or oratory to the tutelar angel or saint of the entrance.

Over the town, and within the four crosses which *The abbot's power over it.* marked its boundaries, the abbot held supreme jurisdiction. All civil and criminal causes came to his court. He had his own prison, and, saving the rights and privileges which the citizens had won or bought from the monks, and which were embodied in their charters, his power was absolute. His spiritual jurisdiction within the crosses which stood a mile *His spiritual jurisdiction.* in each direction from the martyr's tomb, was that of an *abbas nullius*, or one subject to no bishop save the bishop of Rome.[1] Only a legate *a latere*, or the visitor appointed by the English-Benedictine general chapter, could officially inspect the monastery and its dependencies.[2] Like a bishop, the abbot of St. Edmund's could wear the tunic and dalmatic and bestow the solemn blessing with mitre on head and

---

[1] Even an *abbas nullius* not having episcopal consecration was obliged to call in a bishop for ordinations and other strictly episcopal functions.

[2] Hence the abbot of Hulme, deputed by the general chapter held at Northampton, visited the abbey in 1441. (Yates, p. 114.)

crozier in hand. He appointed the parochial clergy in his jurisdiction, and monks, priests and chaplains owed obedience to him according to their order. One restriction, however, was placed upon the abbot. He had no power to tax the borough without the will of the convent, for it belonged to St. Edmund and his altar, and all the profits from it pertained to the convent; unless they voluntarily granted them to the abbot, to the burgesses or to the king. Accordingly, the horn called the *mote horn* and the keys of the town were every year on St. Michael's day delivered to the sacrist in the chapter-house by the town bailiffs; the sacrist delivered them to the prior, who in the same way, through the sacrist, returned them to the town authorities. This observance took place annually, in order to assert the right of the convent over the town, so that, during the vacancy of the abbacy, the king should not take it into his own hands with the abbot's temporalities.

The abbatial jurisdiction over the franchise of St. Edmund.

No limit, however, restricted the abbot's temporal rule outside the limits of the town. Like St. Cuthbert in the north, St. Edmund held an extensive franchise in the east. His possessions embraced a third of Suffolk, besides manors and farms in a dozen other counties, and over these the abbot had quasi-regal rights. The consequent wealth and influence made him a baron of the realm, with the privilege of sitting in parliament with other spiritual peers.

The wealth of the franchise.

The wealth and possessions of St. Edmund were the accumulated growth of centuries. The same principle which induces men now-a-days to erect memorials to Prince Albert, or General Gordon, animated St. Edmund's clients to bring their gifts of gold and land to the monks, the guardians of their hero's tomb. In the course of ages these substantial expressions of devotion or gratitude to St.

Edmund brought in a yearly revenue of £200,000 Its annual revenue. of our money. Yates, who wrote in 1804, ventures the statement that the possessions of the monastery produced an annual income of £500,000. Weever[1] places St. Edmund's Bury as second only to Glastonbury in wealth, privileges and power. He says: "If you demand how great the wealth of this abbey was, a man could hardly tell, and namely how many gifts and oblations were hung upon the tomb alone of St. Edmund; and besides there came in out of lands and revenues a thousand, five hundred and three score pounds (£1,560) of old rent every year." The commissioners of Henry VIII., however, put its annual value at £2,336, or below that of St. Alban's and Canterbury, implying that at the height of its prosperity its ample endowments held only the fourth rank among those of the ecclesiastical and monastic establishments of England. It is well known, however, that Henry's agents were not too scrupulous in their reports, nor too accurate when the figures would tend to their own interests, and hence little reliance can be placed on their statements. In 1278 the monastery, in paying subsidies to the king, admitted a yearly income of £10,000, which, put into modern money, more closely approaches the estimate arrived at by Yates and others.

Such then was St. Edmund's patrimony 700 years A summary. after its beginning, 500 years after the introduction of the Benedictines and just before its final ruin. Thirty-three abbots had held its pastoral staff, many of them illustrious for holiness and learning; monks famous for scholarship and skill in the fine arts had found refuge in its abbey;[2] and great men of the

---

[1] "Funeral Monuments," pp. 463-4.

[2] Some of its most celebrated men were :—Abbot Baldwin (1097); Abbot Samson (1211); Abbot John of Northwold, annalist

realm, kings, noblemen, merchants and honest townsmen, considered it a mark of distinction and honour,
to be enrolled in the fraternity of the guardians of
St. Edmund, or to have allotted to them a grave near
his shrine.

Unimportance of the place previous to St. Edmund's burial there.   The magnificence of its buildings, the extent of
its possessions, the sacredness of its precincts hallowed
by the continuous chant of the choir, the solemn
round of holy services, the daily masses and processions, and the ceaseless stream of pilgrims during
its long tenure of prosperity, all owed their origin and
strength to the name and power of St. Edmund.
Some have, indeed, imagined that the spot had first
been consecrated to druidical worship from the tradition of the procession of the white bull,[1] and from the
Saxon name *Beoderics-gueorth*, meaning *a chief spot for
worship*.[2]   Others have fixed upon it as the Villa
Faustina, *the prosperous town*, or the Villa Faustini,
the seat of Faustinus, of the *Iter* of Antonine, but
accurate measurements do not bear out their theory.
Others again connect it with the Roman Bericus,
whom Suetonius mentions in his account of the
emperor Claudius, the first real conqueror of Britain.
We reach firm ground, however, in the reign of St.
St. Sigebert's connection with it.   Sigebert, who founded a monastery and church on
the spot in honour of St. Mary; in that monastery

---

and voluminous writer (1301); Abbot Hugh of Northwold, afterwards bishop of Ely; Prior Roger, the computist (1360); Jocelin of
Brakelond, chronicler (1214); John Eversden, poet, orator, historian
(1336); Edmund Bromfield, bishop of Llandaff (1389); Boston de
Bury, author and bibliographer (1410); John Lydgate, rhetorician,
mathematician and poet (1446).   Abbot John Melford or Reeve,
who survived the destruction of the monastery only a few months.

[1] An old custom of the townspeople.

[2] Sir Henry Ellis derives this meaning from the Saxon *bede*,
"prayer," *rice*, "power," or "authority," as in "bishopric," and
worth, a "town."

he laid aside his crown and devoted himself
to a religious life.   Afterwards, about the time of
St. Edmund—so the old charters and registers have
it,—being a royal town, it descended to one of
royal blood named Beodricus, Beodricius, or Beodric, Etheling Beodric's.
who gave it to King Edmund.   Whether Beodric
bequeathed it to the saint before or after the martyrdom is uncertain.   More probably he offered it to
Bishop Wilred, when that prelate was seeking some
secure and permanent resting-place for the holy king's
remains.   No spot was more suitable for church,
tomb and monastery, than King Sigebert's royal
town, then known as Beodricsworth, or *Beodric's
estate.*   So Etheling Beodric surrendered it, and Edmund took possession of the fief, over which he
exercised undisputed suzerainty for six hundred years.

For centuries it retained its name of Beodricsworth.
In course of time, however, the people called it
Kingston and Edmundston, St. Edmund's burg, borough,
or town, and lastly St. Edmund's Bury ; not because
St. Edmund was buried there, but by reason of the
splendour of the place, the word *bury* in Anglo-
Saxon signifying "court" or "palace."   Carlyle ex- Carlyle on the growth of St. Edmund's patrimony.
plains the growing importance of the place in the
following words :   "Edmund was seen and felt by
all men to have done verily a man's part in this
life-pilgrimage of his ; and benedictions, and out-
flowing love and admiration from the universal heart,
were his meed.   Well-done !   Well-done !   cried the
hearts of all men.   They raised his slain and martyred
body ; washed its wounds with fast-flowing universal tears ; tears of endless pity, and yet of sacred
joy and triumph. . . . .   Oh ! if all Yankee-
land follow a small good ' Schnüspel the distinguished
novelist ' with blazing torches, dinner-invitations,
universal hep-hep-hurrah, feeling that he, though small,

is something; how might all Angle-land once follow
a hero-martyr and great true son of heaven!" It
is natural to man to worship, but it is a humiliat-
ing fact that he oftentimes worships mere empty
nothings—"Kings' progresses, Lord Mayors' shows and
other gilt-gingerbread phenomena of the worshipful
sort," with other heroes of doubtful character— "these
be thy gods, O Israel!" Is not Edmund better and
nobler than these? The modern world enshrines
its heroes under the dome of St. Paul's, in the aisles
of Westminster abbey, or beneath the monument and
flowers of the suburban cemetery, and even bequeaths
legacies that posterity may keep up the worship.
In similar manner but more reasonably "did the
men of the eastern counties take up the body of
their Edmund, where it lay cast forth in the village
of Hoxne; seek out the severed head, and reverently
reunite the same. They embalmed him. . . . with
love, pity, and all high and awful thoughts: con-
secrating him with a very storm of melodious adoring
admiration and sun-dyed showers of tears; joyfully
yet with awe (as all deep joy has something of the
awful in it) commemorating his noble deeds, and
God-like walk and conversation while on earth;"
till at length all good men, bishops, priests and
people, the Pope of Rome approving, pronounced
that he had in fact led a hero's life in this world,
"and being now gone, was gone to God above and
reaping his reward there."

"The rest of St. Edmund's history, for the reader
sees he has become a saint, is easily conceivable.
Pious munificence provided him a *loculus*, a *feretrum*
or shrine; built for him a wooden chapel, a stone temple
ever widening and growing by new pious gifts;—
such the overflowing heart feels it a blessedness to
solace itself by giving. St. Edmund's shrine glitters

now with diamond flowerages, with a plating of
wrought gold. The wooden chapel, as we say, has
become a stone temple. Stately masonries, long-
drawn arches, cloisters, sounding aisles buttress
it, begirdle it far and wide. Regimented companies
of men. . . . devote themselves in every generation to meditate here on man's Nobleness and
Awfulness, and celebrate and show forth the same,
as they best can; thinking they will do it better
here, in the presence of God the Maker, and of the
so Awful and so Noble made by Him. In one word,
St. Edmund's body has raised a monastery round it . . .

"New gifts,—houses, farms, *katalla* [1]—come ever
in. King Knut. . . . with his crown and gifts, . . .
many others, kings, queens, wise men and noble
loyal women, let Dryasdust and divine silence be
the record!"[2] The devotion of ages has found expression, has become visible and lasting in this pile
of buildings, in this monastery and its monks, in
this town and its burghers, in these vast possessions,
lands and manors which form "the Funeral Monument" of the saint, Edmund.

The first custodians of the shrine were some clerics, *History of St.
Edmund's Bury
before the
coming in of the
Benedictines.*
priests and deacons, who, out of devotion consecrated
their lives to the service of God and St. Edmund.[3]
About the year 925, Athelstan constituted them a
collegium. They then consisted of the four priests *The Canons of
St. Edmund.*
Leofric, Alfric, Bomfield and Edmund, and of the two
deacons Leofric and Kenelm. Within a few years
they increased to fourteen priests and five deacons.

---

[1] "Goods, properties; what we call *chattels*, and still more
singularly *cattle*, says my erudite friend."

[2] Carlyle's "Past and Present," edit. 1843, p. 47 et seq.

[3] They began to live in community about A.D. 925, if not before.
From 903 to 925, they probably served the church, though Oswene
seems to have looked after the shrine.

These keepers of the shrine had care of the property and relics ; they preserved the "Acts" of the saint's life and martyrdom, and registered the miracles. Countless benefactors gave donations to them and to the saint's burial-place, which they guarded. Among others Earl Alfgar and his daughter, the father and sister of the unfortunate youth Leofstan, Early donations made large bequests of land. The very Danes ex-to the shrine. piated past crimes by offerings to the tomb, and the English upheld law and religion, at least in theory, by making Edmund's patrimony grand and over-awing.

The long list of English kings who, by their gifts and charters, laid the foundation and built up the stately memorial to their fellow-sovereign, King Athel- begins with Athelstan the Conqueror. He offered stan's. upon the altar, among his other gifts, a most precious copy of the gospels. His brother and successor King King Edmund's. Edmund in 945 confirmed by charter to the "family"[1] of St. Edmund the possession of Beodricsworth, and granted for the first time the temporal jurisdiction over the district within the four crosses. He more-over endowed his patron and namesake with the permanent revenue of the manor of Fornham Parva. Edwy's. Even the dissolute Edwy respected St. Edmund and gave him the manors of Beccles and Elmswell, and Edgar's. King Edgar and his chancellor Thurketul confirmed all former gifts and added other lands. The relic of the true cross which lay upon the sleeping martyr's breast for a hundred years, was among the valuable legacies of this period. But the Bishops Theodred I., Bishops Theodred I.'s, Theodred II. and Adulph made the richest offerings Theodred II.'s, and Adulph's. at this time in the form of extensive and valuable estates. Theodred's will is still extant and bequeaths to St. Edmund the three manors of Harrings Heath,

---

[1] King Edmund's charter uses the words " familia monasterii."

Ickworth and Whepstead, to which Bishop Adulph
added nine others.

The secular canons in course of time proved The decay of discipline among the secular canons.
unworthy of the guardianship of the shrine which
had been entrusted to them.   They spent upon
themselves the offerings made to the Church and
to St. Edmund, and neglected the tomb which
they had engaged to attend.   The fervour and
enthusiasm of the first founders had evaporated
in less than a century, and their successors disedified
the pilgrims by their careless lives and their resistance to Bishop St. Algar's right to control their
administration or to exact any contributions from
them for the general needs of the Church.   This rough
spirit was in a great measure due to the unsettled
state of the country, but Bishop Algar could not
altogether excuse the neglect of the tomb.   While
leaving the canons, therefore, in possession of the
monastery and church, he entrusted the round chapel
and the shrine within it to the monk Ailwin.

With Ailwin the patrimony of St. Edmund enters The appointment of the monk Ailwin.
upon a new history.   Devout clients gained more
singular favours at the shrine, and in consequence
donations and thank-offerings increased.   The journey
of the sacred body to London, and its return after
three years, spread the fame of St. Edmund far and
wide.   An unwonted enthusiasm was created in his
favour ; and gifts flowed in without stint.   For instance, the Dane, out of himself with gratitude for
his restoration to sight, threw his bracelets and necklace upon the coffin ; the Lord of Stapleford, cured
of a lingering sickness, gave his own manor as a
thank-offering ; and on Ailwin's re-entry into Beodricsworth with the sacred remains, the people loaded
him with joyful offerings.

Next the "carucaginm" ranks as the great tribute

of the East Anglians to St. Edmund, whom they always considered as their proper and only sovereign. It was granted in thanksgiving for the deliverance from King Sweyn. On hearing of the death of King Sweyn by the hand of St. Edmund, "the people lept for joy," says the Register of Abbot Curteys, and, "wishing to make a grateful return to St. Edmund, they determined to bestow on the saint fourpence annually forever for every carucate of land in the whole diocese; which gift on that account is called carucagium." This tax was paid to the saint's church until the next century, when Herbert of Losinga, bishop of Norwich, borrowed it, or, according to some, had it made over to him by the monks, for the building of his cathedral.

King Canute's munificence was another consequence of Sweyn's death. Sweyn had exacted tribute of the royal martyr's freemen, although every king and conqueror since Guthrun had held them exempt. He had even threatened to burn the saint's town and sanctuary, and if he refrained, it was from no feeling of reverence, but because a sudden and extraordinary death prevented him. Canute, unwilling to be a party in his father's crimes or his countryman's irreligion, at once made reparation to St. Edmund on his accession to the throne. "To expiate his father's crimes," runs the old tradition, "being oft affrighted with the vision" of the royal martyr's "seeming ghost," he confirmed the charter granted by Edmund I., "allowing the saint to enjoy the profit arising from the town," giving in addition the "sea-fish which should annually accrue to him in right of toll."

To Canute and Ailwin we owe the establishment of the Benedictines as guardians of St. Edmund's shrine. In the third year of Canute's reign the "monachus et auriga Sti Edmundi," Ailwin, who for thirty years had been the saint's faithful servant, was consecrated bishop of Elmham. This necessitated the entrusting of the custody of the shrine to other hands. The new bishop, convinced that the secular canons, whom Bishop Algar had deprived of the office of custodians, were unfitted to resume it, contemplated their removal altogether, and the introduction into their place of some of his Benedictine brethren of the monastery of Hulme. Finding Elsinus,[1] the abbot of that monastery, favourable to his design, he sought and obtained the support of King Canute. The twelve ecclesiastics who formed the college of canons[2] were provided with suitable maintenance and removed. In their place Ailwin inducted half of the community of Hulme. Count Turchil, before whom Ailwin had fled to London, but who now presided over East Anglia, favoured the entrance of the monks "into that basilica, day and night to serve God, blessed Mary and the body of the holy martyr." Uvius, prior of Hulme, a humble, gentle and benign man, was blessed as first abbot by the bishop of London. The rest of the community comprised Leofstan, the abbot's brother, Edward, Leosden the deacon, Alfric, Bond, Edric, Assiwold, Leofstan, the second of that name, Sparhavoc, and the boys Oswald and Ordric. With a generosity, worthy of imitation in these days, the new community received half the books, furniture, vestments and other goods of the mother-house.

Uvius, first abbot.

The first monks.

---

[1] Also written Elfinus.

[2] The "Registrum Sacristæ," as well as other registers of the abbey, states that "Clerics amounting to XII. were ejected ; to whom, as they were left without any fixed abode, Canute gave the privilege which is yet held by those who are called *Duodeni*." In Abbot Baldwin's time these priests were formed into a college and placed over St. Denis' church, the predecessor of the present St. James' church, although not built on exactly the same site.

The privileges of
the new abbey. Bishop Ailwin gave spiritual jurisdiction to the
new abbot and exempted the monastery and town
within the boundary of the four crosses from all
external interference.   Lastly the king confirmed all
that had been done by the "magnificent prelate
Ailwin."   "Summoning all the prelates, nobles and
magnates of the kingdom to his parliament, he
reminded them of the *deeds* of the said Bishop Ailwin,
viz., of the exemption and other grants made by
him to the aforesaid abbot and monks, and he
graciously confirmed the same by a formal charter,
which he signed with a cross instead of a seal, and
all and each of the prelates and nobles impressed
on it the sign of the cross, and all signed their names
to it immediately after the illustrious name of the
king." [1]

Canute's further
devotion to St.
Edmund. Canute is said to have also made a dyke to mark
the vast and magnificent patrimony of St. Edmund.
Out of reverence and in acknowledgment of the
final subjection of his race to St. Edmund, he moreover uncrowned himself and sent his crown to the
martyr's shrine, and when he founded a college of
white canons at Cambridge, he placed it under the
patronage of St. Edmund. [2]

Queen Emma's
oblation. Queen Emma, moved by her consort's example,
gave, as an annual oblation of " 4,000 eels with the gifts
pertaining to them, with the annual tribute of Laken-
heath."

The building of
the stone church. No sooner had the Benedictines taken charge of
St. Edmund's tomb than, according to the tradition
of their order, they began to build as rich and as
worthy a church as their means would allow.   For
this purpose Bishop Ailwin supplemented Canute's

---

[1] Curteys' "Register."

[2] Harpsfeld, p. 748.

generosity by the *carucagium*. The large but rough
timber church of Bishop Theodred was replaced by
one of stone, only the round chapel of stone, in which
the shrine rested, being allowed to remain.[1] It took
twelve years to complete, and was consecrated by
Agelnoth, archbishop of Canterbury in 1021, in
honour of Christ, St. Mary and St. Edmund.

The new church, however, fell far short of what
Baldwin,[2] the third abbot, thought suitable for his

The great
basilica.

---

[1] Bishop Theodred II. probably built the round chapel in stone
after the attempt to rob the church.

[2] The following is a list of abbots. See Yates' "History of
Bury," p. 208.

1. UVIUS, – 1044.
2. LEOFSTAN, – 1065.
3. BALDWIN, – 1097.
4. ROBERT I. of Chester, 1102, deposed.
5. ROBERT II. of Westminster, – 1112.
6. ALBOLD of Beccles, – 1119, consecrated by Ralph, archbishop of Canterbury.
7. ANSELM of St. Saba's Rome, elected Bishop of London, – 1148.
8. ORDING, – 1156.
9. HUGH I. of Westminster, – 1180.
10. SAMPSON, – 1211.
11. HUGH II. of Northwold, made Bishop of Ely, 1228.
12. RICHARD of Ely, – 1234.
13. HENRY I., – 1248.
14. EDMUND I. de Walpole, – 1256.
15. SIMON de Luton, – 1279.
16. JOHN I. of Northwold, – 1301.
17. THOMAS I. of Totynton, – 1312.
18. THOMAS II. of Draughton, – 1335.
19. WILLIAM I. of Bernham, – 1361, who, when a monk, had the
famous dream about the saint's return to St. Edmund's
Bury.
20. HENRY II. of Hunstanton, LL.B., died on his way to Rome.
21. JOHN II. of Brimkele, LL.B., – 1379.
22. EDMUND II. Bromfield, D.D.
23. JOHN III. de Tymworth, – 1389.
24. WILLIAM II. Cratfield, – 1414.
25. WILLIAM III. Excetre, – 1429.

B B

abbey, and he determined to build a basilica which should eclipse the finest cathedrals north of the Alps. Baldwin had seen the churches of Italy, and, as a Norman, had full cognisance of what the skill and strength of the new nations could accomplish. He accordingly obtained a charter from William the Conqueror, and with stone from Barnack in Northamptonshire and from the still more distant Caen in Normandy began the great church of St. Edmund. Lydgate thus sings of it:

> "In nyne and twentye wynters ye may see,
> A newe cherche he dyec edefie.
> Ston brought from Kane out of Normandye,
> By the se, and set upon the strande
> At Ratlysdene, and carried forth be lande."

The church was built on the plan of the cathedral of Caen.[1] The sacrists Thurstan and Tolinus superintended the erection, and also prepared the newly carved *feretra*, into which the bodies of St. Botulph and St. Firminus were to be translated. The builders spent thirty years on the mere shell, and not till 1095 was "the precious undefiled and uncorrupted body of the most glorious king and martyr St. Edmund" placed within the enclosure of its eastern apse. Once finished, it continued to be the abbatial

26. WILLIAM IV. Curteys, + 1446. In his reign flourished John Lydgate, who wrote the epic of St. Edmund's Life and Passion.

27. WILLIAM V. Babynton, LL.D.

28. JOHN IV. Boon, or Bohun, LL.B., + 1453.

29. ROBERT III. de Ixworth, alias Robert Coote, LL.D., + 1469.

30. ROBERT IV. Hengham, + 1474.

31. THOMAS III. Racclesden, S.T.B., + 1479.

32. WILLIAM VI. Codenham, DD., + 1497.

33. WILLIAM VII. Buntinge, + 1511.

34. JOHN V. Melford, alias Reeve, S.T.B., 1514, + 1540.

[1] Yates (p. 77). The same writer says (p. 80) that Shaftesbury abbey-church was modelled on St. Edmund's.

church till the sixteenth century. Its cathedral proportions suggested to both Bishop Herfast and his
successor, Bishop Herbert de Losinga, the removal to
its sanctuary of the episcopal chair of East Anglia,
and, apart from the additions made in the course
of ages, its vastness and grandeur ranked it as one of
the greatest churches of northern Europe.

With the building of the great church, St. Edmund's The consequent
resting-place began to fill a conspicuous place in importance of
the nation's history. Previous to Abbot Baldwin's
time St. Edmund's influence had made itself felt
throughout the land, but just as the history of
England enters upon a new phase with St. Edward the
Confessor and William the Conqueror, so the historical importance of St. Edmund's Bury begins with
the Norman abbot and his new church. From
Baldwin's time it became the custom for kings to
lay their crowns on the martyr's tomb and redeem
them at their weight in gold. Our sovereigns summoned their parliaments to meet within the abbey
walls. St. Edmund's memorial abbey, church and
liberty thus figure in every page of English History,
for five hundred years. William the Conqueror confirmed the abbey charters; Rufus sent his commissioners to represent him at the translation of the saint
in 1095. In the civil war of Stephen's reign, Prince
Eustace made St. Edmund's Bury the centre of his
resistance. Henry II. was crowned under the vaulted
roof of its basilica, and from its walls he issued
forth with St. Edmund's banner to win the battle
of Fornham. John sought its aid, and his barons
swore at its high altar to maintain the articles of the
great charter. Louis the Dauphin and the French
invaded its cloisters. In 1272, Henry III. assembled
parliament there. Within its great refectory Edward I.
held the famous parliament on ecclesiastical subsidies,

while, in an adjoining room, Archbishop Winchelsey
read to the clergy the papal constitution forbidding
the giving up of ecclesiastical property and revenues to
the secular power without the permission of the Pope.
"King Edward II.," says Stowe, "kept his Christmas
in 1326 at St. Edmund's Bury, sore afraide of the
queene's return, and of those excited people that
were with her, lest they should with a power of
aliens put him downe from his kingly dignitie."[1]
His queen Isabella marched to the abbey on her
landing on the coasts of Suffolk, and there gathered
an army of adherents round her. Jack Straw and
his rabble later on (A.D. 1381), after beheading the
prior and the keepers of St. Edmund's barony,
plundered the abbey, taking away a cross of gold,
a rich chalice, and jewels and ornaments to the
value of a thousand pounds. In the year 1446, on
the feast of St. Scholastica, Henry VI. held the
parliament in the great refectory, during whose sitting
the good Duke Humphrey of Gloucester, regent of
the kingdom, was found dead in his bed in St.
Saviour's hospice, having, it is supposed, been foully
murdered. The imperfect catalogue of events and of
kings, bishops and notables, to which this short
sketch must necessarily confine itself, closes with
Henry VII. and his daughter Mary, the last Catholic
king and queen who knelt in the basilica. Mary,
sister of Henry VIII. and queen of Louis XII. of
France, beheld the venerable abbey in the glory of
its setting, and asked on her death-bed to be buried
near the royal martyr's shrine—a request willingly
granted by the monks.

The gifts of kings and queens.

The illustrious or enthusiastic visitors who so frequently journeyed to St. Edmund's Bury did not
come thither merely for business or to enjoy the liberal

---

[1] "Annals," edit. 1592, p. 338.

hospitality of a Benedictine abbey, but to offer their
homage or make their supplications at the shrine
of the martyr, and they usually left behind some substantial proof of their devotion to the saint and his
servants.   Royal and noble benefactors especially
strove to increase the influence of the institution and
the welfare of its monks.   Thus St. Edward the
Confessor, who as frequently visited St. Edmund's St. Edward the
Confessor
tomb as other kings in after times visited his own,
on one occasion found the young monks eating
coarse barley-bread. "Why," he enquired of Abbot
Leofstan, "were these young men of his kinsmen not better fed?"   The father of the monastery
informs him that the income of the house will not
permit more expensive food. "Ask what you will,"
replied the king, "and I will give it to you, that
they may be better provided for and better enabled
to perform the service of God."   The abbot, after
consultation with the monks, asked for the manor
of Mildenhall with its appurtenances, and the jurisdiction of the eight hundreds and a half, with all Gives the eight
hundreds and a
the royalties of the district afterwards known as half
the franchise of St. Edmund. Edward granted this
great and important privilege, which several succeeding kings confirmed, thus extending the liberty of St.
Edmund beyond the four crosses.

Edward also thought that king St. Edmund should And the privilege of a mint,
have his own royal mint,[1] and therefore he "granted 1065.
that St. Edmund should have his moneyer within
his vill." A long line of kings approved of and confirmed this extraordinary privilege. King Stephen,
Henry II. and King John granted a second and a
third money-die. An exchanger had his bank at the
mint. A moneyer, an assayer and a keeper of the

[1] See the History of the Mint of St. Edmund in the annals of the
coinage of Britain, vol iv. p. 384, 1819.

die (custos cunei), who took the oaths of their office in
the court of the exchequer, protected all rights, and cast
and tested the money. Being St. Edmund's mint, its
coins bore on the obverse the name of the royal martyr.[1]

Other kings and queens proved equally generous
towards the great abbey. They confirmed the charters
of Athelstan, Edmund, Canute and St. Edward, and
added others, till they reached upwards of two hundred.[2]

William I.   The stark Conqueror confirmed the privileges granted
by pope and prince by a special charter signed by
himself, his queen, B. Lanfranc, St. Wulstan, St.
Osmund, his three sons, William, Robert and Henry,
and the principal bishops, abbots and barons of the
realm.   When Doomsday Book was drawn up, the
patrimony of St. Edmund included manors and farms
in Cambridgeshire, Bedfordshire, Northamptonshire,
Essex, Norfolk and Suffolk.   William's queen, Matilda, gave Wereketon towards the building of the
great church, and at her death her consort added
Scadewell in Northamptonshire, and other lands " pro
anima reginæ Matildæ,"—*for the soul of queen Matilda*.

Henry I.   Henry I. granted a six days' fair—three days before
the feast of St. James, the feast itself, and two days
after,—an important privilege in those days.   King
Richard I.   Richard the Lion-Heart, on a visit to St. Edmund
previous to his setting out for the Holy Land, gave
his manor of Aylsham " for the maintenance of
four wax candles to be kept burning for ever round
the shrine of Blessed Edmund."   On his return he
sent the standard of Isaac, king of Cyprus, as an
offering to St. Edmund.   Queen Eleanor, consort of
Henry II., gave her jewels, ten marks of gold and a

---

[1] See plate xii. of Anglo-Saxon coins at the end of Mr. Ruding's
work, nos. 1-6.

[2] The charters of St. Edmund's Bury in the Harleian collection
fill 49 folios.   They are 267 in number.

golden chalice, "in perpetuam eleemosynam. . . .
pro intuitu charitatis et amore beati martyris"—*as
a perpetual alms for charity and for love of the blessed
martyr.* John on a pilgrimage to the abbey, *out* John.
of reverence for the glorious martyr"—"ob reverentiam
martyris Edmundi" (so ran the deed of gift)—offered
a large sapphire, a ruby set in gold, and ten marks
annually at Easter to repair the "feretrum martyris."
Henry III. gave to the church of St. Edmund a Henry III.
"golden cup for the Body of the Lord." Henry VI. Henry VI.
after his visit gave a general remission of all taxes,
and, for those days, the large yearly pension of
£7 13s. 4d. Foreign potentates, nobles and ecclesiastics swelled the list of benefactors, so that, in
the course of centuries, St. Edmund's liberty embraced
a third of Norfolk and Suffolk, and the abbot held
the patronage of 75 benefices and the lordship of 171
vills or manors. [1]

The popes generously seconded the love and The patronage
of the Roman
devotion of the faithful by bestowing abundant Pontiffs.
spiritual gifts. Sixty papal bulls were religiously
preserved in the abbey chests. Abbot Baldwin in
person procured the first confirmation of the privileges of the monastery from Pope Alexander II., Alexander II.,
1061.
and other pontiffs subsequently renewed and amplified
them. Pope Alexander, in issuing the first bull,
invested the abbot with the pastoral staff and ring,
delegated to him the cure of souls, and presented to
St. Edmund's church a porphyry altar [2] with the

---

[1] See Leland's "Collectanea," vol. i. p. 249, and Dugdale's
"Monasticon," vol. iii. p. 165, edit. 1821.

[2] This altar was carefully preserved, with the following inscription
upon it :

> "Altaris mensam cum reliquiis bene comptam
> Dat, sacratque hanc nobis Baldwino Pater orbis,
> Pontificum sydus, Alexanderque secundus."

privilege of celebrating mass upon it even in time
of interdict, provided the church-doors were closed
and the reigning pope had not expressly prohibited
it. Dr. Yates thinks that the precise nature and
extent of the privileges granted to the abbey by the
supreme pontiffs cannot be easily ascertained, but it
is not difficult on examination to see that they
precisely amounted to what is known in ecclesiastical
language as the independence of an *abbas nullius*,
i.e., an abbot exempt from episcopal control and
himself exercising a bishop's jurisdiction over his
abbey and around it.[1] For the ordination of his
subjects, however, and in a few other instances, the
bull of Pope Callixtus II. required him to call in
a Catholic bishop, though he could choose whom
he would. The bulls of Pope Gregory IX. explain
these exemptions more at large. One ordains that
no person except the Roman Pontiff or his legate
a latere shall, in the town of St. Edmund or within
its four crosses, claim to himself any power or right,
or celebrate any public mass, or build any convent,
oratory or chapel, or hold any synod, or exercise any
episcopal office. Pope Alexander III. granted a second
bull of exemption from any interdict pronounced
upon the rest of the country, by which he permitted
the abbot and convent, with doors shut, the interdicted and excommunicated excluded, without the
ringing of bells, and with a low voice, to celebrate
mass and the divine office. The same pontiff made
Abbot Hugh papal legate, an office generally reserved
to the archbishops of Canterbury; and, at the Council
of Tours, Hugh sat before the abbot of St. Alban's,

Callixtus II., 1119.

Gregory IX., 1227.

Alexander III., 1159.

A.D. 1163.

---

[1] Hence one of the devices of the abbey consisted of a mitre and
two keys saltierwise within it, signifying that the abbot was subject
nullo medio to the Pope, the successor of St. Peter, and the holder
of the keys.

who then ranked as the first of the Benedictine abbots of England. Pope Innocent IV. not only exempted the abbey from any visit from his envoy Boniface, archbishop of Canterbury, but he ordered that prelate to excommunicate Richard Earl of Gloucester, who was harassing the monks and trying to force them to surrender certain rights. In consequence of these exemptions, archbishops or bishops, when they visited St. Edmund, averred that they did so saving the rights of his servants, and respecting the privileges granted to them by the apostolic see. Callixtus III. designed the highest honour for St. Edmund's Bury, and thought of raising it to an episcopal see, but, to the monks' joy, he did not carry out his intention. [1]

Innocent IV., 1243.

Callixtus III. 1455.

Made free and independent, temporally and spiritually, the abbots were able to use their wealth and influence for the good of religion, the support of the poor and strangers, and the education of children. This wealth has now indeed fallen into other hands, but not to be better employed. The turf and the gambling hall, the banquet table and the ball-room consume much of what the monks expended for the glory of God and the happiness of the people. For the monastery was not merely the abode of those who kept up the perennial office of the church, it was likewise hospice, school, college, almonry, bank and library,—in a word a public institution, and not the exclusive possession of an individual. Hence to detail the work of the four-and-thirty abbots who in the course of five hundred years ruled St. Edmund's Bury, is merely to describe the growth of a great national and religious foundation,

The work of the abbots.

---

[1] Henry VIII. and Charles I., by that spiritual supremacy supposed to have been given them by act of parliament, both entertained the idea of making St. Edmund's Bury a bishopric.

inspired by the example and virtue of its saintly
patron.

Baldwin was the first abbot of St. Edmund's Bury
who built on a vast scale. He left the great church
as a memorial of his genius and piety. He raised
the Norman tower or "great gateway of the church
of St. Edmund,"—a fair specimen of the work of
this saintly abbot—which competent judges now
pronounce to be unrivalled among the romanesque
structures of Europe.

Robert of Westminster prosecuted the work of
Baldwin. His sacrist, "Godefridus, a man of gigantic
stature, but greater in mind than in body," completed
the refectory, the chapter-house, the infirmary and
the abbot's palace.[1] Abbot Robert also bought
the great bell, which in 1521 was said to be the
largest in England.[2]

Under Anselm, the seventh abbot, the nephew of
St. Anselm, many of the chapels in the basilica
were completed. Baldwin, although he had spent
thirty years in raising the massive thick walls of
flint and boulder cased with smooth stone, had not
even finished the shell of the great church. He left
it to his successors to complete and add the minor
details of chapel and altar. During the reign of
Abbots Robert I., Robert II. and Albold, which
covered a period of twenty-four years, the building
had increased apace, and Abbot Anselm now dedicated
many of its chapels and altars. He placed an altar in
the porch under the protection of St. Saba, in
memory probably of St. Saba's on the Aventine in
Rome, of which he had been abbot. He completed

---

[1] These additions to the monastery necessitated the final demolition of old St. Mary's, which was re-erected on another site. —Battely, p. 57.

[2] Consecrated by Ralph, Archbishop of Canterbury.

Side notes:

Baldwin, 3rd abbot, 1065.

Robert II. of Westminster, 5th abbot, 1102.

Anselm of St. Saba's, 7th abbot, 1119,

and blessed the chapels of St. Martin, St. Faith, virgin and martyr, and the altar of blessed Peter the apostle. He erected the altar of the Holy Cross in the choir, for the "ruby rood" or "pity rood," a copy of the "Holy Face" of Lucca, which abbot Leofstan had caused to be made, and which Abbot Anselm now blessed, after putting many relics behind it.[1]

On becoming abbot, Anselm desired to make a long contemplated pilgrimage to St. James of Compostella, but his counsellors thought it more beneficial for him to stay at home, and build instead a church under the invocation of St. James. Anselm accordingly erected the first parish church of St. James on the site of the present one. It took the place of St. Denis' church,[2] which the abbot ordered to be taken down on account of its close proximity to the great basilica, whose façade it prevented from being widened. On the removal of the church of St. Denis, the builders commenced the north wing of the façade of the basilica, which was to comprise an octagonal tower and two chapels to correspond with the similar constructions of the south wing. The amount of building undertaken and completed at this period, under the sacrists Ralph and Harvey, is almost incredible. The façade of the great church, with its five towers was finished, and also St. James' church with tower and belfry, which Corbeuil, archbishop of Canterbury, opened and consecrated at the invitation of the abbot, at the same time as he dedicated the chapel of St. Michael in

(margin note: builds St. James' church.)

---

[1] The people, says Battely, held this crucifix, which was one of the chief treasures of the abbey, in great veneration. It seems to have stood at various times at the altar of St. Peter, at the altar of the Holy Cross and in the south transept.

[2] Built by Abbot Baldwin in memory of St. Denis', Paris, to which he had belonged.

the infirmary. At this period also, the church of
St. Mary's. blessed Mary was completed, and its tower and belfry
furnished with loud-sounding bells like those in the
St. Margaret's.; tower of St. James'. St. Margaret's, a third church,
was also built on the site of the chapel and tower
which Albold had put up with Abbot Baldwin's
permission.[1] To replace a little stone chapel held in
great veneration, but inconveniently situated near the
river Linnet, which it was desired to widen, the
chapel of St. Andrew in the brethren's cemetery
was finished and painted, so that therein "the whole
community might daily chant the *Placebo* and the
Dirige for all in the cemetery." Ralph and Harvey
likewise built the first wall round the abbey precincts.
The walls round the town and a hospital were built
at the same time, towards which the townspeople
did a part, but "it was as a spring to a river,"
say the registers, compared to Sacrist Harvey's.

The bronze
gates.
In the midst of rough stone and mortar, more
artistic work was not forgotten. Brother Hugh
skilfully wrought the beaten doors of bronze which
adorned the western entrance of the great church
and rivalled those which Abbot Anselm had seen
at Monte Cassino. The same "Master Hugh," with
incomparable skill, painted and adorned the chapels
The library. of the basilica, and also the library of the monastery,
for which Prior Talbot, with the aid of the sacrist,
had caused books to be written.

Ording, 8th
abbot, 1148.
Abbot Ording, the successor of Anselm, dedicated
the chapel of St. Giles, but the sudden destruction of
the monastery interrupted the work of beautifying the
church ; for in the year 1152 a great fire consumed the
abbot's palace, the refectory, dormitory, chapter-house,
infirmary and other buildings. At once, however, the

[1] Abbot Anselm invited John, Bishop of Rochester to consecrate
St. Mary's and St. Margaret's, as well as many of the chapels.

work of reconstruction commenced. The designs for
the new buildings rivalled in splendour those of
Geoffrey, or Godefridus, the sacrist, in the time of
Henry I. The bath was altogether a new construction
by Sacrist Helyas, Ording's nephew. The monks aimed at
re-erecting the buildings on a larger scale and in solid
stone, but unfortunately the treasury failed in the
latter years of Abbot Hugh, who had succeeded
Ording in 1156. Abbot Hugh, in the words of Hugh of
Jocelin, was "a pious and kind man, a good and Westminster, 9th abbot, 1180.
religious monk, but not wise or heedful in worldly
affairs. To be sure good governance and religion
waxed warm in the cloister, but out of doors affairs
were badly managed . . . . The townships of
the abbot and all the hundreds were set out to farm,
and the forests were destroyed, the manor-houses
threatened to fall, and everything daily got worse
and worse. There was but one recourse and relief
to the abbot, and that was to take up moneys on
interest, so that thereby he might be able in some
measure to keep up the dignity of the house." In
other words, Abbot Hugh in his old age became the
prey of the Jews, and when he died, on a pilgrimage to
St. Thomas à Becket's tomb, from a fall from his horse,
he left to his successor, Abbot Samson of Tottingham, a Samson, 10th abbot, 1182
far-stretching pile of unfinished buildings, an exhausted
exchequer and a heap of Jewish bonds. The broad-minded
clear-sighted Samson, the special protégé of St. Edmund
and his devoted servant, was a man admirably fitted
to put things in order. He possessed the qualities
of a good ruler; he knew what men to choose, and
he trusted them; he could be cautious: "We must
first creep and gradually learn to walk," he said of
himself at starting. He had patience with abuses,
till he could correct them. He knew how to seize
his opportunities, well aware that the proper use of

one chance of doing the right thing brings with it twenty others. He had the will and the energy to silently grapple with every difficulty of finance, discipline and government. He applied these qualities of a great ruler to the temporal affairs of his abbey, without, however, neglecting his chief duty, the spiritual welfare of his subjects. He pacified the townsmen by granting them a charter. He arranged with the Jews, and was satisfied only when he saw them safely beyond St. Edmund's liberty. Many of the abbey buildings had been temporarily thatched with reeds. With the assistance of Hugh the sacrist, he roofed them with tiles, the more securely to prevent danger from fire. He took down the guest-house, the almoury and the halls for the entertainment and relief of strangers and pilgrims, which, since the fire, had been constructed of wood, and re-erected them in stone, defraying the expense with part of what "Brother Walter the Physician had acquired by his practice of medicine." He founded and endowed the hospital of St. Saviour at the north gate of the town, and a new free school at the south-east corner of the great cemetery. Every manor, farm and wood in St. Edmund's patrimony was revalued and set in order. The completion of the greater part of the choir, the addition of one storey to the west tower, a pulpit, a new rood with the usual figures, a richly carved abbatial chair, a new palace, and several towers and chapels were among the achievements of Abbot Samson's reign. He also provided a leaden conduit to convey water underground to the abbey from a source two miles off. Under his direction the sacrist, Robert of Gravel, planted and enclosed the vineyard "ad solatium infirmorum et amicorum;" and Prior Walter de Banham began the marble lavatory, which

his successor Prior John of Gosford finished. Above
all he prepared a marble base and a new and costly
shrine for the body of his master and patron Edmund,
whose face on the night of the feast of St. Catherine,
1198, he presumed to uncover and look upon.
Enumerating the rest of the deeds of Abbot Samson,
his biographer, Jocelin, recounts how he became royal
justiciary, confessor of Henry II., the adviser of
Richard and John, and the respected spiritual father
of kings and barons. At last by prudent management, by a careful protection of his abbey from the
encroachments of others and by a new confirmation
of its privileges by Rome, Samson raised his monastery
and church to the highest state of prosperity.[1] He
died full of honour on the 3rd of January, 1211.

His successor, Hugh of Northwold, did little towards
the material improvement of St. Edmund's patrimony.
The political events of the time, the drawing-up of
the articles of Magna Charta, the consequent civil
war, the invasion of the abbey-town by one party
after another, and the final robbery of the martyr's body
by the French,—all concurred to prevent the undertaking of any great work. One memorial, however,
of St. Edmund is connected with Abbot Hugh II.
At the foot of his tomb in the cathedral of Ely, of
which he died bishop, the legend of St. Edmund's
martyrdom is sculptured, as a last sad tribute to
the saint from the abbot in whose reign England
lost the royal martyr's body. From this period, then,
the material improvements to the abbey are few and
far between. The institution was now consolidated,

Hugh II. of Northwold, 11th abbot, 1215.

---

[1] The latter days of Abbot Samson were troubled and stormy.
John's visit to the monastery in 1201 and 1203, the meeting of the
Barons there in 1205, the interdict in 1208, the blowing down of
the great tower in 1210, cast a cloud of sorrow over the noble
abbot's last days.

and its traditions established; and the absence of the martyr's body withdrew the motive power for further improvements and adornments. From time to time, however, the abbots made additions which vied in beauty and solidity with any work of their prede-

Simon de Luton, 15th abbot, 1257.

cessors. Thus Simon de Luton, the 15th abbot, at his own expense and that of his parents, built the Lady Chapel adjoining the north transept.[1] In digging the foundations for this new sanctuary, the monks came across the walls of the ancient round chapel and the stone base in its centre, where St. Edmund's body had rested for 192 years.[2]

John of Northwold, 16th abbot, 1279.

John of Northwold, Simon of Luton's successor, presents another example of abbatial munificence by his foundation and endowment of the chapel in the cemetery, known as the Chapel of the Charnel, "for the perpetual celebration of two masses by two chaplains" for the souls of those buried around. Abbot John of Northwold also founded for the said two chaplains the house of residence, which afterwards grew into the Jesus College of the guild or fraternity of the Holy or Sweet Name of Jesus.

Thomas II. of Draughton, 18th abbot, A.D. 1312.

The wrecking of the abbey by an infuriated mob in 1327 brought about the building of a second massive embattled wall around the precincts. The justices awarded £140,000 as compensation for the damage done, and the insult and indignity to which the rioters had subjected the Abbot, Thomas of Draughton; and although, at King Edward III.'s request, the abbot and convent at first remitted part and then the whole of the fine, they were able to build on a magnificent and extensive scale. The abbot's bridge and the abbey gate-way still remain as samples.[3]

---

[1] A.D. 1272.

[2] From A.D. 903 to A.D. 1095.

[3] After this riot the town obtained independent authority as a corporation with a common seal, custody of the town gates, etc.

It fell to the lot of Abbot William Curteys to William IV. Curteys, 26th abbot, 1430. rebuild the central tower of the church, which in the course of four hundred years had yielded to decay and partly fallen. The Pope granted a plenary indulgence to all contributors, and the abbot was thus able to raise a lantern tower worthy of its surroundings. From these details it is easy to form some idea of the building up of St. Edmund's patrimony.

Learning and holiness distinguished its rulers to General character of the abbots. the last, the happy result of the community retaining the freedom of election, with which even kings dared not interfere from fear of St. Edmund. The known ability and virtue of the abbots of St. Edmund's Bury obtained for them the highest offices of trust in Church and state. Of the later abbots, Cratfield was one of the proctors of Archbishop Arundel at the council held at St. Paul's for the suppression of the Lollard heresy. William Babynton, LL.D., held the office of president of the Benedictine order in England,[1] and the last abbot, John Melford, alias Reeve, in 1520 was one of the king's privy councillors.

The dissolution of the noble and magnificent The dissolution of St. Edmund's patrimony. institution which these pages but faintly delineate, comes like a shock on the historian. Why should it have been so ruthlessly beaten to the ground that scarcely a stone is left upon a stone to mark its site? One of Henry VIII.'s commissioners wrote that "he found nothing suspect as touching his (the abbot's) lyving," and what he said of the abbot he had also to say of the 59 monks who formed the community.[2] He found but "little fault" at the

---

[1] Abbot William Codenham, D.D., was the patron of Thomas—afterwards Cardinal—Wolsey, to whom he presented the rectory of Hengrave.

[2] There were also three monks at Gloucester Hall, Oxford,

time of his visit, yet the abbey was not saved. Four
agents of Cromwell superintended the rifling of the
church and monastery. They burnt or threw away
as rubbish, the relics of St. Edmund, St. Thomas à
Becket, St. Lawrence and even the relic of the holy
cross. By the providence of God the body of the
royal martyr was not there to be subjected to their
impieties. Not so the costly shrine which had
contained it. "Please your lordship," they wrote,
"to be advertised that wee have been at Saynt
Edmond's Bury, where we found a riche shrine,
which was very comberous to deface. We have
taken in the said monastery in gold and silver
MMMMM. (5,000) marks and above; over and
besyds, as well, a rich cross with emeredds as also
dyvers and sundry stones of great value, &c., &c."
What surprises the antiquarian most, is the com-
pleteness of the destruction. Would that the tyrant,
who saved Peterborough because of the tomb of Queen
Catherine, had spared St. Edmund's Bury, the resting-
place of his sister, Mary, queen dowager of France!
If St. Edmund's great church, vaster and more massive
than Durham and not less venerable, had merely been
left deserted and uncared for, exposed to the rains and
storms of three centuries, something more would have
remained than a gateway or a broken arch ; but malice
employed gunpowder to destroy quickly and abso-
lutely this noble architectural monument, this stately
memorial pile, upon a more magnificent than which
"the sun has not shone," and which a few years
previous seemed indestructible. "Greater loss than
this," writes Camden, "so far as the works of man
go, England never suffered." The possessions of the

the English Benedictine house of studies, now Worcester College.
At the dissolution 43 out of the 62 received pensions. (Yates
p. 257.)

royal martyr—lands, churches and houses all over England—passed into other hands, and their present owners probably know little, and think less, of the saint whose patrimony they enjoy.

The curse invoked, in many a charter and deed of gift, upon any who should violate St. Edmund's rights, fell most terribly on the despoilers. The charter of King Canute prayed that "eternal captivity" might seize those who robbed St. Edmund, and that they "might be given to the service of the devil, and with him be bound in inextricable chains." St. Edward's charter ends with the terrifying words, " Si aliquis fuerit ita vesanus per incitamenta diaboli, quod velit hanc libertatem mutare, sive in aliquo adnichillare vel depravare, sit ille anathematizatus, et in gehennam ignis demersus, nisi in vita sua resipuerit."—"If any one shall be so maddened by the incitements of the devil, that he determine to alter the boundaries of St. Edmund's Liberty, or to nullify it or spoil it in any way, let him be anathematized and drowned in the fire of hell, unless he come to his senses in this life." Spelman in his "History of Sacrilege," after mentioning the fate of Prince Eustace and of the young Count Leofstan, relates how the intruders into St. Edmund's manors all perished miserably. John Eyre, for example, purchased the site of the venerable church from Queen Elizabeth on February 4, 1560. Little, even at that time, remained of the ruined and desecrated sanctuary, but the heaps of stones and boulders which lay around were part of the bargain, and the whole was valued at £615, though the purchaser seems to have paid only £412 19s. 4d. The purchaser died childless; and during a period of 244 years, i.e. from 1560 to 1804, twelve families one after the other got possession of the site, never to

<aside>The punishment of the despoilers.</aside>

pass it on from father to son. It is now the property of the town.

The modern patrimony of St. Edmund.

The monks, though they had lost their abbey, did not forget their saint. Forced by the persecutions of the time to seek a refuge abroad, they no sooner rallied again into a congregation than they revived in a foreign land the greater convents of their own. They reconstituted the ancient cathedral chapters, and the succession of the cathedral priors has survived to the present day. In corporate bodies they continued the greater abbeys—St. Alban's at Douai in Flanders; Westminster at Dieulouard in Lorraine; Glastonbury at St. Malo in Normandy; and St. Edmund's Bury at St. Edmund's, Paris. The new St. Edmund's in the Faubourg St. Jacques became almost as illustrious as the old, if not for architectural beauty and extent, at least, by royal benefactions and for the renowned personages who visited it, or lay buried within its enclosure.

Its distinguished monks.

Several of its monks fill an honourable place in the annals of the Benedictine order, like Dom Clement Reyner, one of its first members and the compiler of the "Apostolatus Benedictinus"; the martyr monk Alban Roe; and Dom Placid Gascoigne, prior of the monastery, and afterwards abbot of Lambspring and president of the English Benedictine Congregation; of whom the annalist writes "that he was very exact in that part of the rule which commands the abbot to first practise himself what he commands others to do." Add to these Dom Benet Weldon, the chronicler of the house and order, Father Francis Fenwick, the eloquent preacher and learned theologian, whom James II. sent as his representative to the court of Rome, and Dom Charles, afterwards Bishop, Walmesley, the famous scientist and mathematician,

whom English statesmen consulted before adopting
the Gregorian calendar.

The monastery of St. Edmund at Paris, once founded, The history of
                                                    St. Edmund's at
became the rendezvous of the noble and illustrious Paris.
Catholic and even Protestant English who, for political
or religious reasons, sought refuge in the French
capital ; and great names figure in the list of benefactors who, out of devotion to the royal martyr or
desirous of his protection, endowed his monastery
and its sons with worldly possessions. Of these the
name of Archbishop Giffard, its quasi-founder, stands
first. The monks could afterwards add to the list
Anne of Austria, the queen-mother of Louis XIV.,
and Maria Henrietta, queen of the unfortunate Charles
I., who "on all occasions showed her royal favour to
the house." Louis the Great gave an annual donation
of £25 to the monastery and a gift of 7,000 livres
towards the building of its new church, besides
granting letters patent for the protection of the house.
The monks in return for these favours were to
offer up a solemn mass on the feast of St. Louis for
the health and prosperity of his majesty and his
royal successors for ever. Not satisfied with what
he had done previously, the king in 1671 accorded
to all the professed monks of St. Edmund's the
privilege of naturalisation, so that they became capable
of possessing, for support of their community, such
benefices of the order as might be bestowed upon
them. This privilege he extended to any monk of
the order visiting or residing in St. Edmund's
monastery, provided he continued his studies as far
as master of arts.

The continuity of the new St. Edmund's with Its continuity
                                             with the past.
the past was so far recognised that the owners in
England contemplated the restitution to the monks
of their ancient home. Dom Benet Weldon, the

annalist, writes that "when ye king (James II.) was on ye crown [*sic*], as our house here in Paris bare ye name of ye Holy Martyr, St. Edmund, king of the East Angles; those who had the land of our old great abbey of St. Edmund's in England, frivolously and vainly apprehensive yt we should again re-enter into all, they proposed to ours ye sale of 'em; but his majesty acquainted therewith advised our fathers not to undertake ye affair yt they might not give occasion to publick clamours and noises yt would be seditiously made under pretext yt ye monks were a going to be put into possession of all again; wherefore our fathers humbly submitting to his majesty's sentiment let fall ye affaire."

The building of St. Edmund's church in Paris. In May, 1674, took place an event which ranks with similar ones in the history of old St. Edmund's— the erection of a monastic church in the royal martyr's honour, sadly inferior indeed in size and magnificence to Baldwin's noble basilica, but more stately far than "ye poor old church" which Prior Sherburn began to pull down on St. Joseph's feast, which came that year (1674) on April the 4th. "On May the 29th following, on a Tuesday, the Duke of Orleans' daughter[1] by Henrietta of England, laid the first stone of the new church. My Lord Abbot Montaigne officiated, who gave about £100 to the building. At the time the old church was pulled down, the old dortory was also pulled down." Lord Abbot Montaigne, "first almoner to the queen of England," was not the only benefactor who came forward to help in the building up of the new church. King Louis gave his 7,000 livres, and the archbishop of Paris issued a

---

[1] She afterwards (A.D. 1679) became queen of Spain, and died when she was only 27 years old, after three days of sickness, having received the last sacraments with exemplary piety.

letter soliciting alms, to be read on August the 5th, 1675, in all the churches of his diocese.

The new church of St Edmund could not boast *Its completion* of much architectural beauty. In fact, the site, if nothing else, hindered anything like display. The monks had only a narrow strip of land to build upon, which was hemmed in between the Renaissance glories of the royal Benedictine nunnery of Val-de-Grace and the austere sternness of the Feuillantines, while the great Carmelite convent over against them literally overshadowed it. Instead of thirty years St. Edmund's church at Paris took only three years to erect. The Abbé de Noailles, afterwards archbishop of Paris and Cardinal, blessed it, the Duchess of Cleveland, Sir Henry Tichborne and his lady, and other illustrious personages being present at the inaugural ceremony.

From this date the monastery of St. Edmund *The later history of St. Edmund's,* became still more important, not only by chapters of *Paris.* the English Benedictine Congregation continuing to be held there from time to time, and by the revision of the Anglo-Benedictine constitutions made within its walls, but especially by the vaults at its north-west end becoming the favourite burial-place *It becomes the burial-place of* of English Catholic exiles, and particularly of those *English exiles* who, whether from a false idea of loyalty or not, faithfully followed the fortunes of the Stuart line. The annalist of the monastery gives the names and epitaphs of several of the honoured dead who lay interred there. Sir Francis Anderton, Lord Lostock, a great benefactor to St. Edmund's, found a resting-place in the martyr's church. Lord Lauderdale before his death desired the monks to bury him, and they laid his body in their vaults. Mr. Francis Stafford, whom James II. had sent to St. Edmund's to prepare for death, and who gloried in being a son of that Viscount Stafford, better known as Lord

Stafford, the aged and venerable victim of Titus
Oates' perjury, breathed his last in the monastery
and was laid to rest in its church.

And of the last
Stuart king. Last of all, James II. himself, after his death at
St. Germain-en-Laye, September 16, 1701, was em-
balmed and the next night conveyed in a hearse to
St. Edmund's church. He had always loved St.
Edmund; and his children, notably James III., the
Chevalier St. George, and Charles, the Young
Pretender, frequently visited the monastery, as their
royal ancestors had visited St. Edmund's more stately
abbey in England. Perhaps they regarded St.
Edmund as the patron and protector of kingly
rights, as he certainly was of the people's liberties.
James II. had his own chamber or cell in the
monastery, where, in the days of his adversity, he
used to make his pious retreats; for James in
adversity was a very different man from James in
prosperity. So when he died, the monks received
the last Stuart king and laid him on a hearse in
the chapel which "my Lord Cardigan" had erected;
and the Benedictines of France and England conjointly
performed the sad obsequies according to the rites of
royal funerals in France. The royal corpse reposed
in state unburied and incorrupt for 112 years, awaiting
the day when it should be taken to England and
honourably interred in Westminster Abbey. Wax
tapers were constantly kept burning round the coffin
till the French revolution, for a report had spread
abroad that miracles were wrought at the tomb
of the unfortunate James, who, though anything but
a saint at one period of his life, had been remarkable
for the penance and holiness of his latter days.[1]

---

[1] Agnes Strickland in her history of Queen Ann (edit. 1875)
gives a further account of James II.'s body. The revolutionists
on opening the coffin found the corpse entire and in an

Among other historic names connected with St. Edmund's, Paris, occurs that of Bossuet, the Eagle of Meaux. St. Francis of Sales also, won by the exemplary regularity of the community, visited St. Edmund's whenever he came to Paris, and special mention is

Historic visitors.

---

extraordinary state of preservation. The municipal authorities took possession of the hearse and body, and charged from a son to a franc for admission to see it. In the midst of the infidelity of the Revolution whispers went about of miracles performed by the corpse of James II. Robespierre gave orders for the body to be buried, which was not done, but it was carefully and reverently preserved. When the allies came to Paris in 1813, the corpse of the unfortunate James II. still remained above ground. The strange circumstances having been mentioned to George IV., he ordered the remains of his kinsman to be carried in funeral procession from Paris to St. Germain-en-Laye, and there interred in the church. The long-delayed funeral of James II. then took place with royal grandeur. No mourners of his lineage attended his coffin on its return to St. Germain, for his race had passed away; yet his people followed him to the grave, for most of the English in Paris, setting aside all religious and political differences, attended the cortége in deepest mourning. A monument was raised to his memory in the church.

In "Notes and Queries," vol. 2, p. 243 (quoted by Agnes Strickland), a certain Mr. Fitzsimons writes as follows :

" During the French Revolution of Terror, I was a prisoner in the convent of the English Benedictines, Rue St. Jacques. In the year 1793 or 1794 the body of James II. was still in one of the chapels there, awaiting interment in Westminster Abbey. It had never been buried. The body was in a wooden coffin, enclosed in a leaden one, and that again in one covered with black velvet. While I was there, the Sansculottes broke the coffins to get at the lead, to cast bullets. The body lay exposed a whole day; it had been embalmed. The corpse was beautiful and perfect; the hair and nails were very fine. I moved and bent every finger. I never saw so fine a set of teeth in my life. A young lady, a fellow prisoner, wished much to have a tooth; I tried to get one out for her, but could not, they were so firmly fixed. The feet also were very beautiful. The face and cheeks were just as if he were alive. I rolled his eyes, and the eyeballs were perfectly firm under my fingers. Money was given to the Sansculottes for showing the body. They said he was a good Sansculotte, and that they were

made in the annals of the house of the honour which the saint showed it on more than one occasion. Then as now all the world visited Paris, and English travellers and tourists naturally took an interest in a community which spoke their own tongue. Hence Dr. Johnson, the venerable lexicographer, (who, his chatty biographer tells us, visited Paris with the Thrales in 1778,) wrote in his diary: "I was very kindly treated by the English Benedictines, and had a cell appropriated to me in their convent." The honoured name of Benjamin Franklin likewise occurs in the guest-book of the English monks. While in Paris, Franklin frequently sat at their table, and from them he learnt those principles of government of the common Benedictine law, which he embodied in the American constitution, so that the independence of the United States received its form under the same auspices as the charter of English liberties.

St. Edmund's at Douai.

Thus the new St. Edmund's in many ways rivalled the old. To those who clung to the old faith it was a place of pilgrimage still. In the esteem of the Benedictine order and of the royal line of Stuarts it held its place as of yore. At the great revolution, however, the political and social disturbances in France again scattered the monks and plundered their convent. The Benedictines never entirely abandoned the monastery; the original property is still administered for their benefit, but they have never returned to it. When the storm cleared, they revived the memories of St. Edmund's, Paris, and old

---

going to put him into a hole in the churchyard, like other Sansculottes; and the body was carried away, but whither I never heard. Around the chapel of St. Jacques several wax moulds were hung up at the time of the king's death: the corpse was very like them."

St. Edmund's Bury at St. Edmund's, Douai, where they took up the work of the former English colleges in that venerable city. May they, however, without injury to their present patrimony or diminution of their work in the land of exile, develope one day a central home in their own country, as magnificent and far-stretching as St. Edmund's Bury of old.

Seal of Modern St Edmund's.

Go litel book, be ferfful, quaak for drede,
    Ffor t' appere in so hyh presence.
To alle folk, that the shal seen or reede
    Submytte thysylff with humble reverence.
    To be refourmyd, wher men fynde offence,
Meekly requeryng ; voyde off presumpcion
Wher thow faylest to do correccion.

                                        Lydgate, Harl. MS. 2278.

APPENDIX.

THE hospice of St. Edmund K. M.—an earlier
foundation than that of St. Thomas—owed its
establishment to a Mr. and Mrs. Whyte, assisted by
kind benefactors from England, in the year 1300 (the
first jubilee), or 1350 (the second jubilee). It was
situated in the Campo di Fiori close to the old church
of St. Chrysogonus beyond the Tiber. Its object was
twofold—(1) to support a number of priests, who
would offer Mass and daily devotions for all benefactors living and dead ; (2) to receive into the hospice
and to give spiritual and corporal succour to the
sick and infirm English pilgrims. The hospice was
well supported, and after a short time rebuilt on a
larger scale and endowed with property in the immediate neighbourhood. Since, however, the site of St.
Thomas' Hospice (now the English College in the
Via di Monserrato) was found more healthy, more
central, and in the immediate neighbourhood of
similar institutions for the Spaniards, Swedes, Flemings, etc., it was decided in 1463 to merge the two
English hospices into one. A warden and twelve

chaplains presided over the new institution, officiated
in the church and ministered in the hospital.   They
likewise dispensed *free hospitality* to all national
pilgrims whilst they visited the churches of Rome
and performed their devotions.   The poor had eight
days allowed for this purpose, the noble and rich
three days.   The hospice received and nursed the sick
and infirm pilgrims till they were cured.   The warden
had full parish priest's rights within the precincts of
the hospice.   The dead were buried in the national
cemetery of St. Thomas.   (See "The Catholic Magazine
and Review" from January to December, 1832, vol.
ii. p. 408.   Printed at Birmingham by R. P. Stone.
The particulars are probably taken from the papers
of the English College.   Hence the reference "*Bulla
in Archivio,*" pp. 410-412.)

The chapel of St. Edmund seems to have existed for
some time afterwards independent of the hospice. Hence
Signor Armellini on the churches of Rome ("Le Chiese
di Roma," di Mariano Armellini, pt. ii. p. 682.   Tipogr.
Vatic., 1891.) writes that St. Edmund's was only "a
small oratory of the Trastevere, near the church of
St. John Baptist of the Genoese."   Of it Martinelli
says that it was erected *a quodam Anglo*—"by some
Englishman"—and hence depended on the English
College.   Neither chapel nor hospice now exists,
but the church of the Genoese, near which they stood,
is just behind St. Cecilia's, not far from S. Maria dell'
Orto, St. Chrysogonus', the house of St. Francis of
Rome, etc.   The site—a waste tract of small extent
lying beside the seventh station of the ancient Roman
"Vigili"—is still pointed out by the more erudite
archæologist.   The chapel stood on the part nearest
to St. Cecilia's, and hence most distant from St.
Chrysogonus'.

Some of the old buildings stood till within a few

years, and the arms of England might be seen
sculptured on the marble lintel over the door of what
was once St. Edmund's. The last remains were
pulled down about five years ago, and the arms of
England were destroyed before they could be secured.
A marble slab in a house facing the main street,
and very near the station of the "Vigili," states that
the property "belongs" to the English College, and
thus confirms the almost forgotten tradition.

The following inscription in the sacristy of the
English College at Rome gives the history of the
suppression of St. Edmund's chapel, two hundred
years after the hospice had been amalgamated with
St. Thomas':—

> Decreto S. Congregationis
> Visitationis Apostolicæ ·
> edito die XXIX. Maii MDCLXIV.
> Oratorium S. Edmundi Regis Angliæ
> Transtyberim olim positum
> suppressum fuit
> et obligatio illic celebrandi missas
> ad summum hujus templi altare translata
> aliis omnibus in pristino vigore
> juxta mentem S. Mem.
> Gregorii XIII. permanentibus.

Over the high altar of the present church in the
English College stands a remarkable picture of the
Most Blessed Trinity, to whom the church was once
dedicated, St. Thomas of Canterbury, and a saint
vested in royal robes, who kneels in a suppliant attitude. Behind this latter saint an angel holds three
arrows and a palm. On the ground lie a crown and
a sceptre. The picture formerly hung in the old
church, and, according to tradition, over its high altar.
Donovan says ("Rome Ancient and Modern," vol. ii.

p. 245, edit. 1844): "Over the great altar of the
old church stood a large painting of the Holy Trinity,
with St. Thomas of Canterbury and St. Edward the
Confessor kneeling beneath, executed by Durante
Alberti of Borgo S. Sepolcro, and now" (before the
present church was built) "to be seen in the spacious
hall, which gives admission to the college library."
Cardinal Wiseman ("Last Four Popes," *in vita* Pius VII.)
also says that it is by Durante Alberti, and represents
St. Edward. But do not the arrows and palm, the
inscription in the sacristy and the union of the two
hospices in 1463 imply that St. Edmund the Martyr
is represented rather than St. Edward the Confessor?

INDEX.

www.ingramcontent.com/pod-product-compliance
Lightning Source LLC
Chambersburg PA
CBHW022016110726
47901CB00006B/1547